The Reign of Ta
When Giants Walked the Earth - 2

IN THE SAME SERIES

Kobor Tigan't

The Reign of Ta
When Giants Walked the Earth - 2

by
Christia Sylf

Translated from the French by
Michael Shreve

A Black Coat Press Book

ISBN 978-1-64932-308-8. First Printing: May 2024. Published by Black Coat Press, an imprint of Hollywood Comics.com, LLC, 18321 Ventura Blvd. Suite 915, Tarzana, CA 91356. All rights reserved. Except for review purposes, no part of this book may be reproduced or transmitted in any form or by any means, electronic or mechanical, including photocopying, recording, or by any information storage and retrieval system, without permission in writing from the publisher. The stories and characters depicted in this novel are entirely fictional. Printed in the United States of America.

Introduction

Le Règne de Ta – Chronique des Géants, here translated as *The Reign of Ta – When Giants Walked the Earth* – was initially published by Robert Laffont in 1971. It was a sequel *Kobor Tigan't* (1969), also available in this collection.

Christia Sylf was the pseudonym of Christiane Léonie Adélaïde Richard-Delecluse, born 28 September 1924 in Paris, who passed away on 28 November 1980 in Entrevaux in the Alpes-de-Haute-Provence. She was a major French fantasy writer who remains, even today, mostly underappreciated in France, where fantasy thrives in the shadow of homegrown imitators of J.R.R. Tolkien, Robert E. Howard and J.K. Rowling.

A full biography, bibliography, as well as an autobiographical essay, are inckuded in our first volume and we refer the reader wishing for more information about Ms. Sylf, her work, and inspiration, to them.

Reportedly, she would say that she received visions from ancient times and previous incarnations. In any event, her work was truly unique in the sense that she was able to transform her experiences into novels and, with considerable work, produce fascinating and captivating books, bearing a message of freedom and open-mindedness.

Kobor Tigan't and *The Reign of Ta* were followed by *Markosamo le Sage* [Markosamo the Wise] in 1973, a story featuring reincarnated versions of all her major characters, but taking place twenty thousand years ago, during the age of Atlantis. A fourth volume, *La Reine au Coeur Puissant* [The Strong-Hearted Queen] (1979), carried on with a tale taking place in Ancient China two thousand years ago.

Sylf created a new type of literary fantasy and world-building that owed nothing to the great British and American masters. She rightly deserves to be recognized as a major talent in the field.

Now, read on...

Jean-Marc & Randy Lofficier

CHRISTIA SYLF

chronique des géants
LE RÈGNE DE TA

ROMAN

ROBERT LAFFONT

Prologue

The river of Time drains, rolls and wears down men like pebbles.
But I myself, I roll without wearing down
being of the same nature as the river of Time.

You have met me already. I have spoken to you already.
Remember! Remember!

It is still to you I am speaking. It is about you, still, that I am speaking, hurried wayfarers, too soon scattered by the wind of death...

One moment, just one, stop! Who is chasing you? And what are you chasing? The panic of delirious living is fanning your fatal fire. And, chasers/chased, despite your hurry, you can't escape your enemy or catch the fleeing illusion.

For heaven's sake, stop! And let the Great Memory with its multiple branches reappear in you...

This present wants you to remember at last.

You are not as destitute as your arid thought would like you to believe. There are sources in you where the patient nomadism of meditation can drink its fill. Drink this water and reflect among all your ancient reflections... Ah, you remember like this. Slowly, carefully, remember...

And you, returning from another age, whose innate memory is frightened and confused by the fragmentary flashes of these past lives that haunt you, dare to accept your true inheritance, dare to contemplate what your soul possesses, dare to take back what rightfully belongs to you and dare, finally, to say, like so many others who have awakened: "Yes, it's true, I was there. I remember. It was 30,000 years ago in Kobor Tigan't, the five-fold City of Giants!"

But yes, dare to see it, dare to elaborate it in you, dare to relive the Great Memory! You were there, different from what you became, and yet so similar. You were in Kobor Tigan't, you, a witness, you, a participant, a hero or damned by the all-powerful magical matriarchy for whom our doleful old souls are forever etched with longing.

Me, too, o wayfarers coming back, I was there like you. Remember...

I am called old Kébélé, the Wise Friend.

I am an eternal old man, the timeless, the Ever-Living.

I have many other names, but what never mind! I do not vary. I remain. Whereas you pass on, scattered pollen, across the sky of my being.

Permanence is the status of my life, it is the sphere of my activity. I know no other existence than this ageless duration. I am.

But I am only because it is for you.

It is mine to alter the destiny of those over whom I keep watch.

I cannot interfere but a little. The extra part that you possess, your free will, limits and controls my alterations.

I also weave and embroider. Some, seeing me at work, have called me the Master Weaver and others the Embroiderer, but never mind! From my threads that cross I merge futures. I join the summit to the depths. Thus, angelic beings see their reflections appear in the abyss while it elevates the force of its yearnings toward ideal propositions.

And the right and the left, the more and the less, the heavy and the light, always and forever, in my work, coming into balance, readjust and offset each other while I, in the center, watch over what goes in and out of the heart.

This is the Great Tapestry of Karma.

Time puts its little stitch there in the canvas of space.

My premeditations offer creatures the pure arcs of evolving ways or simple schema favorable to vast liberations, which the acts of men always manage to overburden and complicate with erratic webs… No matter if they hold themselves back! Through my work everything is motion nonetheless, everything is journey, everything is infinite departure and phenomenal return. Everything, humbly, separates to meet again magnified. The solemn cycles carry away the dazzling thread of destiny on their prestigious flights.

Here, over my work, for a brief season, life spreads like a garden. Then comes a long winter of snow, of obliteration. Like nothing ever was. Memory doubts and recollection fails. Who, in all this barrenness of indifference, would still spot the garden? But over there, somewhere else, life crackling in the hearth blazes up at the zenith of its fire. All of sudden, in its gray suit of rags, death comes in, smothering the fire with ashes and leaving the door open, banging in the empty house…

No matter really! Me, Kébélé, I repair the broken threads. The Tapestry is always being spun. The embroidery will be done.

And when it is finished, it will be just a part of the pulsing, cosmic fabric that will give rise elsewhere, otherwise, to another embroidery, different, but whose warp and weft will not be separate from the whole and on whose framework the ancient threads, the very same ones, will come to form the multifaceted image of a new destiny for men.

Thus was Kobor Tigan't (where you also lived), the immense, the unbelievable, the colossal mountain-city, rising successively to touch the sky with its five hierarchical terraces.

Oh, its unequaled brilliance still endures on my Tapestry!

It was, then, the age of plenitude, of vital expansion. An irresistible attraction, an aspiration to the heights favored the massive growth of men, animals and plants. Everything kept rising higher. Bodies as well as souls. They had treasure troves of power, great reserves of passion, they were rich, truly, and all together, without any bargaining needed. From bountiful nature they effortlessly filled silos and cellars.

A true cosmic breath blew over this world. Neither space nor time but the very substance of this principle, of this non-dimensional ocean in which the master-spirits of all creation swim.

It was this that overshadowed Kobor Tigan't. This that the Giants breathed.

Moaning passions, torrential thoughts, storms of primal devotions, dimensions and power, which we cannot even imagine under our skies of dust. The glory of living that would terrify our puny natures that stagger among cramped neuroses in the little that remains to us...

O Kobor Tigan't, it was said: "Whoever knew you kept your memory forever, stored in the imperishable marrow of their being!"

It was 30,000 years ago when the matriarchy expanded the feminine sun of its radiant ovul...

But this splendor does not matter! It is dear to my heart only because those I was watching over lived there.

You were there too. Remember Abim. You knew all about her. Who didn't fear her! And yet she was no longer ruling. And yet she was living alone. But her magic was governing everything. Nothing and no one escaped its influences, from below, in every direction, branched out. And her black egoism kept her from seeing that she was usurping the power of her eldest daughter, Opak, the queen, the Ooh'Rou, as the Giants said, feminizing the name of their sun, Ooh'R.

Great ills befell.

Abim was a dreadful Kali, an Our Lady from under ground.

She loved nothing as much as reveling, alone, in the telluric emanations, which she knew how to raise up through her body and use, unjustly, to amplify her own magical influences.

Installed in the very center of the realm, she committed the crime or if you prefer, to be more exact, the sin of interfering, like a parasite, in the natural channel of communication between Below and Above, between the telluric energies coming from Mother Earth and the solar, logoic energies coming from the Life-Giving Star, the Sun Ooh'R.

Abim will thus disrupt the whole life plan of the Race of Giants.

Remember that Kobor Tigan't had been organized like a marvelous machine for transcendence. It was the Body, built and structured, of the Race of Giants. Every body should live the fullness of the flesh in the exaltation of its cells.

The Human, the microcosm, could operate through this "mesocosm" to accomplish its union, its reuniting with the macrocosm.

Kobor Tigan't was highly functional. The solar seeds descended freely into the feminine exhalations of the earth. The union of their dual forces created a third ambient point, a field of favorable influences in which nature, in balance, bore fruit and the beings advanced in an extraordinary expansion when living was an intoxication.

This mysterious love play of the earth and the sun in Kobor Tigan't formed an analogy on the level of the Ooh'Rou. The fertile queens represented the becoming of the Race and took upon themselves the production of its models. In their sacred wombs where, through the instrument of a chosen male, the counterpart of the solar seed engenders the children of the future in perfect accord with the promised destinies.

But Abim meddled in this happy harmony. And Opak, her daughter, the queen, mysteriously lost her powers of queenship without understanding why. She could not govern nor produce the Great Child they were hoping for.

Fatal events, born of unbalance, came one after another.

The reign of the Ooh'Rous witnessed a change and, perhaps, an end.

It was the fault of Abim, the Huge Mother, the very essence of the matriarchy, which was paradoxically stricken to death.

Everything started falling apart, the strong, sound values crumbled in the panic, alarm and grief.

Amo, the handsomest of the males in the Royal Chamber of Men, whose body and soul could not be sated by love, died trying to exorcise the detestable influence whose origin he had located.

And Angel, the stranger, the Beautiful Being come from elsewhere, set down through space on the holy mountain Kah'B'La, the one whom Opak loved too much and too hard, disappeared that same day, which hurled the queen into sorrow and madness.

And Ta, the princess, her younger sister, lost the likeness of herself, her double, her only beloved, To. She lost him in an instant for having forgotten, just for an instant, my advice to never be separated.

And Abim whose influence over her was thus severed, also met her own end.

… Then came the endless fog and the sadness of the people...

The B'Tah-Gous, the Storytellers, those female bards who teach the men, began dying. Just like the Ananou, the animal-human hybrids, those grand batrachians they raised to become the weird T'Lo, the bisexual love slaves.

Opak turned crazy, locked up in her rooms. She yearned to forget and, who knows, maybe unconsciously to die, in fanatical eroticism with her T'Lo whose psychic drug ravaged her relentlessly.

The entire Race, affected in its very core, was, therefore, as if lifeless, in a daze. The reaction was not coming. Too slow to change, too heavy to move, it was going to stay totally helpless, unable to confront the changes that had become necessary to its survival if Ta had not, in a redemptive surge, taken the reins just in time.

The young woman will find herself in the highest position before realizing it. The sole inheritor of the B'Tah-Gou sages will be at her side…

And now, here it is: Ata-Réè has become her irreplaceable helpmate. She is the predestined sister who supports, assists and councils, who shares everything, joys and sorrows alike.

Now this: in her Chamber of Men deserted by all the males, in the middle of only her T'Lo, crazy Opak stagnates. No, there are no more B'Tah-Gous. Yes, the Ananou are slowly dying off. And shut in her rooms Abim is lying upright in the shell of a mineral death that has made her body a stone.

Now this: the matriarchy is toppling. Other influences are struggling to exert themselves. Mutations are festering. Already, for a long time, more girls than boys are born. The polyandry of the matriarchy will have no more reason to exist.

Ta is the chosen lady of this new age. But she is less a woman than a Being. It falls on her to pave the way for what is to come. Everything depends on her. She will have to create everything. She will have to dare, to innovate constantly. To usher in the coming time.

She will have to clear away the psychic ruins and, at times, voluntarily demolish the structures that are still useful but in truth already rotten. She reigns. And it is a new and immense reign. She gives Kobor Tigan't the spectacle of a queen never seen before. She astonishes, beguiles, subdues. Opinions vary about her, but in the end her progress almost always prevails.

Ta has become the White Ooh'Rou.

She knows that she is building the necessary link, the transition between two ages. She has known from the start that her reign will pass and be replaced by another, completely different, from which she will withdraw after great weariness. Because her only beloved, To, is no longer.

Grief, regret, absence, Ta will suffer them until the end while showing everyone the enigmatic face of a woman who never grows old, whom they imitate but can never equal and whom they love but never really touch.

CHAPTER I

For Kobor Tigan't, which rose there as always in the five-fold foundation of its colossal and extravagant cities, yesterday, recently, before, what did it have?

What dramas, what laughter, what cries, what stirrings in the souls and bowels, what seasonal turning, what face of the sun?

Forgotten! Already forgotten! Almost... No doubt, yes, there were the vital medley and their daily twists. There was a day. A baroque pearl in the infinite necklace... But this day is long gone. It was forgotten, I tell you!

Now night was reigning. Absolutely. Of course, one might believe that it would not persist. It spread out, though. Its gentleness was relentless, its progression perfect, its settlement complete.

Now it had conquered everything. Blossoming! In the end it proliferated, triumphant!

For everything that had groaned and cracked in the narrowness of conscious living, here was immobility, sleep. And beyond, the opening, the escape, liberation: the greater night. That which is black. Here, thick and heavy and also, elsewhere, sleek and thin like funereal satin. The true, black night. The only one. It billowed everywhere, over its narrow gullies, over its bays, the archways and the exits, bearing the neuter flow of silence in which other silences drift, infinitesimal, those pilgrims in long theories of dispersed vacillations...

But Kobor Tigan't, the pyramid of terraces in titanic levels, the five-fold city of Giants, it stood there and did not leave, anchored in the port of its destiny like a five-deck ship.

Down below, in the first city, which was like the earth, in Kob'Lam, the blacker than black was like velvet between the silos and storerooms where the great muteness of the food reserves slept and also the dark dwellings that harbored the old people, the tranquil people, a vast humus of creatures.

Above it, in Kob'Vam, the vegetal, it was the night of leaves, the bushy trees, the formless gardens among the ranks of foam where the water babbled, rivers and waterfalls, torrential turbulence.

Higher, in the middle of Kob'Ram, the wild heart of the night, a pink halo of embers betrayed the dream of the forges. It never slept like the others, this city of metal and activator bellows! Even in sleep it retains the afterimages of its daytime life: sudden roars or bright bursts, jets of fire and flurries of sparks, a little of this opulent and painstaking activity that makes it vibrate, in constant commotion by the crowds enthralled by the work of the Blacksmiths.

Higher still, in the altitudes where the air became pure and thin, in the mists of geysers and the stupendous waterfall that divides the noble city of Kob'Iam, the bountiful architecture faded away.

Beyond the bridges, the spans and the dizzying stairways, at the summit, against the blackness of the sky, gleamed the golden sphere of the Royal City, surrounded by its votive banners, all turned white now. Just below could be glimpsed the myriad of golden domes of the Palace, patterning the layout of the monumental terraces of Kob'Ooh'R where Ta reigned alone henceforth.

… She does not sleep. In her illustrious bedroom whose size makes her solitude even more apparent, she is there, eyes open, sitting in her bed, her back against the pillows rumpled by her insomnia. A veiled light reveals that everything around her, fabrics and furs, is white. She does not want color anymore. She is alone. She tells herself this. Every day. Every night. Alone facing the bustling race. Alone with the Reign. Alone. To is dead.

She sighs. How would she express her suffering today? She is beyond tears. She barely had any time to herself to weep her mourning. The moon has gone through many phases since the upheavals that brought her to power. From one day to the next, without transition, she had to get to work to maintain the realm, to reassure the people, to pull together the nobles of Kob'Ooh'R and Kob'Iam.

She tackled everything right away, tirelessly, fixing the most pressing problems, containing the still possible panic because the disastrous retreat that interrupted her sister's reign had greatly disturbed the race and fears were surfacing in all their minds, alarmed by events never seen before.

For Ta the days flew by in the work, one task after another, so that she could not find one single moment free of urgent solutions to be applied here, there and everywhere. Therefore, she got used to thinking fast, sorting out and making quick decisions. Her actions took on a rigor that the sluggishness of Opak's reign had made necessary.

Too many days had passed, left to themselves, before the new Ooh'Rou applied the often cruel remedy of her determination and her action.

She influenced the realm with all her will. She projected her thought, in advance, ahead of what was often being prepared in the shadows and what Opak had always tolerated ponderously. She anticipated, devised, prepared.

It was a crushing responsibility! During these long lunar cycles, each one repeating the series of the same emergencies that required unflagging vigilance, Ta had many times thought, resignedly, that the aggravation would never stop. This was her fate, forevermore! Because she had not accepted, from the start, secretly in her heart, to give everything, to do everything that was in her power for the whole race to make the transition to the new age gratuitously or for her to assimilate the impulses needed to create in her the indispensable changes to enter this age without passing away...

But now, on this night, there was a pause in the Queen's work. So unexpected, so precious in its sudden emptiness that Ta did not dare waste it on sleep. She wanted to live it.

She felt again her own body, her presence, living, breathing. She listened to her breath. Once again she knew she was there! Like a spellbound twin she followed the course of her thoughts. Once again she knew she was thinking!

Thanks to this—because basically there were fewer emergencies than yesterday, because all her work had repaired the breaches of power—she could, much better, choose and sort through her thoughts. She could, much better, tune them to the mysterious rhythms of the great will that governed all things before her and by which alone she would be free to govern as far as she proved able to respect and direct the constructive harmonies.

She sighed, like before, but almost with contentment. She settled delicately into this suspension of activity. She stretched her slender hands in front of her and let her back sink lazily into the pillows. This sudden relaxation of her body, instead of carrying it off to sleep, by slowing everything down it clarified the flow of her thoughts.

In this peaceful rhythm all her perceptions took on their former finesse. Again, like when she was just Princess Ta and she escaped to Kah'B'La, the holy mountain, she rejoiced thanks to the play of her senses, investigating the world and bringing back the fruits therefrom.

Thus were reestablished her liaisons with the various palpitations of life. Listening, breathing the air, tasting the nocturnal essence on her lips, brushing her cheeks with the tips of her fingers, examining the details of her room, she located herself, a conscious island around which the storm had finally died down.

She took back possession of herself, of her room, of this time. No more need to confront.

Little by little, therefore, she let her attention drift outside. Nothing got in her way. The bay windows were open, the shades parted. It was the mild season. It was not raining but the sun was still veiled. No one was surprised by this: the Spring Festivals had not taken place this year. The crises and sorrows that struck the best of the race were still too close. An evil spell enveloped Opak, the disastrous, whom her sister Ta wisely kept locked up. The people had bestowed devotional trust in her new reign and they patiently waited for her decisions, her decrees and her changes. Nothing was like before. Ta, then, when the time was right, would know what to do.

The young queen knew the thoughts of the people perfectly well. But at this moment she was enjoying the silence, the emptiness of this black night. She was savoring the austere presence, more meaningful for her than the buzzing of devoted crowds, the demands of petitioners or the chattering sycophants who constantly surrounded her, annoying her sometimes to the point of nausea by the incessant activity that they thrust upon her and demanded back from her in return.

Rest, at last! This night was a haven. Ta could reflect, conscientiously, at her leisure, almost voluptuously. She stepped back, mentally, to get a better look at what had happened.

Alone like this she was Ta. No longer the hectic ghost being harassed on all sides by an impotent people who had been unable to act alone for a long time and continually needed to be poked and prodded.

She contemplated in retrospect. She measured the exact extent of the work. Her first reaction was great amazement.

It suddenly seemed to her that since her accession to power she had lived for only one torrid, breathless, numbing day, a whirlwind of screams, clashes, speeches, always on parade, constantly present before her people who were there, waiting, everywhere, all the time.

Awful obligations! One single day of long-suffering eternity. Until her meager slumbers, always haunted by images that were just episodes from the long day!

Ta's eyes stared into the night outside beyond the windows. She saw, gradually, like in a black mirror, the people's game replayed over and over without realizing that she was once again absorbed in herself. Everything she had observed voluntarily, like everything she had suffered unknowingly, had built up in her consciousness until it formed a sum that she questioned all the time, a measure that she classified, forcing herself to assemble the facts, the reactions of the same nature, early signs of events that she always had to try to see coming, to know the inner essence in order to use it or oppose if need be.

Often, what she had reaped like this remained unknown to her. She did not know what to connect or compare it to. She had to make a guess. With a shudder she examined these faceless enigmas.

What embryo was going to hatch from these sealed shells? What kind of springtime would it be? Where would the sunbeam come from that would cause the awakening, the appearance and then the growth?

Sometimes she guessed and she prepared herself accordingly, sure not to forget and to recognize the thing at the right time.

Sometimes also she accepted certain of these unknowns. Her intuition guided her. She did not know what would come, but she welcomed it in advance, convinced of sensing a future harmony or an aide that would show up at the right time.

Thus, she often felt like she was secretly making mysterious pacts, entering into covenants with positive forces that were offering themselves to her discreetly.

This discriminating function engrossed her and even though it took up all her time, it pleased her, aroused her intelligence as it devised a combination of personal actions in order to bring these elements together into the main themes of her pre-established plan. But she rejected other elements. She was merciless. Her decision came down like a cleaver!

She told almost no one about this project, figuring that she was accountable to no one. Only Ata-Réè, whose radiant devotion was guaranteed, did she sometimes trust. Besides, did she not guess everything! But she was too discreet to ask insensitive questions. Even if she already knew, she just smiled and stayed quiet. The harmonies that governed her were the same as Ta's.

The two women, therefore, were in perfect harmony. They looked alike and had the same worries. Faced with problems, they came up with the same solutions. But Ata-Réè offered hers only if there was need.

Above all, she recognized Ta as her queen, the only Ooh'Rou of Kobor Tigan't.

Since her accession Ta had tried to play the role of regulator. It was necessary to keep up the pace for the Race to evolve. Not too slowly, of course. Numbness and idleness are harmful. And these are the particular flaws of the Giants. But not too fast either. For, hastiness in this peaceful people who enjoyed their routines would have created panic and therefore disorder and perhaps violence.

The Giants were changing.

They were changing already, before, when she was a happy, careless princess. And already, despite her youth, despite her obvious disdain for the affairs of the realm, she had seen this, keenly. Now she thought she had been wrong, warned as she had been, to stand apart.

Who knows? Maybe Abim herself, in her monstrous autocracy, had heeded these warnings?

Who knows if the tragedies could not have been avoided by using young, new measures like Ta devised so easily! Abim would have made her an Ooh'Rou right away since she, the Very Huge, had realized to her bitter disappointment that Opak was unable to govern.

The young, lonely queen shook her head sadly: Everything went awry! She should not have stayed apathetic. For, in the end, To is dead! And Amo, the bravest, he who is like the sun, is dead too. The Beautiful Being, the Stranger from Kah'B'La the holy mountain, isn't he dead as well? He disappeared without anyone knowing. Not a trace, ever. So, Opak went mad, Abim stopped existing, they closed the stone doors of her vigil room, the treasured Storytellers of Kobor Tigan't died off, one after another, an Inescapable exit, they left, their bodies faded away in the shadows of their homes... Ata-Réè, the last Storyteller came to Ta... It was necessary to start the reign right away. Without To...

All this, of course, was her own fault. Her remorse was not abating. It sharpened her prudence, her attention, her vigilance. She wanted to redeem herself in her own eyes. This, too, was nobody else's business. Who among the people had even thought that Princess Ta could have so soon prevented the blows of destiny? No one, certainly. Everyone revered her, on the contrary, because she had galvanized them in those cruel hours.

She knew how to reassure them when they were all *just like* children, frightened by losses and strange calamities that came with them. Everyone adored her passionately because she herself had been struck and the last wave of misfortune deprived her forever of her only beloved, To.

She alone knew why he died. In truth, she alone knew the secret motivation. She let him leave. She really sent him to his destiny. She ordered it. She said, "Go!" had not the old man of Kah'B'La warned, "Beautiful children, never separate from each other!"

The young woman rolled her head wearily over her pillows. Always the same thoughts, the same remorse, the same regrets! The shudder before the sobs fluttered in her breast.

Come on, useless! She had no more tears. She forced her thoughts back onto a better course. This was the way she could mend.

... The people. The Race. The coming future. The indispensable changes...

Unusual currents were running through the Giants. They could not safely keep on living like this. The past was suffocating them. It was used up. Nothing could be drawn from it. Their tranquil habits were cracking all over. The absolute reign of women had stopped being the cradle of the future. It was, on the contrary, becoming the quagmire... O Ta, you know it, you who are the first white and manless Ooh'Rou, you who safeguard this hard passage from one age to another, you know it. But how to tell them, everyone of your race who, still so recently, communed in the Fertilization of the Queen, that formidable Ooh'Rou, splendid and golden, whose Chamber of Men contained the most beautiful males, Opak her sister who is languishing, locked up, at the mercy of her T'Lo's drug!

It was impossible to say anything. Nobody would understand. Action was needed. An action designed specifically for transformation and to be kept up over long and patient years. To cleverly replace the mores and customs that no longer really satisfied. To discern, before the people themselves, what would really no longer satisfy. What had stopped having correspondence in the present time and in their souls had to be destroyed. Always put something else in its place. Leave no empty holes. Replace. Compensate. Innovate.

Broad features were being erased while others, previously in the preserve of a minority, were developing, anarchically, looking to be adopted by everyone. They would be invasive and dangerous if Ta did not rein them in beforehand.

This was the case with the T'Lo.

In order to think better, she had just closed her eyes.

It seemed to her that she was not completely accepted by the Devotees of the T'Lo. She often felt reservations, resistance even among the nobles of this kind. They appeared to be attached more than others to the past, to ancestral legends, to old ways of doing things.

Ta disapproved of the use of T'Lo. She knew all the dangers, having seen them at work up close in the royal family. Opak's resignation, her sickness, her madness, came straight from the erotic exhaustion due to the abuse of the T'Lo and the psychic intoxication they caused. There was no example of a Devotee not becoming apathetic toward the end, but alas, the depraved nobles saw this as a refinement, a privilege. They had got used to dying in muddled ecstasy at the end of their exhaustion. "They're rejecting real life," Ta figured. This habit had to be abandoned since it was ravaging the best families.

It had not been the same for the Ancestors who suffered no psychic damage. This was a particularity that Abim liked to recall whenever she prodded Opak to be careful with her T'Lo.

The giants of Kobor Tigan't, over the ages, had become acclimated to the subtle poison that contact with the T'Lo distilled in them. Perhaps the latter were likewise evolving in their comfortable environment, somehow increasing their toxicity?

Wisely, the young woman thought that everything had its time and that a once inoffensive habit was becoming excessively harmful. Things have to change periodically. Often they turned into their opposite when they were no longer necessary but only a stubborn routine.

The Great Ancestors, at the end of their monumental exodus, which had decimated them before bringing them to the High Plains where they built Kobor Tigan't, formed an alliance with the T'Lo only to create servants and helpmates. Over the years, bonds of affection were obviously made between the masters and their humanimals. Gradually they stopped using them. They adopted them. They reveled in raising them. They desired them. Their tender nature blossomed. The devout admiration they had for humans caused them to pay back hundredfold the slightest attention paid them. They were love slaves. They had no other mentality. They probably desired to become humans...

"There you go," Ta thought, "the utility of one era has been transformed into useless perversity! The usage is a poison. The T'Lo are not made to enter the coming time. They are vestiges. Without the care they are surrounded with they would already have disappeared naturally."

Clear signs supported her reasoning.

In the Pit under the palace, the Ananou, those T'Lo not yet domesticated, were they not dying off? Every day, or almost, their number decreased. One after another they sank into apathy before finally falling asleep, never to awaken. It had started just before the death of Abim. There had been moments of lesser carnage, but it always started up again, more or less severe, for longer or shorter periods. It had to be admitted that at some unimaginable point in the future, there would be no more Ananou.

"So," Ta told herself, "maybe the T'Lo would also dwindle away? That would naturally solve the problem." They already seemed to be procreating less than before. The young Ananou born of the T'Lo and put back in the Pit after weaning were becoming rarer. In any case, the very old balance of births that had always compensated for losses was now broken. Ta did not think it would right itself.

From the start of the problem she had enacted severe measures.

She had secretly taken out the corpses during the night and forbidden it to be spoken of. No one came near the Pit anymore. The guards around it were Abim's old guards, enormous men who looked carved out of stone. The young Ooh'Rou made them the elite of her personal guards. Their chief was called Hé-Nark. He hardly ever left the queen and constantly kept watch at her door.

Ta loved to be surrounded by these men who followed all her orders. They were reserved by nature and extremely discreet and serious. They did not chitchat and their presence alone kept away the pests. These men were bound by a fraternity of habits and tastes. They were nourished by lofty sentiments and dedicated to the sun Ooh'R. They were a blend of warrior and priest.

The women, while admiring them, seldom accepted them in the Chamber of Men. Maybe they were too private for their liking? Possibly. Even the most authoritative of women avoided looking straight into their gray eyes because these superior males always smiled and nobody could say what their slightly ironic smile really meant.

From their long service to Abim, who demanded self-control, silence and incorruptibility from them, they had built a rock-solid character. Tough and callous towards anything that did not come from the royal power, they gave to Ta a feeling of safety and strength. They manifested the resolutions of her soul.

Their first public appearances with her had fascinated the crowds. There was a kind of revelation. Having been shut in with Abim for such a long time, they were practically unknown. In addition, they turned out to be very different from the other males.

At first the people naturally thought they represented the new queen's Chamber of Men. She had to deny it publicly but was not sure she was believed. On that day no guards had smiled and a haze of resignation veiled the eyes of Hé-Nark. But what did their feelings matter! The queen respected them and could congratulate herself for the choice. So, they had to settle for that.

But with respect to the Ananou, she also knew it would take very little for the secret to evaporate, even if the trusty guards said nothing, even if the people were docile and unsuspicious. An indiscretion was always possible.

Besides, did not intuitions have a role to play, which so often arouse sudden curiosity? Faced with what must not be seen, the wind of chance stirs up the one and only gossipy child of the whole realm.

Ta had caught snippets of nervous talk from the nobles concerning the Ananou. Since her ascension to the throne, they had made, as usual, requests for adoption of Ananou, which she, because of here disapproval, had not granted, postponing her answers.

The Devotees of the T'Lo, confident in the legitimacy of their rights, were astonished. Still, they had politely waited, figuring that Ta was behaving like this because of the troubled times and anyway it was not an outright refusal. Therefore, they remained on stand-by. But their feelings toward the new Ooh'Rou were mixed from then on. The situation was becoming unmanageable. It was in danger of reaching a critical point.

Now, the young queen was determined not to influence the extinction of the Ananou, which she saw as a sign of the New Age. Without them the Race would be able to purify itself. Moreover, these Devotees were only a minority. All the people had always openly opposed their practices.

Ta had promised, therefore, to lend out none of the Ananou to individuals. This would be a start. She would abolish the custom when the time came. She realized she could not wait too long. But, truth to tell, she did not know how to go about it and especially in what terms she should announce her decision.

At this juncture, Ata-Réè reported other conversations of the Devotees to her, one after another. The agitation was growing. Confused mutterings had apparently been overheard: "We don't understand this

Ooh'Rou Ta anymore. Isn't keeping up the customs the surest guarantee of a quick return to a normal and happy life?"

The did not understand that life, to be kept up, needed change and that like in nature it was necessary to let some creatures die so that others, more in tune with the new intricacies, might take their place and play their role, momentarily as well.

Ta was so thoroughly penetrated by this New Age that she was surprised, annoyed and always saddened to see the reluctance of her kind. "They're all going to perish if I can't change them. They will become like my mother Abim, mineral masses, devoid of their humanity, stuck forever on terraces of dead stone!"

She had to prevent such a fate at all costs! A sudden desire to take immediate action reared its head. She controlled it, being perceptive enough to see that time would accomplish her plan and she need not rush things but on the contrary pretend sometimes to be in agreement with the others.

She had also agreed to see a delegation of the Devotees. The meeting was supposed to take place the next morning in the Audience of the Light. How much she wanted this night to never end!

They had taken a liking to meetings with Ta. She was not like her sister Opak who granted very few and so was hardly ever asked. The pressure of recent tragedies had raised all kinds of latent questions, too long neglected by the Race. Affected by the calamities, yanked out of their quietism, the Giants of Kobor Tigan't were starting to discover their spiritual poverty. Their overindulgent lifestyle was fraying, uncovering the tatters of their secret being. Why, how, how long, what was the meaning of all this, what should they do? Swarms of questions! And the inability to answer them…

They had no imagination. They did not yet know how to make good use of the materials offered nor to try to put them together. They remained passive. So far, with a stunning surfeit of naivety, they had put up with the critical developments that made up all their glory and strength. But this was not enough!

They, too, had realized that this was not enough for a long time. And that Ooh'Rou Opak had not helped them, not governed but only lugged around her massive body among them in a daze without ever thinking about the slow movements of their minds. A bad Ooh'Rou, really! And her noxious influence was certainly responsible for the inexplicable deaths of admirable Amo, of To the beloved of the princess, and of He-Who-Comes-From-Elsewhere, known for too short a time, alas!

The traumatized Giants brooded over their regrets without doing anything…

But since then, at the top, an Ooh'Rou, unthinkable before, clean and white, was finding answers, even anticipating their questions, guessing them as if by magic. Right away, almost from one day to the next, they got used to talking to her and confidently awaiting all her explanations, all her decisions.

Women started repeating, like a chant, "Ooh'Rou Ta knows!" It sounded very precise, very affirmative. Afterward it turned into an expression they used to end difficult conversations between good folk. When an argument reached some thorny deadlock, they sighed and said, "Yes, but She knows." Simply put, this meant they were leaving the solution of the problem to more capable hands.

This simple exclamation comforted them. They used and abused it. They really had dire need of such a queen.

With this thought, Ta, in her half-sleep, smiled faintly. Then the images in her mind became blurrier. Her breath became deeper. She was not really sleeping yet even though she did not open her eyes and her head nodded to the side.

Despite this restful state, her mind suddenly dove into the grievous problem that she knew she would have to confront very soon: Opak!

It had just sprang up out of the worries caused by T'Lo. She could not help thinking of the only one of them who was likeable: T'Lo Dê, Opak's favorite who far surpassed all his kind in intelligence and, truth to tell, in humanity. This last quality was very easy to see in him. Besides, thanks to the compassion of the Beautiful Stranger, he had experienced a truly extraordinary awakening of consciousness. T'Lo Dê had been personalized.

Humbly, Ta had to admit that she had secret respect for him. She tried hard not to show it.

But she wondered if it was not because of him that she was delaying the necessary elimination.

Now she was afraid that T'Lo Dê had caught the same illness as his primitive brothers, the Ananou. Indeed, over the past lunar cycles he had become morose. Sluggish and apathetic, he spent most of his time lying around, alone, in a corner of Opak's room.

If anyone entered, he became even more lethargic, pulled up his knees and half hid behind cushions. He had absolutely no interest in the former Ooh'Rou and never mingled with the other T'Lo who continued to surround and caress her. He even seemed afraid of the violent outbursts and when a fit sent the madwomen into spasmodic howling, he went half crawling in search of help from the nearest guards. Hé-Nark had often witnessed this and had spoken to Ta in his discreet and detached manner. He was the one who suggested to her that the T'Lo was certainly going to have a baby.

So, there would be two births because Opak's pregnancy was reaching its end.

The heart of the young queen beat grievously at this reminder. With her older sister being half-crazy what kind of child would it be? And above all, who would this child be? Was it only from the seed of Amo? Nothing was less sure…

For a long time she had prepared herself to face this ordeal. Ata-Réè would help her. But afterward, once the infant was born? It would no doubt go to join the other sons and daughters of Opak in the Royal Nursery. And if the child, born after so many troubles, bore the sign, the Sign that Abim refused to reveal the exact nature of? A Sign come from Ooh'R the Sun…

Ta has fallen asleep without realizing it. For a long moment she will be very calm.

Outside, little by little, the night is starting to change. Clouds drift in that are now massed into a milk-white ceiling. The air is astir. Winds pick up. The awnings over the windows billow as if they are taking advantage of Ta's sleep to put some clandestine commotion into the formerly calm room.

At first vague, the ocean scent from the Great Va-Hôh, the cursed west, is strong now. It is no longer the black night. Something else is looming. It is like the invisible witnesses of an imminent event are gathering.

But the young woman dreams… She has difficulty moving in the sparkling water falling from very high up onto her who feels neither the weight nor the moisture. It is the big waterfall on the other side of Kah'B'La, the one that sprang out after the disappearance of Angel, the Beautiful Angel. Ta is trying to get to the heart of the element. There is something attracting her there even though she does not know its nature and it is almost impossible to see anything in the midst of all the shimmering. Nevertheless, she strives. She has the feeling that something urgent is soon going to pull her away from this task. She has to find out before they call her back! Abruptly, she runs into the unknown mass that is there in the water and that is glittering broken reflections like a giant gem. Ta cries out, "Angel!"

And her dream breaks off… A loud thump. It is her heart. A dark thump. It is the night, the usual grief. From deep down in the dark To is rising up, imploring, calling her! He is running towards her. Without ever moving closer. Without ever reaching her. She is riveted to her throne. She cannot speak. She cannot do anything for To. Nothing but suffer. Nothing but pant, endlessly, in the lamentation of this double torture… Her heart is pounding…

Ta jumps to her feet. Someone is knocking on her door.

It is Ata-Réè, who enters, preceded by Hé-Nark. His skin looks gray. Despite his self-control he is an emotional man. He must be upset. He salutes and steps back. But his eyes say much.

Ata-Réè whispers hurriedly, "Ooh'Rou, Opak's time is starting. I was there. You have to come now."

She has already thrown a coat over Ta's shoulders. Even in her haste the gesture is soothing, affectionate, imparting the strength that the young woman will have great need of.

Ta thinks, "The ordeal has come." But now she is determined like every time she has to act. Refusing any reply, she rushes off with her assistant. Hé-Nark is waiting in the hallway. She stops to touch his arm. His whole body shivers like always, even when her dress barely grazes him.

"You understand, right?" she asks.

He nods.

"You will never say anything about this night without my order." She hammers out these words. She touches his arm again.

He confirms, "I'll never say anything. You know this very well, Ooh'Rou."

She stares into his eyes. Yes, she knows. She is content with him. "Well then, come with us," she orders.

The guard follows them silently down the hallways that wind around towards Opak's rooms. At their approach the other guards step aside, bowing their heads as the queen passes by.

She swings around to Hé-Nark, "You are responsible for their silence. See to it."

He smiles. No one will dare speak as long as he is around. His authority is not empty and everyone respects it. He is the Chief, their Leader.

Opak's ransacked rooms are no longer those of a queen but of a madwoman.

Contrary to their habit, all the T'Lo were together in a single room far from their mistress. They seemed to have gathered there spontaneously. The lurking anxiety is causing them to look upon everyone and everything with frightened eyes. Some have tears on their cheeks. What is happening to Opak is unnerving them. Their sensitive organism quivers, like a reflection, at what goes on in the nearby bedroom.

When Ta gets there, she barely glances at them. Still, she gets the feeling that T'Lo Dê is not among them. But she does not have time to check. The emergency is elsewhere and too much time has already passed with nobody helping Opak. She can hear her breathing, hoarse and shaky.

She catches the smell of sweat and blood. In order to approach her sister, lying on a pile of gutted pillows, she has to kick her way through the jumble of clothes, jewelry and plates of unfinished meals.

Ata-Réè quickly leans over, clears the way and helps her queen.

Opak dozes, moaning, totally nude. Her huge belly glistens like ripe fruit. Strangely, she has strung a bunch of her jewelry along her left leg: bracelets and necklaces on which she has threaded rings, winding them from her ankle up to her thigh.

"Step aside," Ta utters briefly to her maidservant.

While her assistant politely does what she is told, the young queen swallows her disgust and leans over her sister who seems to be unaware of her presence.

It has been a long time since she has seen her so close. She is struck by all the details of her degradation. Her body, not so long ago celebrated for its harmonious shape, is deformed by fat. Her once so glorious, coppery orange skin has turned pale, riddled with blemishes. Her face is barely recognizable. The erotic abuse of the T'Lo has left its stigmatic marks. Indeed, her temples are deep, mauve hollows that blend into the wide, dark rings around her eyes. Her nose also bears this mark. Other similar stains are starting to mottle her cheeks.

Ta lifts one of her hands to look nervously at her nails. They are mauve too. In furious bitterness she wonders how the families devoted to

29

the T'Lo can consider these marks of the highest nobility, the elegant legacy of a privileged class.

She shakes her head sadly and shares with Ata-Réè, "How far she had fallen! She won't live much longer."

"That's right," the maidservant says. "Her time is up. She has turned away from life. Everything is too much for her now. Except, of course, her T'Lo... But look, for the child, nothing is moving forward. It's going to die if this continues. She doesn't want to make the effort."

Ta sighs, "It's as if she doesn't even know it."

The young woman feels a weird kind of weariness. Who is right? Should we really fight it? This woman has chosen another path, the path of denial. Must we harass her because we are on a different path? Must we force her to snap out of it, to remember all the tragedies that made a wreck of her? Must we force her to play her final role as mother? And what is in her womb? Maybe a monster that we will have to get rid of? Maybe Opak feels like this child should never see the light of day...

But life forces are strong in Ta. Before making a final decision about what to do, she ends up shouting out, "Opak! Do you hear me, Opak?"

Success! An eye opens, just one, shiny, clear, sharp, right in front of her face. She could not help jerking back. It is staring so intensely at her. But does it see her?

She presses, "Opak, it's me, Ta. Do you recognize me?"

The other eye is open now. Alas, this one is all hazy, clouded over, and then it slips to the side, away from the first.

Startled, Ata-Réè cannot hold back a cry. The young queen herself thinks she prefers the face with eyes closed rather than this unsupportable mask! What can one expect from a creature so far gone?

Nevertheless, she grips the shoulders of the prone woman, gently but firmly, to make sure her words get through. "Listen, Opak. You're expecting a child. I told you every day when I came to see you. Do you remember? Now is the moment. Feel your belly! Your child is coming? We have to move you. You have to help it come out."

She stops. The two eyes are closed again. A vague smile (one might call it ironic) crosses the puffy face. Suddenly her face turns red. It looks like her neck is swollen. Her head rolls from side to side. Opak is certainly in pain. But there is no sign that labor is starting—the birth remains at a standstill.

It is obvious that her huge, apathetic bulk is not sending to her brain the true meaning of the visceral labor that is trying to break out. The psychic drug of the T'Lo have destroyed her nerves.

Even still, a dim and distant suffering must be felt somehow because she starts mumbling, "Pain... I want my T'Lo..."

She straightens up a little, tormented, in the arms of Ata-Réè. Her eyelids crack open. Her eyes wander a little less. She is trying to make out the details around her and she reaches out aimlessly. It is Ta whom she touches and who responds to her squeeze.

"My T'Lo. Where are my T'Lo? I want..."

"No," Ta says. "Not now. Later."

Tears well up in Opak's eyes.

Ta tries to comfort her, "You will have them later."

"All?"

"Yes, all. And T'Lo Dê too. But right now, sister, you have to give birth to your child. It wants to come out. Help it!"

She was suddenly stupefied to see Opak shaking with laughter. But since it hurt her, she stopped almost immediately and cried out, "My child! What child? Opak has no child."

Shaken again but this time with a sob, she resumed sounding reproachful.

"You shouldn't make fun of me, sister. You know as well as I that Opak has failed in everything... You're not mean, so don't hold it against poor Opak. There will be no child this year. Everyone knows it just like you and they say nothing. My people are not mean."

She broods a little, like she is about to fall back asleep. Then she lifts a finger in the air and declares, "This year, in which the greatest misfortunes fell upon us, the Sun Ooh'R did not fertilize the Queen of Kobor Tigan't."

The crazed laughter shook her again. She claps her hands. And once again the pain stops her. She starts choking. For an instant she just pants like a wretched animal. Then, between two gasps, she cries out, pleading, "My T'Lo... I want my T'Lo..."

"You will have them. Soon."

Opak calms down, looks at her sister, leans back against Ata'Réè, "You're not mean, Ta, it's true. So, listen..."

Lowering her voice, with terror on her face, she pulls her sister closer by the neck as if to share a secret.

31

"Her, you know, the Very Huge, our Mother Abim, she guessed it! Before everyone. Before I even dared believe in my misfortune, she yelled at me 'Shame! Shame!' I was scared. Her anger is searching for me, always, everywhere, to cast me down... Abim is going to put you in my place! Yes, yes, it's true. You will be the Ooh'Rou. I'll be nothing. The Very Huge is fed up. Hear how she screams!"

In spite of herself, Ta pricked up her ears. Strange whispers can be heard outside. She smells the odor of the Grand Va Hôh that permeates the air.

"It's the wind," she says.

"No, no," Opak shoots back, "it's our Terrible Mother. Everyone will know. Oh, how loud she's shouting! 'Opak has an empty womb! Good people of Kobor, we have a Calamitous Queen!' An empty womb, that's it, the emptiness is hurting me, I'm destitute, my riches have gone, I'm all empty... Oh, it's the emptiness that wants to come out. Oh, how big it is, how heavy..."

She starts beating her belly. The two women have to hold down her arms.

"Come, Ta, send me my T'Lo. I can't go on without them. I need them. Get them here and you will be queen. You want that, right? You just have to take all my men, I don't love them anymore. You'll have the best Chamber of Men, a queen's Chamber... My T'Lo! Just one. Send in T'Lo Dê. Oh, he doesn't love me anymore... Listen and you'll understand. My T'Lo take me far, far away, up on high, into the heart of Ooh'R where the lights spin with bright colors that pour out of all my T'Lo and enter my belly. Then I climax, always, continually, I am alive and I climax. Here, you understand, look, everything's dead, it's full of the dead. I made them all die, me, the Calamitous... the corpses... a roomful! Amo, Amo, it's him! Oh, the Beautiful Amo. But yes, Ta, he's crawling with worms! And he still wants to come with me! No, no, Amo... Angel too is here in his net. Since I captured him on Kah'B'La, he's been dressed up like that. Him too, all decayed! And yours, my sister, your only one, To, he is here..."

Ta was struck with horror, but she cannot bring herself to interrupt the madwoman.

"To is not the same, he flows like mud on the ground... Look, they're coming! All of them! Give me my T'Lo who will take me away... Help! Oh, the dead, they're all pulling my life out!"

She sinks completely into a fit of dementia, howling, drooling. She writhes and twists, trying to break free of invisible restraints. Her agitation kicks off the labor again. She arches her back in the throes of pain. The child is starting to appear.

On the small head Ta sees a tiny lock of hair. Hair so thin, so pale that she cannot help thinking of Angel. The thought flashes through her like lightning. She knows—this is the child of Angel!

She does not say anything. The secret proof has just struck at her very heart.

She forgets everything, her fatigue, her torments, the atrocity of the situation where a poor, crazy woman does not even know she is bringing her son into the world, a son who is, without a doubt, glorious.

Ata-Réè has surely understood, too. Yes, their eyes meet, gleaming.

But Opak is still now, unconscious apparently. Ta makes her decision. The child has to be born. They cannot let the child perish. It is already showing signs of weakness. It does not matter if Opak has to sacrifice her own life. They have to force her and get this new life out of her unconscious belly.

The same determination fires them both up: Ata-Réè and her Queen work together, fervently. The child, save the child! Opak's tortured body lurches. But the fruit is plucked out of it.

It is time! The baby, a small male, is blue and not moving. But it cries shrilly.

Worn out, soaked in blood, disheveled, Ta is clutching it to her own bosom, her, the widow, sterile, the Ooh'Rou without a man.

Ata-Réè gently dries off the tiny creature. The baby cries and quivers. They can find nothing to say. They just look at what they are holding there without really believing it.

And then, as the baby starts kicking, Ta sees on the sole of one foot a mark—round, orange, encircled by rays.

Her whole body shivers. "The Great Child!" she utters reverently.

The Great Child! She has identified the solar sign, the mark of Ooh'R, the Gift of Ooh'R, that Abim refused to reveal. No possible doubt about it. On this child, born in such extraordinary circumstances, where life and death merged, on the borders of madness and sanity, is unquestionably put the mark of the Sun, which destines him to reign. So far only females bore the mark. They alone, the future Ooh'Rous, were called like this to their exceptional reigns. They had always been recognized like this.

But this time it is a male. The first to be chosen like this. Ooh'R knows, too, that the reign of women over Kobor Tigan't is coming to an end...

"I am the last Ooh'Rou," Ta says.

Ata-Réè leans over and kisses her shoulder.

The young queen calls in Hé-Nark. She hands him the child swaddled in soft sheets. "Carry him to my bedroom. Don't let yourself be seen. He won't make a sound. He's sleeping. Watch over him until I come."

Ta sends Ata-Réè to get some women from the Royal Nursery to take care of Opak. She has made the very quick decision to keep this son of Angel and Opak , The Great Child, near her. She has made a rapid assessment of the situation. Her conclusion is clear.

She does not want this child in the Royal Nursery. He would be raised there without education like all the others. That is not at all what she wants. So, she will care for it personally with the help of Ata-Réè.

For now, it does not seem the right time to reveal its existence. This would bring only more complications. The people are not prepared. She must do a little more beforehand, gradually set up new institutions that will allow her to make the whole race accept the future rule of a male.

During all this preliminary work the child will grow up. She understands that there will be a first stage in her plan when she will be at liberty to talk about him, to unveil his parentage and show him. But nothing more. He will be welcomed. She had no doubt about it. The memory of Angel, the Beautiful Stranger, is still very vivid. When he was among them, everyone wanted to see him take a prominent position in Kobor Tigan't at the side of Opak before the disasters struck, for which she was judged responsible.

Now that she is alone in the room and Ta, shaking off these thoughts, goes to her sister.

Blood is still flowing. It is time for the women to come...

Very clearly, very calmly, she talks to Opak, "Listen and listen well. You've brought the Great Child into the world, He who carries the Mark of Ooh'R. Listen up. It's Angel, the Beautiful Being, who gave it to you."

Did she hear, just lying there? She is staring at Ta with big, tranquil eyes. A royal solemnity haloes her for a moment.

The affirming words ring out again: "It's the Great Child, yours. He whom you loved so much, the Beautiful Being fertilized you."

Everything shuts down. Her eyelids close. A gray mask, almost a death mask already, settles on her peaceful face. She is asleep.

Blood keeps seeping out. Too much for Ta as she grows impatient. When the Nursery women get there and immediately start panicking, she lays into them hard and coldly, then with Ata-Réè's support, supervises their work.

When the room is tidied up, the bed remade, Opak cleaned up and subdued by her weakness, the women are sent away. Thankful to be free so quickly, they hurry out without further ado. The contact of a calamitous Ooh'Rou is always fearsome. The less they see her, they better they will be. The young queen knows this. She figures they will not gossip much because the Giants do not like to tempt evil with careless speech.

Ata-Réè steps up to her. "You should lie down, Ooh'R. It's not yet sunrise. You're tired. And soon there's that meeting in which you'll have to be wide-awake."

"I know," Ta smiled at her concern. "You're right, but I still have things to do. It's not over yet. Stay here with Opak. Come get me if you need anything. I'm going to send Hé-Nark to you with the baby. As long as Opak is alive, she'll nurse her son. You're in charge from now on."

A hushed noise makes them turn around. It is the T'Lo who are coming back timidly to gather around Opak. They lie down, sit or squat without taking their golden eyes off her. But they make no move toward her.

Nonetheless, Ata-Réè's reflex is to chase them off, but Ta stops her, "Leave them! What are you worried about? That they'll bother her? No, look, you know how they are. They'll respect her and help her as long as the child isn't weaned. Until then, they'll keep their eroticism in check. Let's hope the same goes for her."

She sighs before continuing.

"You can watch her watch over her in peace with them. If you have to move Opak, ask for their help. You'll see, they're clever, they're quick to understand what you want from them. They only ever want to obey and they don't have a hint of maliciousness.

Ata-Réè replies, "It's true. Deep down, for devotion and loyalty they're almost perfect."

"Well," Ta concludes with half a smile, "they are T'Lo…"

All of a sudden a tiny little whine is heard nearby only to break off right away. Puzzled, they look at each other and listen. It seemed to have come from a cramped, dark room off the bedroom where they stored the cushions, furs and blankets.

"What was that?" the young queen wonders aloud. "It sounded like a small creature... but it can't be a child, right?"

She lingers for a moment, waiting for another whine. Then, with one of those flashes of inspiration that she is used to, she realizes that something as strange as the birth of the Great Child might very well be happening. She heads straight for the small room. As she goes she calls out, "T'Lo Dê?" Knowing perfectly well that he cannot answer since like all T'Lo he is mute.

However, they hear a rustling noise from the back of the big closet. Ta leans forward and asks nervously, "Is that you, T'Lo Dê?"

She can see nothing. Ata-Réè snatches up a lamp.

The cry erupts again, pressing, angry.

Ta mutters, "Yes, it's a little creature. Not a T'Lo since it's calling out. But what a forceful cry! How angry it sounds!"

The lamp throws dark, crooked shadows onto the walls: the corners of the piled-up cushions, lumps and slivers of blankets and covers, and the round head of T'Lo Dê suddenly visible. From deep inside this lair he is struggling to come out, but he falls back. His giving birth must have been very recent. However, in the light his eyes glitter with an extraordinary fire and his face has an expression of boundless pride. Too weak to move, with a touching impulse he holds out a frisky little being that looks contorted with rage and whose furious wails get louder at Ta's approach.

She sees then, up close, the unbelievable: this creature born of T'Lo Dê is not an Ananou. It has only one sex—it is a girl whose head is already crowned with flaming red hair.

The young queen is dumbstruck. Her heart is pounding because she feels that another truth has just been made clear.

Furthermore, still susceptible to picking up thoughts, T'Lo Dê is already waiting for her to tell him what she has just guessed but dare not say.

She whispers, "She is from Amo, isn't she?"

T'Lo Dê nods enthusiastically. Grateful love is ablaze in him. For the first time in Kobor Tigan't a human seed has successfully crossed with a T'Lo. He knows it. He sits up. He smiles. He points out that the child is not mute. He, T'Lo Dê, has created what he loves more than anything in the world—he has created a human!

His joy brims over. With his long, delicate fingers he exhibits the limbs of his daughter to show Ta all her perfections. He spreads her tiny fingers, tenderly touching the webbing between them, but he holds up his own hand to show that hers are much thinner. He points to the amber skin and brings her up to his cheek to compare with his own pinker, less beautiful skin. As a comment, he shakes his head, sighs and smirks as if embarrassed for himself. Finally, solemnly, with the greatest signs of respect, touching them one by one, he indicates the two poles of his masterpiece: the hair of fire and the tiny genitalia, the simple sex of a girl…

Ta feels overwhelmed. This joy captures her heart. She sees the lamp trembling in the hand of Ata-Réè.

But how to avoid thinking of the what comes after this incident? What will become of this hybrid? More human than T'Lo or more T'Lo than human? How will these two natures, the T'Lo ancestry and the human ancestry, be reconciled? There will be battles and tensions in this infant. No doubt the mighty blood of Amo will triumph over the humanimal blood by awakening its qualities of courage, kindness, uprightness and, above all, solar love…

It should certainly be raised as a human. It must be closely watched over and brought up.

The baby's cries have not stopped. Ta is suddenly aware of them and surprised to feel so annoyed by them. She looks at the child. It really does seem to be lashing out against everything around it. Its limbs thrash about but with surprising determination.

Ata-Réè looks gloomy. She gazes at Ta with her faraway look of a prophetess. "She's going to be very mean. She's going to do harm. Always and in every possible way. It'd be better if she'd died."

T'Lo Dê turns green. It is his way of growing pale. He hugs his child tightly. But his baby finds a breast, takes it and suckles greedily.

"We will raise it here with the Great Child. They will both receive the same royal education. I'll see to it myself."

Ta has spoken and there is no going back once her decision has been made. She wants to honor the memory of Amo whom she has always held in particular esteem.

She addressed T'Lo Dê now, "Opak has brought the Great Child into the world while you gave birth to this girl. This is an historic moment for Kobor Tigan't."

Relieved and delighted, T'Lo Dê makes the typical deep bow of the T'Lo as Ta leaves the room.

Ata-Réè bows, too, without another word. She knows, sadly, that she has to keep a close eye on her beloved queen because from this day forward a danger is growing here... A very powerful danger, she thinks as she glances one last time at the baby feeding almost savagely already and squeezing the breast in rhythm with its tiny, forceful hands.

She has gone back without saying a word to take her station at Opak's bedside. Most of the T'Lo are dozing around her. They are as calm and gentle as always. T'Lo Dê stays to himself.

The young queen walks slowly back to her rooms through the maze of stone corridors. She meets nobody. The guards have gone. Hé-Nark has done his duty. Now he just has to bring the child back to Opak. He has to wait for the order. On the way, Ta feels the weight of her fatigue. The nights of insomnia have worn her down. What happened to her safe sleep in the arms of To? A tearless sob.

She gets to the door. Hé-Nark looks at her with his insightful affection. She bites her lip and distracts him. "The child?"

"He's resting. He doesn't cry. He's a good baby, queen."

"Yes, Hé-Nark, he is destined to great things."

"I'll watch over him just like over you. But if the same danger threatens you both someday and I can only save one, it will you, Ooh'Rou, whom I will save."

Ta snaps back, "No, Hé-Nark, your duty from now on is first of all to the Great Child."

She shows him the two solar marks.

The guard pales a little, then a brave smile brightens his face. "Well, I'll save you both, no matter what happens."

He leaves with the newborn whose little blonde lock of hair, all cleaned up and glistening like a silky snowflake, is all that can be seen.

The memory of Angel is suddenly so present, so palpable in the room that the young woman shivers with loneliness and looks around, disoriented, expecting to see some apparition jump out. But there is nothing but the wind blowing, twice as hard as before.

To get a little rest she has to close the shudders, whose awnings are flapping or plastered against the walls. Ta remembers how Angel was like an angry bird when caught in the vile net on Kah'B'La and had thrashed about...

Before closing them she takes a look outside. The cloudy night is agitated. The rippled sky is fraying. Is a storm coming out of Grand Va-Hôh? It would be a bad omen. She leans out to get a whiff of the weather? Far down below, like in a chasm where the remains of the black night have congealed, she gazes down the plunging perspective of the tiered cities. Halfway down, in Kob'Ram, the pink glow of the forges softens its halo. Ta loves the forges and the metalwork that is done there. She reminds herself to make use of the Blacksmiths. They are interesting people and creators. She will go get a closer look one of these days.

She will also get a closer look at the Royal Nursery. She should get to know the children there. They are the noble caste. She thinks, "They are my closest family. Opak has turned out to be a disaster. She was a great progenitor and in this sense truly royal. Her fruits were always, without exception, beautiful and healthy. But then the women in the Nursery, although they are sweet and tender, are completely incompetent to give the children any individual distinction. Me, I want them all different! I'll have to keep them close to me. I'll have to pay more attention to their couplings from now on. As soon as they're old enough, the girls should have their choice from the Chambers of Men. To do like the Ooh'Rou!

"This might make the Nursery women laugh. Whims and unbridled freedom—they let the children do anything! Their naughtiest mischief is just looked at as something amusing. Because of this leniency, the kids get bored quickly. As soon as they're adults, most of them turn into devotees of the T'Lo, more fanatical than others."

She is thinking this, already sliding the stone shutters closed, when she notices down in the garden of Kob'Iam a light moving. It is a woman, then a man going out along with three of their T'Lo!

She cannot believe her eyes. This is contrary to all customs, to all discreet use of the T'Lo, which have always been respected so far. A T'Lo never goes outside, except during very rare ceremonies. Important funerals, for example, are one of these exceptions.

But here, now, these people are walking off their property! And they are—she cannot doubt it—going across other people's property. Now they are going down, step by step, into the empty streets of Kob'Ram; With their T'Lo!

Ta goes to lie down on her bed. She will not sleep. She has too many worries.

Ata-Réè leans over wistfully. She is holding the son of Opak in her arms. She had to keep it because every time she put the newborn up to his mother's breast, in her deep sleep, with a muffled groan, she rejected him. The T'Lo grouped around her jumped each time, overwrought, and started trembling as they looked at Ata-Réè. She knows they hate any kind of violence and very often they can see what is coming. She could also read in their expressive eyes what they were trying to say. It was a warning against Opak's possible reactions—the infant was not safe near her.

Ata-Réè, therefore, took him without forcing him to feed. Even though he did not suckle, he is quiet. He is sleeping, perhaps exhausted from the birth.

T'Lo Dê has come to see him, hugging his tiny daughter against his breast. She has drunk so much milk already that she spit some up, which barely wakes her up with her possessive little hands gripping the T'Lo's breast.

All is calm in the drowsy atmosphere. Ata-Réè feels her body relax on the covers and cushions that support her. Still, she is not sleepy. Her thoughts lighten up and drift back to memories that are dear to her.

She hears a kind of ethereal music that floats in space, far above Kobor Tigan't. Tenuous sounds, wrapped in echoes wherever they fan out, bouncing back and forth, composing a multi-voiced speech open to all. A part of her rises up to engage with it, for this bath in harmonious waves from which she always comes out refreshed and that often takes the place of sleep for her.

But also, since this domain was opened to her by Angel, she thinks of the Beautiful Being come from Elsewhere, brutally captured by Opak who loved him to the point of violence.

Ata-Réè recalls her one and only meeting with him. It still haunts her.

It was the evening of Amo's last day in Kobor Tigan't because he, the most beautiful of the Queen's men, left. And Angel, too, who went with him. Both of them together ran far away from Opak. Angel because he had never loved her but only put up with her, as a prisoner, despite (or probably because of) all the honors she heaped on him. Amo because he had loved her too much, tried to join with her through worship of the senses whereas she never wanted to do anything but consume him. So, this love that Amo bore, in the end, eclipsed her, its very essence carrying beyond the image of the Ooh'Rou to crystallize on the animating principle of her—the only Sun, Ooh'R.

It was another time, before Opak's madness, before To's disappearance, before Abim's death...

Tenderness washes over her heart because Méè-Nê, the B'Tah-Gou, whose psychic heir she was, still had a little time left to live, even though she was already fading, stricken by that same rejection of life as all the other Storytellers. Her disciple, at her side, piously received from her the final transmission of knowledge. That night, they were both waiting in their cozy atmosphere. In the back of their house the resinous wood was burning low, wafting its scent…

They spoke little. For a long time it was easier for them to share their thoughts without words. They had both, at the same time, as usual, felt the visit coming. Their keen senses followed the approach. And they waited, patiently, fearlessly. Resigned to fate, they knew how to wait with all the practices of patience. They understood what could be changed and what could not. With this enlightened acceptance of the decrees of fate, they felt at great peace.

When remembering how the door opened on that night, Ata-Réè's heart skipped a beat, just like then… The two men emerged without a word, outlined against the dark night by the dancing flames. They were holding hands. How dilated their eyes were! They were two very dissimilar men. Amo, heavy and muscular, tall like a human tree, his face hardened under the foliage of his flaming red hair; Angel was wispy—a body about to fly away—all curves capable of lightning quick reflexes, without any visible muscles, but strong in his nerves, with the pallor of the invincible.

These two should have fought each other in the turmoil of passions swirling around them! But no, they joined together to come here this evening. But it was only to go off in a better way and farther away.

Méè-Nê's house in the Low City was their first stop after which they would run farther down, silently, escaping from the Ooh'Rou up on high by descending through all the other Cities. But who knows if it might not be their only stop? Because it was clear that the two men would let nothing, neither rest nor repose, stop them from reaching their final goal.

Amo left. And with him—for, he was the living symbol of it—the time of the fertility festivals went too, the broad smiles of the springtime men, the powerful rituals of the generative forces offered to the infusion of the sun.

Angel left as well. And with him was lost the contact with the celestial Elsewhere, which had been offered by this intermediary and which they had only glimpsed without forming an alliance.

On seeing them, one could not really tell which of the two was leading the other nor whose greater despair had convinced the other.

No matter! They left, permanently, both together, both of one mind.
Their common decision united them. It was as if the wind was already
blowing around them, uprooting them. Yes, soon, they would disappear,
swept away by a storm of silence all the way to obliteration.

They could no longer live in Kobor Tigan't. They had become,
through their trials and tribulations, too subtle in their desires to continue
to live in the material density that belonged to the Race and the Place.

When they entered, there was an unusual freshness around them.
The future, already, perhaps?

Something that was still holding steady a little, completely collapsed. The New Time had just secretly begun!

Amo stepped forward to say goodbye to Méè-Nê, his B'Tah-Gou.
He was not coming to hear her talk tonight. He was going to topple the
Standing Stone of Grand Va-Hôh by which the illicit power of Abim had
endured. The Very Huge could only be affected through her Stone. He
knew this. They could only topple her by toppling the Stone. Therefore,
he would sacrifice himself.

Ata-Réè had stood up on seeing Angel. He went to her alone. An irresistible current streamed between them, emanations flowing back and
forth, elated to discover, depressing to have to lose. Angel spoke, his
long hand held out to the girl. He wanted to give her his own blessing:
the gift that he had of hearing the voice of the ineffable heavens that
watch over men and work above them.

He wanted her, like him, not only hear but to repeat, to communicate it to her circle, this multi-faceted vibration, this utterance of the
clouds, these reflections of the birds, these voices of thunder and springs,
outcries of lightning, stairways of echoing laughter, cascading, caroming
pearls from chains of broken time, crackling souls in blue flames and the
bated breaths swimming in the dark of night: Music, all the essential Music and the power to sing it to others!

Like that, Angel had sung for the girl, translating for her as he went
along, the communication he perceived. And because he so badly wanted
it and willed it so, she heard it at the same time as him. And like him, but
from a clumsy throat, she sang in unison for the first and last time with
him…

Since then, her gift had developed. The perception became clearer
and more conscious. Her vocal chords became more flexible. Ata-Réè

was then able to reproduce what she heard. Already, troubled but respectful, they say that the voice of the Beautiful Stranger comes through her. They listen. They are quiet. They sink deeply into thought. Their easily influenced hearts race. Images visit their astonished souls.

They do not know how to sing in Kobor Tigan't. Music is unknown to them.

Atta-Réè has decided to teach the young, budding B'Tah-Gous whom she has picked up and who live in the palace with her.

She is thinking about all this when the contact of the small, prudent hand, a little cold, makes her jump. She recoils but regrets it right away. T'Lo Dê has obediently withdrawn his hand.

He, too, knew Angel. He had just caught her thoughts and wanted to tell her that he, too, remembered him, missed him, was hopeful.

So much light flowed into those golden eyes, raised so pitifully toward Ata-Réè that without another thought to her own feelings, she laid a sympathetic hand on his arm.

And it felt so nice to stay there, communing silently in the same images that the Storyteller wondered what half-revealed beings were imprisoned in the mute destiny of the T'Lo…

CHAPTER II

After a night of insomnia, Ta regained her strength only by watching the light advance. It was almost always like this. With the first rays of dawn she dragged herself out of bed to sit in a high chair from which she could see everything from the corner of the window with the shutters open.

She breathed the fresh air with a kind of gratitude. She felt numbed by weariness. Her limbs were heavy. She could not even think about moving. To have to talk again, to give orders was a loathsome prospect. Her whole being recoiled at resuming the royal office. Her desire to run away was never as strong as at these moments.

In the distance across from her the cone of the holy mountain Kah'B'La jutted out of the first blue mists exhaled by the sleep of the valleys hollowed out beneath her. Very slowly it became clearer, lighter—a balm for Ta's soul—it became almost translucent, its edges fringed with a pinkish gold that was peace and tenderness.

The young woman mused every time that this mountain must have feelings, maybe thoughts that were communicated round about.

Then the Sun Ooh'R was there, white, radiant, devouring everything in its glory. Kah'B'La was its first springboard. After jumping off from there it reached everything.

It was day! As the young woman let out a sigh of relief, the birds swept in. They came from everywhere in swirling clouds and started rising above the mists. The rumbling of some big animals, although faint in the distance, could be heard on a gust of wind that also blew in a honeyed scent.

Now Ta was breathing with relish. Life was streaming back to her. She stood up and leaned out to see the waves of birds washing over Kobor Tigan't like every morning. Different flocks had preferences for one city over another. Ta identified them and cheered up as always. She would have been irate if anyone bothered her at this moment.

She knew the somewhat drab plumage, the kind of savage but bold look of the ones visiting only the Low City as if their wings could not carry them higher. "Lazy but clever, the silo looters," she judged kindly.

To the higher cities, Kob'Vâm and Kob'Râm, came bigger, stronger, more colorful birds that chirped a little like fowl and often forgot their eggs, which were gathered up.

But the finest birds were like a reward for Ta and the best motivation to start her day. These ones came later, always the last. More than once she had to leave for a morning meeting before she could see them, a bitter moment for one with so few personal pleasures… It was hard to tell what direction they would come from. It was always different. Most of the time it was a surprise, one of the things that made it so delightful! They were mixed up with the others and then all of a sudden they were there, up close, flying in front of the window like big butterflies.

This morning they were there again before she saw them coming. She was looking to the right when they came from the left. Those fickle feathers. Ta laughed. They were of every color but the hues of fire were predominant. They flitted every which way, taking visible pleasure in cutting across each other with not a trace of fear.

The young queen lowered her head suddenly. They were the same birds as on Kah'B'La when the Old Man had passed by and said, "Beautiful children, never separate! Don't let them separate you!" And To's eyes sparkled with love. To's eyes still alive!

The young woman was standing up. She stormed away from the window. The Ooh'Rou's day was starting! She had heard her servants coming to her door. On the round terrace the tall figure of Hé-Nark had passed by. The hammering forges of Kob'Râm were pounding again. The cohort of food distributors had gone through Kob'Lâm and were now entering Kob'Vâm. The sound of the big waterfall was very loud today. It must have had a lot of water.

In her room Opak was awake. She had moaned and sighed almost the whole time. Her eyes, with white circles tinted slightly mauve, struggled to open.

The previous night's birth had left her very weak. Her milk-laden breasts must have been hurting her. Thinking to comfort her, Ata-Réè talked softly, presenting the child. She did not seem to see or hear. But dark fears suddenly troubled her and she cried out for her T'Lo, which exhausted her out. She reached out feebly, then let her arms drop limply.

The T'Lo came up but did not touch her. For them she was a mother and stopped being an object of desire. The odor of milk had an anti-aphrodisiac effect on them. They even pulled away when she tried to pull one of them onto her bed. Then she cried a lot, without moving, a pitiful bulk, too weak to truly sob.

The T'Lo also cried in their silent way, but they did not budge.

Ata-Réè used Opak's despondence to slyly slip the newborn onto her breast and it started sucking greedily. Opak howled in fear and tried wildly to pull the infant off. T'Lo Dê, who was right there, grabbed her hand just in time and leaned over her face to look her in the eye. She calmed down, mumbled some inarticulate sounds and fell into a kind of hypnosis as her eyes rolled back a little. Her lips parted. Almost a smile.

The baby kept drinking. He had not cried during the squirming. His eyes just opened wide.

"I believe he's already a brave one," Ta remarked as she stepped into the room. Seeing Ata-Réè's face light up, she said, "Yes, but he will take less than T'Lo Dê's girl."

Indeed, the baby was already full and pushing away from Opak who was once again fading into lethargy.

With great pride, T'Lo Dê was looking at his own child. Pink skinned, red haired, rounded belly, she was sleeping on a purple pillow in the sunlight.

The women from the Royal Nursery showed up with their worried looks and clumsy attitudes. Just like the night before they took care of calamitous Opak grudgingly.

Ta was quick to scold them. "I hate skittish women like you! What harm do you think is going to come to you? Don't you see that my sister is heading towards her final end? Touching her won't bring any trouble to you, except what you'll get from me it you don't do your duty well."

She laughed at this last comment. The women felt reassured, then they brightened up and clapped their hands when she announced her upcoming visit to the Royal Nursery. Before leaving with Ata-Réè the young queen bent over Opak's son.

"I name you R'Ang!" she decreed as she put her finger on the child's head.

T'Lo Dê held out his daughter in his arms. Ta made the same gesture, "You will be Dê-Ta'Am!"

Her assistant sighed as she looked on.

"Yes," Ta said, "I know what you're thinking. But she won't be able to turn bad because we'll raise her with great care along with R'Ang, isn't that right?"

The Storyteller looked away.

The young Ooh'Rou put on a brave face, "Well, never mind, we shall see." She led her assistant away to accompany her to the meeting with the T'Lo devotees.

Hé-Nark was waiting outside. Ta said, "You haven't slept much!"

"No less than you, Ooh'Rou," he replied with his usual meekness.

The three of them smiled at one another, briefly. Then just as quickly, at the same time, each took their hierarchical place and headed to the audience hall, the guard in front of the Queen with her assistant behind her.

The hall where the Audience of Light was held had gigantic dimensions. It was flooded with morning sunlight because on the east side it opened onto a huge, overhanging terrace decorated with blossoming trees from Kah'B'La whose outline could be seen in the distance exactly in the middle of the terrace.

In the hall, 20 cyclopean monoliths carved out of blue stone found nowhere else supported a golden ceiling whose plates could be opened to let in even more light.

One had the extraordinary feeling of royal magnificence in this place.

During her reign, Opak, who shirked her advisory responsibilities, came here very seldom. Ta, on the contrary, judged it indispensable to the influence of her authority, even though she did not, by nature, enjoy the consultations, which were often muddled, unproductive and a waste of time among the trampling crowds who were never sure to fully understand. But in the end, she had realized that the people remembered these sessions. They talked about them beforehand and afterward, even if the results had been disappointing for them, they took pleasure in telling others about it, embellishing their own role.

The new Ooh'Rou, therefore, had refurbished the hall. The skillful Blacksmiths came up from Kob'Râm to install golden joints between the shiny stone tiles on the floor. They had also encased the Ooh'Rou's high stone seat with plates of hammered gold. At present it was softened with skins and white cushions, decorated with garlands of flowers and leaves as Ta liked it, which they were starting to imitate everywhere with nostalgic reminders that the Beautiful Stranger come from Elsewhere had been the first to do such things in Kobor Tigan't.

The young queen sat down, flanked by her guard and her assistant. She contemplated the outlines of the people gathered together, too obscure against the light from the open windows.

Without a word, just a gesture, she ordered the ceiling hatches to be opened. In the breathless silence they listened to the plates sliding open. Light came flooding in.

Now Ta could see what she had guessed. Her eyes turned slightly harder. In front of her all the Devotees were openly wearing their badges of membership to the cult of T'Lo, the thin bracelets usually hidden under bigger bracelets. Flaunting them like this outside their homes was like walking around naked. Plus, it was an exceptional gesture, bold, risky and secret since they only bared these bracelets during their unions with the T'Lo. Never in public. In such a place as this, under these circumstances, it was a provocation.

The Devotees, with Oda-Néè at the head of the delegation, stood bedecked like this in front of their queen. All the important women had around them the most handsome of their Chambers of Men. They looked serious, aware of their rank, while the men, more naive, grinned a little, self-satisfied and enjoying their effect.

There was a short silence. Hé-Nark had furrowed his brow while Ata-Réè standing next to the throne scrutinized all the faces. The badges of the cult glittered in the sunlight. The Devotees spread out their arms to show them off.

Externally, Ta was like ice. Not a single muscle on her face twitched. One might think she had noticed nothing. But her thoughts were spinning wildly in her indignant mind. She knew, however, that she had to contain her anger.

Discreetly, she touched Ata-Réè's hand and she responded with a soothing squeeze. Yes, she had to stay in control… Hé-Nark met her eyes. He was asking if she needed help. No, they had both already helped her enough! Strength flowed through her body. She felt better all of a sudden, ready for a fight, sure of herself, of her power, of her right to exercise it.

She let her eyes fall casually on Oda-Néè who arrogantly straightened up while the other women looked surprised and the men narrowed their big eyes.

Calmly, Ta gave her a knowing smile, full of callous disregard, which unsettled her immediately because she could not hold back a low, spiteful growl. The queen was not treating her according to her rank! It would have been normal for the Ooh'Rou to ask her to sit nearby. Well, Ta showed no intention of doing this. The customary invitation, awaited by all, would not come. Quite the contrary, she just looked away to casually address the assembly.

Her voice was clear, sounding almost amused. "Must I really bring in some T'Lo so you can romp and revel in front of me, Devotees! Or should I rather ask you the very subtle reason for you baring your intimate bracelets? Because, seeing that you petitioned me, I might think you're trying to mock the Ooh'Rou like this, which would obviously work against your interests."

The Devotees knew they had made a mistake. Their intention had been unmasked and their blunder was likely to backfire on them.

A brief panic ran through their ranks as they stole glances at one another. Some tried, so very discreetly, to cover their bracelets, but Oda-Néè, seeing the need for diplomacy, was already stepping up to justify them. She was friendly, almost flattering. Still, the insincerity in her voice grated bitterly on the ears of the young queen.

"Our badges?" the Devotee said. "But it's to show that we honor you with our trust, Ooh'Rou. Aren't we, who represent the tradition of the Ancestors, in very intimate company with you who incarnate the spirit of the race? You rule, so you know your needs. You rule, so you protect your possessions and those you love. For, where do our beloved T'Lo come from if not from the precious Ananou, part of the royal power, which has always been granted to us as a special privilege. I know that to others our present attitude before you might seem odd since, as you know, they say that you, the queen, have no T'Lo. But we can't believe this. It's good for the low people of Kob'Lâm to spread such gossip that has nothing to do with us, right?"

She was smiling, friendly, imitated by all the other women trying to smooth the way for a peaceful settlement.

But Ta coldly denied this overture, "You're wrong. The people are right. I don't have any T'Lo. I condemn the custom. Too old for me. Times have changed since our ancestors. Our bodies are different. Nature around us is different. We don't think in the same way. We don't have the same needs. We have other needs that are more urgent and that we must satisfy, we must fulfill. Our minds have to stay clear and lucid. Life today demands many ideas from us and the strength to implement these ideas. Things, events, beings have come to us over time. Remember Angel! Who knows if others of his kind won't show up one day on Kah'B'La or just right within our walls? What will you do then? You have no idea. Because you don't think about it. Because you don't think ahead like you should. Yes, these beings, these events, these things are considered evil by us or not considered at all. But when they come, we'll still have to accept them, integrate them, make use of them and without violence…"

Eqin-Go brazenly interrupted her, "All of us Devotees condemn violence!"

"I know that," Ta said."

"We love. Isn't that enough? We revel and rejoice like only a Devotee can do. Isn't that enough? Through our noble practices we reach good and sweet ecstasy…"

"…which kills you prematurely after having turned you into crying babies! Isn't that enough for me to condemn it? You drool and vomit, crawl around on all fours with a purple face and black fingernails because the T'Lo, who are dangerous now, ravage you with their drug that saturates your bodies. Isn't that enough for me to condemn it?"

Her voice had risen. But she kept going, not giving them time to interrupt her. If they had dared, she would have shut them up! Furious but powerless, the women tapped their feet. Ta had them firmly under her thumb.

"Have you ever considered that you serve no purpose?" she ignored their scandalized reaction. "Have you ever considered that you're completely useless to our race? You're not even an obstacle to its progression, which won't tolerate your languors. Look at how the people despise your practices!"

"O Queen," Ka'Ok, a friend of Eqin-Go, pleaded, "what are you saying? Your words are frightening us. We can't believe what we're hearing!"

Oda-Néè added, "O Queen, the people always despise what's too much for them."

"Do you think they understand you?" a tall, haughty woman tossed out.

Oda-Néè forced herself to stay calm, "Our practice comes from The Elders, the origins of the race. What use are we, you ask? O Queen, we persevere while everything else, as you can see, is changing, deteriorating, since those tragic events that afflicted Ooh'Rou Opak. We believe that the health of the race resides in us who keep contact with our origins, who don't forget our Great Ancestors."

Ta took up the gauntlet and snarled, "I don't forget them either."

Oda-Néè shrank back and turned humble, "That's not what I meant, O Queen, but we are dedicated to proving ourselves worthy of them and especially of always being like them. As if they were still here."

"Yes," the tall woman spoke again. "As if we really were the ancestors."

"Well," Ta felt another burst of irony come out, "believe me, Devotees, if our ancestors were here at this moment, they wouldn't face what's coming by wearing themselves out with their T'Lo! First of all, they would be trying to find what decisions should be made, new ways of doing things for the new age. Moreover, you seem to forget that the T'Lo were created long ago during a period of scarcity, of adaptation when the race had been decimated by a long exodus and the Times of Fear. The T'Lo, for our ancestors, were useful servants. Now, I ask you, what are they good for?"

The question remained unanswered, unheeded. The Devotees were appalled. That an Ooh'Rou would talk like this was more than they could ever have imagined. They cast startled looks at one another and were breathing loudly, their hearts racing. Their bewilderment was too deep for them to react. Their eyes were full of tears.

Ta watched them with obvious contempt, repeating her question, "What are the T'Lo good for now?"

It was Oda-Néè who suddenly burst out. Shaking off her men, who tried to hold her back, she lunged forward, red with rage and aggression. She started shouting, almost in the queen's face:

"What do you mean, what are they good for? Our incomparable T'Lo who give to humans more than the banal orgasm—the Other Pleasure, The Endless! But who are you to speak of such things? Do you understand? Do you respect anything? You didn't ask me to sit at your side! Your sister Opak would have. She observed the customs and you've locked her up without telling us the real reason why... Abim, the Very Huge, would she have tolerated this heresy you proclaim? All the great Ooh'Rous who preceded you communed with us in the worship. Is it because of her love for the T'Lo that you took your sister's place on the throne? Of course, you were a strange princess, but who you have become..."

Ta, who had not opened her mouth so far, cut her off there. "I have become Ooh'Rou Ta. She who rules over you and your kind and who will rule over you until the end."

She made a sign to Né-Nark who came forward, grabbed Oda-Néè by the shoulder and before she knew what happened he pushed her back among the Devotees. All the women started clamoring. He went back to his place without a trace of emotion, but he kept his eye on Oda-Néè, who was scared, didn't dare say anything, just rubbed her aching shoulder where the marks of the guard's fingers were still red.

This incident, more than anything else, stupefied the Devotees.

That a man—an underling to boot!—not even part of any Chamber of Men, dared to brutalize a woman of Oda-Néè's social standing—this was unthinkable, completely unheard of, an outrage worse than an insult: a defilement!

United in their disgrace, the women were flushed and the their men could only grumble and groan. Then the voice of the queen rang out again to state the facts:

"You see, I am Ooh'Rou Ta, different from the others. Just like Princess Ta was different. I believe you understand that I will make every effort to convince you! Hé-Nark is here to make sure my ideas are respected and my power is enforced. There are and there will be others like him. I like to use their strength and their skills in other things besides sex and hunting. He is a new kind of man whom I am training. They are free in my service, free to belong to a woman or not. As you all know, I have no Chamber of Men and I have no intention of ever having one. One alone was Mine: To, who is no longer. No one can replace him. The desire for the Choice of Men is gone forever from me... So, I will remain the White Ooh'Rou. My role is to prepare you, with full knowledge of the facts, for who will come after me. Men like Hé-Nark make up a new caste around my throne. I will honor them with broad powers if they earn it. They are the manifestation of my authority over all of you."

She paused a moment and then with a graceful, forgiving wave of her hand she said, "Now that this has been cleared up, let's move on to why you have come here? What's the reason?"

She had already guessed it but she wanted to hear them say it so that she could study their attitudes while they tried to win her over. Plus, by asking them to explain themselves, she struck another blow because for these furious Devotees, convinced of being beaten, her friendly invitation had the effect of a cold shower and by confusing them it kept them under control more than another exercise of authority.

The women stood agape. Oda-Néè was still too shocked to speak. Therefore, all they could do was babble pitifully through the trembling voice of Ka'Ok, "O Queen, the Ananou are passing away…"

"So they say," she conceded nonchalantly as she smoothed out a wrinkle of her garment.

Astounded by such little interest, all the Devotees just gazed at this little gesture.

Ka'Ok did not speak again until the Queen looked up, awaiting what would follow. "O Queen," she implored, "don't you realize, the Ananou are dying!"

"I realize it. Yes, indeed, they're dying. But don't torture yourselves over it—they're not suffering. Their time is up, that's all. Nature is extinguishing them very gently."

The Devotees found this spoken with an unbelievable hint of cruelty and had the awful feeling of not really being understood.

In fact, Ta was playing with them. The closer she watched them, the more ridiculous she found them. The signs of their unhealthy eroticism, those purplish marks on their temples, their sluggishness, their forced tameness, those poses, their reactions always taken too far—it was all extremely annoying to her. She saw in their eyes a kind of strange savagery. She figured that it was soon going to be necessary to protect the race from them.

But Oda-Néè had pulled herself together and spoke more urgently, "We don't want them to die! We want to take them, to take care of them…"

"Why?" Ta asked, driving her into a corner.

Oda-Néè saw what she was doing but righteously stood firm, "To make our T'Lo of course!"

"More T'Lo!" the Queen exclaimed sarcastically. "Don't you have enough already!"

"O Queen," Eqin-Go remarked sadly, "we see very well that you're cruelly making fun of our cause. It's unacceptable to us that the Ananou die."

One woman looked Ta in the eyes and pleaded, "O Queen, you can't believe what you're saying! You're testing us, right? Since the Ananou are the treasure of all the Ooh'Rous, since, by always granting them to us, the Ooh'Rous have thus bound our loyalty to the crown. I ask you, has there ever been a single traitor among the Devotees? We have always respected our duties to the realm. Our families are always the closest to the throne, always the most steadfast. We always offer our precious metals. We give our profits from the hunt. We take care of the food for everyone. The best Dongdwo egg gatherers are mostly from us. An Ooh'Rou can always ask anything of a Devotee, that's the tradition!"

"I know, I know," the young Queen muttered, "you are loyal folk. But for this, must something remain dormant in you? The people of Kob'Lâm are calm and loyal and ask nothing in exchange. It doesn't even cross their minds."

Her question was not answered. They were starting to hate her. She was too different from them. It cast a shadowy fear over their hearts.

"Grant us the last Ananou!" Oda-Néè burst out in a mix of plea and threat. "For, O Queen, it is obvious that for your reign to be effective, with all your eccentricities, it will need more than ever the traditional support of our faction. What do the Ananou and what we do with them matter to you since you don't care about them? We'll save them. We'll make T'Lo. I promise you that when we die they will, as always, be thrown back into the Palace Pit, thus belonging once again to the crown until we ask again, bearing gifts…"

She stopped because the Queen was talking.

"Listen, Devotees, I know very well all your reasons. There's no need to enumerate them to me. I also know, thoroughly, from seeing the fatal progress of my sister Opak every day, the dangers of your practices. I repeat once and for all: the old times are gone. You're different from your ancestors. You don't have as much strength. The T'Lo you've brought up in your families, generation after generation, have stored harmful toxins in their nature. You're weaker than them. By coupling with them incessantly like you do, because once you've got a taste you can never control yourselves, you're letting a subtle poison saturate your humanity. I'm telling you that very quickly, in short time, your T'Lo will become even more dangerous and you will degenerate even more rapidly. That's why I absolutely refuse to give out any Ananou. That's also why, knowing that you're all draining yourselves out, in the days ahead I will put no pressure on you in any way, leaving nature to wipe you out since you're asking for it and certainly after the Ananou have died off, your T'Lo won't be far behind."

The Devotees gasped and cried in horror, louder and louder as the speech went on. The final words, however, fell on utter silence. Oda-Néè opened her mouth. No sound came forth. She was livid with rage.

Hé-Nark was thinking that Ta had just made a dangerous enemy. Ata-Réè thought the same thing. They both looked at each other from either side of the Queen.

Ta stood up. "This meeting has lasted too long. I knew what would come of it so I could have saved myself the trouble, but I wanted to give you my reasons and especially to make you understand. Think about it and force yourself to admit the truth. Have no fear. Your T'Lo belong to you until they die. But I intend to keep your practices from spreading beyond your walls. I will see to it."

She walked out, preceded by Hé-Nark and followed by Ata-Réè, leaving the Devotees standing there, looking at one another in astonishment, muttering together with seething rage. They ended up leaving, trudging through Kob'Ooh'R. The people they passed were troubled seeing them so gloomy. Some asked them what had happened in the palace, but they did not answer because those people were not part of their circle.

The news of the Devotees' indignation spread through the five cities. The people of Kob'Lâm thoroughly enjoyed it and hoped that the new Ooh'Rou would do more of the same. The arrogant Devotees had certainly been put in their place!

After leaving the Audience Hall, Ta harbored no illusions about the possibility of ever convincing the Devotees of the harm of their practices. They would resist with all their might if she tried in any way to back them into a corner. Their resistance would go to their head and they would become even more vain. How quickly they put themselves on a pedestal! Did they not consider themselves as the greatest of the Race right after the Ooh'Rou!

Mulling this over she went with Ata-Réè to Opak's rooms. When they got there, the scene was dramatic. Yet Opak was sleeping, on the floor this time, soaked in sweat and her clothes in rags, the pillows torn apart bearing witness to the violence of her furies.

In one corner, the women from the Nursery, still trembling, were wiping away tears. The T'Lo were protecting R'Ang the best they could, forming a wall between him and Opak. T'Lo Dê had set him on some covers and dared not do anything else. He tried to comfort him by caressing his forehead with one finger. The newborn had withdrawn into a strange calm and was waving his little fists in the air.

For the third time Ta got angry with the Nursery women. Ashamed, they scampered around to repair the damage, straighten up the mess and take care of baby R'Ang with an expertise that the young queen was pleased to see and which reassured her as to their skill in raising children.

When Opak was put back on her tidied bed, she did not wake up. All those present had a bad feeling. And they all looked at one another at the same time.

Ta had just leaned over her sister. The paleness was turning to white. Sweat continued to pour down her forehead even though they had several times wiped it dry. There was a bruise on her cheek. Her hair was clumped in long strands. Impending sorrow loomed over all this woe.

Would the senseless woman ever snap out this stupor? It was frightening how deep it seemed. Obviously, with every fit, she was losing a little more of her vital potential because each lazy stupor lasted longer than the previous one. At first she had come out of it and devoured huge amounts of food. But her gorging had diminished. Now she forgot to eat and asked for nothing. They had to force-feed her while she was in a twilight of consciousness.

The helpful T'Lo watched over her with gentle caresses and remarkable intuition. She accepted everything from them, even when unconscious. Her life seemed to depend on their magnetism.

Ta sighed, "And yet she has to feed her baby for as long as possible."

CHAPTER III

The Royal Nursery—its moors, orchards, gardens, woods, waterfalls pouring into pools that opened into canals—occupied a large, protected, sunny area in the southeast of Kob'Ooh'R.

The huge, bright children's palace was there, surrounded by individual dwellings, each on its own property, where the royal offspring often chose to live as adults with their families instead of the Ooh'Rou's palace.

In the southwest there was a thick forest whose ageless trees, all woven together, bound by vines, dense and disordered, were a little scary but sure enough stopped the storms blowing down from Grand Va-Hôh.

From this part of Kobor Tigan't the mountain Kah'B'La could not be seen but on the horizon was a jagged, steep, impassable mountain range covered with dense vegetation two-thirds up its sides, the rest just sheer cliffs and bare walls usually lost in mists or buried behind clouds. It seemed like thick banks of fog were always amassed behind these mountains.

The Giants of Kobor did not like the fog, which discouraged them from going to see what there was on the other side. Moreover, they readily restrained themselves from the troubled nomadism of their Ancestors, which still ran through their veins. This was their idea of peace and comfort.

All told, the Royal Nursery was almost a world unto itself with its specialized denizens who were surely a little indifferent to what happened to the others in the other Cities, including Kob'Ooh'R, because here it was not really Kobor but The Nursery, a privileged universe of royal descendants!

In the first place, it looked like they did not grow old here. Did they even die? Nothing was less sure!

Ta was thinking these things, scrutinizing everything around her, in detail, because it was a nice change from her glum reflections.

She understood why those who lived here from infancy were so content, why they stayed so willingly, always sorry to leave and then only under pressure of some greater interest.

There was a kind of rustic charm to the place. The wondrous power of childhood was spread a little everywhere. You could laugh here. And you had to play. Everything was cheerful, friendly, made to be easy, for a carefree life because it was all protected, privileged.

In fact, more than anywhere else, the water of the small waterfalls, of the canals or the springs laughed and glimmered. The foliage, all so bright, expressed its joy in the breeze. The mildness lay over all the mossy rocks. The crossing paths invited chasing. The thickets offered hiding places and all kinds of red, yellow and purple berries for the girls to make necklaces. Dazzling stones allured the boys.

Ta was pleased to breathe in the blend of grass, fruit and earth, while telling herself that here you had to be light-hearted, easy-going, slow-moving. She remembered her own childhood, not so long past. Hadn't she been more light-hearted, more easy-going than anyone else? To the extent that it was practically a fairy tale and that now people were respectfully startled that she had adopted such a strict attitude. Yes, the death of To had changed everything. All of Kobor knew this and sympathized.

"At least," she was thinking, "they could never accuse me of being lazy. But it's true that this fault is so common in the Race that it's hardly ever criticized."

She smiled a little. She stopped to catch her breath because she was now in sight of the Children's Palace whose mass of white stone could be seen through the trees.

She realized that Hé-Nark was there. Lost so deep in thought the entire way, she had forgotten about him. He did not once disturb her in any way, just walked with her. He knew the art of being inconspicuous while still remaining vigilant.

She thanked him, "You're as nice as one of these trees."

She pointed to a particularly majestic one. The guard smiled. His face was all kindness, respect and discretion. He never fished for compliments, did not like them and was suspicious when they came from others. But from her he accepted them, albeit uneasily.

"You know," she abruptly changed the subject, "I think the whole Race is lazy. It's sleeping when it should be wide awake. But I'll get there, you'll see, I'll get there!"

She was mumbling, less to him than to herself. He smiled again a little kindly. There was compassion in his eyes for the young woman who was bearing such weight on her shoulders and whose youth was being given to the realm to the point of forgetting all about herself.

The Queen was a perpetual source of astonishment and admiration to him. He tried hard to understand her. He did not always succeed. Her strange boldness sometimes scared him.

Ta did not see the expression on Hé-Nark's face. Once again forgetting about him, she was on the march again, hurrying a little on the slope leading down to the palace. It formed a kind of avenue, mostly paved, a gentle descent of very flat, almost imperceptible steps. A pleasant and relaxing stroll, well shaded, bordered by funny-shaped, moss-covered rocks sitting in pools of spring water. Huge fern groves alternated with these rocks. Flocks of birds, not wild, followed them, surrounded by big insects glistening like metal.

Then a noise came through ferns, which suddenly parted, making way for a clumsy Mouh-Tou dragging its udders and stalked by a gang of laughing boys and girls who wanted its milk that was already dripping on its own. Jumping around, flushed with joy, holding garlands in their hands, they bounded after the animal without paying any attention to Ta as she stopped to watch them.

Back on her way, she encountered more and more of them.

Lively groups, almost naked, with pretty jewelry and leaves in their hair, scattered around the whole Domain, eating fruits, picking flowers, teasing the domesticated animals.

The girls led the boys with fitting authority. Each girl was out to round up a few boys to be subjected to her juvenile charms, but they bickered too much among themselves, each claiming possession of anther's boys! The boys loved to cause a fuss that flattered their pride. They strutted around and flexed their young muscles while the girls fell into very serious discussion about possible arrangements. Most often, after suffering through this indispensable trial, they agreed to let the coveted boy go free.

The first girl to catch him again by throwing her abduction belt around him became the owner... until the next squabble! And then more tongue-wagging, shouting, giggling, stomping and frantic chasing that ended in victorious captures in the middle of an admiring circle.

The girls worked at fixing up the grottoes, decorating them with moss cushions and fern mattresses. They called them, obviously, their Chambers of Men and brought their boys there to try out their childish eroticism and their craving for sensations in which they overflowed with imagination.

There were also other games that Ta remembered playing in her youth as she watched them. Sitting, standing or running, by twos, threes or ten together, depending on the rules, the children played "Na-Nood said" or "Scaredy Dongdwo" or "Escape from Grand Va-Hôh" or "Pretty Ooh-Rou runs off" or "Where is the Very Huge?" or even "The silent T'Lo" or "The clapping Ananou" and also "Jump Mouh-Tou".

Seeing them all like this, Ta smiled, stopping once again to watch them. The children were healthy, happy and beautiful. Judging by their age they were all Opak's...

Back on her way with Hé-Nark on her heels, she thought sadly of her sister's fate. Before hating her the people had loved her as a triumph of fertility because from a young age she had been very prolific and later, defying time, staying strong as she aged, which is a special trait of the Race of Giants, she had regularly brought more and more children into the world. Yes, for a long time, she had given the image of a marvelous Ooh'Rou, a royal female whose males were all exceptional and an inexhaustible mother whose every child magically strengthened the blessed destiny of Kobor Tigan't. Until the day when...

Halfway to the palace Ta was yanked out of these depressing thoughts by the Women of the Nursery rushing out to welcome her. They brought other children in their arms or hanging onto their clothes. Ta admired how pink and plump they were and started asking questions as they went.

She was concerned about how the children were being raised, what they were eating, where they slept, what toys they had and why they came so rarely to the palace of Kob-Ooh'R so that she, Ooh'Rou Ta, had so far known practically none of her sister's offspring.

The women answered her candidly, with naïve confidence. Ta saw that they were good, bursting with vitality, laughing glibly at trivial matters, completely carefree and, to tell the truth, empty-headed. These beautiful, chubby women had the mentality and the vanity of children. The Nursery was all they needed to be happy. They were not curious about anything else. The rest was of no interest to them. They did not feel concerned by anything else.

Moreover, they repeated this every chance they got with a kind of mischievous pride. With a privileged feeling, they knew only that they were raising the children of the Sun Ooh'R and deep down the identity of the Ooh'Rou, mother of these children, did not matter to them! They had no special devotion to her. Not even the admiration felt by all the other inhabitants everywhere in Kobor Tigan't.

Ta realized that in their eyes she herself was just an incomprehensible monstrosity because she had remained sterile so far and now (they knew it but could not believe it) she had no Chamber of Men.

The Women of the Nursery, on principle, looked down on anything that did not concern them directly and they certainly (alas!) communicated this attitude to the children. They were called the Great Breeders. What a title! What more could be asked of them?

They were surprised at the Queen's consideration as she drilled them cautiously. They were almost upset. What, were they incompetent? Wasn't everything in order in the Nursery? How could any one, even just little, question their skills? This had never been seen before!

Ta had to calm their sensitivity with some clever compliments. Then, when she saw they were appeased, since she wanted to learn more about their characters, she kept them talking by flattering them. The women opened up immediately, forgetting everything else. Yes, they said, they had the most honorary duty in all the realm! Yes, everything here was peaceful, with plenty of food and healthy bodies. The other cities? They knew nothing about them. What was the point of going to see what was happening there when everything was comfortable here? As for Kob'Ooh'R and the palace, they went there, of course, every time they were asked. But sure, that was all and they did not think about it. They were the Women of the Nursery, they raised the children. There had always been children. They never left.

Ta perceived a new cause for worry about the future. These women were all just good for feeding babies but what was their care doing to the older children? Pushing them aimlessly, without guidance, into total ignorance of the rest of Kobor Tigan't and of their place with respect to others.

When she was sitting on the bright terrace of the Children's Palace, relaxing with the other women, she put aside the big problems so they could talk about more pressing subjects. And so she learned that several generations lived together on the Nursery grounds.

Firstly, highest in rank, pampered, admired, even revered because they were Sons and Daughters of the Sun Ooh'R, came the children Opak had from the various men of her Chamber. In the royal caste, they paid no attention to the father since the real spouse of the Ooh'Rous was the sun.

61

These children, from toddlers to teenagers, lived in total freedom. The women tolerated everything from them and surrendered, almost ritually, to all their whims. Apparently no one in the Nursery ever had the slightest thought of contradicting, even just a little, the children's desires, no matter how crazy they might be.

Ta figured that such tolerance must have serious consequences. On examining the children she found them almost all the same: nice but selfish, greedy, authoritarian and outlandishly lustful. All qualities that were the pride and joy of the Breeders.

None of these children seemed to have the royal flame that kindled the mind to take a real interest in others. They thought only of themselves, far away from the Race as a whole, just like their Breeders, as the young queen was expecting. She told them about the other cities, about the people of Kob'Lâm. They yawned. She used words they could understand to describe the charms of the holy mountain Kah'B'La, the fearless search for eggs in the swamps of the old Dongdwos. They made faces, showing no interest whatsoever. Their intelligence was limited and smug.

Ta saw such indifference and dull boredom in their eyes that she let them go, thinking wearily that they all had the same defects as Opak.

She asked about the older ones whom she did not see. The Women answered proudly, "All of them have already mated."

Indeed, when barely of age, the Daughters of Opak had nothing better to do than vainly build their Chamber of Men just like their royal mother. They put in some of their own brothers who pleased them and also other males, older than themselves, whom were a source of great pride. They had chosen from the royal caste, from the descendants of Abim who lived on forever in the Nursery by leading a very dissolute life.

"I have the feeling," the young queen muttered with a half-smile, "that the Spring Festival for the Choice of Men takes place here many times a year."

The Women laughed a lot at this comment. They took it for a compliment.

Satisfied with how the conversation was going, they then boasted that the customs were well maintained and that many of the most refined T'Lo adorned almost all of the Chambers of Men because the Ooh'Rou had always thought of giving them as gifts to her daughters and was very often generous with other families of her caste.

So, Ta had just found out the main problem. Here, too, it was raging. She was almost scared. But this corroborated her view that Opak's children, except for a few, rare examples still to be discovered, would be good for nothing in the future life of the realm. She would not count of them, therefore, to be part of her entourage. Her thoughts turned instead to the young B'Tah-Gous around Ata-Réè and the respectable men, in ever-growing numbers, under the command of Hé-Nark whose prestige was continually on the rise. These would be a true elite.

She went to visit a few of the beautiful properties where the complicated branches of her own lineage lived well, but indifferent and self-indulgent. She was welcomed everywhere with great honor in which her keen sensitivity to human sentiments picked up a kind of suspicion, if not distrust.

She saw herself in none of them. The were all anachronous, outdated. She recognized a few of the T'Lo Devotees who had been in the delegation that morning. So, these women were part of her family and she did not even know it! They were not sulking. On the contrary, all of them, as if it were prearranged, made a great show of their T'Lo. Men and women in all the houses were sporting their Devotee bracelets.

The presence of Hé-Nark was very intriguing to them all, especially his self-control and discretion, which contrasted so sharply with the nonchalant exuberance of the other men. But even more baffling was his neutral relationship with the Ooh'Rou. They saw and felt no familiarity between the two of them. They barely talked to each other and kept their distance. Why? Was Hé-Nark not, then, one of Ta's males? They insisted on believing that for some inexplicable reason she did not want to admit that she had a Chamber of Men.

Their curiosity was piqued to the utmost. But, either out of respect for the Ooh'Rou or because the gray eyes of the Guard kept them in check, no one made the slightest mention of it.

The visitor, as well as Hé-Nark, noticed all of this. Since their thoughts often coincided, quite naturally and now quite routinely, they exchanged knowing glances, with a hint of amusement. It seemed, however, to the Guard that the queen was a little irritated whereas in his gray eyes she spied once again, despite the playful glance, a mist of sadness.

Nevertheless, the very strangeness that they felt from Hé-Nark after meeting him made him an object of great interest to the rich women who opened their Chamber of Men to the Queen. He made more than one T'Lo flustered as well. But he stayed like stone.

During all this time, Ta let none of her feelings show. She visited everything, haughty and calm, talking to the men, women, children and T'Lo in few words but politely. She generously admired everything they showed her and knew when to give a compliment to prevent any uncertainty. So well did she play her role that the Devotees, who were ready to make some waves after the morning's incident, no longer knew what to think.

The Men of the Chambers she had seen were mellowed because, all the same, the White Ooh'Rou was beautiful. She had a weird, pale beauty that was striking among all the plump, golden women. But contrary to the men, the women were no calmer when Ta's back was turned.

The high-ranking Devotees, figuring that they were once again being mocked, went to tell Oda-Néè since this woman of Kob'Iâm was already renowned among the Devotees and they expected a lot from her imagination and the decisions she never failed to make.

Hé-Nark overheard them talking about it but said nothing. When the moment allowed, he whispered to the Queen. But all she did was shrug her shoulders—she had no need to hear what she had already surmised.

He-Nark thought to himself that the Queen might not be wary enough of the Devotees and he swore he would watch them more closely.

Ta got tired suddenly. All these people were getting on her nerves. Therefore, she ordered the Women of the Nursery to leave her alone. She intended to make the rest of the visit through the forest by herself. Later, before leaving, she would pass by the Children's palace. Annoyed and showing it, the Breeders rounded up all the children by promising them sweets and stormed off.

Ta could wander at will. Hé-Nark followed at a respectable distance so as not to disturb anything but her shadow. Lost in thought, she did appreciate the stroll until at the edge of the forest she saw a pretty property full of rare, carefully arranged plants in the middle of which stood a truly cheery house very different from the others.

She was won over by the charm of the place. It was even more intriguing as she saw children (more than one) scampering in, whimpering with a scraped cheek or bruised knee.

She followed after them on the end of a long, winding path that led to the house where they gathered around a young woman with long, straight hair. They whined to her about their booboos so that she would take care of them. Which she did, with much finesse, rubbing on ointments that were certainly plant extracts kept in various stone or bark containers. Ta noticed that the children immediately quieted down as soon as the woman touched them. She must have had a gift.

At the sight of the queen she jumped to her feet. Her hair was thrown back, revealing a long face full of quiet determination with two very dark eyes that took note of things and beings, embracing them without expressing anything but the sole desire to help. Such beautiful eyes with such a rare quality that Ta, won over, smiled right away.

But the woman was already greeting her, unsurprised, unembarrassed, as relaxed and polite as could be, "Blessings and praise unto you, White Ooh'Rou!"

She was the first here to call her by her full title. The young queen was pleased. Her fatigue was already fading away. But the woman went on, offering a hollowed out seat covered with a thick layer of fresh leaves.

"Sit down and relax. These leaves are refreshing. You need it. The children are leaving right now. I've taken care of them. They are no longer hurting. They are comforted."

She sent them off with a gentle wave that was obviously irresistible because the children obeyed at once, scattering towards the exit.

"But," Ta said, "please, keep your children by you!"

The other chuckled, "They're not my children."

"But you seem to love them so dearly."

Another little laugh, even more amused, "No, White Ooh'Rou, don't believe it. On the contrary, they tired me out. But I don't like suffering. I don't like what hurts the body. I like healing. Now, it so happens that the children often get hurt and I can easily see what's wrong, even if it's hidden. I also see what cure is needed and where it can be found. So, the children come. They all know this."

While talking she was arranging the barks, plants and roots that were spread out on the table before her. But she was not watching her hands, which seemed to have a mind of their own and instinctively know everything she touched. She just looked at Ta.

"Oh, you don't sleep at night," she sighed, but then added, "I think it's because you don't *want* to sleep."

The young queen slumped in the leaves that did indeed relax her. Her eyes half-closed, she spoke frankly, a little taken aback at letting herself go like this, "I have a bad dream. The same every night. And my sleep is disturbed."

"Yes," the woman urged apologetically, "but believe me, Ooh'Rou, it's also, it's especially because you want to think, to contemplate during the night on top of the day. It's the new time that's speaking through you. Someone needs to be listening. And that's you, alone, attentive, every night."

Ta sat up, astonished at so much insight. The woman's hands, however, apparently found what they had been searching for all alone because they were gathering up some brown scraps.

The woman had not stopped talking. "But Ooh'Rou, your strength will flag if you keep on like this every night! Here's some bark. Put them in the water you drink and you won't need to sleep much. Your strength will be renewed. And maybe you'll never even grow old!"

Ta was enthralled by all this knowledge as much as by the innate harmony she felt between the two of them. "Who inspired you with such things?"

Her host looked embarrassed. She had just sat down at her feet. Her hands passed over her eyes. "O Queen, sometimes there's a voice in my sleep. And this sleep is not like the others. Whenever it gets hold of me I can't fight it. It's the voice I hear first, calling me to sleep... the voice of an old man..."

The Queen flinched while the woman went on.

"... telling me, 'Go see in such or such place, this plant or this tree that has this color or this shape. Pick this fruit or this leaf or take this root.' The voice goes on to tell me if the plant has to be dried in the shade or in the sun, if it should be mixed with others, cooked over a fire or in the oven. And it always says, 'It's for this or this condition.' That's it, O Queen, and it's the truth."

"The old man," Ta asked, "do you know him? Have you seen him?"

"No. He told me not to be curious about him. I obey. I'm simple. I don't like what upsets the order, what interferes. That's why I hate to see bodies that are hurt and injured. I love what is free. The little, colorful birds, for example..."

Ta shuddered because she was thinking of the Old Man on Kah'B'La surrounded by his birds perched on his shoulders or clinging to his hair, birds like those she looked forward to seeing every morning.

Her eyes fell upon Hé-Nark standing apart in the garden as abstract as a rock. She had enough self-control to hide her emotions. "Do you realize you haven't told me your name," she put her hand on the young woman's shoulder.

The woman started laughing, a little confused, and answered, "O Queen, it's because I feel like I've always talked to you: I am Gan'd. Don't be surprised at my character or at this ease of understanding between us. It's because I, too, was born of Abim. Oh, before you, of course. I've always lived here. You know, our Very Huge ignored what issued from her Chamber of Men. Only you and your sister Opak were singled out by her. With good reason. None of us would've had the capacity to intervene in the realm. We don't like much to leave the confines of the Nursery. Kobor Tigan't is another world to us, hard and dangerous, which holds no attraction. Here we feel better. We have everything we need. The tranquility is incomparable. The food distributors always bring us plenty of the finest fare. Even some Dongdwo eggs since we are very noble beings!"

She paused to laugh, sounding so disillusioned that Ta stared at her in surprise and asked, "But are you yourself satisfied with this kind of life?"

"Me?" Gan'd replied, "I like it here, but not for the same reasons as everyone. I'm not an example, you know. You'll see this right away. Don't rely on me to understand things. Still, I'll explain them to you. It's true that no one here yearns for anything more than what we get. It's simple. The nobles' happiness lies in the observance of the rights and duties of tradition. So, the women of my bloodline are all big Devotees. That's all they think about. Nothing but this passion that inflames and consumes them! They have their T'Lo meetings, their T'Lo cult, their T'Lo inventions, their T'Lo worship! They trade them, compare them, cover them with jewelry and their men do exactly the same thing, just as madly passionate and fanatical about their T'Lo. Everyone lives in an erotic fog that enraptures them in ecstasy. The older women are already decimated, in the last stage of Devotee drunkenness and they're considered great beings, nobler than the noblest. Oh, you know how proud the Devotees are!"

Ta was surprised at what she was hearing. She suddenly wondered about something she noticed. "But you don't wear the badge of membership. Are you more discreet than all the other women I've met?"

Gan'd looked at her almost severely and her voice was hard, "White Ooh'Rou, it's better that you know my truth. I have no T'Lo. I'm not a Devotee. In this sense you can consider me like an ordinary woman, a woman from Kob'Lâm. I'm not afraid to tell you that I think it's crazy to give yourself to the T'Lo. I know they distill a venom even it they don't mean to—they're gentle creatures. But the vital cloud that envelops them is stronger than ours. It takes the place of ours and we dissolve in it."

Ta stared hard at her. So, Gan'd was an ally! She grabbed her hand, "Me too, I disapprove of the use of T'Lo. Did you know?"

Gan'd had a big smile, "I knew it. And I'm glad for it. Enormously. You are what's needed, Ooh'Rou, what's needed to lead a great realm! I will give you plants to help you govern. You will expand your power of thought. You will find in your mind the things never done before and never spoken of, which will cure our race of its erosion."

Muddled voices and muffled sounds arose in the silent house. It drew Ta back to a sense of decorum and she asked politely, "Gan'd, would you do me the honor of showing me your Chamber of Men?"

She was already standing up, but the young woman held her back with the same forceful look in her eyes as before, "White Ooh'Rou, here's another truth about me: I'm like you, if what they say is true. I have no Chamber of Men. Or rather, no longer. And believe me, I don't want one!"

Ta was stupefied. "What happened?"

"Not much, really. I told you, I like tranquility, nature, silence. I like being alone so the voice can speak freely to me. I like to go whenever I want, day or night, to pick my plants. Therefore, I've chosen very few men for my Chamber. Only three. It's a scandal to my relatives. And to the others too, even the women of the Nursery. Everyone came to see me, out of curiosity, and of course a little suspicious. They criticized me, in disgust, for deteriorating my nobility with lower-class pettiness. I didn't even try to make them understand that I was different from them and I was living in accord with my nature. What's the use! They loathe everything that's not part of their tradition. They adore making scandals. It's a way to get them noticed. So, they left me alone and spread weird rumors about me. As a result, some women hid in the bushes around my property to question the men as the passed by? Did I have any particular vices? Was I cruel to them? After this they got worried and two used the excuse of the lack of T'Lo in my Chamber to demand their freedom. They ended up in other Chambers."

"So, there's only one left?"

"No," Gan'd sounded more sober, "no, I'm alone. The last didn't come back from a hunt in the forest. He was a little reckless. Maybe he fell into pit or something. And the vile birds, maybe 'Those Birds', disposed of his body... I don't want to think about it," she ended abruptly.

Then she headed toward the house. "I'll show you what I have." She came back out almost right away holding a little girl in her arms, almost still a baby. "She's from him. You may not believe it after seeing all the children around me when you got here, but I have only her. Her name's Do'A-Roo. She's very well behaved."

Indeed, the baby was quiet, looking at Ta with serious eyes. The child emanated a kind of attentive silence that seemed to be her distinctive quality.

The young queen had a premonition that this sweet Do'A-Roo, in the future, would be playing a significant role at her side. And she was also sure that from this moment on Gan'd was a partner.

In fact, when she was ready to bid farewell, the woman spoke so amiably, so effortlessly, with a perfect blend of respect and familiarity: "White Ooh'Rou, I will come to see you. I feel that the voice of the old man wants to tell me the plants you need. I'll find them and bring them to you."

She bowed. Her eyes were a little glazed over when she looked at Ta and almost whispered, "Oh, by the gift of Ooh'R, you're going to need help! You're so brave... but that won't be enough... Count on me, Ooh'Rou! I'll always come as quickly as possible. Send a guard to get me anytime you want!"

Hé-Nark had come up to them and nodded. Gan'd with her child accompanied the queen through the paths to the exit. Lost in thought, they kept quiet. Hé-Nark followed behind. Then he thought of something, went back and took the bark for Ta, which the two women had forgotten. He smiled when he caught up to them. When they saw what he was carrying, they laughed at their absent-mindedness.

With one final goodbye Ta marched off. It was getting late and they had to be back in Kob'Ooh'R before nightfall. She realized, pleasantly, that she felt totally relaxed. Gan'd's house was a soothing island of vitality. Thankful, she turned around to wave. The young woman standing at the edge of her domain bowed again. She did not return to her house right away. She watched her visitors going away. It was not the sharp outline of the queen that drew her attention but the solid one of Hé-Nark.

A turn in the path swallowed them. Gan'd lowered her eyes. She stayed there, sighing, kicking pebbles. When her daughter started babbling, she snapped out of her reverie and answered merrily in gibberish.

On the way back, which passed by the Children's Palace, Hé-Nark came beside Ta. She had waved him forward. She was sorry for her reaction when he had warned her against the Devotees. She was ready to listen. He was visibly pleased. Tactfully, he shared his feelings. He felt the need to be extremely vigilant. He told her that Ata-Réè shared his opinion that the Devotees would never obey. If one was not firm, meaning if one did not control them in time, some surprise would be in store.

Ta reminded him that she disapproved of all violence, any kind of restrictive measure and that she would never expect the Devotees to become allies. "All I want is to stop them from spreading. They'll end up wasting away in time."

Hé-Nark reflected and replied that he was not so sure and unfortunately just keeping an eye on their schemes would not control them. But he would not press his point. He moved on to some details that it was good for the queen to be aware of.

Thus it was that she learned that the influential Devotees, led by Oda-Néè, were scheming earnestly against her. Through the Men of their Chambers, all of them quite chatty gossip-mongers, they were spreading awful rumors. The cities of Kob'Iâm and Kob'Râm were festering. It was said that Ta had taken power by force, locked up Opak and the events of the last season were a cover for this takeover. It was also assumed that the new Ooh'Rou hated her sister because she, like all the traditional Ooh'Rous, was a great Devotee who reached communal climaxes with her T'Lo that were so intense it bothered Ta who was naturally incapable of rising to the sublime!

To support their claims, they kept mentioning the fact that she had no Chamber of Men, that she was obviously abnormal, that she had unnatural cravings that drove her to this unbelievable cruelty of wanting the death of the T'Lo!

With this Ta sighed, telling Hé-Nark (as if he needed to be reassured of the purity of her intentions) that she did not want any creature to die but she already knew the T'Lo and Ananou had no place in the new ways of life. What was the point of forcing them to live when nature was exterminating them? And especially when it was warning humans, in a way, by making the T'Lo venomous!

"Fear not, O my Queen," Hé-Nark replied, "I'm your guard and your servant. You have no need to justify yourself to me. I think you're always right and the true essence of Ooh'R inspires you to take the measures that will protect our race."

The Women of the Nursery were waiting for the return of their visitor in front of the Children's Palace. As soon as they saw her, they scrambled out to meet her so they could escort her to the exit. They offered baskets of fruit and flowers, which Hé-Nark took charge of.

They all seemed to have completely forgotten their recent sulking. Flushed and full of energy, fighting to be next to the Queen, they twittered and jabbered back and forth as they related, as if of paramount importance, stories about the Nursery.

Ta listened to them absentmindedly. She had decided to amuse herself, so she slyly observed their faces while remembering to smile at their expressions of naïve exuberance. In order not to avoid talking she threw in some "Ohs" and "Ahs" and the timely "Really?", which caused torrents of explanations that she couldn't care less about!

Swarms of children babbled around them. When it was time to say goodbye, a few women became serious and dared to ask questions. Ta recognized them as the ones who had been at Opak's bedside. Shy but determined, they asked her if her sister's child had lived. After an affirmative response they looked relieved.

"It's because we haven't seen him," they said as an excuse.

"You'll see him," the Queen replied. "But later."

The women gushed, "Of course, of course, later, like always, when he's been weaned by his mother, they'll take the greatest care of him! Ta might want to choose ahead of time which one will be specially appointed for this role?"

"No," Ta said calmly, "no, he'll be raised in the palace by me."

All the women were stunned. As if Ooh'R was exploding in front of their eyes.

There was a painful silence. They looked at one another. The White Ooh'Rou was starting to scare them! Was not this decision, so opposed to tradition, hiding some dreadful scheme?

Ta saw suspicion flash in their eyes. She was getting used to it.

She was about to console them when one of the more daring took the shot: "But in that case, O Queen, what will become of the tradition of the Great Child? We were hoping that our new Ooh'Rou was coming to see us about this matter. It's our glory when the Great Child is discovered and recognized among those we raise! The Very Huge had this privilege. But maybe she didn't pass it on to our new Ooh'Rou? Maybe our new Ooh'Rou is unable to recognize the Great Child?"

The woman was standing straight and firm, aware of the role she was playing before her comrades. Her impoliteness bordered on insult.

The eyes of Hé-Nark had turned to stone. He turned them to the Queen. She gave him a little gesture of restraint: This was just a common Breeder. She answered dismissively with a smile on her face.

"Don't worry, Woman, and rest assured, all of you, I'm not as helpless as you fear. The Great Child is for later. For now, however, I can guarantee you that you will get to know him. Yes, don't worry, my intentions are pure!"

She turned her back and started walking away in silence, putting distance between them because the women, being slow to understand, just stood there. They were wondering what to do with such insolence toward their sovereign.

Hé-Nark caught up to Ta, "You'll have to remember this, O Queen!" he whispered.

She shrugged her shoulders, stoical. No matter! The Women of the Nursery were certainly the stupidest creatures of the realm... But the Breeders came up to them in a flurry. They were giggling and clapping their hands. They thought they had understood. Traditionally, the Great Child, destined to become a transcendent Ooh'Rou, was always a girl. The women had just made a guess about Opak's mysterious newborn that Ta was going to raise in the palace. Proudly, they brayed, "So, Opak's infant is not a girl!"

"It's a Son," Ta said. And she left, for good, without paying any more attention to them.

The women watched her go. They understood nothing. What kind of being was this Ooh'Rou Ta, so inscrutable and confusing?

CHAPTER IV

During the return, the twilight darkened quickly. The road became difficult. The big, felt-winged night birds started hunting silently everywhere at the same time.

"We won't get back before nightfall," Ta said.

"Don't worry," Hé-Nark replied, "I thought of that. Do you see those lights coming toward us?"

Indeed, torch-bearing guards, running from the royal city, suddenly appeared before them. The last leg of the journey was covered without incident.

At Kob'Ooh'R, Ata-Réè and her young B'Tah-Gous were waiting for the queen's return on a high terrace where scented torches burned. She had had a meal prepared. Food the queen loved: honey, fruit, sweet roots cooked in Mou-Touh milk rather than meat. Habits inherited from the Beautiful Stranger, which were starting to spread through the five Cities.

Ta was glad to see her companion. She put her hand on her shoulder as she so often did and drew her closer to ask for news of Opak.

"She's calm. The day went well. The T'Lo are good sentries. They watched over her very well."

"Better, I suppose, than the Women of the Nursery would!" the young queen laughed heartily.

She sat down to eat. She passed around the flowers and fruit brought by the calm young girls who bustled around, serving her with delicate movements. Ta admired their luminous smiles and could not help comparing their faces to the royal offspring in the Nursery. The comparison was not favorable to the latter!

A cheerful conversation unfolded during the meal. Ata-Réè happily explained that her pupils, guided by her, were starting to hear the lofty music revealed by Angel a that some of them were already trying to reproduce.

On the next terrace the guards were also eating. Gathered around the incontestable prestige of Hé-Nark they sat together in great harmony. They laughed a lot but not raucously, rather calm and composed. Their dignified voices and attitudes seemed to be their common ground. They were truly different from the other men, whom they openly accuse of being frivolous. This seriousness, in any case, must have been contagious because every new recruit very quickly acted the same, as if by mimicry. They were very fraternal, took care of one another and thus formed a true corps, remarkably cohesive, whose guiding soul emanated from Hé-Nark.

For the moment they were talking about the great figure, Amo, and the example he had set. It was their favorite subject of conversation. They often came back to it. They attributed to Amo a mysterious continuation of life in the invisible. They felt like they were being touched by him. They saw his presence in the evening shadows and, for them, his voice fused in the storms coming from Grand Va-Hôh.

With reverence they called him "The Man of Ooh'R" and they remembered his affection for Angel, from now on identifying him with the Beautiful Stranger come from Elsewhere whom they all hoped confidently would return.

They were not the only ones to think regularly about these two remarkable figures. In all of Kobor Tigan't, from the highest to the lowest of the five Cities, the double legend, in various ways, absorbed their hearts and minds.

Now the Guards were quiet, relaxed. The meal was over. In silence they drank up the evening air, in slow lungfuls, sighing sometimes with serenity. They watched the movements of the B'Tah-Gous whose light-colored clothes fluttered around the queen under the flickering torches. To them the young girls looked like emanations of the White Ooh'Rou. They felt united. They were affected by girls. They dreamed of them. Did not the will of the Queen weave secret bonds between these two elite corps? The Guards liked to think so.

The other women did not interest them. They had almost all refused to belong to any Chamber of Men, no matter how honorable, and this was a great surprise to the women, given their status. As for those who did belong to these Chambers, they were gradually regretting it.

The chatter on the royal terrace paused. The Guards leaned over, all ears. The voice of Ata-Réè rose up, strange, sweet and solitary like the blue Na-Nood that had just appeared in the sky.

She was singing her first official song whose simple words deeply moved the followers of the new Ooh'Rou:

We have a White Ooh'Rou.
She is not like the others.

Would she know another Sun,
Father of the One we love?
We have a White Ooh'Rou.
Her Chamber of Men is empty.
She stands alone before us.
And yet she is the one who broke our solitude.
We have a White Ooh'Rou.
The one before was golden
And had plenty of Men.
But did her glory nourish our hearts?
We have a White Ooh'Rou.
She does not only live
She sees us and speaks to us.
She teaches us what we can become.
We have a White Ooh'Rou.
She is not like the others.

The voice died out. There was not another sound or movement. Ta had fallen into deep meditation. Her head tilted to the side, she was dreaming of the future. Wrapped up in thoughts, she considered those around her less as beings than as movable and perfectible elements of this future. Her eyes wandered from her Guards to the flock of B'Tah-Gous. She united these two groups in her mind. She was going to carry these men and women, together, to the heights of realization. Around her, they had to become, for the others, enviable models of the desirable future of the race. Secretly inspired, she knew she could help them to be the first to go through the necessary transformations. They were complementary. That was why she had so easily gathered them around her.

She knew she was strong enough to unite them.

Like Ata-Réè, Hé-Nark also perceived what the Queen was thinking and he approved of it. With his haughty patience, he suffered the sting of the exclusive emotion he felt for his sovereign. He wanted nothing for himself, nothing but to serve her like no one else could ever do.

She was a woman of unknown essence. By understanding her, he was enriching himself. By spending time with her, he was making progress and maybe even a little before the others. Just by being in her radiant presence, he was freeing himself from the crowd. He, Hé-Nark, was the Guard of the White Ooh'Rou...

Tonight, barely having got home, Ta went out again. She wanted to extend her journey by paying a nocturnal visit to Abim, her mother, the Very Huge.

The desire had come to her abruptly, like an obligation, even though she was dead tired. She had often dreaded having to do it, to the extent that her thoughts would turn away from her mother, sometimes suppressing even the memory of her.

But tonight Ta needed to provoke this titanic shadow. She wanted to measure the acidity of her young power on the stubborn cohesion that kept all of Abim's remnants together. Even though she was still there, unchanged, motionless as always, she did not seem defeated by death. She wanted to know why/ She wanted to know how and how far or deep it might go.

She had not gone back to this part of the palace since the last season. Nobody lived there. Nobody visited there. The huge rooms remained empty, unused. And nobody even talked about the place or about Her who was there.

While living, the Very Huge had, by not showing herself, nipped all curiosity in the bud. Ruling through absence, ordering through silence, a click had always secretly materialized all her wishes. She could topple any obstacle so completely that the undisputed prestige of her invisible government sealed all lips. The Giants feared unleashing her rage by gossiping. Furthermore, just by pronouncing her name they were afraid of attracting her attention, said to be always on the watch, even in the spirit of the times.

In the grip of her occult reign, therefore, as a precaution, no one spoke out consciously. Now they continued to stay quiet as a precaution but this time because they did not know in what way the Very Huge was lingering on in death and if by chance she had lost her memory they did not want to call her back to the living by pronouncing, however faintly, her name.

The people of Kob'Lâm were fantastic at this safeguard, which the higher cities of Kob'Vâm and Kob'Râm also observed, but less strictly, whereas the aristocrats of Kob'Iâm scoffed or even pretended to ignore it.

From the Devotees, for a while, as a reaction against Ta, a different tendency had arisen: they started talking about Abim like an Ancestor. They openly mentioned her position just over the Ananou Pit. There were some who said she descended from the mythic Ooh'Rou who had once conceived from her beloved T'Lo. Wasn't the Very Huge, therefore, in her well-guarded secret, a kind of extraordinary T'Lo, fantastic and misunderstood by those around her, especially her own family? They knew her not! Who knew if Ta, who was certainly not her daughter, hadn't discovered the secret last season and out of hatred of the T'Lo imprisoned Abim to death in the same way she was imprisoning Opak?

The rooms of the Very Huge had not been opened since Ta had turned her back one day last season, leaving her mother alone to die off in mute and motionless agony. On that day, Hé-Nark terminated his duties as Master of the Guard for the Very Huge to enter the service of the young Ooh'Rou with the other guards under his command.

There had been no protest or grumbling, not a moment's hesitation. Agreed. Ta's clear voice barely spoke her orders when the big guards, with the silence and long vigils finally broken, got moving to do everything she asked before following her calmly into the other part of the palace.

Thus, as they went away with her they closed all the doors, one by one, to the forbidden hallways that snaked through the shadows into the very heart of the palace, into the center of the influence seized by Abim and where, even dead, she remained present, inflicting the presence of her death all over Kobor Tigan't, above all forcing the stoppage and stasis of the telluric energies that she had unlawfully diverted.

Ta was walking through the hallways without saying a word. Hé-Nark was in front holding a torch. The other guards followed behind in a long train, also carrying lights. It was like a homecoming.

Hé-Nark opened the doors, cautiously, one by one. They creaked. At each one, Ta prudently slowed her step and behind her, docilely, the men slackened their pace. But they did not really stop. The procession marched on. As soon as the door was opened Hé-Nark jumped through and ran to the next one while the others came through. Like that, gradually, in an active silence full of thoughts. Like that, in staggered rhythms, all these men, this woman, this other man alone in front, continually throwing his muscles into the task, creak after creak...

Coming from afar in the rear, the wind entered with them. The dust from the imprint of their feet rose in lazy curls. The torches crackled. It was like the sound of ideas, busy like bees in the suddenly discovered orchard of the imagination under a feverish sun.

None of them could stop thinking. What were they going to encounter there at the end where the Presence was getting denser behind the tallest, heaviest, most massive door… Yes, what was on the other side of this last door that opened without creaking before the stayed hand of Hé-Nark and where Ta entered alone, taking her guard's torch?

They lined up along the opposite wall in the hallway. They started to fear for their young Ooh'Rou. They held their breath to listen. When she would cry out, would they hear her call?

Hé-Nark stayed right next to the door. His men gave him questioning looks…

Inside, it smelled of balms and dust, the cooled fire and the faint musk of a reptile that had holed up deep in one of the walls to hibernate.

Ta had taken three steps. She had only one thought before everything in her head stopped. This thought flashed out: "Nothing has changed. She's here!"

No, nothing had changed here in the wedges of shadow and light revealed by the torch. From the entrance you bumped into the same obstacle: The Very Huge.

She was still here. Who would have believed otherwise even for the briefest instant. She was still sitting. A little more crooked maybe. But sitting she was just like before, like always, as tall as a man standing.

Abim was enthroned, unequaled, unrivaled and proving it. She was enthroned in her death like in her life. Sitting in death. Sitting on her realm.

She was black, mountainous, rugged, deeply hostile to everything that was not her. She was fixed in the permanence of her difference.

Who had ever been like Abim while alive?

Who could ever be like Abim in death?

For, in this state as well she manifested her essentiality: the difference in her being with respect to everyone else. Different in life, she remained different in death.

She had not collapsed. No decay whatsoever. She had not dissolved into dust. She had not swollen up with gas, with foul swamp bubbles. No, not even dried out. Not crumbled in the slightest. No.

On the contrary, quite orderly, in her place, she had densified her nature: *she had mineralized.*

And now in Ta's total silence—one of those exceptional mental silences in which no thought dares to venture out—and in her gaping, defenseless gaze, in this empty opening, the Stone Abim was embedded!

The young woman took a deep breath. She shook herself free of the grip. Her thoughts flowed freely again. She started to be less hypnotized by what she was seeing and simply to see and to make sense of what she was seeing.

Since the last season she had become Ooh'Rou Ta. It was, therefore, no longer the girl that her mother was forcing to endlessly brush her vast, white hair. She was no longer the girl coming in here with the duty to report in detail everything that was being said and done in the five Cities.

So, she stepped forward, holding the torch out so that all the details would appear in the light. She looked at her mother, intensely, with a calm eye, like looking at some huge structure encountered in the jungle. The invisible forests of death and shadow kept this massive structure leaning weirdly to one side.

Abim was an empty temple. Her thighs formed a base from which the frozen stairs of her belly fat lumbered up to her chest with its two dismal wine-skins of breasts.

Ta shined the light on the face. It still overlooked her! Between the hardened shoulders the round mass of her head jutted out, still assertive under the dry stream of hair. Her chin rested on the top of her chest. Mouth and eyes closed, a face walled up in the final refusal. She had given in to nothing. She had entered her death without renouncing anything, without denying anything at all of her nature.

A block.

Ta took in these details without fear, without emotion, without disgust, but with peaceful sadness.

"Well then," she murmured, "my Very Huge Mother, you really are a Stone. You were never anything else. A Stone, monstrous and magical, like those standing on the Grand Va-Hôh where your mind used to go to animate the Central Stone, the tallest one. Yes, you were that Stone, o Mother, you took on the features of a giant queen to come and sit here in the realm, in the center... It, too, over there, it's leaning like you. It's almost fallen. Amo, the brave man, damaged its base. He only succeeded halfway, didn't he? Otherwise, for sure, you, too, would have fallen. You're just leaning, Mother... No matter! You can't do anything now. You're here, that's all. Your ancient chain of power has disappeared. The Ananou are dying off. It's probably your fault. Your magic wore them out."

She stopped talking for a moment. She felt like her words were becoming strangely slower as they passed through the very thick density towards the unlocated place where Abim was listening in. She was sure that she heard her. She just had given the words time to reach her.

But Abim's response could not be heard. Withdrawn too far. In too much pride. Too distracted in her monolithic sulking.

Suddenly, in the dust at her feet Ta picked up a comb, the same one she had used the last season. She put the torch on a nearby tripod and with a little smile, muttering again, she swept the comb slowly through the long hair within reach.

"An old habit of ours, isn't it, my Very Huge Mother! You who were so demanding don't ask for it anymore. But why not do a little like then since today I have big news to tell you."

She paused and leaned closer to the looming presence.

"Mother, the Great Child has been born!"

...Down there, elsewhere, there was a stir, an impact. And something expanded, like attention, in a round, gaping, black cavity...

Ta sounded almost cruel triumphant, "The Great Child, yes, Very Huge! Oh, you didn't want to recognize it! You didn't want to tell me the Sign either. You kept the knowledge to yourself. Mostly because you feared the child would come from Amo whom you hate so much. Bah! Your worst fear was useless. The Great Child is Angel's. And you loved him. I recognized the Child. I guessed and identified the Sign. The indisputable Sign of Ooh'R's favor on this mating. The Sun Cross is on the son's feet! Yes, you heard me, I said the Son! This time it's not a daughter. Women are done with the Reign. Here, Mother, I'm the last. After it will be Him, the Son. I'll put him on the throne myself."

She nodded her head.

"Basically, despite your awful ploys you didn't really win. Whatever you might have wanted—hear this—now things are such that there won't even be a real Ooh'Rou, spouse of Ooh'R. No, Mother, the currents have deviated, see. What was circulating is now stagnant. What was from the sun on high is no longer spread down below on Earth through Kobor Tigan't as it once was. For too long you clogged the hollow pillar of the rightful union. You're still blocking it! So, the sun scattered its seeds beyond this matrix of this profound Earth on which you persist, from which you sucked out all its strength from below. That's why there is this White Ooh'Rou that I am, sterile and robbed by you of a man! What irony! The Very Huge Mother, eroding the principle of the magic reign of Woman so badly that she ushers in the reign of Man! Your selfishness pushed you too far. By sticking to your one and only goal, you ended up doing the opposite... By marking the Son, Ooh'R gave his final, most meaningful gift. Consequently, he will reign."

She grabbed her torch. She had just thrown the comb into the dust. Everything was said.

However, before opening the door she changed her mind and went back. "I believe you would've been capable, even on seeing him, to prevent this male from reaching the throne. You wouldn't have announced him, I'm sure. You who were excess personified! But now the Time has come when to keep on living everything has to change, to reverse…"

She headed back to the door. When she got there she turned around one last time to barely even whisper, confidentially, "In fact, between us, Very Huge, in this mystery of your feet, which you never showed, was it because there was also the wheel of Ooh'R?"

She went back to her rooms. Everything was ready for her: soft lamps, perfumes, garlands of flowers, tasty fruits. The cushions on the bed were calling her to sleep. The windows were open to the night. Through one door, like an invitation, you could see the private garden, closed and protected, full of leafy plants, the scent of flowers, and in the middle in a deep pool, the water was constantly circulating, where the queen loved to soak her body.

Ta did not see all this. For her, it was night again, like yesterday and before. It was lethargy. Everything had been done today, of course, but how could it be enough, where was the reward? Since it was solitude like yesterday and before. The night of the heart. The cessation of the feelings. The desire for man was gone forever after the death of To.

She was just a White Ooh'Rou, overworked with more yet to do, a woman alone whom every evening brought back to herself, pitilessly, so that she might lose every vanity. And indeed, she found herself standing exposed and confused before a huge, passive population with their backs against the sky of an incomprehensible future!

Yes, she was scared. She hid it vehemently.

After a few moments of silent panic, she managed to shake off her despair and go bathe in the garden pool. When she came back, moving more relaxed, she felt better. She lay down on the bed to fall into a brief sleep. She came out of it screaming.

She had confronted the same dream as every night: To, pleading, unreachable.

Sitting up, holding her head with both hands, she noticed on her nightstand, in a cup, put there intentionally, the bark concoction prepared by Gan'd.

She took it then lay down to await the effects. She felt like she was falling straight down and cut off from all her senses. How long did it last? She could not say. But suddenly she was sitting up, her mind clear and bright. New strength was flowing in her. She felt incredibly present, aggressive, alive!

It was on that night that she realized the need for a great speech and composed it.

CHAPTER V

All the people are assembled, crowded together around the main terrace of Kob'Râm, the city of fire and forges.

To speak to everybody Ta wanted to be in the very heart of Kobor Tigan't. That was why she chose the City in the middle. The people of Kob'Tâm came down while those from Kob'Vâm and Kob'Lâm came up.

Everyone is there. Everyone is waiting, anxious. It is a big day. What are they going to learn? What is the White Ooh'Rou, always full of surprises, going to say? The sun beats down on their heads. The crowd packs closer together, stamping their feet. The murmuring wanes. The moment has come for silence. And no one dares to move or make a sound.

The swell of faces looks up expectantly at her. Ta sees it in sharp relief down there at her feet. She hears how they quiet down and knows what kind of silence it is. It is a chasm she must jump into.

She makes one last check around her. The echo stones are in place. Her voice will carry far. And whoever does not hear will, as always, be told the words in the evening by those who are proud to have remembered them.

Behind her, on one side, are the young B'Tah-Gous. The Guards are on the other. The Girls are all in white, the Guards too. The same as Hé-Nark and Ata-Réè, to her right and left respectively. She herself is sparkling in white on a raised seat covered with immaculate skins.

In the center of a lily setting that refracts the bright light onto the audience, the presence of the new Ooh'Rou takes on uncommon import. It is all the solitude of the royal grandeur that Kobor Tigan't feels. But they do not know how to explain it. The white is more striking and astonishing because, as always, they wear bright colors.

Row upon row, at the sight of her, whisper at first, "She's still dressing like the Beautiful Stranger!"

Because of this they suspect mysteries. Did Angel really disappear? Is the Ooh'Rou meeting him? Is he the one inspiring these weird new ways? They hope so. They loved the Beautiful Stranger. They miss him. They almost look for him through Ta.

Down below, in front of the Ooh'Rou, there is the perpetual crucible of molten metal. Just before speaking her eyes plunge into the glow. She believes she sees the inside of her own heart...

"People of Kobor Tigan't, people of Giants, all of you, my Race!"

She pauses. Her voice softens.

"You, my people!"

All the hearts are beating. The word carries. In the excitement they accept this royal possession. Among the Devotees in the front row Oda-Néè purses her lips.

"I have great concern for you, my people. I think of you day and night. I live with you. But it seems to me that you don't understand me very well. It seems to me that my character surprises and disturbs you. It's my fault, certainly. I didn't explain the reasons that compel me. I've confused you."

The pale figure of the Ooh'Rou is an island of solitude and yet her voice slips comfortably into all their minds. Everyone hears her for themselves alone. Each of them feels trust.

"You see, my people, I didn't have time to bring you together. I had to act first, as quickly as possible, for your good, for you, to save you from harm, from fear, from all the bad things assaulting you. Everything was so hectic last season when the relentless fog was menacing and the reptiles came out of everywhere! You remember, don't you, like me, that time of evil that it seemed we'd never get out of?"

Yes, the people remember! Each in their way is communicating mutely with her who is speaking like this. The White Ooh'Rou had found at the onset the voice to capture all their attention. The heart of her people is open.

She can, therefore, trace the history of recent tragedies and explain the events that remain obscure. First of all, she denounces the demonic wiles of Abim, her nefarious actions, her confiscation of power. She is clever enough to make them understand, in simple terms, how the general balance had been upset.

Her audacity to speak of this taboo subject shocks the people. At the mention of the doings of the Very Huge, gasps and groans of scandal run through the audience.

Among the Devotees it is different. They do not participate, they pretend to be cold, they still scowl and whisper bitterly that the Ooh'Rou is slandering the Very Huge, that venerable image of the Ancestors, only to cover up her own deceits.

On hearing this, those closest to the Devotees are astonished. They worriedly repeat what they say. What deceits are the Devotees referring to? What do they know that the others don't? They look really sure of what they are insinuating.

In the meantime, to wind up her first part, Ta has officially announced the extinction of Abim. This causes a greater shock. But the Devotees are saying, "It's not true, it's false!" Their neighbors look at them and become agitated.

Now the voice of the queen drifting over everyone tells of the heroism and insight of Amo. For, everything must be remembered, omitting nothing, in order that in their minds everything work out to clear up the confusion of misguided imaginations. So, she tells them why and how Amo sacrificed himself. She tells them how horribly he probably died by the magical onslaught of the Very Huge's fury. She boldly describes the Standing Stone of the Grand Va-Hôh, the counterpart of Abim and the relay of power.

Everyone follows her, passionately. Everyone takes part. They hang on every word. They expect everything from her. At the mention of Amo's death, tears flow. Even among the Devotees they cannot fight their emotions: Eqin-Go who was the bosom brother of Amo weeps openly.

Oda-Néè is enraged when she realizes the influence Ta can have so easily. She figures that it will take a long and bitter fight to get rid of her. She swears she will succeed. She will galvanize her Men who are too easily swayed anyway. The T'Lo will help her. She is still young and their psychic drug has, for the moment, only a stimulating effect on her that just heightens her abilities. Her ideas flow very quickly and she is the admiration of her peers for her ability to always come up with new plans.

However, despite all this, she cannot help admiring Ta. For her body, for the mystery she sees in her, for her clear voice with such subtle nuances, for her art of persuasion. She finds herself listening eagerly when she tells of the radiant person who was Angel, that Beautiful Stranger, found on Kah'B'La the Holy Mountain.

All around her their eyes sparkle, their lips are parted. She, like everyone starts looking in the clouds for those golden-headed white birds, the companions of the Beautiful Being whom Ta's speech seems about to bring back!

Oda-Néè looks down and stamps her foot. This White Ooh'Rou is so powerful! It would be wrong to underestimate her!

Everyone's attention is centered on Ata-Réè because they know that she received from Angel the gift of hearing the celestial music. It is an extraordinary ability, a transcendent power that no one has ever had before in Kobor Tigan't. The Queen reminds them of this at the right moment. Her solemnity passes straight to the audience a feeling of the sacred.

Then they pay even closer attention because she is explaining the nature of the tragedy unleashed by the clumsy behavior of Opak towards the Beautiful Being and how he revolted rather than stay with them, choosing to disappear with Amo.

Full of regrets, the crowd sighs together. Will the Stranger, of whom not a trace remains, ever come back from his incomprehensible Elsewhere?

A glum sadness passes. Ta tells frankly of the love despair that drove Opak mad. And here, unafraid, she goes on to say that this madness is the end result of her sister's excesses, of her overindulging in the drug of the T'Lo.

The crowd reacts. Waves of movement, jumps and jostling. They are standing on tiptoes. The people of Kob'Lâm are burning with interest. Others are more divided. The Queen has come to the heart of the matter. Is she really going to leave nothing in the dark?

The hostility of the Devotees becomes obvious to all. They form a block, defying Ta with their looks. They have uncovered their badges. People are quivering. The nervousness passes. Excitement and anguish now. What is going to happen?

Nothing. Nothing but the inevitable continuation of Ta's speech. Yes, she has decided to say everything so that there be no more uncertainty between her and her people. She wants them, with all her might, to fully understand the merits of her actions.

Nothing, therefore, is going to stop her. She explains calmly, goes into detail. She covers everything as clearly as can be.

There are, however, some things that are hard to explain, like the weakening of the Ananou who are dozing off into death, slowly, one after another. It is hard to explain the strengthening of the T'Lo's toxicity and the ravages they cause and that they will cause more and more as time fortifies their venom.

"Lies!" the Devotees shout.

Hé-Nark steps forward. The other Guards as well.

Ta keeps going. She does so with the utmost simplicity, as if nothing happened. They admire her, they listen. She explains well. Oh, yes, they want to understand! Kob'Lâm is all for her, unreservedly. The people of this City cast dark looks at the Devotees, who dare not make a move. They are already despised!

Wisely, they do not budge. It would not be ill-advised. Oda-Néè got it. A sign from her holds back all the nobles of her ilk. The Women calm their Men's anger. But the menacing reaction of the Devotees has escaped nobody's notice.

For her part, Ata-Réè, disturbed by premonitions, has turned pale. She fears for her queen because she saw how the black currents of bitterness were swirling over the Devotees' heads. Her aperceptive gift is never wrong. Thanks to it she already knows that from this day on the Devotees will not stop trying to topple the White Ooh'Rou.

Images, still fuzzy but that only need to be clarified, stream before her inner eyes. All of sudden there is a flash of a young, red-haired woman dragging behind her line of T'Lo. A counter-queen! Ta is going to be directly threatened with the loss of her throne and her life... By pure willpower the seer stops the vision. She searches the crowd ferociously to find the redhead she had glimpsed. There is no one like her. She feels, she understands that it is for later.

But already Ta, with her courage, is facing and even fanning the first flames of the very real danger. Her speech is forcing people to sort through their opinions. Even among the Devotees. All of them are not so rigid. Some might be receptive. The erotic enchantment of the T'Lo have still not reached their vital sources. More strongly animated than others perhaps, they are still free in their choices and decisions. Their spirits have preserved normal appetites. The future that Ta is presenting to them is compelling and they want to participate actively.

Ata-Réè is the first to notice this. She sees the thought sparkle in the eyes of some of the most influential women. The ones, moreover, allured by the queen's personality, who have adopted some of her habits. Like her they wear light-colored clothes and are unusually sober in their elegance, for example replacing their jewelry with woven flower ornaments, as was the wont of the Beautiful Stranger.

They are intelligent women. The Men of their Chambers have greater freedom of movement and are much less dependent than others. At their homes they are starting to get together less for banquets and erotic games than for conversation in which their passionate minds can question and comment on countless subjects.

The uncompromising Devotees make fun of these women, saying that with all their pretty talk they obviously want to take the place of the dead Storytellers!

As the speech progresses, the Queen's insight also picks up on these women whose sympathy reaches her as if it is being diffused. Automatically turning towards this wave of warmth, she meets their bright eyes and sees them offering smiles and signs of approval. She is comforted and then starts addressing that side which is showing more and more enthusiasm for her words. She wants to ally with these women. She feels they are ready. They need it! If she convinces them, she will start this very evening to break apart the Devotees!

To focus more directly, having quickly selected one of these women, she speaks as if only to her:

"O woman, you are beautiful, grand, noble, strong in body but stronger in mind. Me, your Ooh'Rou, I salute you as the incarnation of my race. And I tell you this: I want you to live; I want you to meet the future with all your power and all your strength. I don't want you to become, in a few Ooh'R cycles, like one of your T'Lo, soft, weak and dull. I don't want you, o beautiful woman of my race, to be like my sister Opak who's been given that terrible name Calamitous. No, not you! I told you this. Understand, my lovely, there is no future for your poor T'Lo. They won't become humans! But we humans, arriving at this great turning point of the Ages, we are going to become like the T'Lo if we don't watch out! They are hooked onto us like weak but pernicious plants that can only survive by wrapping themselves around a tree. It's our sap they're thriving on. It's from their inability to live that you, yes you, are in danger of dying!"

The people are holding their breath. Everyone feels like they are this single woman to whom the Ooh'Rou is speaking with such severe love.

Ta's voice twists into lamentation. "You're going to die! If you don't use what's stirring in your head, what's flickering in your heart, what allows you to talk face to face with the sun, what allows you to walk in the dark night, forcing the shadows to answer you! You're going to die too soon! Don't fool yourself! Everyone who feeds the T'Lo with their vital sap will die too soon. And you know how they die! Everyone knows. Even though they say the opposite, it is not a glorious death. It's just a withering on the vine. There's no grandeur, no dignity in bearing the purple stigmata on your cheeks, eyes and forehead. It's not true! I know. They say in your families that it's the Tradition, our Ancestors did it before us. That's a lie because the conditions weren't the same, our Ancestors weren't weakened by their T'Lo who weren't so harmful then. None of our Ancestors would have tolerated this. If they'd let themselves waste away in this pointless eroticism that gnaws away at you with endlessly repeated dreams and sensations without ever satisfying you, our Ancestors would not have built Kobor Tigan't!"

An ovation explodes. The Devotees are grim-faced, unsmiling. They are withdrawn into contempt. They sever themselves openly from the crowd. Oda-Néè has decided to do all she can to make sure that sooner or later this impious Ooh'Rou will disappear. But a weird regret stings her heart and surprises her again. She realizes that despite herself Ta's radiance has seduced her. She realizes that she has not stopped staring at her and finding her, at this moment, beautiful, alluring and... convincing! But she would rather die than admit it!

With this realization comes sorrow: Alas, why is this truly wonderful Ooh'Rou, so alluring and radiant, trying to destroy the tradition of the T'Lo with arguments that are so unworthy of a Queen and only good for the small-minded people of Kob'Lâm? She cannot understand. For, she knows how special and delightful are the infinite orgasms that the T'Lo alone, so generous in their love, can give humans! Without the T'Lo who would know the inebriating oddities of lights and colors in which they all whirl as if eternally!

And isn't it sweet, isn't it noble, this extinction of recent times for a pure Devotee when she floats beyond the world, climaxing again and again? The world is but an orgasm, that's the supreme revelation! Transcendent death is but an orgasm!

Her conviction blazes so brightly that without listening to the Queen anymore, she suddenly starts to yell out the aphorism of the Devotees, "Only the T'Lo know love and give love!"

All the Devotees chime in, "Everyone must come together, through the T'Lo, in love!"

The guards sweep down on them and force them to stay quiet. They obey, but with contempt.

For the second time Oda-Néè is facing Hé-Nark. He grabs her arm. His gray eyes are ironic. She is furious. Still, she thinks he would make a fine addition to her Chamber of Men. She has no man like him. He sees what she is thinking and the irony in his eyes drifts down to his mouth in a slow smile.

He returns to his place, leaving her stifled. She promises to have him nevertheless! Isn't there a rumor that he is one of the Ooh'Rou's secret Men? One more reason to have him!

When calm is restored, Ta looks down again at the pretty woman who is the support for her eloquence. She refutes the outburst of the Devotees:

"O beautiful woman, I tell you this: That love is just an illusion! Where does it take you? Nowhere! Because you drank and then you were thirsty, much thirstier than before. You drink thirst by looking for love in your T'Lo. Everything a T'Lo appears to give you is just an illusion, bitter and barren. All they give you that's real, finally, is death and decay! The T'Lo doesn't give, only takes—your time, your strength and passion, which you could devote to all kinds of other things that would be truly beneficial to you. Whoever persists in the custom of T'Lo from now on is damaging the whole Race because they are putting themselves above the interests of all. By knowingly weakening themselves, they can do nothing for themselves or others. They forsake us. They desert us to embrace a false love. To embrace death! We won't go far, I tell you, if our elites, the strongest of body and mind, are consumed by the intoxication of wrong-doing and non-being, which is the lie attached to the T'Lo. That's not what love is! It's not dying in the fumes of your evaporated senses. It's the opposite—it's thinking of those like us who are coming after us and it's building, setting up for those who follow us like we followed our Ancestors."

The Blacksmiths of Kob'Râm, strong men, who listen eagerly, are burning with the desire to run to their forges to start the monumental and momentous work. The Tanners of Kob'Lâm are thinking they must find a way to work the skins more delicately. And the Hunters feel the urge to fill all the food reserves to bursting.

Countless conflicting sentiments torment the Devotees. Revolt and anger for most of them. Confusion for others who feel, more or less, their convictions being shaken and no longer know which side to take. For a few the words of Ta go directly into their consciousness and they are already almost decided to get rid of their T'Lo. They, obviously, are uncertain of what might happen if they make this decision. The new and unprecedented situation scares them. Will they dare decide?

The young Queen keeps developing her thoughts:

"It's love that builds. We must choose the best materials and the strongest builders. For, we always have to face and prepare for the future to triumph over it. Now, what have we been doing lately? Nothing! We're still living in the structures of our Ancestors. They knew how to think of them for us in advance! But now that a great, transforming wind has come, what have we really done for our future? Not much, do you think, o people of Kobor Tigan't? Me, I say nothing! We've been creeping around in ennui for ages. We don't really create anything like our Ancestors did. We're happy just repeating what they did. And what's worse, we do it badly, we weaken it, deform it. So, we just sit around yawning without really becoming. We're becoming nothing at all. Ennui and sluggishness and death have slipped into our lives. Thus, we tolerate our poor T'Lo telling ourselves that it's noble and beautiful. We raise parasites who, if we don't watch out, will get the better of our race. For, what do the T'Lo do for us, for our future?"

"They love us," Oda-Néè shouts.

"They love us and they wear us down!" the orator replies. "They are useless and dangerous. They build nothing. They aren't blacksmiths or egg hunters or anything. Nothing! We've been dying for a long time from the custom of T'Lo. They live off the life they take from us. Nature proves this since the Ananou, who aren't replenished by mingling their bodies with ours, are slowly dying. The T'Lo have to die in turn. They're the residue of bygone days. Every Giant worthy of our Race commits a crime against us all by continuing to give care and vital energy to the T'Lo. The future is coming. We have to change. Like nature changes in the seasons. This is a new Season of Man that is about to start and we have to live differently by getting rid of everything that weakens us."

Her voice rises with astonishing force. The echo stones resonate so well that the farthest away wonder who this transcendent person is who speaks like this with so much power. Whispers pass through the crowd all the way up to the front row. "Ooh'R inspires her! Ooh'R is speaking through her!"

And the fact is that she looks grander. Her weird paleness is still striking but now it looks almost luminous against the bright white of her clothes. She looks surrounded by a halo. The magnetism of her eyes pierce the audience. Her voice resonates, metallically. She strikes the people's sensibility. Every word shoots out like accurate little arrows. She vibrates with such conviction, such penetrating enthusiasm that all their nerves are strained and all their breaths quicken to the accelerated rhythm of their beating hearts.

The Queen decrees:

"As a result of everything I've just said, starting right now all who have T'Lo are advised to give them back to the Pit. Thanks to the traditional drink of oblivion they will become simple Ananou once again. And they will die off like the others, without suffering, as nature and the New Age will it by extinguishing their vital flame. I will grant high honors to the Devotees who are wise enough to heed my advice before it becomes an order."

Now Ta turns more menacing:

"Don't be stubborn, Devotees, in the name of an outdated tradition! I've decided to abolish it forever! I will consider everyone who persists in this custom as impious and opponents of my power. They will be rejected by me and stripped of their rank. Access to Kob'Ooh'R will be forbidden to them. And my sentence will apply to anyone who, though not like them, still visits them too often."

Her words cause a sensation. They are not used to such determination. The Devotees, utterly silent, cannot believe their ears. Oda-Néè whispers to her companions that they are just empty words and the Queen would never dare do what she says. Then seeing Hé-Nark staring at her, she looks more contemptuous than ever as she listens to the rest.

In secret, however, she feels deeply stunned by this unveiling of the royal character. She has to admit that she evens admires her. Her mind is seduced by her. She envies her. And this makes her more anxious than ever to fight. She wants to be like her, to speak like her, dominate like her and see her words transform into action.

Ta has just said that she was hoping to be understood by the best and that from now on the Devotees, who were decided, could go take their T'Lo to the Pit. Guards would be willing to help them. She assured them that these T'Lo that turned back into Ananou through the drink of oblivion would be well treated and just like before they would suffer no harm.

She smiles suddenly because the beautiful Devotee who has supported her from the start has just made a sign to her that she would be the first to do it.

Ta is jubilant. She uses her renewed strength to launch into the final phase of her speech:

92

"Yes, my people, I know, you think my reign is as harsh as it is confusing. You think I have deliberately neglected things that you were expecting from me, things that all the Ooh'Rous have always hurried to accomplish. Like I haven't yet embedded the gems confirming my reign on the R'Lil of Ooh'Rous. But as I've told you more urgent matters are pressing and I'd rather work for you before sacrificing time to royal ceremonies. That's why our Traditional Festivals haven't happened. Neither the Choice of Men nor the Fertilization of the Queen. But, really, I ask you, my people, what is a White Ooh'Rou like me going to do in the Spring Festivals? I don't belong there since I have no Chamber of Men. Since Ta died. Since my desires died with him and I have nothing to choose and no child will be coming from me. That's the way things are and they must be accepted. Times are changing. The Reign too. I'm different from everything you've known because I represent the time that's coming, that it's my duty to lead you into. Therefore, here are the modifications I've decided to make to our customary ceremonies. From now on, it won't be me, your Ooh'Rou who will preside over these festivals. I will choose a beautiful young woman to take my place who will be worthy in every respect to represent for you the Spring Ooh'Rou, the Ooh'Rou of Love whom the Sun Ooh'R will accept. She will be fertilized divinely and it will be her child that I will integrate into the royal line. I will raise it in the Royal Nursery. And when it's grown, it will be among those who come to me in the Palace. So it will be. For every cycle of the renewal of nature, I will choose the most beautiful woman for the Festivals."

Ta spoke a little while longer, announcing the upcoming for the Festivals and promising other developments. She ended with an invocation, calling upon the blessing of Ooh'R for her people.

After a round silence that religiously preserved the final echoes of her voice, an unbelievable ovation broke out. The enthusiasm of seeing and hearing her had triumphed over all their reservations. Fears flew away. They finally knew the White Ooh'Rou better. She held her people in her hand!

Hé-Nark was keeping a wary eye on the Devotees. But they did not make a sound. They just stood there silently, unmoving, while everyone around them clapped and shouted with joy.

Ta had called up the Devotee whose intelligent sympathy had been so supportive. She talked to her for a long time and learned that all her Men dreamed of entering the Royal Guard.

After her speech Ta dealt with the Blacksmiths. She called them over and spoke with them. This was her opportunity to observe them up close. She wanted to see if what was said about their speech was true. She asked them about their work. At first timid, they quickly warmed up.

Walking slowly during their conversation, to the everyone's astonishment she headed for the forges. Without seeming to she was able to follow her plan to find out more intimately about certain aspects of the life of Kobor Tigan't. In view of future arrangements known only to herself, she was looking ahead for possible anchor points, focusing on signs of anticipation for the arrangements and where and how they might be accepted.

Consequently, she was less interested in the forges than in the Blacksmiths! It was a race of rather peculiar men. She figured right away, on seeing them up close, that they were a little like her Guards and she liked the resemblance. She noted, however, that they were less spiritual. The women of Kobor all said, "With a Blacksmith anything can happen!" Which did not mean that they were temperamental but that they had a strong independent spirit.

In fact, the Blacksmiths did not really live like other men. For example, they went back to the Chamber of Men less regularly than others or during the Choice of Men they might refuse the woman who chose them. Sometimes they even left their Chamber of their own accord and never went back. Also, unlike other men they openly frequented the prostitutes of Kob'Lâm, those outcast women who were neither B'Tah-Gou nor caretakers of the elderly nor Chamber mistresses but a little of all these at the same time. It was believed that the men frequenting them got something special which the other women could feel even though they complained about it, naturally!

Moreover, a woman could always be surprised to find a Blacksmith sneaking into their Chamber!

These peculiarities amused the Queen and she liked them. She thought she should use them and that the Blacksmiths would add enthusiasm and perseverance to their independent spirits to play an important and brand-new role in the coming cycles.

She watched them work. They took pleasure in eagerly explaining to her their jobs. She smiled, listening to them. And they, in front of this White Ooh'Rou whose every action was a source of bewilderment for the people, they felt happy, in harmony and as if carried away beyond their usual possibilities. Never had the metal and fire felt so exhilarating!

On seeing them work Ta remembered that they had a reputation for being passionate males. It was for this proven quality that a lot of their foibles were forgiven. And yet, in their gestures, words, looks and attitude, they seemed less erotic than the other men.

Intelligent men, knowing how to stay free, less passive than average. Men of the future.

Yes, that was it, like she had foreseen, a branch of this changed generation that it was her mission to develop.

The Queen knew, furthermore, that the Blacksmiths did not like the T'Lo. As a result, in the Devotees' Chambers there were very few men from the forges.

These men drew their raw materials from metal-bearing veins, which they knew how to recognize and utilize. However, in everyone's eyes, including their own, the fact of discovering and possessing precious metals was just a charming talent since it was not the possession of material goods that made one superior in Kobor Tigan't.

The Blacksmiths' gold circulated, therefore, inside Kobor Tigan't, from one to another, in a vital circuit that gave life to all, a little like blood. When someone wanted a golden object—a weapon, cup or jewelry—they asked the Blacksmiths. According to private standards of their own conscience, they either accepted, or not, to make the object. They were never unreasonable or frivolous but their decision, positive or negative, was always final. They had a science of their own about appropriate times and everyone knew that, in the case of a refusal, the object would have been malevolent or woeful. So, they waited for a more favorable period.

On the other hand, the Blacksmiths were obliged to accept all royal demands, as the Ooh'Rou took counsel only from herself.

Among the Giants, the value of things was determined more by the intentions attached to them, at least for what was man-made. They always knew, for example, that such or such an object had been made for such or such an occasion with particular feelings attached to it thereafter.

An object of love or friendship or beauty, an object of reconciliation or confession—there were all kinds of these because they did not like to stay angry!—or simply an object for oneself to feel happy, something personal. There was not one single useful object that did not have its reason for being made. Everything, therefore, had a soul.

Every creation was like the birth of an individualized being. And every creator, the Blacksmiths first and foremost were highly conscious of helping the spark to enter the well-defined soul in the matter being shaped. The Blacksmiths called this "picking the flowers of Ooh'R". In Kobor Tigan't they considered an object without intention inanimate and therefore troublesome. So, no creative act was "gratuitous". Everything mattered. Everything was part of the whole. Everything was alive. Everything spoke.

That was why the Great Faces made by Amo before his death attracted so many people, sneaking up to see them through the window of the room in which they were kept.

The young Queen thought of this often and once again while watching the Blacksmiths her thoughts drifted back to it.

Creating the House of Great Faces to offer them to the people's devotion was one of her most pressing projects. But she had not done it yet. She felt like it was missing something. She could not get rid of this feeling. And that was what had held her back so far... It was aggravating.

Yearning for it to be done, knowing its value, its urgency really, and not being able to despite being determined to accomplish it—what a vexing dilemma! She felt like she was caught in a tangled net and was struggling in vain to break free.

Every time, inevitably, she ended up thinking of Angel. She saw him again captured in his net without understanding why this image came sharp and clear whenever she broached this problem. She had to decide nonetheless. She promised herself to go that evening with Hé-Nark to see the Great Faces again. Maybe the reluctant secret would reveal itself? She did not really expect it. What was missing for the Great Faces to fit together perfectly?

Ta shook her head, realizing that the Blacksmiths stood puzzled before her!

As a distraction after complimenting the Blacksmiths, she proposed a stroll through Kob'Lâm. A proposition that left everyone speechless because such a thing had never been done by an Ooh'Rou. The Queens did not come down into the Low City.

They mentioned this timidly and Ta, starting off with a sprightly step, replied, "Well, see, now the Ooh'Rou is doing it!"

"The Ooh'Rou is doing it, the Ooh'Rou is doing it!" The crowd repeated it. The laughter and enthusiasm exploded as the Queen's retinue got moving with the crowd reveling behind it: they were going to Kob'Lâm!

Kob'Lâm, the Black City, the one at the bottom, the last or maybe in the secret of what is truly important, the First, who knows! Because everything rests on it. It is the earthly base of the titanic tree named Kobor Tigan't. It is the Foundation. It is in its flanks that lie the riches, the future, the safety too since it contains the food stores, all kinds of reserves, the silos and the whole mass of people that are also a kind of reserve, renewable, renewed and of consistent quality.

Kob'Lâm is, in essence, a custodian. A custodian of good things. There has never been any tendency to any kind of perversion in this City. They live well. They live stable. They live loyal. Tranquil. They love the Ooh'Rous. They never buck against the laws. Everything that contributes to strengthening the Race is welcomed here.

That is why their local tradition makes them hate the T'Lo, for whom they feel nothing but disgust, and they abhor the Devotees whom they consider depraved. The affliction of the Race, as they say.

Ta knows very well that everything in Kobor Tigan't is sustained by this Low City. The other Queens before her seemed to have forgotten this, as ungrateful as they were. They never deigned to visit Kob'Lâm. So, inevitably, this City lived a little far from the power of influence, however beneficial to it, receiving, unfortunately, only scraps that it was wise enough to settle for.

Ta wants to make up for this deficiency, to reconquer the City—or else to conquer it for good seeing that, all things considered, it seems that since the time of the Great Ancestors, who built the invulnerable foundations, they have always neglected Kob'Lâm. Maybe because it had no problems like in the higher Cities!

With the people of her entourage (still somewhat stunned by her decision), the White Ooh'Rou entered the Low City.

From the very first moment she feels like she is diving into the very heart of the vortex of life! She almost stops breathing. She never imagined such a tumult or so much excitement.

After the initial shock has worn off she is filled with joy and energy. Her first thought is whispered to Ata-Réè: "Kob'Lâm is generous!"

The faithful companion nods, happy now that her anxieties have vanished.

Hé-Nark cheers up. Nevertheless, his vigilant eyes sweep the crowd. The quickly understands that danger resides not in the ranks of these exuberant people but still among the Devotees who gather up their clothes as if they have walked into a pigsty but they stay up front near the Queen. Noblesse oblige!

At the entrance to the City, the young B'Tah-Gous, surprised by the crowd, had huddled together, appealing to the Guards for protection with hounded eyes. Now they are reassured, so they smile and babble, captivated by the countless details they had never imagined. Soon they will giggle, gasp and clap their hands. Ata-Réè will have to give them a kindly warning with her eyes to calm down their youthful enthusiasm.

The Devotees are already making disparaging remarks.

But the good people are different. They do not even try to hide their reactions. How could they not be delighted, absolutely thrilled that an Ooh'Rou is finally walking within their walls and taking such obvious and serene pleasure in it!

An Ooh'Rou here! This has never been seen before.

So, through the labyrinth of streets, between the massive houses, there is a rush. The terraces are teeming. They wave long, white banners. All the houses open up like ripe fruit spilling out entire families. In the windows whose shutters are thrown wide open, the curious press together, shoulder to shoulder. Clusters of children are perched on the railings. They are all eager to see an Ooh'Rou up close—a fairy tale figure for them!

When Ta smiles at them they twitter and wave to hold her back, to stop her and talk with her. The boys say, "I want to be a Royal Guard!" The girls cut in, as they should, "I'll be a B'Tah-Gou! I'll be a Breeder in the Royal Nursery! I'll have a Chamber of Men in Kob'Ooh'R!" They have more imagination than the boys. Even an adorable toddler, still in her crib the day before, wobbling on her little legs, lisps, "I'll be Ooh'Rou way up on high!" The other girls laugh but the boys are embarrassed by such ambition and scold her, even though in her innocence she understands nothing and repeats her conviction like a chirping baby bird.

The people flock together, crushing one another as Ta walks calmly through the human tide streaming into her white wake. What an incredible blend of scents and sounds!

They clap their hands. They shout out. They wave. They laugh. They sneak a touch of that strange white garment that caresses as it floats by. All their voices blend together. It is total chaos. All the daily tasks have been left behind. The artisans have deserted their workshops. The perfume-makers offer balms in homage to the Queen. An entire street has been hastily lined with braziers in which the finest scents are burning. But these mingle with the aroma of the burnt food that was forgotten in the kitchens! In the district of dyers the vats of boiling dye spew bitter fumes to the point that Hé-Nark wants to redirect the procession.

Ta does not agree with him. She goes through everywhere. Nobody should be neglected. She has to see everything.

The sun beats down. The heat is overwhelming. Everyone is sweating. They notice that the Queen, unfazed, is a source of coolness. Her face is not flushed. This is very remarkable. They talk of it. It is like she is sliding, gliding, unreal, over the torrential turmoil that does not splatter her with even a drop.

They also say the Grand B'Tah-Gou, her companion, is probably of the same marvelous substance since she too seems untouched by the heat or dust.

The young B'Tah-Gous are splendidly pink. Their hair slips out of the headbands. More than usual the Royal Guard, whose bodies glisten with sweat, look upon them with a very special love.

The people are not shy about gawking at all the Devotees who are wildly dressed in bright clothes and covered in jewelry. The arrogance and pompousness in their gestures, the splendor they show off and especially the signs of the cult that they continue to show openly, all cause a scandal.

People mumble and groan as they walk by. Sometimes even showing contempt by making sure to stay out of their way so as to avoid contact. Some of the elders in the front do not hesitate to spit out heartfelt remarks completely lacking civility.

"There goes the ruin of the Race!"

They snicker loud enough to be heard.

"They haven't been looking too good lately, our Devotees!"

They toss out sarcastic questions.

"So, are those good old Ananou feeling better?"

The furious Devotees just shrug their shoulders. What can they say to this riffraff? But Oda-Néè is singled out. A huge old man with full beard and curly hair, magnificent like a tree covered in the cycles of Ooh'R, grabs her as she goes by.

"You won't grow as old as me, far from it, Pretty Mistress!" he growls.

She is scared. She screams. Her men are already rushing forward. But Hé-Nark is faster. In a flash he sets things straight and Oda-Néè scampers on with Eqin-Go and Ka'Ok on her heels while the old man guffaws, bowing to the Head Guard.

"By the strength of the R'Lil! If I were younger, I'd ask to be one of your men!"

"I'd accept you on the spot, Old Man," Hé-Nark replies.

Up ahead, Ta has witnessed the scene. She sends back one of her Guards to the Old Man. He carries a white scarf from her and the assurance that the old man will be welcomed in the Palace.

"It's so absolutely tacky!" Oda-Néè snarls. "She wallows in the mud!"

Eqin-Go nods her head. Ka-Ok does the same more slowly. But the two of them think the second part of this comment is unjust since it is impossible to imagine this White Ooh'Rou getting the least spot of dirt on her. She is so beautiful! Their eyes say it so eloquently.

The Devotee sulks. She tries to control herself while walking, but her rage bursts out, in a whisper, "No, we weren't bold enough. We should've brought our T'Lo. The next time, we'll do it…"

Her Men do not look enthused. They glance at one another. It sounds preposterous. There is Hé-Nark and the other Guards watching them! And Ta, definitely, is tolerant up to a point that is better not to challenge.

Seeing the growing anger of the Devotee who is expecting approval, Eqin-Go ends up playing the diplomat and mutters, "You know, it'd be better to accomplish our plans without provocation."

Oda-Néè has to agree.

In the course of the visit, after the early excitement had passed, they realize that Ta has come not just for a stroll but really to investigate and examine everything. It was less a spontaneous whim, which they could have believed at first, than the fulfillment of a long-awaited project.

The realized quickly that she would neglect nothing and nothing would escape her notice.

Indeed, she wanted to see everything, to get close and understand everything. Unashamed, she had whatever she did not understand explained to her: certain processes of an artisan, for example. She asked a lot of questions. She cleverly suggested certain improvements. She proposed changes.

It was, in fact, a field study.

As always, the excitement of learning new things dispelled her fatigue and she did not see that she was tiring her entourage. Or if she did see, she did not care!

To the dismay of the Devotees. Delicate by nature, they were soon complaining, sick of being duped into an adventure they could not get away from, stuck as they were at the front of the procession!

Ta saw they were becoming jittery and took great pleasure in it. A few words whispered to Hé-Nark and they were so completely surrounded by Guards and B'Tah-Gous that, like it or not, they had to follow along until the end!

Oda-Néè was exhausted and got her Men to carry her, quickly imitated by all the other Devotees.

Eqin-Go had a sense of humor. He whispered loudly enough to be heard, "Just imagine if we'd brought the T'Lo!"

Ta wanted to see the cloth-makers and their vats for soaking the plants. She wanted to see the ones treating animal hides. She also wanted to inspect the food reserves, the cellars and silos, the pride of the City. She knew that concerning this all was well since the harvest and the hunts renewed the provisions for everyone after the daily distribution. It was still an honor for the best Men to take care of this. She knew, but this was not enough. She had to see for herself in order to fully appreciate everything.

She talked with the Dongdwo egg hunters. She had always had a soft spot for them, first of all because they were brave, then in memory of To who had been one of them and who died on his last expedition. But she noticed that no Devotee was among them, which was unusual.

She learned that the Dongdwo eggs were still getting rarer. She thought to herself right away that they had to find an energy food to replace them. Her thought drifted to Gan'd whose extensive knowledge of plants would no doubt be of help.

She also learned that it was true that no Devotee Man participated in the hunt. The others were surprised but they believed they understood. Ta glowered when one of the hunters told her that the Devotees were probably plundering the swamps in secret. Moreover, the eggs they had stored up had disappeared—the ground all around had been trampled and they had found an object nearby…

For this revelation the man had lowered his voice and his companions formed a circle so that only Ta and Hé-Nark next to her could see the object: a Devotee badge.

Lastly she learned that the Devotees no longer gave the fruits of their hunts to the general provisions but kept them for themselves.

Ta quickly thanked the hunter and invited him to the Palace for a personal meeting to hear more.

She figured that the Devotees must be using the Dongdwo eggs for both their rejuvenating and aphrodisiac qualities to compensate for the loss of vitality caused by their T'Lo. It was a serious matter. They were openly rebelling against the crown.

Nevertheless, Ta did not let this overshadow her visit. The day was too nice and the people's zeal gave her real hope as to the qualities of the Race.

Fully determined, in spite (or because) of all the Devotees' reluctance, she expressed the desire to see the strange prostitutes of Kob'Lâm whom they only spoke of in veiled terms because they were sterile and contrary to tradition it was the men who chose them, going in secret and coming back, according to what they said, with a masculine radiance like no other.

In their district, where the Devotees hastened to veil their faces (which made her laugh), she found that the women were not only beautiful but smart, courageous and free of the matriarchal exhaustion, so to speak.

She conversed with them peacefully and saw that her reform projects were well reflected there.

When she left these women, as calmly as she had come, she had formed her opinion and considered them beneficial because the frequent visits restored the men's desire and capacity to choose, which the matriarchy had stifled.

A startled and admiring glimmer danced in Hé-Nark's eyes. The other Guards gazed upon their beloved B'Tah-Gous realizing that they had already chosen them!

Ta finished her stroll in Kob'Lâm by going to another district to visit the houses of the deceased B'Tah-Gous. She wanted to see up close if they had been immured as she had ordered. Ta had forbidden them to disturb the bodies. She wanted the bodies to remain in the holy lodgings without being profaned by the slightest touch.

The Queen chose the house of Méè-Né, the greatest of the storytellers, who had trained Ata-Réè who remained quiet, somber, flooded with memories. The others also fell silent because the death of all the Storytellers, those memory brains of the Race, had coincided with the disastrous events of the past season.

For the residents of the district the evenings had become sad without the Storytellers around. They missed their warm words that materialized so well in the dark when the elite Men came to them for instruction!

Ta figured it best not to brood too long over this. She snapped everyone out of it, "Come on, don't be sad! Our grand B'Tah-Gous are at peace. Besides, they're still here in their wonderful heirs, the young B'Tah-Gous being trained by Ata-Réè, the living extension of Méè-Né."

She strode off, away from the sepulchers on which shrubs were already growing, which she had ordered not to be cut, leaving it to nature to cover over and obliterate their death under the profusion of plant life. Soon it would be just a big garden full of birds and flowers...

"To wrap up, let's go see the sacred pool of our Storytellers!"

Her order rang cheerfully. The Devotees, who were lagging, perked up at the words "To wrap up".

Ta led them to the sacred pool. The atmosphere was bursting with emotion.

The pool contained a green liquid that was traditionally linked to the B'Tah-Gous' astrality. It was believed that their gift of prophecy, their particular magic, all their qualities, their very life depended on being near this liquid.

Well, they were deeply concerned last season when the B'Tah-Gous were dying helplessly and this liquid started dissipating. Ta urgently order the pool to be covered to stop people worrying uselessly over its level.

Now with the covered removed she saw that the level had not changed. She stressed this fact. It was a good omen. "Look, everyone! The calamities are over, over for good! The sacred pool is no longer shrinking. Everything is in balance. It's a sign of the return to life."

They applauded. But she went on.

"The ancient tree of instruction of our old B'Tah-Gous is dried up but hasn't the main branch remained so alive and strong that I can lean on it? And what pretty seeds are all around this tree!"

She smiled as she took Ata-Réè's arm and motioned to the young girls.

"You see, nothing is ever lost. Everything starts to grow again. Our young Storytellers will go farther than their elders because, as you all know, before his disappearance the Beautiful Being transmitted to Ata-

Réè the ability to hear the solar foliage that constantly rustles around Ooh'R while paying homage."

Very quickly, the captivated audience repeated her words to those behind them and they to those behind them and so on.

But Ta, like in the throes of a fever, leaving them no time to think, kept up her momentum.

"And not only does Ata-Réè hear the solar voices, but she can, like Angel did to please us, reproduce the harmonious messages. Her Daughters do too. They have the throats of birds! And the echoes of the glory of On High that they express down below delights Ooh'R and invites his passions to join with us!"

Her enthusiasm was contagious—a herald of the imminent announcement of great things. She felt it and she was suddenly compelled to give to her people everything they wanted. That was why she ordered from the Blacksmiths present a golden bowl in which the green liquid of the B'Tah-Gous would be put and kept in the House of Great Faces where the people of Kob'Lâm along with the other cities could come to hear the song of the B'Tah-Gous and by means of the Great Faces they would receive the boons emanating from the bygone heroes!

She had spoken as if in one of those dreams in which nothing seems to make sense... It was the din of the enthusiastic response bursting out after her final words that brought her back to herself. She rubbed her eyes and could not believe it.

"What did I say? What did I just say?"

She was flabbergasted. But the decision had been made! It was impossible now to go back...

Ata-Réè was holding her firmly by the elbow, "And so it had to be, O Queen!"

CHAPTER VI

All was quiet in Kob'Ooh'R. Not a light anywhere. Not a sound could be heard.

Ta was standing before the room where they kept the Great Faces. She hardly raised her voice, "Open it," she said to Hé-Nark who was awaiting orders.

The door was stubborn. The Master Guard had some trouble with it. The stone had not moved for a long time. Finally, it gave way and Hé-Nark went in first to set up around the room the lamps and torches he had brought.

Ta followed him cautiously. She fought against the cold. But she was nervous because she feared the moment when she would see To's face again, sculpted by Amo before he died. In the end, she gritted her teeth and marched in bravely, preparing for the tears that would inevitably well up at the sight of that beloved face. She did not want Hé-Nark to see her sorrow.

She was paying little attention to the room before the Guard finished his task, but two things still intrigued her. There was a strange scent in the air, a sweet smell like a resinous balm. And then there was a kind of shimmer from the Great Faces lined up against the walls. To her it was like a light-reflecting crystal. Maybe her eyes were tired? She blinked but the weird shimmer just spread out and floated there like a cloud.

She asked Hé-Nark, "Do you see that shimmering veil on the wall?"

Surprised, he shook his head, "I don't see anything, Ooh'Rou."

She forced a laugh, "I must've stared at the sun too long today."

Nevertheless, she knew that the crystalline cloud was not an optical illusion but that she could really see it. It was better, therefore, to say nothing. The phenomenon was too pleasant.

Having done his duty and lit the room the Master Guard left quietly, leaving the door ajar as the Queen had asked. He stood watch in the hallway, waiting, reining in his wandering thoughts. He let himself feel nothing but the bliss of serving the Ooh'Rou. Nothing else. No other thought should slip into his heart. It would be impious. Besides, the vigilance expected of him could not be compromised for any reason. Not even the contemplation of the Queen's beauty…

In the room, the young woman stood motionless a moment to receive the invisible messages. She felt like she was suddenly in the throes of intense activity: thoughts whirred around her like leaves tossed by the wind.

"The Great Faces are alive!" she said softly.

It was like her thought was heard and they liked it.

The aromatic scent grew stronger. The crystalline cloud rose above the Great Faces that Ta could now behold in peace.

Immense, deified by Amo's genius, they stood before her and seemed to be waiting for her to come meet them. The first to catch her attention, in the middle of the others, was the one of the Old Man of Kah'B'La. His beard cascaded down like a waterfall and his hair was a forest.

"Come! There's no harm…"

She heard him. A wave of happiness flowed through her.

Comforted, confident that she could look bravely at To's face, she walked over, going from one to another, stopping before each one to gaze freely upon it. Each of them gave her a message. And from each she took away a blessing and strength. For, all the masks were alive now with sacred life. Amo had converted their humanity into divinity. They had become or rather become again the archetypes of themselves.

In the confinement of the room where they had been waiting for Ta's visit a powerful cohesion developed that united them as one like a holy family.

They had truly become one: Ancestors and as such worthy to receive the devotion of the crowds.

Moreover, all the secret visitors whom they had so often caught hanging outside the window, admiring, had they not, little by little, fed them with their thoughts?

"O Great Faces," the Queen murmured, "you have awakened. Much more than I would've dared to believe! From Ooh'R you all were bearing a spark of fire that did not go out with your disappearance but it remained here in you… Even you, my sister, whom I see before me, totally solarized!"

Indeed, the transcended mask of Opak, whom Amo's hands had fashioned in coppery ocher earth, was the one of the fertile spouse of the Sun, a Queen such as he had dreamed of, both struck and revealed by the lightning bolt of solar love.

It was a mask of plenitude. The eyes were dilated, the nostrils flared, the lips parted.

"Truly, you are all her in your truth. Whether this truth had been realized or not..." Ta nodded. "I will bring you all to your House and from you will come our inspirations and needed support."

After Opak she examined Angel's Face, which Amo had made out of clay that was almost white. Long and narrow with two huge eyes that stared up and far away. Ta felt an impulse come from him and enter her.

"Search... Search for me..."

What did he mean? She thought she was getting something else:

"Search for me... I have to come back here... with you... I'm not far... All of me."

She was trembling. Was this the solution, what was missing?

"Where are you? O Angel, tell me!"

A sudden and intense dizziness. The shimmer of the crystal surrounded her, so dense that she thought she could feel it. At the same time a collective voice assailed her, apparently coming from all the Great Faces together:

"Kah'B'La!"

She felt herself whirling. When she opened her eyes, she was leaning on the mask of the Old Man and with the crystal cloud almost gone, along with the dizziness, she heard very clearly, "Go to Kah'B'La! Search! And you will find."

"Very well, I'll go."

Everything was suddenly calm. She knew now that nothing was standing in the way of her project for the House of Great Faces. The missing link was on Kah'B'La, the Holy Mountain.

Then she was able to cope with To's Face without trembling. A long silence during which the irreparable gulf caused by the loss of her beloved was widened in her heart...

When she turned away, satisfied, she had not suffered. She was just empty. Empty and indifferent. She passed by her own Face and then stopped for a long time before the multiple attempts at the mysterious character who had been the Friend of the sculpture and whose face had been reshaped ten times without ever being adequately finished. Who was he, this one whose every aspect was like a single facet of a Whole impossible to render?

She pondered. Each seemed good enough to represent the essence of one quality. She saw: Wisdom here, Peace next to it, Mercy over there,

Kindness elsewhere, Intelligence, but above all the mystery of a humanity more refined than the Giants. Angel had been the first emissary of this humanity, maybe celestial, to which all these Faces ultimately belonged.

Ta stepped back, automatically, because the crystal cloud was coming back. It broke up into as many parts as there were Faces of the Friend. Each one shined, briefly, above. Then the cloud reunited and disappeared. It could have been an illusion. But Ta knew that it was an answer and the intelligences were making sure to enlighten her.

She figured that the visit was now over. She was about to leave when she realized that among the Faces of the Friend, there were others she did not recognize and in particular, to her great surprise, a Face of Amo.

Now, she knew that he had not made one of his own face. Had he come back?

Her heart pounding, torch in hand, she rushed over to get a better look. And she saw wet streaks on the floor. She followed them to a big pile of fresh clay next to a rough outline.

She heard a stealthy noise and bent down to look between the wall and the line of Faces. She saw a young child, very thin, scared, standing there before her, with a defensive look and dirty hands.

Ta called out, "Hé-Nark!"

He was there in an instant. But before he could make a move the child jumped to the windowsill and slipped between the bars.

"Run! Bring him back to me! Don't hurt him!"

Hé-Nark ran off silently, taking a shortcut that would lead him onto the lower terraces where the child would have to pass by. Ta leaned out the window. She caught sight of the fugitive youth scrambling down the terraces. He turned back to see her. It was at that very moment that Hé-Nark jumped out and cut off the escape route.

He literally jumped into the arms of the master Guard who just had to hug him tightly to bring him back quietly as the prey struggled fiercely but without uttering a sound. This did not fail to astonish the Queen.

Wondering about all this, she awaited the return of Hé-Nark while fidgeting with a piece of the wet clay. So, this child was fashioning Faces all alone! He was continuing the miraculous creation started by Amo and even taking it farther! Comparing the work of the child with Amo's she found no difference. The expressive boldness, the feeling of transcendence, the magical life infused in the resemblance, they were the same.

At this point Hé-Nark came back. He stood his captive in front of Ta not roughly but firmly enough to remove any possible desire to flee again. "Greet the Ooh'Rou, child!" he said.

The child looked up at Ta, then lowered his eyes immediately, but she had time to feel a shock from those dark, serious pupils. He did not say a word.

So, she took the lead, "Tell me what you were doing here!"

He did not answer. But his eyes looked up again. She saw a plea in them, an admission of the impossible, something very touching that was trembling there.

"I'll help you," she said. "You just have to respond. Let's see, the other Faces here were made by your hands?"

He bowed his head in acknowledgment.

"They're beautiful, as beautiful as Amo's!" the Queen acclaimed.

Once again the child's eyes looked up, this time for a little longer. A faint smile crossed his lips. But he did not break the silence, just stood still, head bowed and arms hanging loosely at his sides. He showed no signs of wanting to run away.

Ta was taken aback. She looked at Hé-Nark who tried to encourage the child to speak, "Come on, kid, the White Ooh'Rou is asking you questions. You have to answer. Don't worry, the Queen isn't angry with you."

"On the contrary," Ta added.

The child looked up at her, so totally surrendered to her will that she shuddered while he opened his mouth but uttered not a sound, shaking his head sadly.

She thought she understood and with a great wave of pity said, "Ooh'R have mercy on you, child! You can't talk, is that it?"

That was it! The child was mute. A long, deep silence. And countless inexpressible thoughts burst through those young hands that Ta was holding now in her own.

"Did you know Amo?"

He nodded, happy to be understood. He did not pull back his hands.

The Queen went on, gently picking pieces of clay off the child's fingers. "Of course, you watched him work?"

He nodded again, more eagerly and always happier.

"So, he showed you how? He taught you?"

He shook his head. That was a no. And he looked very sorry. Obviously, he had not dared to come forward to Amo.

"But then how did you do it?"

Oh, it was simple. He laughed, silently, squinting his eyes, pulled away his hands respectfully, which Hé-Nark was glad to see. Then he went and squatted by his work, took some clay, waved them over and went back to modeling.

The Master Guard and the Queen watched on in wonder. It was soon obvious that he had forgotten all about them. They heard him breathing like people who are very concentrated, with that throaty sound like in sleep. But he was not sleeping, far from it! His hands were forming an unfamiliar Face, lofty, weird, with none of the characteristics of the Giants.

Ta noticed that the child was working while looking straight ahead at nothing. But apparently he saw his model.

The Queen asked Hé-Nark like at the beginning, "Do you see, isn't there a reflection there?"

The Guard squinted to get a better look. But he shook his head. No, he saw nothing.

Ta gave him a reassuring smile and did not press. She herself, once again, could see the crystal cloud.

But the child saw much more than she since it was from the heart of this cloud that he was capturing the Face of his model!

Ta touched his shoulder. He shuddered, pulled back to reality. "Do whatever you want here. You are a great creator. Don't hide from me anymore. I authorize you to create all the Faces you deem fit. They'll be put together in a palace they deserve along with all the others. And the people will gaze on them in silence. Do you like that?"

He clapped his hands together, overjoyed, went back to work and let his passion express his contentment.

"Come," Ta said to Hé-Nark, "let's leave him alone. Ooh'R is inspiring him."

The next morning her servants yelped in surprise to find a still wet clay bird at her doorstep. They were trembling with excitement when they brought it to her. Ta took it, recognized it as one of the golden-crested white birds that had accompanied Angel to Kobor Tigan't before disappearing with him.

"Great marvels come from the hands of that child," she said. "It's another sign of what I believe. So, let's go to Kah'B'La! There are surprises awaiting us!"

She left with Hé-Nark and a few of his most trusted Guards.

She leaned on Ata-Réè's arm and said, "For a while now I've been dreaming of a great crystal."

On Kah'B'La, when they got to the summit, a little light-headed as always from the mighty stature of the Holy Mountain where plants and trees spoke to the soul, they could see the Land of the Other Side.

The anticipated surprise appeared in all its magnitude: the huge waterfall that had unexpectedly sprang forth after the disappearance of Amo and Angel, was gone!

Not even a trickle of water remained. All the rocks on this side were dry. The moss and the plants that had grown had fallen to dust. Down below, the plain of the Dead Land, which had turned into a muddy lake, was slowly drying up. Mists were blurring its liquid horizon so that they could not see how far the meager water reached.

Ta and the others stood speechless for a moment. They were all shaken up. Really, why did they come here? Was it just to see the disappearance of the waterfall without making sense of it?

The guards secretly wished to leave immediately. A glance from Hé-Nark, reading their thoughts, reminded them of their duty.

Ta kept quiet. A wave of memories, added to the fatigue from the rapid climb she led, were clouding her view a little. She could not stop the flood of cherished images rising up from her youth here with To and that reawakened that exhilarating day of their discovery when they saw Angel, the mysterious stranger, lying in the hollow of rock while above him, like a heavenly host, the golden-crested white birds soared around... Youth, love, passion, promising wonders, where were they all now?

She snapped out it before the others noticed her agitation.

Besides, Ata-Réè was leaning over, full of excitement, pulling her arm and pointing down the mountain. "Look, look, in that hollow, there's something there, something shiny!"

It was true. Ta saw it clearly—knowing right away that she had come here for this—a block, oblong-shaped, reflecting all the colors of the sun. Her recurring dreams in which she wandered under the waterfall and bumped into a glittering bulk, came rushing to mind.

At the same time the B'Tah-Gou cried out, "O Queen, I told you, right, it's the Great Crystal of my dream!"

"We dreamed the same thing, Sister!" Ta replied affectionately.

The guards were leaning over as well, wondering at what really did look like an unusually big gem.

111

But what should they do?

On impulse Ta ordered them to go and see whether the precious block was joined to the rock it was set in or free-standing.

She sat and waited. Ata-Réè stood opposite her. Hé-Nark turned away from them to watch his men descending.

There was a subtle change in the air. A few small, colorful birds came out of nowhere. Ta saw Ata-Réè's face freeze. Her body stiffened. Her eyes stopped blinking. Then the Grand Old Man of Kah'B'La appeared and in three strides came to sit casually next to the Queen. She took a deep breath; she was not as forsaken as she thought!

"No," the Old Man responded to her thought, "no, I'm here a lot more often than you think. Only, you're so busy that you don't have time to concentrate on seeing me."

He took her hand. She felt good. She felt reassured. To would not be gone forever. A time would come when...

"Yes," the Old Man said, "you will see him again, I promise. It won't be long. You took on a heavy burden and you have to see it through to the end. Go forth, then, bravely, and let nothing hold you back. Trials await you, certainly, many of them. And you will have little rest. But when all is over you will be reunited with To."

She glimpsed this single point of light in the depths of a dark shadow...

"My Daughter," the Old Man went on, "don't think, however, that you are entitled to more than this single light. Happiness will come to you. A tender happiness. Strange but tender. Remember this! And also enormous ecstasies in which all of heaven will be in love along with you, sacredly..."

He was getting up to leave. Already?

"I'll be back."

The little birds were whirling around. The Old Man's white beard shined, blinding bright, and she almost had to close her eyes because it was unbearable to behold his beauty, joy and vitality while his voice woke all the echoes of the mountain!

"Put the Crystal in the House of Great Faces!"

Ata-Réè was leaning over the Queen who was whispering to her, "Put the Crystal in the House of the Great Faces."

Thus it was decided.

Hé-Nark looked very satisfied. His men were coming back up with news: the Crystal was not stuck in the rock. But since it was very heavy and they did not want to risk damaging it, they agree to send for more men to bring it back to Kobor Tigan't. Hé-Nark, therefore, left some Guards on site to wait for the reinforcements.

Ta went back with a smaller escort. She walked calmly, picking flowers on the way. Hé-Nark was amazed watching her—she seemed to be back to the young Princess Ta. Ata-Réè noticed, too. She smiled as she held a flower taken from the Queen's bouquet.

The Guards who stayed behind on Kah'B'La later told that during that night a bluish fluorescence appeared around the crystal block several times, that a strangely sweet sound could be heard, that invisible birds were constantly flying around them, that unrecognizable scents had almost knocked them out and that the weirdest part of it all was that they never felt afraid in the least.

The Great Crystal was brought back to Kobor Tigan't without any serious problems. Everyone came out to see it pass by. A feeling of religious gravity floated in the air. The crowd was speechless and felt like they had been transported back to the time when Angel was brought in except that this time there was no sadness to accompany the arrival.

The construction of the House of Great Faces was started on a big empty lot in Kob'Ooh'R. The people of Kob'Lâm were glad to learn that they, too, could visit it.

Meanwhile, the Great Crystal was put in with the Great Faces. The child sculptor became its official guardian. He put the Face of Angel on one side of it and on the other that of Amo and between the two the Old Man of Kah'B'La.

Ta was thinking that behind his muteness lay a treasure of knowledge. She had him discreetly and tenderly taken care of sometimes by Gan'd, sometimes by Ata-Réè. The latter came often to meditate before the Great Crystal. She was surprised that it was not transparent. An inner vapor seemed to float in an oblong cavity at the heart of the gigantic gem.

Ata-Réè passionately yearned for this vapor to dissipate.

CHAPTER VII

The new Festivals announced by Ta in her big speech could not take place on the scheduled date. Opak died and her funeral had a great emotional impact on the Giants of Kobor Tigan't.

From the lowest to the highest City they realized that an era was vanishing along with the former Ooh'Rou. A page was turning. They were really going to have to enter this new Age that the White Ooh'Rou talked about so urgently.

When the news of the death of Opak was announced from city to city by the Royal Guards, the people retired to their homes, as was the custom, for a silent, three-day wake. Behind their closed shutters, making sure that no light filtered in from outside, they lit their braziers to burn the heavy, evocative scents of sadness. During these three days they remembered in detail the brilliant images of the reign of the Ooh'Rou who was so beautiful after all, but so negligent of the real needs of the people.

Opak had died quietly. Since the birth of her son R'Ang she had grown weaker. She had never regained her sanity. She survived like a shadow through the languid days. Her fury had completely vanished after a final fit when she tried to kill her baby, which she refused to nurse.

T'Lo Dê was there fortunately and he could take the infant away from her. He had already seen that R'Ang was wasting away and without being noticed had started feeding him along with his own daughter.

After this episode, with her milk dried up, Opak grew rapidly thinner. In the end she was no longer recognizable. Ta could not see her without hiding afterward to weep in anger at this decline, which nothing could stop.

Gan'd came several times with her herbs and bark. But she shook her head saying that the Old Man just recommended semi-darkness, silence, in short, peacefulness around the dying woman.

With her nerves on edge Ta feared that Opak was suffering. Gan'd assured her that it was unlikely. If it happened, Ata-Réè would chant at her bedside those harmonies that she heard in the heavenly spheres she could visit.

So, Opak lay there in a daze, not moving, not doing anything. They barely saw her breathing. She did not even moan. She slept or stared without reacting to anything. Apparently she did not see or hear because not even a sudden crash could startle her.

Ta and Ata-Réè spoke to her softly, called to her, hoping to bring her back a little to consciousness, but to no avail.

They had to force-feed her. Her compassionate T'Lo watched over her constantly with the most admirable patience. Able to enter a kind of altered state that allowed them to keep fatigue at bay, they did not sleep at night, kept constant watch over Opak, ready to provide whatever she needed. They gave her liquids, got her fresh air when her fever rose or covered her when she shivered. They looked deeply sad, cried a lot in each other's arms and, to be honest, made the young Ooh'Rou take pity on them since her tender heart and clear mind could not reconcile the two feelings they aroused in her.

On the one hand, their sheer gentleness, their perfect devotion, their obvious love for their human masters disturbed her while, on the other hand, the toxic emanation of their presence and their contact horrified her, made them, in spite of everything, dangers to be absolutely avoided.

Ta, however, did not want to hurt them. She had already thought of their life in the palace after Opak's death. It was possible. They would be happy and comfortable until their own death. But they would have to be carefully watched so that no human become erotically involved with them again. She figured that this was a merciful solution but very dangerous in all the unforeseeable possibilities. She knew that the temptation of T'Lo love was sometimes almost impossible to avert. She remembered having been troubled by them, at certain times of her life, when she was Princess Ta before To showed up and that she was angry then at all the males in her Chamber of Men…

In the end, wouldn't it be better to give them the drink of oblivion that would erase their brains, make them simple Ananou again so that they could be easily put back in the Pit? They would not suffer. Even their grief at the loss of Opak would be taken away from them. Wouldn't that be better? She would suggest this to the Devotees! This had to be done to set an example.

She understood all the merits of the plan but could not help feeling sorry for them. Still, she preferred this to the risk of keeping them in the Palace in their T'Lo state.

For T'Lo Dê it was different. His unusual personality had always earned Ta's sympathetic indulgence. She did not consider him a simple T'Lo but saw in him something else: a reflection of humanity, so impressive that she had to respect him and so always allowed him a privileged place.

Then the extraordinary birth of Dê-Ta'Am was added to this. And that was not all. In fact, out of necessity, T'Lo Dê was now the nurse of R'Ang.

Of course, at first, when they found out the T'Lo was filling in for Opak who kept rejecting her baby, they got a nurse for R'Ang. It was a woman from the Nursery, simple and healthy, from a branch of the royal family. But the baby, perhaps already used to the T'Lo's milk, did not accept this woman. Usually so calm the baby would not stop wailing. He vomited with a kind of rage. They tried other nurses without success. The infant withered so quickly that there was nothing they could do but to give it to T'Lo Dê who had become so woeful that it pained the Queen.

Afterward, everything went back to normal. R'Ang regained his strength more quickly than he had lost it and was back to himself: a calm child with big, observant eyes that the fits of his "sister" Dê-Ta'Am rarely disturbed and that the "motherly" tenderness of T'Lo Dê put at ease. The love that he spread around "his kids" was deeply moving. His skill in caring for them no less so. He sometimes went about better than a mother because of his psychic abilities whereby he could divine the nature of the babies' every need. Moreover, the infants felt protected and thus they thrived.

R'Ang was back to his normal weight. Ta, however, was a little worried because he was drinking only the T'Lo's milk. But what else could she do? The habit had been formed.

Since Opak had entered the beginning of the end, they had moved T'Lo Dê out of her room and put him in a big, cheerful room full of sunlight and quiet so that he could raise R'Ang and Dê-Ta'Am whose turbulent energy would have exhausted anyone else.

Despite the privileged situation, despite the exhilarating joy of seeing the two human babies growing more beautiful, T'Lo Dê sometimes let his inner vision wander into Opak's room. Then he, too, cried. But he shut it out right away and dried his tears because their bitter scent made the babies cry. And he could not stand hurting them in any way.

Ta, who had been to see him, was mulling all this over at Opak's bedside along with Ata-Réè, Gan'd and Hé-Nark who was standing guard at the door. All the T'Lo were huddled around in a tense and silent circle. They were trembling.

Ta knew that they had read her mind. The T'Lo were telepathic and often saw through walls or at a distance. These qualities were innate in them and were, admittedly, their most appreciated traits because they could thereby warn their masters of unexpected dangers.

In the vast hallway leading to Opak's rooms all the Royal Guards had been summoned quietly.

The young B'Tah-Gous were also waiting together outside on a nearby terrace. When the breeze lifted the curtain a little they could be seen holding hands, close together, heads bowed. A pure and calm radiance emanated from them, almost palpable, whose effect could be felt all the way in the bedroom where it blended, in a way, with the powerful presence of the Guards who were ready to defend the dying woman from attacks that were always possible out of the dark. They all knew that the death throes called forth horrifying creatures that surged out of the cracks in the floor or from holes in the stone walls.

But today there was not a cloud in the sky and the shining sun was saying, "Ooh'R sympathizes with her who was his Ooh'Rou. He himself is keeping the shadows at bay. May Opak die before nightfall!"

All of a sudden, as they looked on, Opak sat up unexpectedly. She stared in front of her with desperate eyes. But it was obvious that she saw nobody. Her lips moved but no words came forth. She reached out to call forth and drive away. No way to tell which.

Gan'd touched Ata-Réè's arm, "Listen. Up on high, far away, way up there, listen. And sing what you hear!"

The B'Tah-Gou did so. Her tense expression changed, giving way to such gentleness. Indeed, she was hearing.

An odd tone, linear, almost lulling, came out of her breast. First she hummed with her mouth closed, as if to attract the wandering sense of the dying woman. Almost immediately Opak turned her blind eyes in her direction. The fear in her face started fading away.

The T'Lo were trembling, pitifully. Ta clenched her jaw. Hé-Nark stiffened at the door, turning pale.

Ata-Réè approached Opak, raising the depth and the strength of her incantation. From her mouth streamed an otherworldly melody, light, winged, expression of joy that men could certainly not know.

Opak's eyes closed. But she remained sitting straight up in the same position. To all appearances she was listening, following the song, thoroughly engrossed. Then, when the song rose up into a sudden burst of liberating ecstasy, she opened her eyes wide. The sun coming in through the window lit her from behind. Her face, therefore, was shadowed but her soft red hair glowed like a halo. Her eyes grew even bigger, then she seemed to wake up, breaking out in a smile.

She said, "Angel!"

Then she fell back, the smile wiped off her face, and she died on the spot. She was nothing but a long, shadowy, empty thing, an envelope consumed by wear and tear.

Ta jumped up, chilled, and hugged Ata-Réè who had turned silent again.

The keen eye of Gan'd was gauging their emotion and already planning what would be needed for the funeral preparations.

As for the T'Lo, with Opak's final breath they leaped back against the wall and plastered themselves to it before sliding slowly to the floor. Their hands covered their eyes. They turned around, faced the wall and did not move.

Hé-Nark opened the door to let the Guards in as they all pulled down the mourning headdress over their eyes. Orders passed down the rank and while some went bearing the news to all of Kobor Tigan't, others fanned out to surround the Palace.

For her part, Ata-Réè had leaned out the window and signaled to her Daughters who also veiled their heads with part of their clothes. A slow, modulating chant rose from their midst.

The B'Tah-Gou veiled herself in turn. Gan'd had already done so. Only Ta remained bareheaded.

Meanwhile, the sun had set. But they did not light the lamps in the Palace, which had to stay in the dark until the body of the deceased was laid to rest. A red afterglow lingered in the sky. They opened the curtains to see better. Everything was bathed in a soft, crimson light.

"What does that mean?" the young Queen murmured. "I've never seen the light of Ooh'R last so long after he's gone."

In fact, the eerie redness lasted all night long. It just darkened a little, but it was in this glow that Gan'd washed Opak's body with her aromatic herbs whose powerful perfume masked the noxious air of death. When she was done, they covered the body with every single piece of her jewelry. Her ceremonial weapons were laid around her. Later, they would be ritually smelted in the Kob'Râm crucible.

Then they left, closing the door behind them. Ata-Réè joined her Daughters. Hé-Nark went to his men. Gan'd wanted to go back to her house in the Nursery. She was not afraid of walking in the night and had smiled a little mockingly when Hé-Nark offered to have some men escort her. She realized almost right away that she had only turned him down like this in the hope that he would accompany her himself. But he did not go. She was disappointed. Especially in seeing her own weakness.

Ta went back to her rooms. She bathed in the pool in her private garden like she was washing away the defilement of death. She sighed in relief at this feeling of being purified.

She thought about almost nothing this night. She was astonished. Was it due to the red night when it seemed that everything was on hold, held back, reclusive and faraway? Leaning on the edge of the terrace, she felt like she was in another time and another place, a kind of double of Kobor Tigan't, unknown to her until now. She gazed curiously below the railing at the unfolding panorama. The indescribable afterglow that en-shrouded everything seemed to be coming out of the buildings so that the Cities looked made of the same material as the red sky where everything merged together.

Because of this celestial phenomenon everyone was outside in nerv-ous groups. The lack of light from the Palace and Kob'Ooh'R foretold to them the mournful news. They were waiting anxiously for confirmation.

From her high observation point the Queen saw that they were start-ing to go back home. The movement began in the nearest Cities and spread with the Guards sent out by Hé-Nark announcing the news. The streets emptied. The lights went out, one by one, from high to low.

How long did she stay there watching the spectacle? Ta could not say. She had lost all sense of time. Then, at a certain point she shivered. The last lights, way down in Kob'Lâm, had just gone out.

Alone in the red night she slowly straightened up. She felt totally abandoned.

Then, with the tears of a child, she wept for her sister for a long time.

In Opak's room the T'Lo were rocking to a slow rhythm to lament her in their way.

Not far away, in the big room that had been allocated to him, T'Lo Dê was seeing them through the walls. He was rocking too and even though he was crying it was probably more to put to sleep the infants he was holding.

The third night after Opak's death, in the middle of the night—and this time the sun left no afterglow—the royal funeral ceremonies started.

The first signal left from Kob'Râm. The forges, which had been quiet up to now, suddenly rang out with sharp banging on the anvils. Bounced by the echo stones, they sounded like bells. The clear, rarefied air carried them far.

In all the Cities, the people who were awaiting the signal left their houses to line up silently along the way that the procession would take. They did not speak and moved without a sound, very orderly. Nothing had yet appeared from Kob'Ooh'R. The shadows were dark up there. For three days no light had shined behind the stone shutters.

Then, as expected, everything that was closed opened at the same time, all of a sudden, everywhere, and from the windows of the Palace sprang forth the brightest lights. They reflected off the golden surfaces and all of Kob'Ooh'R was sprinkled with this glory.

Soon, they saw the first torches leading the procession come out of one of doors of the City. Their bearers had been chosen from the best known Chambers of Men and represented the delegation of such in homage to the deceased Queen. Their duty was to light all the torches and braziers along the way because the procession had to march in the brightest light possible.

Behind the torch-bearers, completely isolated, Ta came alone, aloof, secluded. She wore a kind of long coat of white hide, very thin and supple, which fell straight off her shoulders to her feet, which were also sheathed in the same white hide. She had one piece of jewelry. Her loosened hair was uncovered, as opposed to everyone else.

She walked slowly, steadily, with a kind of forced calm and looked at nobody. Her indifferent eyes wandered over the people as if they were objects. Her simplicity, the cold severity of her appearance made the harshest contrast with the splendor of Opak's remains, which they carried standing up like a statue not far behind her. The deceased was decked out in an unusual, lavish manner, loaded with jewelry that sparkled in the light and clicked and crackled along the way.

In everyone's eyes, this grand, funereal object, completely stiff and fragrant with herbs, was less Queen Opak than the old reign brought lifeless in its dead splendor to its ultimate submersion.

As they approached everyone fell silent in the grip of anguish. They were aware of the road already traveled since Ta's accession. Opak's domination already seemed so far away to everyone. They were surprised they had lived through it without complaining. Almost unintentionally they weighed the differences. And they were surprised that the funeral had not taken place earlier.

The Giants of Kobor Tigan't believed that they were now being carried forward by the irresistible force that their new Ooh'Rou had transmitted to them.

Losing Opak was like losing a little of themselves. They were separating, almost unintentionally, in a fatal but certainly beneficial move, from a part of their ancient being. It was like the molting in a fabulous springtime—they were leaving behind the skin of the past season, a heavy skin unfit for today, in order to enjoy a new day that demanded they be sharper, faster and more agile.

They were a little scared, of course, but they could not help feeling exhilarated. Deep down inside they were feeling a great need for renewal, an unbelievable yearning for the unknown.

Nevertheless, right now there was deep mourning. They were all affected and by grieving for the Queen whose power was cut short, whose destiny was ruined, they were grieving for themselves.

The Men who had belonged to Opak's Chamber surrounded the body carrying her ceremonial weapons. They looked haggard because the nearness of the corpse of the one whose intimate heat they had shared filled them with horror.

Then, according to custom (but for the last time, Ta had said) the T'Lo came after the deceased. With their strange, sinuous look, a little lost finding themselves free and out in the open like this, they held each other's hand. Their grief was beyond measure. They wept in their pitiful way, mutely. T'Lo Dê was at their head. His being a mother softened the grief he felt for Opak's death. He cried mostly out of camaraderie and because the sight of the crowd traumatized him. He had only one desire: to go back to the Palace and be with his two children. Gan'd was watching them. He had trusted her from the start, but he was afraid that the children would get hungry during his absence. More than anything else, he lamented being away from the Palace and thought only of how to get back there.

Behind Opak's T'Lo came all the Devotees along their own T'Lo whom they watched over jealously, driving off any fear or fatigue from them. They made a gaudy group. They had all taken great pains to dress traditionally in an orgy of colors and precious accessories. They showed off their Devotee badges and, also a tradition, they had their T'Lo wear their most beautiful jewelry.

Their heads were tightly veiled to prove the extent of their sorrow. It made an odd contrast to the eroticism that exuded from them.

Oda-Néè with Eqin-Go, other Men from her Chamber and some close friends were in the front row. Once in a while she turned around to whisper a few words to those behind her who immediately told those behind them and so on until it reached the back row.

On the sides of the procession, in two long, parallel lines, on one side marched the Royal Guards and Ta while on the other were the young B'Tah-Gous. They were led respectively by Hé-Nark and Ata-Réè who were thus level with the remains of Opak.

Hé-Nark was not at ease. He kept looking over his shoulder at the Devotees. He sensed some treacherous danger from them.

Oda-Néè had surprised her following and after audaciously removing her mourning veil she had met his gaze with insolent arrogance. She saw only alert coldness. She had to admit that it would be better not to clash with him and that her cunning alone would facilitate her plans.

She stopped giving messages. After all, her plan was all ready. She had assigned the roles and they knew what they had to do.

When the procession had started moving out of the Royal City, the Blacksmiths in Kob'Râm had changed their drumming. The loud bangs on the anvils turned into a slow and somber beat from striking a kind of metal shield whose low tones affected the crowd that felt more tightly gripped by the funeral.

Kob'Iâm was crossed slowly as all the inhabitants gradually joined the column. Then they went into Kob'Râm where the weapons-melting ceremony was to take place.

On the big central terrace where the crucible glowed red, only Ta entered at first and she stood in the center, followed by Opak's body which the bearers kept upright before her, facing the crucible. Then, when the muted rhythm gave way to silence, the Men of the deceased came in turn. One after another, going by the crucible, they threw the weapons into the molten magma.

Not a word was said. Torches crackled everywhere, casting strange fires on the features of the crowd that packed tightly and quietly around the spectacle.

When it was over the Blacksmiths resumed their drumming.

The procession got back in line and continued its slow descent, City by City, emptying all of Kob'Râm, then the people of Kob'Vâm, then Kob'Lâm.

Ta at the head arrived at the exit on the bridge that crossed the chasm beyond the ramparts of Kob'Lâm. She barely hesitated before striding forth on the road that led to the cliffs overlooking the Dongdwo swamp.

Everybody followed. Soon, through the mysteries of nocturnal nature, the eerie procession broke up, rolling out in ponderous waves on which floated sails of fire, the vast fleet of torches.

The slow sound pulse of the Blacksmiths, who had taken their place in the procession, reverberated in the echoes of the night.

Frightened animals fled every which way, shadowly, while the hushed whirl of the phosphorous-eyed birds soared off.

When the last pilgrims started to leave Kob'Lâm, the front ranks were reaching the Dongdwo swamp where they could already hear the hoarse squawking.

The very last man to leave the Low City turned around when he had crossed the bridge. What he saw shocked him because nothing was more extraordinary than Kobor Tigan't, drained of its people and blazing in solitude from high to low through the five Cities with all the lights lit by the funeral servants.

To begin the final ceremonies on the plain over the swamp, they waited for all the participants to arrive. Little by little, they squeezed together, shuffling their feet. The tense, anguished atmosphere was hard for everyone to bear.

The Blacksmiths kept up their beat. When they stopped, it would be the culminating moment of the funeral, the final act that was to throw the body of the deceased from the top of the cliff into the depths of the swamp.

In the light of the torches the shimmering of the silt was enlivened down below. They saw murky masses starting to move. It was the Dongdwo, the old dragons, who were gathering for the lamentation. In fact, at all the funerals of important people they always groaned and growled and grumbled. This time was no different and their moans wove quickly into a litany.

Those listening shuddered. Was this not the very voice of the mythic Ancestors expressing their wrathful grief?

The body of the deceased was stood at the edge of the cliff. Behind it Ta waited patiently, placidly, flanked by Hé-Nark and Ata-Réè whose warm vigilance enveloped her. The Guards were on one side, the young B'Tah-Gous on the other. The Men of the Opak's Chamber stood behind

Ta. Between them and the Devotees they had put Opak's T'Lo, slightly removed so that they could not see the corpse.

It was customary to spare their overactive sensitivity the final images of the funeral. Otherwise, in a kind of delirium, they might dive into the swamp after the mortal remains. It had happened before. They remembered those suicides and did not want to run the risk. Ta more than the others because she figured that a tragedy involving the T'Lo was less than ever desirable.

Suddenly the Blacksmiths stopped drumming.

In deepest silence, then, they started to extinguish all the torches except those around Opak.

T'Lo Dê in the muddled crowd of his peers fell victim to an uncontrollable horror and felt like he was spinning around in space, falling from very high through an unreal rain whose silvered darts were piercing his heart. He was going to die! But the illusion stopped as suddenly as it had begun. The darkness was almost complete. He felt the milk throbbing in his breasts. His mind flew back to the Palace where his transcendent sight saw the two children crying in the arms of Gan'd.

Taking advantage of the shadows, T'Lo Dê slipped away without being seen.

Everyone's attention was focused on Opak's body, which the bearers were lifting up as high as possible over their heads so that all could see it one last time.

The Devotees started slowly encircling Opak's T'Lo who were far too scared to resist anything and so were quickly mixed with the other T'Lo, then nudged back behind the Devotees where Oda-Néè and her cronies were waiting in the darkest shadows to take them away while the other Devotees screened off the abduction.

Breaths were held. Opak's body had just disappeared. They heard the splash in the swamp.

The people on the edge of the cliff crowded closer to see it sink. The gold covering flashed for an instant, then went out.

Ta stepped back. They also threw the Blacksmiths' drum shields into the swamp along with the spears and their votive banners.

The Dongdwo's groans reached a frenzied climax. Ta went back with her Guards and the B'Tah-Gous while the crowd started dispersing.

They relit all the torches.

That was when Hé-Nark realized that Opak's T'Lo had disappeared. He cried out, alerted his troops and without a moment's hesitation went

124

looking for them. The Devotees joined in rounding up the people, running all over the place in a hypocritical panic. It resulted in such confusion and turmoil that they did not notice the absence of Oda-Néè and her cronies.

The crowd was astir, excited by the turn of events. They imagined they had seen the T'Lo here, there and everywhere. Hadn't they ended up jumping into the swamp? They leaned over the edge but saw nothing but the Dongdwo, unmoving, still moaning.

The atmosphere was completely crazy. The Devotees accused Ta of cruel and maybe intentional negligence. The poor T'Lo were insufficiently protected and had no doubt seen the end of Opak's sinking. Panic and grief threw them into madness! Maybe they ran into the wilderness and are now at the mercy of all the treacheries of the night?

They said so much and so convincingly that even the people of Kob'Lâm, forgetting their revulsion of the T'Lo, were sympathizing with them.

When the incident had erupted Ta had only said one thing: "T'Lo Dê!" Then she bit her lips before starting back to Kobor Tigan't with her entourage.

She found T'Lo Dê at the Palace, peaceful, next to Gan'd who was no less peaceful. He was feeding the two infants in utmost serenity. It was a picture of such domestic bliss after everything that had happened that Ta broke out laughing so hard it brought tears to her eyes.

The next day, after hearing the reports from her Guards and from Hé-Nark in particular, she was firmly convinced that the Devotees were behind it.

Hé-Nark made a strong case for this by presenting his evidence. All it would take, he said, would be to search their houses. They would soon find all the missing T'Lo.

Ta did not agree. She did not want the houses to be violated. But she had her decision announced: all the Devotees were henceforth banned from Kob'Ooh'R unless they converted and gave their T'Lo back to the Pit. To them the Queen promised leniency and just as for the few who had already done it she guaranteed her support.

But for the stubborn who insisted on resisting her, their traditional place at her side would from now on be taken by the young B'Tah-Gous and the Royal Guards whom she intended to make her new, personal nobility.

Hé-Nark thought she was not being hard enough. Grim-faced, he predicted great troubles from the Devotees. Ata-Réè added her own predictions to his. But the Queen would not bend.

"That's enough," she said. "I don't want violence. Time, in this matter, will do more for us than useless brutality, which will justifiably scandalize the people."

Without saying a word Hé-Nark doubled the guard around the Pit of the Ananou.

CHAPTER VIII

The Pit of Ananaou is a dismal place. Especially at night. The gigantic mass of the Palace overlooking it completely crushes it and makes it look deeper and darker.

There is no sound. Even when they die the Ananou do not moan. They are mute from birth. And they stay so after being raised to become T'Lo.

Since the death of Abim they have been clapping their hands like when they felt her magic coming down to plunder the reserves of their astrality.

Perhaps they are dying of inaction, of boundless ennui? Perhaps, mysteriously, they had felt a kind of despair in the absence of Abim? Perhaps she had drained their vital reserves or perhaps, more likely, they are no longer destined to know the future?

But who can really know? They do not know themselves. Their evolved brothers, the T'Lo, do not know either. None of the T'Lo care about the Ananou. They would say that they do not remember being Ananou. Does the butterfly remember the caterpillar?

The state of the Ananou, for a T'Lo, is a former state of larvae, almost mindless. To be an Ananou is to vegetate while waiting to be chosen. Without being at all aware that you might be chosen to become a T'Lo and thereby reach a higher stage of development, a different qualification that through contact with the Human reveals another plane of life.

To be chosen is to escape non-being, miraculously. Since the Ananou are only seedlings of T'Lo that belong to the Human to cultivate or not. From an Ananou they can make a T'Lo. They never become one alone.

Formerly, in the time of the Ancestors, everything was fine. The Race of Giants was strong and the T'Lo were not harmful. But now everything has changed. Life is withdrawing from the Ananou and the T'Lo are a venom.

Now the Giants have more all-consuming thoughts and less instincts to satisfy than their Ancestors. In them, the vegetating soul has captured the divine spark and, being personalized, it strives to be translated through the mind in order to be identified and recognized.

The problems arise at the higher level. The brain fervently sucks in all the burning essences of the body to feed its forge. And even if the body does not really weaken, it still thins out and loses its defenses. The true vital interests are no longer in the protection or delight of the body.

But the T'Lo, who do not have a spiritualized soul, have developed their physical radiation, their bodies of desire, to the point of excess, to try to earn the inaccessible title of being human, which they cannot claim as humanimals.

Unconsciously, they ignore the law of evolution. They are parasites of Man in order to enter the future at the same time as them.

As Ta says very logically, "They are dangerous because desire takes the place of spirit in them while in our Race spirit is starting to take the place of desire."

All this makes the shores of the Pit a gloomy place.

The Guards get bored. They easily become lazy and morose as if the apathy of the Ananou were contagious.

In this place, day and night, the Guards come and go, forgetting over time to talk to each other. They sigh a lot. Nothing ever happens, nothing goes on. Or very little!

Of course, once in a while, ruing the evening inspection when Hé-Nark comes, with his unerring eye, they find a corpse in the Pit, which they remove discreetly and, respecting Ta's order, they go and throw it secretly into the chasm at the exit of Kob'Lâm.

The carrion birds, the despised "Them" take care of making the remains disappear.

In an unspoken agreement the people do not try to spy on the operation. On the contrary, they avoid it, figuring that the discretion demanded by the Ooh'Rou is quite healthy and they are better off dealing with less putrid things.

The people are always very worried about their own mental health. By pure instinct. That is why Ta appreciates them so much and places great hope in them.

From time to time also, after her speech, it happens that the converted Devotees bring their rejected T'Lo to the Pit. This is always a welcome distraction for the Guards.

The T'Lo brought by their Mistresses are knocked out by the drink of oblivion that wipes out their memory and they wake up simple Ananou. It all happens quietly with a great deal of tenderness. They salute. The atmosphere is charged with solemnity and melancholy. The

Guards open the Pit silently. The Ananou move aside passively, indifferently, while they gently lower the body of the sleeping T'Lo. Then, it is closed again, the Devotee, the Mistress whose Chamber the T'Lo belonged to, strips off her badge that will later be offered to the Ooh'Rou as a pledge of total allegiance.

There is always an emotional moment before the end. They are turning a page. They are taking sides. They are starting off on a new path marked out by the Queen. They are, therefore, entrusting themselves to her.

The Guards do their best to help the converted Devotees in their sad task. It has quickly become a custom, once the T'Lo are gone, to share with guards a farewell drink during which they talk gravely about the future destiny of the Race and the grandeur of the White Ooh'Rou.

But, in truth, conversations with the Devotees are rare. So much so that the destiny looks very bitter to the Guards shuffling glumly around the Pit. They prefer to be elsewhere, doing anything else but watching this silent hole where they see, between the bars, floating, pug-nosed faces void of expression; empty, golden eyes staring straight ahead into nothingness.

This passivity of the Ananou stings the Guards. Isn't it a silent call? Do they need help?

Full of pity, then, the men squat near the Pit. Can they communicate with the Ananou? Talk gently to them maybe? All the Guards have tried, day after day, with perseverance that deserves more reward.

But these creatures barely react! They come up and just stand there, giving no indication of why. Calling them closer does no good. If you clap your hands, they are not scared, but they still do not move.

The Ananou make vague gestures that nobody understands because they obviously mean nothing or else because the meaning is beyond the ken of man. There is, then, no way to communicate with them. It is sad. It is mortifying. They feel a kind of remorse or guilt because maybe they, too, want to talk but find it impossible to translate.

This feeling makes all the Guards unhappy. Like all the humans in Kobor Tigan't they hate to cause suffering. And here, no matter what they do or don't do, everything seems to torture the Ananou!

So, they give them lots of food and sweets, but how disappointing it is! They never know if it gives them the slightest pleasure. They do not show it. Not a smile or sparkle in their eyes. No eagerness either. Offer them something? They take it delicately, eat it slowly and make no sound. Not a sigh or a groan. Nothing. Silence. No expression. When they have eaten the morsel, they do not ask for more. You can give them more—they will accept or not, you never know…

The Guards told Hé-Nark that if they have to stay there too long it will break their hearts. He knew that something had to be done. When they have finished their shift, he sends them off to combat exercise or to hunt.

He also scolds them for this over-sentimentality because these are orders from the Queen. Why care about what is dying? Are they not acting a little like the Devotees by taking pity on these Ananou?

Hé-Nark is pretty severe. He is a little annoyed seeing his best men turning soft like this. "I caught you sleeping on duty!" he says. "That's not how we guard!"

The men wonder privately what it is they are guarding. What is to fear from these sleepy creatures?

When Hé-Nark has left, they just shrug their shoulders. The Master Guard is a worrier. Still, they will check to see if he is not right to remind them of their duty. But by the time they know for sure, it will be too late. The incident is going to take them by surprise when they least expect it.

It happens one evening. Ooh'R has not completely set. The day had been particularly dismal. They yawn waiting to be relieved. They are hoping for no distractions at the end of the day.

Oda-Néè arrives with Eqin-Go, followed by Ka'Ok and almost all the men of her Chamber. They are very carefully carrying some of their T'Lo who are sleeping on litters. They look distressed but determined.

The Guards are terribly surprised. They jump to their feet, fully awake, fully intrigued. What's this, the most renowned Devotee, the one who is so inflexible, giving in to the Queen's appeals?

Oda-Néè orders the litters put down. She looks devastated as she sits next to one of them and pets the hand of the T'Lo. "Farewell, you who were beloved among all our beloved. The Ooh'Rou has won, I have to leave you."

She calls upon the Guards as witnesses, "Oh, brave men, you see before you Oda-Néè, she whom they said would never give in to the Queen. And yet… Her speech has worked its way into my heart. I understand. I'm giving up my old customs. I want to embrace the new way. I will bring my badges to the Queen."

An astonished Guard dares a sensible question, "O Devotee, your act is praiseworthy but allow me to wonder why, if I'm not mistaken, all your T'Lo are not here?"

Behind her lowered eyelids, the eyes of Oda-Néè flash. She answers very softly, "I was expecting such a logical question, O Guard. It's because I couldn't give all my T'Lo the oblivion drink at the same time. You know how many there are. I'll come back later with the last of my beloved."

"Very well," the Guard says.

The Pit is opened. The sleeping T'Lo are placed inside. Oda-Néè cries as she pulls off her badges. But her strength abandons her. She has to sit down.

"Let's have the farewell drink together," she offers. "Then I'll have the courage to do what must be done."

The Guards nod. The drinks are passed out. The conversation centers on the outstanding merits of the White Ooh'Rou.

Oda-Néè proclaims, "To the Ooh'Rou belongs the future and our destiny."

The Guards cheer.

Oda-Néè smiles, treacherously…

When Hé-Nark arrived that night on his rounds, it was immediately on alert. His men had disappeared. The Pit was left wide open. And it was empty.

He ran to the Palace and warned the Queen. He was furious and wanted to invade the Devotees' properties, knowing full well who was responsible.

But Ta forbade him, "No, fate has decided otherwise. I don't want violence. You won't go to the Devotees, but starting today I will forbid anyone to visit them. A sign will be posted at their properties to enforce my ban. Anyone entering will be considered one of them and their houses will have the same sign posted. Go, look for your men and find them! I want to believe they have suffered no harm. They're my real worry because it'd take great cunning to fool them."

The Master Guard saw that Ta, even in this clemency, was very angry. And even though he thought that she was wrong not to break the Devotees by force, he obeyed her and got busy looking for his men.

Early in the morning they found them, wandering in the woods by the Nursery. They were acting like children, playing with the kids they had met. They were brought back peacefully. They remembered nothing.

Gan'd was called and observed them. She said they had been given the drink of oblivion. She knew how to cure them. They would gradually come back to themselves but, unfortunately, never fully recover.

Ta was heart-broken. As for Hé-Nark, it took a long time for him to calm down. Even afterwards it was cause for his deep-seated resentment against the Devotees and Oda-Néè in particular because he had made clever inquiries to substantiate his suspicions of their guilt.

The infamous sign was posted on the properties of the Devotees who could now visit only each other. Satisfied for the moment at least they did not cause a public scandal.

CHAPTER IX

It is night. T'Lo Dê is listening. He is not sleeping. His senses are on alert. A light fever throbs in his head. He is thirsty. But drinking does not soothe him.

Delicate, flute-like sounds prick up his questioning ears. He sees iridescent waves pass before his eyes. They, too, are calling out and looking for him. It feels like his sense of touch, already so sensitive, is reaching out, pouring out of his fingers, fondling the colored waves that are also fragrant and pleasing to his sense of smell.

The scents, the colors, the vibrations, a whole language that he understands, an urgent call. He recognizes the egregore, the collective mind of the T'Lo who are looking for him.

He has not experienced such things since he gave birth. His erotic desire is in total remission, which is normal for his kind in such a state when their feminine nature takes over. But tonight, even though his heart is panting with tenderness for his two babies sleeping next to him, his thoughts wander, tormented by vivid images that bring with them great melancholy. He cannot get rid of them.

He sees Opak again, the dead queen. A body like fruit. Copper, gold and honey. Bright and cheery, savage and sweet, completely abandoned to her amorous raptures, never sated, always triumphantly rejuvenated.

How he, the T'Lo loved her! He is surprised to remember, so intensely, those moments when he conjoined with her through the male organ of his dual nature.

He looks at his body, at his resting male organ sleeping the sleep of nature that will only end when he is finished lactating, when his daughter is weaned and he is less exclusively a mother so he can turn back into a T'Lo, both male and female, accessible to all loves and desiring them.

For now, he does not really desire physical pleasure. It is something else tormenting him. He struggles to understand what is happening and misses his former peace. But he tells himself that being the only T'Lo in the Palace he is obviously pining for his kind.

Yes, it is them he wants to see again. It is them he needs. Them who are worried about him and sending constant messages to him in the heart of this auspicious night.

Still, he hesitates. He adjusts the light blanket covering the babies. He touches their foreheads. Are they too hot? No, they are fine. He smiles, happy. His pug-nosed face beams. His golden eyes are full of light. Oh, these children, they are the treasures! He, T'Lo Dê, is rich! He is glorious! What T'Lo before him has realized this miracle of giving birth to something other than an Ananoou, the larva of T'Lo that only attains intelligent life through the cultivation of men! He, T'Lo Dê, he has a child who is completely human!

He caresses Dê-Ta'Am, careful not to wake her. He gently opens her hands. Between the tiny fingers this thin membrane! She is his, the T'Lo! It is the only sign that he he has passed on to her. For the rest, she is totally human. And oh how she cries loudly all day long! He loves to hear her since he is always a little scared when she is quiet because for him who has no voice, who is always silent, the cries of his baby are the proclamation of this miracle—the birth of a human girl from a T'Lo!

He also looks at R'Ang, his foster son. He is very proud of him, too, because he sees the distinctive features of his father, Angel, the Beautiful Stranger whose absence is cruel. The features are his pale blond hair and especially those hands with the little fingers longer than the others.

"The children mustn't wake up before morning." T'Lo Dê wonders why. He finds no answer. And yet, the strict order is etched in his brain. The dear children have to get a good sleep... It will make everything possible... Because he, T'Lo Dê, is being called away and he cannot resist for long. His fate as a T'Lo is summoning him. The egregore of the other T'Lo grows stronger in the night: "Come, brother! We're looking for you. Where are you? We miss you. Come to us who yearn to commune with you. Come to replenish your strength and your magic in our love!"

He has to leave. They are waiting for him.

T'Lo Dê has spread his hands over the two babies whose sleep is getting deeper. Yes, only the day will awaken them now. And he, T'Lo Dê will be back by then. But if, by chance, when he is gone, something bothers them, he will know right away, wherever he is, and he will run back. His telepathic sense is infallible.

Now he is sure that everything is ready. He can set out on the adventure awaiting him.

With his sight that penetrates any thickness, he scans around. The walls become quivering mist. He sees that the Guards are on duty in another part of the Palace. Nothing will get in his way. He leaves quietly through the terrace off the children's room.

...Ah, no, it is not a night of men out here, all around him, as the invisible invitations caress his whole body...

In agile leaps he goes down the terraces, one by one. He is weightless. He is almost flying. All his movements, conscious or not, carry him along effortlessly to where he knows he has to go, the place of shadows where passions are yearning for him. He is heading there, safe, secure, but he is still surprised at his surroundings.

Is it really night? Is this night? Yes, obviously, for those who sleep without knowing, their round mouths open, swallowing dreams they will forget at dawn in the shadows of their quiet homes.

But for those who are awake, who are traveling down below here, what is it then? Neither night nor day. Something else. A hybrid moment that partakes of both. And yet it is not twilight...

Not a sound. Everything is suspended. Breathing normally would be shattering. Walking tall without looking where you go would be foolhardy... Slip from pale shadow to pale shadow, yourself a colorless shadow. In the garden foliage you walk along, become leaves and your progress is but the swaying of plants. If mist sits in a hollow, wrap yourself in it and you will rise up like steam... Who would know except those of your sect? Hold back your emotion, your haste, your desire. Are you suddenly scared? Slow down your breathing, wait, and fear not your failure to arrive... Your kin are on the way, searching for you, awaiting you. You are going to join them for reasons you know and in expectation you swoon in pleasure...

The warm air does not move. The sky is covered in white clouds. The season is on your side. Nature is your accomplice.

Strange, languid, cloudy, it is a night—call it by its name nonetheless—a night to celebrate mysteries in which the acolytes meet secretly, silently, stealthily, with expansive sight, ready to join together in the union of the same secret.

Go! Soon, with your kind, with the Devotees, your mistresses, whom you love so utterly, and in perfect harmony you will reel out the rhythm of obscure acts, the forbidden eroticism. It is a night of T'Lo...

Oda-Néè's domain is surrounded by a thick stand of fragrant trees that are the pride of the owner. They are like no other. Oda'Néè had them brought in specially. She has consented to give cuttings to her real friends. It is a way of measuring her approval because she has become a secret power whose influence spreads covertly every day. From her are sent out all the orders and all the insight to the other Devotees, her Brothers, oppressed by Ta the fake Ooh'Rou...

These trees, laden with huge, green flowers whose broad petals only open at night, are called Dot'Ooh'R, which is an odd paradox for night-flowers!

These flowers are often taken as an emblem of the Devotees who display them gladly because they bear the round fruit they use to maintain their intoxication during their ceremonial orgies. They say that under the influence their senses are sharpened and heightened becoming almost as intense as their T'Lo whom they can talk to more easily mind to mind. The Devotees' goal is to perfect the ability to

hear the thoughts of their T'Lo. They have known for a long time that the T'Lo can read theirs with ease. So, they want to be able to exchange freely with them.

The use of this fruit is one Oda-Néè's discoveries. She is full of inventions to better serve her erotic mysticism.

T'Lo Dê is there on the edge of the property. He does not dare enter. And yet, he knows that he will be welcome. He burns with desire to finally tell his fellow T'Lo the news: a girl was born from him, not an Ananou!

He cautiously sniffs the odors coming from the big garden and the more evocative ones from the big house with the windows open onto the Chamber of Men. He can hear passionate whispers and that unanimous moan of those who are reveling in penetrating or being penetrated by their T'Lo.

But this makes no particular impression on him. He did not come here looking for ecstasy. He came only to reunite a little with his kind and their tenderness. His thoughts condense into a summoning cloud that will float into the house through an open window.

In a very short time the shade is raised. The shaved head of a T'Lo appears. Clearly, he is listening. T'Lo Dê send out another call, more insistent. The shade falls back down. A door cracks open. Light footsteps hurry across the garden. There, behind the bordering trees, a tickling, questioning contact.

The inquisitive thought that reaches T'Lo Dê is stunned, "Is it true? Is it really a T'Lo here, all alone, outside?"

T'Lo Dê assures him he is and asks to go inside with him.

The T'Lo who came timidly out into the garden says, "What will the mistress say if she catches me! It's forbidden to go outside."

"It doesn't matter! Come on, I'm T'Lo Dê!"

The other was startled and excited, "It's me, T'Lo Gâ. Oh, how my mistresses have talked about you!"

"I'm bored. I'm the only one left in the Palace."

T'Lo Gâ puts his arm around his shoulder and his cheek against the other's, "Come with us. All your kind from the royal Chamber of Men are here. Our beloved mistress, Oda-Néè, will be overjoyed because she's worried about you who were Opak's favorite. Come quickly, come! She'll open all her fruit and you'll be possessed by all her males. Come to bliss, come to life. You shouldn't be so deprived of love!"

The psychic waves of T'Lo Gâ pause. He steps back from his companion. He puts his hand on the swollen breasts. He shudders. His face turns pale. His thought puffs up in slow, gentle wisps, expressing his respect.

"Oh, T'Lo Dê, it's true, then, what some say they've picked up while thinking in your direction? You've had a baby?"

T'Lo Dê's blurts out an answer, "I've given birth to a daughter of man!" The psychic flow of the other stopped completely. T'Lo Dê pressed on, "I said a girl. With only one sex. It's not an Ananou!"

T'Lo Gâ's mind was in a flurry. Panting, he squeezed the visitor's hands. "The most sensitive of us said as much. We thought they were crazy, utterly mistaken. But are you really sure? It's really a girl? A human girl?"

"Yes," T'Lo Dê confirms. "She is human, with the sex of a girl, just a girl, and she cries, she's not mute!"

"Oh! I'd like to have one too!" All his questions come pouring out. "What's she like? Black, white, pink? Does she have hair? What kind? What are her hands like? Has she already opened her eyes?"

"Come," T'Lo Dê says, "I'll show her to you. Then you can see the other baby, very glorious, a male, the last from the queen. I'm feeding him too."

How could T'Lo Gâ resist? He forgets all about the restrictions. He walks off into the night holding T'Lo Dê's hand, heading for Kob'Ooh'R.

There in the Palace, after being enchanted by the miraculous infants, they think of their mistress, of the joy she would have felt at such an event and the consequences.

He manages to persuade T'Lo Dê to bring the babies to show Oda-Néè. And they will not bring them back to the Palace if T'Lo Dê wants to live in a Chamber of Men again. He understands perfectly well...

T'Lo Dê accepts. They leave again in the night. They are so careful and so gentle that the two children they carry do not wake up. T'Lo Dê is holding his daughter while his companion has baby R'Ang.

This is how they enter the Chamber of Men where Oda-Néè, wearing nothing but her jewelry, still moist from love sweats, is having a light meal with her Men and her T'Lo. Indescribable surprise: Oda-Néè jumps up and runs to T'Lo Dê. She understands perfectly well all his explanations. What's more, he gives the name of the father—Amo the Solar, the fabulous male who was Queen Opak's favorite!

The excitement is at its peak. The Men form a circle with the T'Lo who clap their hands and weep for joy. They touch Dê-Ta'Am very delicately but she wakes up and strangely instead of crying as usual she smiles and babbles. She is obviously in an environment she likes.

For the moment they pay no attention to the second baby, R'Ang, who keeps sleeping in the arms of T'Lo Gâ who stays back. Dê-Ta'Am's cuteness is enchanting everyone. She has a voice and flaming red hair. How her eyes sparkle! What a beauty! What a success! They fondle the mauve webbing between her fingers. All the T'Lo are laughing in their mute fashion and panting. They spread their own fingers to compare their webbing.

Eqin-Go along with Ka'Ok share the joyful hysteria. Oda-Néè addresses everyone present:

"What glory for the Devotees! This miraculous child embodies all our hopes, all our ambitions! At last, our incomparable T'Lo fertilized by human sperm can give birth to other beings than the poor Ananou who are so desperately fading away." She stands tall, formidable, to make an ominous declaration. "By the treachery of the Aâz, the usurper Ta will not triumph over us! I'm sure of it now that our great T'Lo Dê has given us this proof. Time will not destroy us as that woman secretly desires. I tell you this—a new race will crown our holy unions. The Human with the T'Lo will be truly merged. And then nothing and no one will stop us!"

She takes Dê-Ta'Am in her arms and raises her above her head. The infant babbles and wriggles with delight.

"Look everyone! Here is our highest symbol, the symbol of our ultimate triumph, a living symbol. She is our future. Dê-Ta'Am!"

Everyone goes wild. Then, once the initial excitement dies down, Oda-Néè picks T'Lo Dê's brain for more information after sitting him next to her in great honor. She is interested to learn from him certain details about the queen. But this inquiring fervor does not please the T'Lo. He abruptly cuts off his thought transmission.

Oda-Néè is taken aback. "You don't like my questions? Or do you live in such seclusion that you know nothing about the queen?"

He just smiles. He does not like to be forced. He is independent. More even, since he takes seriously the raising of these two children. And then he loves Ta a lot. She gave Dê-Ta'Am her name.

Oda-Néè does not press him. Besides, her attention is now turned solely to T'Lo Gâ. She reaches out and says, "But what have we here? Another baby? Not another one of yours, is it, T'Lo Dê?"

He shakes his head, still smiling. T'Lo Gâ cautiously brings R'Ang over to meet the Devotee. Once again they gather round this other marvel.

T'Lo Dê acquiesces and sends out explanations so that Oda-Néè understands that this is the last born of the dead queen and his father is none other than the Beautiful Stranger, Angel.

The Devotees have nothing against him, quite the opposite since they remember his friendship with T'Lo Dê. They honestly adore R'Ang and pray that T'Lo Dê will teach him sound principles. Oda-Néè wants to hold him. He wakes up suddenly and on seeing her scrunches up his little face and starts howling. A real fit of anger and fear! Never has such a thing happened before. Oda-Néè realizes this from the confusion of thoughts coming from T'Lo Dê, to whom she quickly hands over the twitching baby R'Ang.

It is contagious and Dê-Ta'Am starts crying too. But a caress from Oda-Néè calms her down white T'Lo Dê cannot soothe R'Ang whose tear-soaked face is turning purple.

T'Lo Dê decides to cut short his visit. He wants to leave. He cannot stand seeing his foster son like this. He is tormented by regret. He snatches away his daughter and gives her to T'Lo Gâ whom he psychically tells to follow him.

It is almost a flight. He forgets all the respect and politeness that T'Lo owe their mistresses. But he does not care. He answers only to himself.

Ka'Ok, who has always greatly admired this T'Lo, wants to hold him back, but Oda-Néè, with a wave of her hand, stops her. She knows that nothing will convince him to stay. She just orders Eqin-Go to go with the two T'Lo to the Palace so that T'Lo Gâ will not have to come back alone.

T'Lo Dê gives T'Lo Gâ a brief caress before running off to his rooms. He has had enough of the adventure. The magical night is withering all around him—R'Ang is crying pitifully. It is no longer rage, it is grief. It is sadness.

And Dê-Ta'Am has fallen into the worst fit of anger she has ever had!

The infants cry so loudly and for so long that Hé-Nark, who happens to be passing by on his rounds, comes to ask what is the matter. He finds T'Lo Dê distraught, not knowing what to do. His daughter has finally quieted down but R'Ang now has the hiccups like a sick baby.

Hé-Nark touches the baby's forehead and brushes away a stray lock of wet hair. That makes the baby cry a little less and breath a little more smoothly. Finally, he falls asleep.

T'Lo Dê is grateful. He puts his forehead on the hand of the Master Guard and looks up at him, so tall standing there over him. Oh, how strong the eyes of Hé-Nark are! The T'Lo feels his heart melt. "If he knew about tonight's crazy escapade, it would be so terrible!" T'Lo Dê is trembling.

"Get some rest," Hé-Nark turns to leave, "your children are wearing you out."

The doors closes behind him. The T'Lo is glad he did not tell Oda-Néè the truth about R'Ang—she does not know that he is the Great Child.

"She cannot find out!"

He shudders. That quiet voice! Who spoke here in the dark right in his ear? Is it Angel? An eerie wave passes through him, inarticulate. He feels like it is repeating the same message and is coming from the same source... Angel taught him to weave wreaths of flowers and leaves. One day he, T'Lo Dê, came up with the idea to mix in little feathers. Angel loved it so! He will teach his two children to do the same thing later on. They will go together to pick the flowers... And he will make them read his mind about the history of the Beautiful Stranger at whose feet it was so nice to curl up...

He falls asleep and dreams of raining feathers, blue, yellow, red. In his slumber his fingers make weaving motions.

After the adventure the telepathic line between him and T'Lo Gâ got stronger from the fact that they shared a very real sympathy. Oda-Néè, moreover, encouraged the budding attachment so that once he got over his initial regret T'Lo Dê went back to the Devotee rather often.

He was welcomed there with countless displays of tenderness, both from the humans and his brother T'Lo. They also flattered him a lot because for everyone he had become a person of utmost importance. T'Lo Gâ did his best to serve him, to anticipate all his desires.

He brought his children with him or not. They were begging for Dê-Ta'Am whom the Devotees were madly infatuated with. Full of self-importance after being implored, T'Lo Dê sometimes brought her. They coddled her. They stuffed her with sweets. She laughed.

Little by little Od-Néè's home became familiar to T'Lo Dê. He adopted new and old habits. It was part of his life.

Every time he came the Devotee honored him and treated him like she did her favorite T'Lo, showering him with all her respect. And since her favorite was T'Lo Gâ there was no rivalry but rather a shared tenderness.

In time, after the breast-feeding was over, the double, male and female, eroticism woke up in T'Lo Dê, which was normal for him like for all his kind. Oda-Néè had waited patiently for this moment because to act otherwise was considered insensitive, if not downright rude, by the Devotees. She could, therefore, express all the desires that she had suppressed, as was fitting, following their particular code of propriety.

T'Lo Dê, having been trained by his long service in the Royal Chamber, responded to these desires with peaceful courtesy and with his male organ now at full strength he possessed Oda-Néè ecstatically, proving himself in this domain as well to be a master T'Lo whose erotic reputation, already great while Opak was alive, was in no way overrated. He found Oda-Néè's humanness pleasant and tried to repay all the attention she had given him.

He was happy, extremely, to be able to give her the Long Ecstasy. Oda-Néè came out of her swoon as if illuminated with magical life.

Eqin-Go and Ka'Ok, who were lusting after T'Lo Dê for a long time, took him rapturously in his female part, which he offered them. They both dreamed of fertilizing him themselves!

But T'Lo Dê did not conceive or even become attached to the Devotees.

He felt no affection except for his two children whom he hurried back to. His absences were always brief and, all in all, against Oda-Néè's wishes, his visit were rare. Neither time nor habit increased the number. And he never showed any desire at all to move into the beautiful Devotee's house.

Oda-Néè did not try to force him. She figured it would be very useful to have an ally in the Palace. She knew how to take her time. And the time had not yet come to act on behalf of the Devotees' cause. It was necessary to pretend to accept the queen's decrees so that they could build up strength, add to their numbers a little, educate further their beloved T'Lo, in short become a secret State within the State.

There was, however, one point on which T'Lo disappointed her a lot. She had hoped, at the start, to get lots of information about life in the Palace, especially about the queen and those close to her, their plans and prospects. But this was not the case for the simple reason that T'Lo did not like this way of thinking. He was wary, unwilling to cause any harm to the queen whom he saw as a special being, like Angel whose memory he held sacred, so he made sure to close off access to his mind every time Oda-Néè tried to broach the matter.

She could not break through this barrier. He, on the other hand, in good humor, always ended up changing the subject as if by magic. She only realized it later and was bewildered.

But she did not get mad at him. On the contrary, she admired his intelligence and self-control. T'Lo Dê was quite the glory and much too loving to bear the slightest grudge against him.

Besides, she figured she could always have his thoughts probed by another of his kind, T'Lo Gâ, for example, who could then tell her.

When he was made aware of this T'Lo Gâ recoiled. He loved T'Lo Dê and did not want to force him or above all to betray him. Surprisingly, however, he apparently obeyed his mistress. But the information she happened to get was so paltry that she gave up for the time being until she could spy better later on.

Still, she wondered whether the two T'Lo had not conspired to wear her down, all the while pretending to reveal a few details to her. No matter! She had great hope in Dê-Ta'Am. She was the future!

The fated child had to grow up so that she could play a crucial role in the conquest of power for the Devotees.

Time, time alone would act in their favor…

CHAPTER X

Day after day the heat waned. They were heading slowly into the foggy season when the mornings are late and gray and the evenings come early to enshroud everything, luring men, animals and plants into long, deep slumbering. But it was still mild. Enough to daydream peacefully outside on the borders of night…

Ta is sitting in her personal garden. She has just bathed. She feels relaxed even with the busy day she had lumbered through. But she allows herself to feel satisfied. Really, another day and everything was done, nothing neglected… Ready for tomorrow with other tasks resulting from these. All is connected…

Among the plants with their leaves as big as a man's chest, among the trees and flowering bushes, she sees the first lights in the Cities go on down below. She watches them with a kind of languid affection—these are her people! Torches roam between the houses. (They are visiting each other, going out or going home.) Some torches float together. (They are talking to each other.) The braziers are lit on the terraces. The faint aroma of food is occasionally smelled, depending on the breeze.

The sky that Ooh'R is deserting is pale pink with a few fruity clusters bursting out—red like pulp embedded with seeds of fire.

On the other hand, Kah'B'La is already starting to assume its nocturnal glow beneath the reflected pinkness that covers it like a veil.

Kobor Tigan't! Never more than at these moments, never more than in this season, the Queen feels its hold. She knows her entire country down to the last detail. She can foresee its every reaction and yet, because she is this White Ooh'Rou, timeless, really, a sacrificial pivot point on which hinge two opposing eras, she feels like an awestruck stranger before it.

"O Kobor Tigan't, even though I govern you and you draw your whole essence from me, even though my ideas generate your actions, you're greater than me and you astonish me! Who, having known you, could ever forget you! O Kobor, even in the wind of death every speck of dust still bears your name…"

Such is her reverie.

Ata-Réè has come to sit by her without bothering her. Their thoughts have merged together, seamlessly, drifting on the same wavelength. The fraternity between them is strong.

"My secret twin," Ta calls her affectionately.

There is the renewal of a pact. Ata-Réè gave herself to the queen and became an extension of her. The B'Tah-Gou often acts as her diligent double. Through her, mysteriously, the mystical part of Ta's work gets done. Never a need for long explanations between them. Their consciousnesses mesh together.

After a circular wave that takes in both the view and the moment, the queen takes her hand and says, "Look, here we are, just like back when you climbed up to me waiting at the top of Kob'Ooh'R."

The B'Tah-Gou smiles, "An entire cycle of Ooh'R has passed. It went fast. It's still recent but at your side, Ooh'Rou, I feel like I've lived two lives!"

"It's because you've done a lot of things."

"Yes, but the people also feel like me. From Kob'Lâm to Kob'Iâm, they say the last seasons are as far away as our Ancestors."

"Really?" Ta was surprised but interested.

"Really. They even say that you caused more things to happen in one Ooh'R cycle than is normal. And that this is great magic. And that it's even greater magic because these things are all great events. Doors have been opened by your hand. They are all thinking of the future now. All your speeches are taking seed in their consciousness."

"Yes, I know, they expect more from me. I'll have to give them everything and then find a way to give them more, even if I have nothing left."

She lightens the melancholy mood with a refreshing laugh, almost an excuse, but her companion is not fooled.

"O Queen, who can take this away from you! Ooh'R, in secret, is constantly renewing you. You have a deeper, broader relationship with him than all the former Ooh'Rous. They all had pretty wombs in which Ooh'R was happy to plant his seeds. Before you, an Ooh'Rou, down below here, was a great, dark sun, an inverse reflection of Ooh'R, casting warmth, not light, in the incubating darkness. Whereas you, you stand up tall, in the center, you know how to clarify what is below as well as what is above and you share and you organize this Life allotted by Ooh'R."

"Perhaps, perhaps," Ta muttered dreamily. "You might be right."

They will talk a while longer. Their mutual harmony is a relief. They are relaxed together, grateful to each other for this kindness they share.

In short phrases, looking at each other, smiling, holding hands, self-reflections basically, they talk about all the little things that weave the fabric of life.

The B'Tah-Gou says that R'Ang, the Great Child, is growing up well. He is serious, well-behaved, a striking contrast to Dê-Ta'Am. T'Lo Dê's daughter is nothing but screaming, squirming and temper tantrums. But in spite of everything, the T'Lo's gentleness and his desire for peace manages to pacify her because when he figures the girl has gone too far, he is able to will her to sleep with his hypnotic golden eyes. And how he smiles if anyone happens to walk in on him! He puts his finger to his mouth and shows off the adorable sleeping baby who is pink and soft and round even though a few moments earlier she was a clenched-up little ball of howling fury.

After mentioning this, Ata-Réè, like almost every time, cannot help reminding Ta of her fears about the future of Dê-Ta'Am.

"There's a perpetual battle in this being. The blood of the T'Lo and the blood of Amo struggle for peace. I don't know how the child was created, but I have the feeling that something somehow exploited Amo to get his seed."

"But," the Queen objected, "don't you think that Amo's virtues, his strength, courage, sense of honor and kindness will finally prevail in Dê-Ta'Am?"

"I'd like to believe so, my Queen! But I can't lie to you. I'm convinced that the strength will turn into brutality, the courage into unstoppable recklessness, the honor into pride and the kindness into favoritism for a chosen few…"

"But that power of love that Amo had, do you think it, too, is destined to be deformed?"

"I hope not. Excuse me for telling you so directly, but I want to keep you on your toes about this because it is this that is your enemy."

Ta shudders. She knows, obscurely, that all this is true. But since she is on the path of changing and improving her people gradually, can it not be the same for this child?

"No," the other insists, shaking her head, "no, don't believe it. Just be on your guard. Love, in her, will be purely eroticism and vicious possessiveness."

The B'Tah-Gou stops talking. Her eyes dilate. A smile blooms on her lips. On impulse she grabs Ta's hand.

"Oh, what does it matter! In the end you triumph, White Ooh'Rou. And you come out of these ordeals rejuvenated and more alive than ever. We who love you will never abandon you."

This "we" means Hé-Nark, Gan'd, the Royal Guards, the B'Tah-Gous and others whose numbers were growing every day and whose trusting love supports the White Ooh'Rou.

Here now Ta is alone again. Ata-Réè has gone. The Queen's thoughts have resumed their course.

How many things have been accomplished since spring! Countless little deeds spring up and fade away in her consciousness as she recalls them. Faces rise up, which she tries to read. What is their destiny? What connections connect them to others? Here is the face of Gan'd, all steadfast but gentle, on a background of leaves whose supple foliage blends with her hair. She is holding plants and roots.

Her knowledge grows every day. Everyone knows how much respect she has for the Queen. They talk about her. They are starting to appreciate the benefits of her knowledge. They come to her for wounds, fevers, for sadness. They are learning from her how to recognize certain herbs to use. The young B'Tah-Gous, Ata-Réè's entourage, see her regularly, share in her research, listen to her explanations. The Queen encourages them on this path. Ata-Réè's inspirations often make helpful contributions that Gan'd never neglects.

Yes, she has a beautiful face, Gan'd. Ta is always happy to envisage it. And yet, she wonders whether the young woman's eyes don't sometimes betray distress. They sneak peeks at Hé-Nark... Gan'd has a heavy heart, for sure. But her lips remain sealed. She does not complain and blushes, offended, if you try to broach the subject. She is proud, independent. She believes the Master Guard sees nothing. Ta smiles thinking about it because it is not true: he looks at Gan'd when her back is turned, when she goes back home to the Royal Nursery. And his attitude changes, he loosens up a little, breathes deeply, hangs his head. And if, by chance, Gan'd happens to stumble, he starts to reach out as if to hold her up from afar. At these moments Ta is always struck by the great kindness that radiates from his face.

The Master Guard says nothing either. His feeling is not the same as Gan'd's. Nevertheless, he knows how beautiful and desirable she is. And he wholeheartedly admires her knowledge and her devotion in caring for others.

... Another face theirs. It is no less radiant, a pure beauty and with a kind of passionate zeal: it is the Devotee who was the first to convert after Ta's speech and whose Men all joined the Royal Guard. She is the one the Queen chose to represent her at the new Ooh'R Festival.

Arousing a lot of enthusiasm, she was the Ooh'Rou of love, fertilized by her prettiest male on the platform at the top of Kob'Ooh'R like Opak did before the shame cut her down and the people withheld their zeal for her. After long delay, after the ordeals and grief, the Race's joy exploded during the Festival. The changes in the ritual implemented by Ta were too subtle to be noticed and adopted at once—their satisfaction swept away any misgivings.

All the vital passions, simmering for a long while, were suddenly unleashed. They said this New Festival was even better than the spring! It was the burning of the full sun, the verticality of Ooh'R.

Fearlessly the joy of love washed over Kobor Tigan't like molten golden lava.

The Choice of Men, which enabled the renewal of the Chambers of love, took place. As usual among the rustic nature of Kob'Vâm, through the gardens and orchards, along the rivers and the lake shore, the long, carefree running twisted and turned and at the end of the traditional hunt the Females threw their symbolic belts around their chosen males' waists.

However, there were some minor changes in these games, which Ta had considered carefully, seeing the spontaneous signs of a change in customs. In fact, foregoing their usual passivity, the men whom the noble women had chosen could refuse for various reasons without causing any resentment. Surprisingly, everything was well received.

A few of these men tried to join the Royal Guards. Others, instead of accepting being chosen, confessed calmly their preference for other women who were informed and acquiesced to their desire by adding them to their own males.

There were also a few cases in which very young couples were formed, untraditionally, of just two, one man and one woman. They went themselves to tell the White Ooh'Rou that they intended to live like this, as a couple, to commemorate what she had done with To. She was moved beyond expression and promised them a place at her side in the Palace.

Ta took no part in any of the Festival. She watched from her rooms, a white and lonely shadow above the torrential wave of the procreative force that her Race drenched itself in.

Then, when the jubilation finally abated on the last day, the young B'Tah-Gous sang for a long time, gathered around Ata-Réè on special terraces of the Palace. The Royal Guards came to hear them.

Hé-Nark told the Queen that the bonds of love were starting to form between many of his men and the B'Tah-Gous who were not unresponsive. Ata-Réè was consulted on the matter and confirmed it, saying that the time had come for favorable unions to be made between her girls and this masculine elite.

Ta was happy to agree. This, too, was a good sign. She had already thought about it before it came to light, wondering how it could be encouraged. Now she would not have to bother...

After the Festival a mellowness settled everywhere. Everyone was happy, easy-going, relaxed. The heat slowed down their usual activities. They savored the art of living. The souls were comforted. Nothing threatened anyone. Therefore, they sought plenitude again. They knew they owed it to the Queen.

In the newly formed Chambers of Men the erotic intoxication of the first days gave way to refined tenderness, to slowly exchanged games of love. The bold Blacksmiths who, as usual, had slipped into Chambers without warning to surprise the beautiful Mistresses regained their freedom. They returned happy and carefree to their forges that rang out gleefully.

As for the Devotees, they had made it a point of honor not to participate in the Festival. It was not forbidden them, but they preferred to get together alone and meet in their homes, henceforth marked with the sign that the Queen had mandated. Their parallel Festival of T'Lo took place... on an extraordinary scale.

Ta knew that it would get worse at every cycle of the Ooh'R.

The Devotees were entering the new era in their own way. But still, contrary to what Hé-Nark feared, they did not cause the slightest public scandal and all their affairs were carried out in private, even more secretly than before.

... The thoughts of Ta go off in a different direction. She thinks of the building of the House of Great Faces that is well on its way.

From her garden she sees the heavy walls in the middle of a vast plot of ground below Kob'Ooh'R near one of the gates connecting to

Kob'Iâm. The forecourt had been covered with very smooth paving stones of a creamy color with gold jointing.

For the building, whose final splendor could already be envisioned, they are using a completely different kind of stone, a very dark blue-black, which looks similar to the marble substance of the R'Lil, those rocky mountains whose twin silhouettes at the bottom of the valley are so dear to the hearts of the Giants.

It crosses Ta's mind that she has not yet, like former Ooh'Rous, embedded the gems in the R'Lil, which will testify to her reign. She promises herself to remedy the situation as soon as possible. The people always need ceremonies to rekindle their enthusiasm. One must never neglect to stoke such fires when they are beneficial...

However, the construction of the House of Great Faces seems, for the moment, enough in itself to keep people excited. Everyone is eager to see it finished.

Delegations often come from the Cities requesting audience with the Queen for the mere pleasure of hearing her repeat her projects for the new building and the ceremonies that will take place there with all the B'Tah-Gous and the Royal Guards around the Great Faces that will finally be displayed together in the place.

The idea of heroes like Amo and To or great beings of mystery like Angel, the Friend and the Grand Old Man, have penetrated deep into the hearts of the Giants. That a brilliant creator materialized their faces has caused utter astonishment because before Amo there had never been any representational image in Kobor Tigan't. Everyone thinks it miraculous. This materialization is a sacred act that some even consider terrifying.

They come in absolute silence to the room where the Great Faces are presently held, where the child sculptor—the respected guardian and the admired creator thanks to Ta—continues to work on others with serene slowness. He sets them in an order known only to himself around the Great Crystal, which he forbids everyone to approach except for Ata-Réè and the Queen.

Outside, by the window, people are constantly huddling together to gaze in wonder at the pantheon. They listen. Does their sensitivity pick up any message? Possibly, since they leave, all of them, looking happy with bright faces and sparkling eyes.

Habits have already been formed. They come with specific goals. They ask. And they receive...

The hunters of Dongdwo eggs, whose art is hard and dangerous, no longer go off on expeditions without first addressing silent thoughts to the effigy of Amo. They are convinced they get more strength, endurance and agility from it. As for the Royal Guards, they have a very special devotion to it.

Irrespective of rank, all the people turn to the effigy of Angel. His memory is so precious and so lively. They want so badly for him to return!

They cry over To so as to share, in a way, the grief of the Queen. He will become the center of the devotion of the newly formed couples who want to live as only two.

As for the huge oblong Crystal brought back from Kah'B'La, it is sometimes surrounded by strange luminescence, blue or green. People come at twilight to see it better. They whisper and shudder. What is this mystery?

Ata-Réè wonders the same thing. She figures they have to wait for a certain time before getting an answer. She is impatient. She guesses... She dares not follow through with her thought however. Her heart beats too fast with too much mad hope. And she cannot help feeling a kind of irritation when she leans close to the Crystal whose misty interior conceals the heart of it... Will it never become perfectly transparent?

Ta has gotten up. She is pacing up and down the paths of her garden. She stops before the big pool where she had taken her bath. But it is not to stare at her reflection. She sees nothing. She is thinking only that the Devotees said this House of Great Faces would prove the Queen's heresy because they would certainly not be seeing the true Ancestors like Abim there.

"They'd also like to see the first real T'Lo!" the young queen hissed, then shrugged her shoulders.

She goes to sit down, hoping that this last declaration is not prophetic because with these Devotees, one never knows. They are full of ideas. Didn't Oda-Néè say that they, too, would build their own House...

"Will they really do it? And what would they put inside?"

Ta is worried. She will send some watchers. She needs to be informed all the time.

She sighs. Why stir up these troubles, constantly! She is being so irrational when she should be resting! The night is so serene. A light breeze brushes her shoulders. She feels like she can cup her hands and catch a trickle from the stars that refreshes and comforts her soul. The dryness of being a woman alone hurts less than during the day. A kind of drowsiness comes over her that she cannot fight. She gives in, happily. Her limbs are numb, but what a delightful fatigue! And how relaxing! She remembers nothing more. Nothing. She is receptive. Breathing is a holy thing. She feels like she is drinking from the very springs of the night...

The Old Man of Kah'B'La, weaving his sparkling threads in front of her, says, "Like me, like me, young queen, you weave carefully without even knowing you can do it. And still, I have entrusted you, for the rest of your life with many threads of my Tapestry. Don't you feel that you stand beside me? Come now, don't stop! Cross and recross all these threads you are guiding. Alone, beings of your kind, ordained from Above, reigning solemnly, collaborate in my Work and join their work to mine on the same loom. Be strong! Do what you know you have to do. When the Work is over, for you, as a reward, there awaits conscious liberation and To, whom you will see again!"

The vision vanishes. Nothing remains but a slight sheen in the air. Ta comes back to herself. Totally at peace.

Lately, the Old Man has appeared more frequently like this. At any time, day or night, it does not matter, alone or with others. In the middle of crowd, which always seems to catch her, the Old Man pops up for a short message, sometimes just for a smile. He wants to encourage her.

She believes he is a strong support for her and she is thankful to him. For, she thought, after the disasters, that he had abandoned her and she had felt a bitter sense of guilt. But now all is well. The Old Man's presence has magnified everything. The transfigured shadow had to be admired.

Ta bent back her neck to look at the sky... Yes, a night pulsing with celestial fires. A night still serene, still warm. Peace and certainly, with respect to the contingencies of life, happiness.

Being here, sitting and relaxing, feeling that her work has been honestly accomplished...

The old, haunting dreams grant you a reprieve... They are somewhere else, held in check, of no use tonight. And do not go looking for them. They will come back, by themselves, later! But what does it matter if they come back later with their stubborn little pains, for now they are nowhere to be seen... It is the great truce with yourself. Because the center of being is content and thereby lets you live a little, breathe a little, dare to be a little...

Is freedom, then, this inexpressible state, this moment of stillness? Should it be given a name? It has none.

The eternal tides of being subject you to change with the waves that go out as if forever and then come surging back, a little crazed, for an attack. Nothing is ever sure. It is devastating when they leave. It is a violent shock when they return. You go from one jolt to another, from being sorry to being sorrowful. That's what it is to live...

And yet, grace intervenes in the middle of all this wear and tear. It is the moment when the opposing forces are equal—the one that carries away and the one that brings back—so there is a truce, a brief balance that is suddenly peace, a dream, bliss.

Grace is this "outside of time".

To savor this, fully, consciously, to live fully, without remorse, to live like this "in the velvet of solitude", with all its clear physical sensations and its state of mind organizing them for you like a good servant, this is what it is to be free!

But is this not the natural state of "prayer"? It does seem to be how you pray, how you reunite with the whole universe. Everything around you is suddenly present, active, useful, reasonable, explicable. Because you feel yourself there with everything. When you become truly present, when you remember, accurately, yourself without falling into the image that you foist on others, then everything along with you, all at once, returns harmoniously to the Totality.

"Everything holds together," Ta sighs with plenitude.

And it was true, banal perhaps but true, and needed to be said. It was like the first words of the prayer. One must always start by affirming the divine cohesion of the world.

The young woman welcomed the universe into her. She was indeed this universe. Not separated from anything. Bound to all by myriad threads, vibrating exquisitely, ensuring her life. She thought gratefully of the Old Man of Kah'B'La...

How nice it was, at this moment, that nothing happened! Nothing but this expanding confrontation in which every certainty reinforced all the others.

The queen thought that if anybody could have shared this moment with her it would have been instantly annihilated. If an outsider interrupted, no matter how close they might be to her, this freedom, whose wild structure defied any intrusion, would be gone.

Her spirit was wandering through tranquil islands in the vastness of living.

All of a sudden she is a little startled to realize that there is no light anywhere. The sky is dark. Na-Nood, the moon, is not there.

In the silence, the big waterfall is flowing steadily.

How long has Ta been sitting like this? Her limbs are numb. Her brain contains only slow, formless thoughts. Her soul aches. What, after such peace, you have to fall so quickly! Can't you keep anything of what soothes you? Alas, it is hard even to remember…

She goes to lean over the railing. She does it automatically. She feels a little jolt because she spots Hé-Nark on a lower terrace. His back is turned and he does not hear her.

So late at night and he isn't sleeping? The queen is surprised. Has he, like her, acquired nocturnal habits? She stares hard at him without him suspecting her presence. His silhouette is tall and straight on the edge of the terrace. He is like someone standing still in order to keep in check some suffering. But no, it is not that. He is awake, that is all, and his thoughts are deep, surely… But what is he thinking about?

Ta steps away, abruptly, not knowing why, surprised by her movement. Why shrink back when the Master Guard has not budged?

Hidden by the leaves she shudders, wrapping herself up more tightly. So much loneliness around Hé-Nark! She is alarmed by it and quickly gauges her own. Isn't it absurd to lie like this? Her body is supple, her blood is hot, her breasts are still like a girl's…

Yes, she knows what Hé-Nark is thinking about. She knows very well. She thinks about it too. That is why she stepped back.

And yet, she just has to call him. That would put an end to lying about their intimate glances. It would seal their fraternal union of souls in their bodies. Isn't she free? Isn't the Ooh'Rou all-powerful?

Without a sound she goes back to her bedroom.

Bad weather comes and then springtime is back, so the cycles of Ooh'R pass! How could she restart her life as a woman, so abruptly frozen when To died! To, not moving, who runs in place towards her but never reaches her, while she forces herself to approach him but never getting there. Distance endures. The distance of one word when she told him, "Go!", driving him away from her for the first time.

"Don't separate, ever, beautiful children!" the Old Man of Kah'B'La had told them.

… The dead don't grow old. Ta is still betrothed to the permanence of To. That is why she, too, endures without growing old. She is no longer really in the circle of life. But next to it, outside of it…

Hé-Nark is awake down below. He is breathing. His heart pumps. His thoughts stream. His eyes probe the night. He is alive.

In Ta's bedroom, as she sleeps, a crystalline formation watches over her at the foot of the bed…

CHAPTER XI

Autumn looms. Soon the season will turn. Then the fog will come, like unto a visible sleep. Fortunately, it is still far away. Maybe, if she does not think about it too much, the arrival will be delayed?

Live and breathe! There is ripened fruit. The laden branches bow to the ground, waiting for us to come by. We will go pick everything! There in the open husks are grains. In the ground are roots full of sumptuous sap. It must be taken. Run fast!

Picking, gathering, in the orchards of Kobor, in the nearby countryside, on the sides of Kah'B'La, weave their wreaths of action.

Baskets and buckets, leather sacks and bark bowls are filled, emptied, brought back and filled again. It is a game. The air resounds with laughter and shouts.

In the Royal Nursery the girls put on necklaces of red or purple berries while the boys, under their watchful eyes, stand before the grottoes—their childish Chambers of Men—the bark doors covered with thick moss. It will be so much fun to hide, to eat the sticky pulp...

In the Palace of infants, the Breeders, who are restless as a matter of principle, watch the sky and the clouds and round up their toddlers a little earlier every evening...

From time to time, the Great Va-Hôh (where brew the storms) raises its voice. It is just a warning. The bad season is for later, for much later. But if, this time, it were to come? A White Ooh'Rou has to act on time... Surely, surely there will be no storms!

The branches are lightened and rise up.

Kob'Lâm plays its important role; the crops start drying on the countless racks; the silos are closed, overflowing.

Outside, far away, everywhere, in the grass, on the heights, in the valleys, the hunters are at work. There are big fires every night. They prepare the game. The pungent fumes whet the appetite. The preserved meat goes into the storerooms in Kob-Lâm where they are dried and smoked.

Yes, the gray season can come. They are ready to face it. The ample reserves guarantee life, peace and the daily approval of man. They can rest. Their thickened blood is drowsy and kindled with love. The vital fire is simmering, glowing red.

Now the crimsoned gold of the leaves evaporates. Now the smell of the scorched pastures fades away. Neither fruity balm nor animal musk remain. The scent of the earth that endures after the others lasts only a short while… The fog rises on the horizon. It creeps forward…

It is time to go home. Some of the tame birds of Kobor Tigan't roost in the crevices of the walls all around the Cities. Others take flight all together one morning to head to the warm valleys.

The old people meet in the squares with timid laughter. They are like groups of tall trees, dry and knotty. They talk. They do not want to go to bed so early. But the women who take care of them come looking for them. They tease them a little. Come now, stop dawdling! They have brought warm clothes. The old people wrap themselves up, with their usual gripes. Deep down they are glad because they feel a little tired. The women hurry them home. They stumble and yawn…

Then, throughout the five-fold Cities, they get organized. In Kob'Vâm they protect the precious plants. In Kob'Râm the forges that had been open all season rumble behind closed doors. In Kob'Iâm the pools ripple. Kob'Ooh'R shines coldly with all its gold.

The streets are empty everywhere. The impending night will guard a curious silence. And then, starting the next day, the fog will be there.

Softly, every morning, Ooh'R rises behind his veil. The coming days are all the same. You don't age, you endure. The days slip by, one after another, without you realizing it. This semi-living is gentle.

But active joy is inside the houses in the luxurious comfort of the Chambers of Men where eroticism lazes, unwinding its sensual coils. Loving long and tenderly, whispering, seducing…

Through their exquisite perceptions, through all their sensitivity, which is so vibrant in the Giants for whom thought is first and foremost a sensation, the New Age seeps in, creeps in, bringing with it explorations, astonishment, discoveries… Intelligence.

There is a honey cake on the queen's table. The furs are warm under her feet. She is thinking about her people.

Ata-Réè has found a dead bee on the terrace. She picks it up. How dry the bee is already! Can it really be that the Beautiful Stranger will never come back? She looks up: there is fog up above.

The young B'Tah-Gous are dreaming, singing with their mouths closed. They hold hands and sway.

The Guards march more slowly. They start steadily, then stop, then go again.

Hé-Nark? He is there, ready, able. Nothing changes him, no season has hold over him. He awaits an order from the queen. He carries out an order from the queen. He is her extension. He is her functioning. He is the Master Guard.

Gan'd knows it. She sighs... Still, sometimes Hé-Nark goes to her house in the Royal Nursery. He seems curious about the plants she picks and their use. He likes to have quiet talks with her. When he speaks, she always feels like there is some other conversation going on behind his words, in their shadow. She dares not say anything because she is not sure that it is the same thing for Hé-Nark.

He is also interested in Do'A-Roo, the daughter of Gan'd. She has grown and is not longer a baby. He helped her take her first steps. What a smile he had then! Gan'd sighs... What is this unspoken question that she sees rising, obscurely, in the eyes of the Master Guard? What does he want to ask her? Certainly he does not love her. But does he desire her? It seems unlikely! Besides, what woman would strive to bother someone so totally devoted to the Queen.

He never stays long enough for it to be an issue... He goes back to the Palace. Some say that he is Ta's secret Man... He turns around two or three times to wave. Do'A-Roo laughs in the arms of her mother and claps her hands at him... You can never be jealous of the Queen, it is impossible... There now, he is far, no more turning around. It was a good day.

But for Gan'd, nothing has changed.

When they will later claim that Hé-Nark visits the prostitutes in Kob'Lâm, she will get terribly angry and lash out at the cruel accusations. He will listen to her without saying a word, with a kind of tender sadness. He will not even interrupt her and when she starts crying he will stroke her hair and simply murmur, "So, you love me, Gan'd."

She will not deny it, overwhelmed by her emotion. But she will declare, "And yet I don't want a Chamber of Men."

He will barely even sigh then, "And yet I don't want to belong to any Chamber of Men."

Gan'd will gasp, seeing the obvious, "You love the Queen!"

He bows his head, "You also love her."

This, too, is true. Gan'd feels herself turning pale. The Master Guard carries her in his arms to the back of her house...

Later he returns to the Palace as usual. He will come back. And thus time will pass. But there will not be a Chamber of Men at Gan'd's or ever love for her from Hé-Nark, but only dependability, kindness and a fraternal sharing of physical joy.

What really unites them is their love for the Queen and their loyalty to her. They are her most faithful allies. The incorruptible whiteness of this Ooh'Rou fascinates their souls.

They will not dare talk to her about their moments of intimacy. Will she guess? They will think so because Ta will often find excuses, beyond governmental duties, to send Hé-Nark to the Nursery or to summon Gan'd to the Palace.

Some people feel bold enough to hint about it before the Queen. They are curtly put in place.

Ta openly showers Gan'd with favors, sits her next to the Master Guard at formal dinners. It is understood that she is pleased with things as they are.

The gossip stops. The White Ooh'Rou looms over everything.

But when the eyes of Hé-Nark delve deeply into hers, she allows the Master Guard to lift his heart up to hers. Alone he often casts a long, dark shadow, when no one sees him. It is because every time he penetrates the body of Gan'd, the image of Ta replaces her in his blurred vision...

And then... And then life goes on, where everything is changing, except the Queen who mysteriously provides all the necessary incitements for her people. The Giants evolve under her gentle but constant pressure. So white, so upright, so pure, so vigorous ultimately, she sets the example for them of the type of being they are all heading towards. They want to be like her. But they only follow in her wake.

The women copied her voice, her walk, her mannerisms. All the men wanted to join the Guards. But the selection had become strict.

Everyone like the Royal Guards and the young B'Tah-Gous, the students of Ata-Réè were from now on part of institutions.

And how could they live from now on without the ceremonies of the House of Great Faces! The building has been finished for a long time. Hasn't it always existed! They are so used to it that they tend to believe it!

The cycles of Ooh'R turn. The fog comes and goes while many times the spring warming fades as the lights renew.

Flowers and leaves disappear, only to come back even better! Old scents and new perfumes. Every seedling too. Like yesterday. Like before. Everything will sprout tomorrow and the next day. Falling asleep in the grayness, they awaken in full sunlight, head raised, to run outside.

And then, in their rightful place, the springs rejoice and catch fire. How beautiful is this time of dazzling light that falls straight onto the unshakable, always young Ooh'Rou whose passionate speeches fire up their spirits!

They run to hear her. They listen to her like drinking from the clearest springs. And they implement everything she says, everything she proposes and even everything she has only suggested.

At every return of the Feasts of Love, the honorary Ooh'Rous are appointed by her and they all conceived children who are raised as true royal children in the Nursery after they are weaned. The Queen keeps her promises.

The Breeders quickly undergo a strict selection. Only those who have no T'Lo and no links to the Devotees will be kept. Those not accepted will go serve the latter and raise their children in the ancient ways of indolence and sensual sloth. The Devotees will brag that they finally have their own Nursery!

But Ta does not care. As long as they do not step out of their assigned boundaries, she will tolerate their right to privacy, relying on time to lead them to extinction. For, they procreate little, certainly, and the number of their T'Lo continues decreasing, although very slowly now. "And it's likely to slow down even more!" Hé-Nark grumbles, always the pessimist on their subject.

The Breeders in the Royal nursery, authorized by the Queen, are obliged, therefore, to adopt new ways. The young B'Tah-Gous come to teach the vocal art to the children and the Royal Guards show them how to run, jump, use the spear and bow. These children are not at all like those of Opak. They are lively and proud, in a word, royal.

Ta comes to see them often. She enjoys asking them questions. They are constantly developing and the competitive spirits is strong in them. The Queen is counting on this generation. As adults they will form the new thinking structure of the Giants, a new class of nobles, no longer weak and degenerate but regenerated. She gives them special food.

Very soon the Girls join the corps of B'Tah-Gous and the Boys swell the ranks of the Royal Guards.

But some of these children, of both sexes, will prove to be creators. They will model and sculpt under the tutelage of the inspired mute whom Ta found among the Great Faces. Because of them, the crude architecture of Kobor will gradually change. The countless expressions of their genius will decorate the facades. The Blacksmiths will teach them to plate their works with precious metals.

Others will prefer to learn the secret of plants from Gan'd. Her daughter, Do'A-Roo, knows many things already. She is very serious. She would like to get closer to R'Ang, as they are growing up, but she has to give up the idea because Dê-Ta'Am's jealousy is a barrier. These two have almost never left each other's side since birth. They are more than brother and sister and the maternal love of T'Lo Dê, who coddles them with all his care, only brings them closer.

But whereas R'Ang profited from the lessons of Hé-Nark, which made him strong and intrepid, Dê-Ta'Am, on the other hand, rebelled against Ata-Réè and against all the B'Tah-Gous in general to the point that they had to give up educating her in a rational way. Nevertheless, the girl will surprise everyone and show an intelligence and precociousness in the heart of her perpetual rebellion. Nothing will have control over her. Moreover, T'Lo Dê will always pamper her.

On the subject of Dê-Ta'Am and R'Ang, many rumors will spread over time as the Breeders cannot stop gossiping. Very early on they will say that one of the two babies whom they see scooting around on a terrace in the Palace is the last son of Opak, fathered by the Beautiful Stranger who came from Elsewhere. And they will say that the other baby is no less extraordinary since it is T'Lo Dê, who is always around them, who was impregnated by a Man of the Royal Chamber, maybe by Amo himself. And they will say that it is for this reason only that the Queen tolerates this T'Lo in the Palace.

Ta hears of this and is angered. A lush garden is set up on the children's terraces so that it will hide them from the curious. Guards are stationed all around it.

But time is the grand master who settles everything. They will get used to these two children. Everyone will accept them as another part of the Queen's sacred entourage. They will assume she has excellent reasons, known only to herself, to keep and cherish these children and that, no doubt, this T'Lo has certain qualities that set him apart from the others.

Thus it all blows over. Ta, in secret, keeps preparing the reign of the Great Child who will be a male this time. Yes, R'Ang will be on the throne.

She tells no one about this. And little R'Ang, who is becoming self-conscious, is not at all proud of the weird marks on the bottom of his feet. He never brags about it.

A crystalline formation continues to appear in the Queen's chamber and she eventually gets used to it since no harm, no dread ever comes from it. Quite the contrary: she has got the feeling that this enigmatic presence is a secret protection.

Nobody else is aware of it. She has asked those around her a few guarded, indirect questions.

But they are the same crystallinities that appeared around the Great Faces that night long ago when she found the child sculptor who also saw them but could say nothing. Now they are all gathered together in the House of Great Faces. They never leave, except for the one that comes at night to the foot of her bed.

At first shapeless with indistinct outlines, it has evolved slowly, gradually becoming ovoid. It is taller than Hé-Nark. It is upright. It barely ever changes. It appears or disappears. It is there or not. That is all.

Ta feels as if she is being watched by an intelligence foreign to her own and she wants to communicate with it. But her spirit is not powerful enough. Not yet...

The day when the House of the Great Faces (the first "temple" in Kobor Tigan't) was finished and decorated, instead of being happy like everyone else, Ata-Réè felt worried.

Night was falling. She had left her students earlier than usual. She was alone in the Palace on her favorite terrace as she wanted. Despite this, she felt uncomfortable, felt the desire to flee and, in the end, knew not where to go or what to do. She contemplated this. Even this demanded unusual effort.

The next day the inauguration ceremonies of the House of Great Faces was supposed to take place with all the people present. Everything was ready. Kobor Tigan't, which had watched the building of the "temple" with passionate zeal had been waiting for this day in a whirl devotion and gravity that had excited the Queen. She was to preside over the inauguration. All the young B'Tah-Gous, led by Ata-Réè, and all the Royal Guards, led by Hé-Nark, were supposed to give life to the House so that the people could come every day to receive wise inspiration.

Well, unlike everyone else, Ata-réè was nervous. She felt disappointed, absurdly betrayed, truly frustrated and especially alone.

For, the Crystal of Kah'B'La was no longer in the room of the Palace where she so often went to see it without realizing how much her mystical universe was focused on it!

It sat now in the House of Great Faces at the back of the "naos" on a pedestal.

And all this was done according to the inner instructions received both by herself and by her Queen.

But it was far away from her! It still remained very opaque with its interior cloud that never dissipated!

And it was an inexplicable refusal. Fearfully she discovered that she had lived, up until now, solely in the expectation of a miracle that would make it clear. Was she wrong, then, to believe in this "promise"?

Her nervousness grows. She paces around the terrace. Her transcendent perceptions make her suffer because the usual celestial harmonies from where she draws her inspiration have just shifted into a hyper-acute mode that she has never felt before. She cannot get away from it. She squeezes her forehead with both hands. Up above, some bizarre activity is spinning into a sound spiral, crackling, swishing and suddenly shooting into the unthinkable where it vanishes while abruptly, in the vastness, silence falls.

The sun has just set. Shadows are rising. Ata-Réè is scared, gripping the railing. What should she do? What is she supposed to do?

Now there is a sound, very faint, coming to her. She takes it all in, trembling with delight. It is the answer to her hope. It is a call: she is expected! She runs, scrambles down the stairs, over the walkways, towards the House of Great Faces. She is like a feather, like a bubble floating in the air. It is a dream.

When she arrives at the dark door of the temple she does not feel a bit tired, like she has not moved. Her desire was there. She became one with her desire.

She has to go in now… A torch is lit for the night, which she grabs to see her way through the kind, watchful Great Faces that are accomplices.

Her footsteps echo under the gigantic vaulted ceiling. Shadows and lights twitch around her. She has the weird feeling of traveling inside herself to reach an ineffable point of her being.

She skirts around the golden pool in the middle of the nave that holds the green liquid from the dead B'Tah-Gous of Kob'Lâm.

Then, what's happening? She realizes that she is already standing at the top of the pedestal without remembering climbing the steps! And there, before her, in her light, in the vast simplicity of true miracles, the Crystal faces her, *clear*.

At the heart of the marvelous gem, intact, itself crystal, lies the body of Angel, transfigured into its perennial state.

The Priestess has found her angelic spouse!

Henceforth the miracle is permanent. Raised above herself, Ata-Réè communicates with the remnant of the Beautiful Stranger. She transmits the messages.

Kobor Tigan't learns that the sky is watching over their destinies and that Ooh'R will send Sons of Light like the Beautiful Stranger, other "Angels"... The Priestess communes, foretells and quivers. She prophesies.

In the House of the Great Faces a ritual is formed. It is no longer the worship of the procreative forces of Ooh'R. It is the religion offered to Him through the intermediary of his celestial mediators whose messages are symbolically translated by Ata-Réè, the prophetess.

She has likewise become aware of the crystalline formations that fill the temple. None but her can touch the Great Crystal. She knows now that an explosive force lies within and that you can only safely put your hands on it in a certain way.

During the periods when the sky is quiet, the cloud gathers again, hiding the presence of the Beautiful Being. It is this restored translucence that alerts Ata-Réè that she will receive new messages.

On special occasions chosen ones are called to contemplate Angel. The people say of them that "they have seen The Presence" and they pay them great honor afterwards.

Ta reigns. With a tender heart she watches the religious development of her faithful companion. But she herself does not really participate in this mystic because she knows that, gradually, her spirit will get strong enough to receive not the shimmering symbols that clothe the truth but The Truth itself, which the true queens must face alone if they are to understand that the whole sky is operational and that it is frequently objectified on earth...

Yes, at this time, in this place, with this spirit and this mission, the White Ooh'Rou of Kobor Tigan't is truly an immeasurable solitude!

To whom can she entrust her knowledge?

She has to wait for the Great Child to grow up. R'Ang will receive the sum of this knowledge that she knows will become more distinct until it is part of the secret powers of life that watch over the Race.

The Old Man of Kah'B'La often comes to talk to her and tell her to focus on the crystalline cloud that protects her in her bedroom. She does so. Slowly, she feels changes in her being. The White Ooh'Rou is different from those around her. She does not belong to this time but only to her mission. A timeless sovereign…

And yet, she has to sacrifice to contingency. Therefore, the gems that represent this White Ooh'Rou have been embedded in the smooth, black side of one of the two R'Lil like the other Ooh'Rous.

Hé-Nark, like Amo before him, comes secretly to dream before these diamonds that are placed after Opak's rubies.

Ta reigns. The stream of becoming that her will channels to her people will pass over her without touching her in the least. She will remain intact, unchanged, in her beauty and youth. To see her admirable permanence you would think her happy. All her people think so and thus call her "The Radiant".

But Ata-Réè, Hé-Nark, Gan'd, they know how hard are her nights when the image of To keeps coming back to her…

What matters the grief of a woman, the fatigue of a queen! The world goes on being weaved. Nothing can stop it. One thing leads to another. The causes give rise to the effects. This makes for strange springtimes of events, good and bad, happy and sad. Here is uncertainty. Here is hope. Night and day, one after another. Clouds pass. Thoughts slip by. The wind blows. Forgetting enables the dawn. The rising sun thinks not of its tragic setting the night before. Mercy means moving forward. And so men live, breath. Their hearts beat. It is sweet to accept sleeping. Or dying. There is always awakening after sleeping. After death.

Yes, it is the infinite voyage of living. But the Giants of Kobor do not see themselves as sedentary even though the big races have been run by them. Thinking about it, the Queen smiles all alone!

They do not realize that they are still nomads, being hurled into the future by the will of a White Ooh'Rou who will grant them no respite, her race to be selected so as to shed its useless excess.

Only the elite will reach the clear heights of the New Age!

Ta reigns. She will rest at the end. She knows it. It will be a crystal repose.

In the meantime, beforehand, as it should be, in order to set an ever-inspiring example for all of Kobor Tigan't, the Palace starts living according to the new rules.

The whole Race now gazes upon this beacon with its sometimes surprising lights.

Ta has made her revolution. On the well-woven web of her convictions, she manages to materialize her ideas by incarnating them, in a way, in the people around her who are thus used as supports.

Finally, having come out of the preparatory stage, this sovereign can enter the active phase of her reign, which consists in extinguishing the last dark fires of the Matriarchy, now outdated, to light the clear fire of the emancipation of males.

Therefore, in the Palace in Kob'Ooh'R her court forms around her, quickly growing through the cycles of Ooh'R.

It was made up of all the advanced people of the Race, duly recognized and selected. And the preeminence was systematically given to the males.

In truth, less a court and less courtiers than a gathering, almost a cell, by affinities with the White Ooh'Rou who was the demiurgic model for all to follow and thanks to whom the archetypes for the New Age were crystallized.

All who congregated around her thus lived off and through her because she mysteriously fed them with the white substance of her feminine magic, the luminous "milk" of her suggestions, always so adept at penetrating psyches. Inspired by her, they were truly active members of her invisible Power Body and especially, truly, for all of them, the anchor points of her egregore.

There were now different sections of the Royal Guards that the queen's Group of Young Servants joined, superior young men among whom, obviously, were the first children of the Honorary Ooh'Rou.

Almost all the Blacksmiths of Kob'Râm formed a special section without having to abandon their work at the forges.

Hé-Nark had authority over all, being unanimously recognized and respected as the most direct emanation of the Queen's will.

All the new Men of Kob'Ooh'R were, in sum, before their time. They maintained order, internal and external, by exercising their physical prowess and, through a ritualistic service to the House of Great Faces, their mystical prowess. Furthermore, they were free, no longer bound to the obligations of a Chamber of Men.

During the annual festivities either they did not participate or they refused the Choice of Men. Besides, this festival was going out of fashion because they knew the Queen saw it as an obsolete practice. Knowing this, she still did not abolish it. Little by little, as she expected, the Women felt ridiculous throwing their belts around the Men like before when all the segments of Society were starting to choose instead of being chosen.

Only the Devotees stayed strictly, stubbornly faithful to the ancient festivals, claiming it pure Tradition that they were now the sole custodians of. Most of the Giants did not take them seriously. The Devotees lived so isolated that in the general opinion they had become "backward", some even said "unruly". But since the Queen tolerated them, it would have been ungracious not to do the same.

However, on the other hand, their isolation from society whipped up imaginations. It had become common, pretty much everywhere, to spread all kinds of rumors about them. As a matter of fact, the people were interested in them, so they spied on them to keep abreast of how their lives developed.

They lived in a closed system, often joining their lands together when they were neighbors, chiefly in Kob'Iâm and the Nursery. These huge domains were almost always fringed with prying eyes!

But like it or not it became a State within a State. There was an ever-growing gap between the Devotees and the rest of the population, overshadowed by the vigilance of Ta.

The Queen was completely aware. But she kept running into the same problem: it was impossible to force them to renounce their practices since she could, under no circumstances, decide to adopt solutions that she judged brutal. It would have been easy with the forces at her disposal to annihilate them. Her Royal Guards would march together as one, trained by Hé-Nark who saw this as the only solution. They would have to invade the domains, separate the T'Lo, toss them into the Pit of Ananou, or even, the Master Guard admitted, kill them... Outrage and outcries, heart-wrenching scenes and above all blood would flow over Kobor Tigan't... This had to avoided at all costs! Ta always ended up with this conclusion.

She forced herself, heroically, to just maintain, to just contain the matter... Time, perhaps, would present a progressive solution without clashes? She hoped so, though she did not really believe it!

This subject caused a quiet discontent in Hé-Nark who saw what the Queen was thinking. He himself had no hope. He knew that they were just postponing a tragic outcome.

The Devotees were relatively calm. For some time, however, unexpectedly, some young people were joining them under the pretext of finding "more love". At least this was what the Devotees claimed.

They had built their House of Great Ancestors on the vast domain of Oda-Néè to oppose the official House of Great Faces. And performing there the orgiastic rites (a mystery because they, too, had progressed) they were starting to attract a kind of fascination in certain minds...

Ta was fully aware. She could only defeat them by the growing luminosity of her character among her people, whom she thus galvanized by stimulating them as far as she could, always giving them new ideas to explore, conscious breakthroughs.

But the larvae of the dark, the quiet instincts, the fermentation of the psyche, the egregore as well of the Devotees, directly hostile to the queen's, worked stealthily, leading to the search for affinities.

In the end, the Devotees started growing. Their internal tension grew too.

Hé-Nark knew that they would break the dam one day. He hated himself for knowing this. His life was poisoned by it. He was dying of fear for the Queen.

CHAPTER XII

Since Ta's decrees against them in the first year of her reign, the Devotees had retreated into a kind of moral exile. They basked in it for most of her reign until R'Ang's became an adolescent.

Their eviction from Kob'Ooh'R had only added to their pompous pride. They spread rumors that the country was in the hands of a usurper who could only lead them to their doom by destroying all the old institutions of which they were the noblest representatives.

Consequently, they started living apart, not even participating in the ceremonies that were not forbidden to them. They did, on the other hand, spend a lot of time visiting one another, feeling like they were establishing a fraternity, which was even more pitiful than their erotic methods, which were officially condemned.

They quickly slid into an extreme sentimentality. They alone loved! They alone vibrated with love! They alone, out of compassion, could give the so cruelly frustrated Race the benefits they possessed!

They got in the habit of visiting, talking and worrying about one another, becoming passionate about everything that happened in their individual spheres. They went with all their T'Lo from one friend's domain to another. They gave each other support and encouragement. They soon dreamed of convincing other people and bringing them into their movement. Recruitment seemed a dazzling goal. They wanted goodness and happiness for all. They wanted to save the Race. Their ambition, their craving for power increased every day.

In everyone's eyes they were starting to be haloed in mystery. The less they knew about them, the more they thought about them, the more they talked about them. They fascinated the public, which did not realize the danger in growing used to their weirdness (weirder every day) whose exotic zest was needed to spice up the stories spread by word of mouth.

People hid on the borders of their domains, lying in wait to discover some new detail about their life.

Oda-Néè had taken the leading role. She had become the soul and brain of the Devotees. They did nothing that she had not imagined and decided. Orders, impulses, inspirations came from her. Everyone rallied around her indomitable will.

Her own personality intoxicated her. She zealously saw the effects of her influence grow. She lived in a constant state of rapture that, through osmosis, spread to those around her.

With this perpetual stimulation the Cult of the T'Lo shortly became a real secret society, an ethics, a politics, a religion, in short a complete State within a State that targeted nothing less than the overthrow of Ta to replace her system with the Cult of T'Lo extended to all. This, according to them, was the only means of salvation.

Without being aware of it, spurred on by the jealous and secret admiration of Oda-Néè for the White Ooh'Rou, the Devotees were gradually being led to mimic the Queen in all her achievements. In so doing, by one of those ironies of fate that always tend to enlighten—but they were blind to it!--they underwent a constant, continual, obvious deformation in all their projects. As a result of this warping and distorting—because their mastermind, Oda-Néè, in her heart of hearts wanted to both do and not do everything the Queen did—they turned into the opposite of the Queen, into a mockery of her. They proclaimed themselves radiant, but they offered only the antithesis of light, the dark, destructive and deceptive face.

They were the first to be deceived.

Oda-Néè lived waiting for the achievements of the Queen. Maybe because she was not really capable herself of innovating. In fact, Oda-Néè was more a political strategist, a manipulator of influences, than a creator who can organize her creations in the time, space and hearts of people.

But there was one crucial difference between these two women with their different titles but both capable of power and magnetic attraction, it was that Ta loved her people with a cold passion in an alchemical state of the "fusion" of her whole, sacrificial being by a controlled fire for the sole benefit of her Race, whereas Oda-Néè, in her dazzling dream in which she believed she loved the Race, was really only practicing onanism... All narcissism is masturbation. Oda-Néè was only posturing in front of a mirror.

Unfortunately, this shard of mirror was such that the countless Devotees were reflected in it as well.

It was at this time that Ta would inaugurate the House of Great Faces and the Devotees would want their House of Great Ancestors. Oda-Néè, therefore, offered her domain. As soon as the temple was built, to copy the clever boy found by the Queen, she sought creators of forms.

These artists made clay models of the weird creatures they encountered during their drunken sessions with the T'Lo. Thus the Devotees surrounded themselves with the materialization of their fantasies whose physical presence could only deepen their enchantment.

The erotic egregore (that collective entity) flourished thanks to these perfectly matched representations. By animating them with their desire, with their orgasms, so with the most vital part of themselves, the Devotees unknowingly got a result that filled them with joy: the health of their T'Lo was stabilized and strengthened so that they started dying much less often. A circulation of fluids withdrew into itself. Once inside it, one never came out again.

In this House of the Great Ancestors, the Devotees gave priority to the memory of the Very Huge. Her statue was the focal point of the sanctuary. But it was an extreme version of Abim because the drugged artist had accentuated all its "black" and "other" features until it basically represented her as a gigantic, monolithic T'Lo. They had truly captured the "shadow" of the Very Huge, her aberrant and demonic side, to the detriment of everything positive she had done in her reign during which shadow and light had been so oddly mixed.

This representation lived a magical life. When you entered the place, you were under its spell because the artist, who had portrayed her so convincingly, had an undeniable gift of giving life to whatever his hands molded.

In truth, to those who knew her, it was not Abim. The more time passed, charging it with an artificial animation, the more this "golem" became different from its model.

The Devotees found in it (without admitting so) a good reason to worship the semi-deified T'Lo.

But even in this, the deforming fatality that latches on and spoils their intentions brought out, once again, only the dreadful side, the cursed aspect of their humanity.

What emanated from this idol said: capture and devour, despotism and slavery. It did not say: happiness but wild chase. It did not say: love but erotic mania.

And, in the end, this was precisely what characterized the Sect of T'Lo Worshippers when, later, they cast their slimy nets over others!

But for the moment, they were more of a curiosity for all of Kobor and a lurking concern for the Queen.

As for Hé-Nark, he was chomping at the bit every time the subject came up. He advocated radical solutions. He had not given up his initial opinions. For him the Devotees were malicious vermin that would only multiply if not utterly destroyed.

When Ta heard him speaking like this she reminded him of her sworn duty to mercy. Why use disgraceful violence to rush what time won't fail to bring about, meaning the progressive extinction of the T'Lo?"

Hé-Nark was not convinced. He protested, often backed up by Gan'd who suggested the possible use of certain plants slipped into their food. But she smiled when she said such things because she knew very well that the Ooh'Rou would be offended and angry before she would laugh, even being aware that virtuous Gan'd did not believe a word of what she was saying.

There was a memorable incident among the Devotees. Remembering the sympathy shown by the Beautiful Stranger to T'Lo Dê and through him extending to all the T'Lo for whom his compassion was piqued, the Devotees decreed that, all in all, the White Ooh'Rou had unjustly appropriated the prestigious Crystal. They wanted possession of it, were jealous of the transcendent messages emanating from it. This preoccupied them for a long time. Oda-Néè and her most active partisans made it the recurrent subject of their talk and claimed that those who kept the Crystal could use its enchantments to better control the people.

It was, therefore, regretful, no even worse, shameful to leave it in Ta's power since she was using it only to support her own despotism.

Who knew, they said, maybe the Beautiful Stranger was suffering the most deplorable torments? Maybe he was a prisoner or even reduced to the state of a mysterious slave exploited by the crown?

They talked so often and so convincingly that their goading created a conspiracy to steal the Crystal. After many secret meetings and meticulous preparation, they managed to sneak into the sanctuary one night with Oda-Néè at their head.

As soon as they entered, they felt disturbed as if lost in a higher, utterly foreign world in which they, the Devotees, were totally alien. And yet nothing hostile confronted them. But they were surprised and almost frightened to see the crystalline shapes in the back of the holy place, floating together around the Crystal with a faint humming like a swarm of bees.

They were startled and froze in place. They narrowed their eyes but could find no explanation for what they were seeing. Then, realizing that the shapes were paying no attention to their presence, they slowly worked up the courage to tiptoe to the stairs leading to the top of the pedestal.

Closer to the enigmatic manifestations that now looked like they were made of Light Water, they suddenly felt a cool breeze. It made them shiver and they fell back. But since nothing else happened, they advanced again, spurred on by Oda-Néè's nervous whispers. She was furious with herself for her emotional reactions.

When they stepped forward again, more determined than the first time, just as they reached the manifestations, all the shapes shifted smoothly in an apparently coordinated move. Their circle opened for the Devotees like clouds drifting apart in the sky or like the morning mist being whisked away by a breeze.

The Devotees were stunned and stopped again. They noticed that the buzzing grew even fainter. Nothing was standing in their way. So, they were free to do as they pleased. This, at least, was what they were trying to tell themselves... They had passed the middle of the temple with the enclosed pool where the green liquid from Kob'Lâm lay dormant. They took no notice of it.

Right above them stood the tall pedestal whose platform held the mysterious Crystal. The Devotees were nervous now. Their breathing had the annoying habit of stopping abruptly. They had to use their willpower to fill up their lungs. They also felt a kind of numbness and they knew not why. A sudden sluggishness washed over them. It made them loathe to take any action.

They all looked around. They saw better than when they first arrived the manifold presence of the Great Faces. Withdrawn in the shadows they formed a surprisingly cohesive set. They were all dreadfully attentive, really *seeing* their defilers and apparently waiting for them to perform their profanity! How sure were they of being the true custodians of the Crystal? What did they know about the fate in store for those coming so indecently?

Scrutinizing the shadowy collection, thinking such things, some of the Devotees wondered what they had come here to do tonight! Their expedition was absurd!

With their enthusiasm completely quashed, they just wanted to go back, as quickly as possible, to be with their own, quiet and calm, among their beloved T'Lo.

After suffering a moment of personal doubt, Oda-Néè saw her militia's zeal waning. Her anger exploded. In a few furious words she ordered her men to get to work.

Like being stung, like sleepers being startled awake, they bounded forward with a weird clumsiness that surprised them—they did not have complete control of their limbs. Oda-Néè gaped at them. She could not figure out why they were so clumsy. Bumping into one another, stumbling over the steps, they still somehow managed to reach the platform.

The first to arrive leaned over the Crystal.

There was a screeching explosion, a short, diamond flame, and the man tumbled backward off the platform without a sound. He crashed to the floor at the feet of Oda-Néè. His companions panicked, scrambled down the stairs and leaned over him. He was dead.

They were confused. This was not possible. They all stood there, petrified, staring at Oda-Néè. She felt paralyzed, unable to say a word. She was fighting against the desire to vomit. Cold sweat was running down her spine.

It was then that they noticed all the crystalline shapes closing in on them. The buzzing was loud and getting louder. The Great Faces seemed to be eyeing them eagerly. The scent of a storm tickled the Devotees' nostrils. Up above, the Crystal was starting to shine blue.

Oda-Néè panicked now. Her pride, however, found an excuse. "It's not the Crystal of Angel!" she blurted out while turning around.

They fled, carrying the corpse of their unfortunate companion.

Because of this expedition (which obviously could have been a lot worse) Oda-Néè became very bitter. It was a defeat. Ta had indirectly inflicted a cruel blow on her. She tried to find the irony in it and maybe even premeditation. Who knew if what they had encountered in the House of Great Faces was not set up beforehand! It was a trap they fell into foolishly. They had surely been spied on.

Oda-Néè let her embittered imagination reshape the event. She and her companions completely changed things while talking about it.

They were welcomed back like surviving heroes whose purity had been defiled by a horrible trick.

There was no longer any question of freeing Angel because (they swore) "the Crystal was a monstrous fake designed by the White Ooh'Rou."

Ta was indeed a dangerous being!

The grief was extreme and almost insane among the Devotees. They had a delirious funeral for the victim, sneaking up to the Dongwo swamps to throw the body in even though it was meant only for the noble dead.

The chief sculptor made a likeness. The Devotees put this image in their House of Great Ancestors. It quickly became an entity that was popular to invoke and beseech for anything at all. He was the martyr, the eternally lamented. They boasted of his courage. They exalted his sacrifice. He was, for the Devotees, the same as Amo.

Oda-Néè, once again, had imitated a feature of the official worship!

The Devotee whose Chamber of Men the victim had belonged to, sank into melodramatic depression and to show it off she planned a voluntary death by the erotic consumption of her T'Lo. This drama was accompanied by such orgiastic splendor that many others wanted to share in her pious ecstasies.

She succeeded admirably in her project. Her death was considered as the height of dignity. And the image of this woman joined that of the victim in the House of Great Ancestors.

They called her suicide "The Great Act". For a while it remained an exceptional case, but later the Devotees propagated the practice in their sanctuary during certain ceremonies of their cult. Later still, the old Devotees chose this kind of death more and more frequently. It became widespread in circles that considered it the noblest and purest.

To support the grandeur of this practice, they boldly referred to Opak who, they said, was the first to choose this kind of death…

However, they had not gone so far at the time of the attempted theft of the Crystal. The following day, during the morning service in the House of Great Faces, Ata-Réè got a message telling her about the desecraters coming in the night but she did not have to worry about them coming back because they had been punished as they deserved.

She ran to report this to the Queen who listened thoughtfully and waited for confirmation to come from outside. Since no trace was left in the sanctuary she wondered what punishment had been imposed. She learned soon enough because despite some precautions the turmoil among the Devotees did not go unnoticed. People thought they heard lamentations for the dead during an unusual ceremony in the House of Great Ancestors. Moreover, a hunter happened to catch sight of them at the Dongdwo swamp.

Other details slowly leaked in and the whole story, not changed too much in its circulation among the people ended up reaching the Queen. She had nothing to add to what they said. She just nodded knowingly. She even smiled. But just a little, then turned gloomy because she hated such dramas. These Devotees were crazy and conceited enough to push one of their own to suicide! Oh, what punishment ruthless! But there was no talk of the measures taken by the invisible for the Crystal Sanctuary.

Hé-Nark, unrelenting in his opinion about the Devotees, grumbled that it was a pity they all hadn't gone through it.

The event had its use in the meaning that it put a halt to the external ambitions of the Devotees. Afterwards, they turned inward, focusing on their secret side without causing any trouble or scandal outside.

Ta knew very well that this would not last. They would reawaken sooner or later, in one way or another. It all depended on the reactions of everyone else and on other events, which was always hard to foresee.

But she trusted her mysterious alliances. They asked her to buy time, to hold on, to stay brave until… She did not know until what. She obeyed. That was all. The slightest breach of her cherished principles destroyed her peace and she could not bear the offense.

The Devotees, therefore, focused all their ambitions on their T'Lo whose delicate nature caused them grave concerns because some of them, even though they were not uncultivated Ananou and their owners showered them with attention, still they became sluggish and died, too often to the liking of the devout.

The death of a T'Lo before its normal lifespan was always dishonorable to the Chamber of Men it belonged to. That was tradition. A love slave ought to enjoy life and happiness. They tended to think that a T'Lo died only from lack of attention and, above all, lack of affection.

The families that suffered this misfortune saw the word OL'T (T'Lo backwards) added to their name as a sign of suspicion and disgrace. They were suspected of cruelty. In Kobor Tigan't it was the worst stigma! Moreover, in such cases, the fact of having to admit to being a OL'T, which made even non-Devotees wince in contempt, was in itself punishment enough.

175

Before the reign of the White Ooh'Rou it was the queen's responsibility to decide these cases, adding or subtracting to the punishment. But now it had already changed a little.

The Devotees, because of the exceptional state of things, decided to abolish the custom. It was no longer required for the like-minded to disgrace themselves. The silent conspiracy against Ta's power united them.

They strove, therefore, to prevent these deaths, to heal the sick and especially to stop their proliferation because when a T'Lo died all the other T'Lo in its group had a tendency to sink into the same lethargy. So, they isolated the affected T'Lo and took greater, special care of them, mainly based on a diet of Dongdwo eggs, which had always been reserved for the noble caste but proved so invigorating for the T'Lo that it was like a miraculous cure bringing them back to life from the verge of an imminent death!

Thus, they stuffed sick T'Lo full of them. Getting these treats became a heroic act that the fanatical temperament of the Devotees raised to the level of an action of holy rebellion against the power of the White Ooh'Rou.

Some clever Devotees managed to get into some of the cellars in Kob'Lâm where the stores of these eggs had been put away for poor seasons. They took just enough and shrewdly enough that for a long time nobody suspected anything.

It was hard indeed to get the eggs from the source now because the Dongdwo swamp was being watched ever since they had found a Devotee badge near traces of their plundering. The regular egg hunters, like the other hunters who continued to give all they caught to the public storerooms of Kobor Tigan't, despised the Devotees because they had stopped obeying this custom; they hunted and gathered selfishly, keeping everything for themselves without ever contributing anything to the good of others.

Obviously, in this case especially, the Devotees protested against their being marginalized by the Queen. Well, since they were being excluded from public affairs, they didn't feel obliged to restock the provisions! Therefore, they let the food rot at their doorsteps every day when it was left by the royal officials and they said they were providing for themselves. Faced with this stubbornness it did not take long for Ta to stop sending them food. Starting from that moment they lived in complete independence. Their domains gradually changed into segregated camps where no one but their own kind entered.

The public curiosity about them grew steadily over the cycles of Ooh'R.

They were still free to move around. Only Kob'R and the Palace were off limits to them. But they rarely mixed with the people. They had become scornful, more than before, of everyone who did not pledge them allegiance and whom they called "the crass".

They never followed any new trends that over time were changing the ways of Kobor Tigan't, spurred on by the innovating drive of Ta. On the contrary, they held fast to the old ways so firmly that they were quickly antiquated compared to the other Giants who were wearing less heavy, less dark clothes, eating differently, talking and walking with more energy, adopting attitudes often copied from the Ooh'Rou whose influence everyone felt to the point that the beautiful women used ointments prepared by Gan'd to have lighter skin like Ta.

The jewelry was lighter, less bulky, more intricate. They decorated the front of their houses with garlands of flowers and leaves. Their perfumes were less heady…

But the Devotees closed their world to all outside influence and they became fossilized.

In the name of Tradition, distorted in their view, they lived in a persistent Yesterday. They became a burdensome obstacle against which the flowing river of life crashed as it rushed towards other tomorrows.

In trying to be custodians of Tradition, in their plans to ruin the innovative Queen, they cluttered their minds with dead ideas. All the psychic corpses of a bygone age fascinated them.

The Devotees were unrelenting! They ignored time. No, they would not change. As proof they wore only heavy clothes that eventually became a mark of their Sect more than a memory of outdated fashion.

They became pompous, religiously apathetic, excessive in everything, always too much or too little. From the collective, orgiastic drunkenness to the funeral debacles for a dead T'Lo, they swung from one extreme to another. And for them, who could not take one step without their gobs of jewelry banging together, it was the height of refinement and the superior behavior of an elite far above the rabble!

Among them the families judged their degree of nobility on the number of T'Lo owned. The erotic skill of these T'Lo added a nuance of "holiness", more or less exalted, to the families. Whence the extraordinary competition of mysticism in the love cells built inside their House of Great Ancestors up and down the nave.

The Devotees claimed that Ooh'R himself had sent the T'Lo to humans so that through the intervention of these instruments of love, stewards of "The Long Climax", they might reach a state of solar communion whose blessings would fall back upon the rest of their community.

The principle might have been very useful in the distant past, in a different context, in very primitive devotions. But was it really? Nothing was less sure. And yet the Devotees took it as their fundamental principle.

So, they cultivated their T'Lo like luxurious plants. They protected them from anything tiring or irritating. They showered them with care and attention. In the morning every family bathed their T'Lo in front of everyone. They rubbed them with scented oils used only on them. After that they held long discussions about what jewelry to wear for the day. Once this work of art was ready they stepped back and cried out in admiration all throughout the house. Then the families visited one another to wonder at these precious beloved ones!

Everything the T'Lo did or did not do was worthy of praise. All their behavior had a secret meaning, innuendos, mysterious messages. Telepathic communication with them became commonplace among the Devotees.

It was easy for the T'Lo to enter the human mind and make themselves understood. The symbiosis became tighter. With such treatment the humanimals became more refined, obviously. But they were also perverted more than before. Their originally gentle and tolerant character lost its humility. They had whims that had to be satisfied no matter how absurd they were if one did not want to be reprimanded by the entire Sect!

The T'Lo became greedier than ever for human love. A living, intelligent drug, a parasite whose roots, tendrils and barbs sank deeper into the human tree!

Little by little, very aware of their influence, they started enjoying the torments of passion they affected so easily. A fluttering eyelid, a little pout and the families were shattered, accusing one another of cruelty and above all of "lack of love"!

The T'Lo loved the ritual devotions of the House of Great Ancestors that pushed some to the sacrifice called "The Grand Act", that is voluntary suicide by erotic exhaustion.

Eventually only T'Lo Dê, who lived apart in the Palace, with his exceptional destiny, stayed like the T'Lo of old, meaning humble, good and truly loving. All the others of his species changed into vain, per-verse, spoiled pets, dilettantes of disturbance, insatiable and possessive.

For, they made their owners understand that they would only die if they did not get enough affection. When the Devotees heard this, they hit the ceiling, they beat their breasts for not having seen this before! So, they loved them harder, to excess, which became a sign of the real psy-chic slavery of the Devotees. It was what the T'Lo demanded. They died less often since to survive they were finally rooted right into the sapwood of the human tree.

As a result, the hold over the Devotees was irreversible. All their aspirations were reduced to one common denominator: the T'Lo!

They dreamed of the Age of T'Lo. Of the T'Lo-Sun. Of many ridic-ulous and foolish things.

In the end they became dangerous because madness is contagious, excess is explosive and aberrant eroticism taxes the ever-unsatisfied hu-man imagination with the deceptive lure of hypnotic mirages...

Kobor Tigan't, without knowing it, was brewing in its depths the most pernicious peril of its long history.

CHAPTER XIII

R'Ang's childhood was hard, full of unforeseen setbacks, sometimes almost chaotic, and Dê-Ta'Am's was no less so. She was inseparable from him, lived at his side, like his twin, under the over-indulgent shadow of T'Lo Dê, which the palace court tried to restrain, but unsuccessfully because of the strong and special ties between the two children.

But whereas R'Ang, in fact, was always drawn to the light and to the elevation of his being, Dê-Ta'Am, on the contrary, with experience (not all good), plunged headlong into the darkest shadows where her instincts for pleasure and possession could flourish.

Very early on, therefore, she was an evil spirit for R'Ang whom he could not, sadly, live without because she spiced everything up and there was never an end to adventures with her!

It must be said the R'Ang hated dullness. His personality needed to be surprised. Thanks to Dê-Ta'Am's particular talent, always complicating things, stimulation was never lacking. The worst mischief he got into was always stirred up if not cooked up by Dê-Ta'Am.

For a long time he seemed unable to say no to her in anything. She pushed and prodded him to try everything, to see everything, to dare everything. She constantly aroused his already excitable sense of freedom. So, he wanted to do everything and nothing could really hold him back.

Maybe after all it was necessary for him to gain such experience? Ta thought so as she watched over him. Powerful souls have to try everything, sure, to their own peril in order to know later (having ignored nothing in this game of life) how to judge wisely the value of things and not be fooled by mere appearances?

With this in mind, R'Ang received a truly royal education in the highest sense of the word! Without knowing it the perverse little hand that pushed him to the verge of all possible abysses played the role of a fearless guide. His whole childhood was a kind of initiation, a journey through pitfalls, dangers, temptations and terrors. Dê-Ta'Am kept the fire burning throughout the odyssey they ventured on together.

If R'Ang did not crumble in all the corrosion from the shadows that Dê-Ta'Am enjoyed exploring, he owed it to his personal stability. His inner metal was thus forged. Everything was a hammering blow against him destined to test his resilience and moral fiber, which made him stronger and never broke him.

His inner self could have fallen apart many times because of the whims of the adorable demon, his shadow, beloved in her way, and all-consuming, that Dê-Ta'Am who wanted to make him like her while he kept trying to make her more like him.

From their earliest age there was a passionate struggle between them. Which of the two would have the greater influence over the other?

Ata-Rèé, Hé-Nark and Gan'd watched over these two children in different roles. They all went through the many surprises, speculations and worries. It had the result, over time, of uniting the three of them. They met and talked so often about the children and suffered so many turmoils in their own lives that their mutual respect and affection created strong bonds between them. They were soon as close-knit as a family around Ta because of R'Ang and Dê-Ta'Am. As for Ta, she felt more torments than the three of them put together!

Luckily, difficulties were her passion. More than anything she loved trying to understand the weird and wild and she enjoyed fixing problems. It was a kind of triumph, even if mostly hidden and silent. All alone she enjoyed the greater rewards of the occult victories. "The mover, the useful and the real are generally invisible. What becomes visible and what people usually rally around in awe is just a tiny part of the royal work." That was what she told herself.

As expected, R'Ang and Dê-Ta'Am, up until puberty, provided her with many an opportunity to practice her talents of sympathy, understanding, patience and also authority because she never failed to put her foot down when called for.

She could wait out situations that alarmed and the panicked others into wanting to interfere. She calmly explained to them that there was no danger and the lesson learned from the experience, as hard as it might be, was more valuable to the children than a useless punishment halfway through!

Indeed, she was right. R'Ang and Dê-Ta'Am remembered the disasters they caused or that happened to them much more than punishments suffered for a short time before regaining their freedom.

R'Ang was not a real rascal; he was truly charming. His apparent mischief was often just an intense desire for an immediate gratification. He could not stand waiting. Still less putting something off until later. When he figured it was the time to act, he felt a little scandalized if an adult tried to stop him. An experience delayed or diluted threw him into a rage that astonished even him but that he was powerless to control.

These fits delighted Dê-Ta'Am who adored the violence. The older she got, the more thrilled she got, laughing and crying, her eyes sparkling as she leapt around R'Ang in a kind of frenzied and already sensual jig. Sometimes she joined in with his anger. Then they became two wild animals who had to be tamed before they collapsed exhausted and hoarse from all their stomping and screaming. In these extreme cases Hé-Nark stepped in. He rarely touched R'Ang. Knowing the cause he usually grabbed Dê-Ta'Am instead and dragged her away despite her scratching and hollering. She, however, calmed down very quickly, turning her fury into laughter. She submitted to the Master Guard's authority. Then she uttered such beguiling babble, trying to charm him with all the cunning of her immature femininity.

Hé-Nark shook his head, a little stern but forgiving. He did not forget the prophecies of Ata-Réè and wondered what disasters would result from this child who was too precociously gifted and sometimes had an almost frightening amount of energy.

Indeed, Dê-Ta'Am seemed tireless. She slept little, like the T'Lo, and no doubt knew, naturally, another kind of rest that calmed her down occasionally, with here big eyes open as she sucked in all the lifeblood of those around her. The Master Guard had seen it happen many times. He had seen how her cheeks got color back while the people around her started yawning.

So, he knew all about her and felt a strange mix of interest and aversion for her. His interest not on an emotional level. She piqued his curiosity. An enigma. He wanted to get ahead of her, in some way, before she was fully developed, to curb the blossoming evil at the right moment. That was why he always wanted to know what she was up to.

The little tease quickly figured out that she was seducing Hé-Nark. She loved to disrupt his duty to the Queen because she was jealous of Ta. But she did not succeed very often. It was hard since she still feared the Master Guard, as pompous as she was, and a glare from those gray eyes was sometimes enough to send her running, which made her curse later when her fury turned the froth on her lips very red.

On the other hand, Hé-Nark showered tender loving care on R'Ang. He answered in kind, just like with Gan'd and Ata-Réè who earned his great affection and could share, on the melancholy days, his daydreams.

But the love of his soul, before he really understood it, was entirely for Ta and her majesty that he always treated with absolute respect. Dê-Ta'Am did not dare to mock the Queen in his presence because he laid into her for it even when she cried later about how badly he hurt her.

Beneath R'Ang's gentleness was always hiding this violence, which he took great pains to control the older he got because he quickly saw the damage that this violence could do.

It was obvious that the opposite natures of Angel and Opak carried on in him. He was their heir. Their conflicts had not been resolved. R'Ang gradually turned into a kind of closed arena where the battle of influences sought closure.

This lasted until he found out about himself. He had to constantly overcome these vestiges to preserve only the constructive principles, purified of their dross. In this state of constantly working on himself he suffered a lot. It often reached the point of inner torture. But he did not want to admit it, even though it did not escape the Queen's notice. She guessed it and show him great compassion, which he was grateful for, without needing to say so in the silent pact between them because they were both very modest about expressing emotions.

Progress was not made in a day. Far from it. Pulled in two directions, R'Ang was continually swinging back and forth from one pole to another, finding no balance or peace with these two inseparable conditions. Sometimes Angel with his lofty graces rose up and other times it was Opak who drown him with her surging vitality, her arrogance, her massive naivety and her terrible appetites. As a result, one never knew how he was going to act in any given situation.

Dê-Ta'Am took too much pleasure in pushing him from one extreme to another. Which only made things worse. He himself realized this even as a child.

Subjected to these forces, R'Ang was like a storm system: sometimes he brooded and grumbled, heaping his thoughts into black clouds, sometimes he exploded, spluttered, blazed and bellowed, raining panic and disaster all around him, and sometimes he seemed utterly drowned in sorrow. All this because he hated to get upset but he did anyway.

He was sincerely sorry every time. Without knowing him, just by looking at him, one would think it was the last time he would have to repent. But Dê-Ta'Am whispered in his ear and it started all over again!

Ta and Ata-Réè lost hope, more than once, of educating him, of ever managing to unify his impetuous character, all mood swings and sudden impulses and then abrupt and total reversals.

It was always excess! When R'Ang pouted or was sad, one never knew how long the gloominess would last. It might last a few moments or days even weeks on end. In the latter case his health declined and Ta told Gan'd who came with fruit, herbs and roots to help his body tolerate the purge of all its heavy elements.

Then R'Ang sank into a world of contemplation that led him to surprising feats of self-control. He organized his thoughts and feelings. He would sigh a lot like someone waking up from a bad dream. He gazed at the trees, the sky, faced up to nature mildly and generally showed a welcome interest in everything around him. He sat with his teachers for longer. These were the happy moments for Ata-Réè, Hé-Nark and of course for Ta whom ha practically never left, staying by her side all day long, a discreet witness to all her royal activities.

Gentleness and charm would exhale their tender plumes from him. Everyone was won over! It was not really peace but its fragile beginnings—"the peaceful". R'Ang looked wreathed by a touch of sadness that fit well his slender form. His hair was melancholy—gently wavy. His weird hands with the little finger long than the others traced the mysterious gestures that only Angel could make.

Ata-Réè was silent when watching him without his knowing. And she turned a little pale with a faint smile on her lips.

During these periods R'Ang absorbed lots of wisdom and, truth to tell, made up for lost time.

Dê-Ta'Am did not like these periods to last too long because she did not want to participate in the enthusiasm he showed and from which she felt excluded. And also the irony and hint of pity she spied in the eyes of Hé-Nark got on her nerves.

Angry at no longer being R'Ang's intimate ally and thus being pushed to the side in a kind of humiliating neighbor, she tried every which way to get his attention. He had to remember she was there instead of staying like this, like an idiot, talking about the sun, stars and moon with adults!

So, she whizzed around him, goading him, buzzing all kinds of absurdities out loud, pricked with wicked laughter.

R'Ang ended up snubbing her. He treated her like a scary Aâz and comparing her to those dangerous plants that are deadly for lost travelers.

184

He said she was like them, soft, sticky, cold and perfectly detestable! Which, however, was completely wrong because Dê-Ta'Am with her red mane of hair and her sparkling eyes was more like fire and all the burning passions.

But the insult hit harder than hoped for. It always worked and R'Ang, relieved but with a malicious twinkle in his eye, watched the defeated enemy run away.

Dê-Ta'Am put her fists up to her mouth to hold in the screams. He ran off to some corner but never stayed long. She always sneaked back to linger around nearby. Of course, it was just to wait for a new opportunity to bother the boy. It was also, above all, because she could not stand being kept away from him in any way at all.

Unfortunately for R'Ang, he was not yet able to assimilate any of the received wisdom for long. It vanished abruptly when Dê-Ta'Am, the shrewd one, saw a breach in his defenses, grabbed his hand and dragged him off to other adventures, always dangerous and sometimes scandalous.

They groaned in the Palace as they prepared to confront all the consequences of a new cycle starting over again for R'Ang!

He got goofy, loud, lazy, vane, greedy. He stuffed himself with food until his belly swelled, wore luxurious clothes and loaded himself with so much jewelry that he wobbled under their weight. Dê-Ta'Am egged him on, delighting in all these quirks.

The two children stood together against everyone, making decrees and giving orders. They mainly tyrannized T'Lo Dê whose kindness lasted all the way until he figured the moment was right to submerge them in hypnotic sleep, which was a welcome relief to everyone around.

When his mood soon swung back, R'Ang turned suddenly solemn, silent and sophisticated. He ate little, three fruits and some herbs, slimmed down gracefully, kept an eye out for birds in the sky, listened effortlessly to the perennial music of the spaces where Ata-Réè drew her inspiration. He grew pale, refused the most modest of accessories and stopped laughing.

Then he forgot everything to go off skipping, running and jumping, to dive into the big waterfall, no matter what season, if he felt like it. Still wet, he strolled around in the wind but never got sick.

Dê-Ta'Am did the same, heroically, his rival in recklessness. They often ran away together. The Guards, then, had to find them. They locked them up for short time in the vain hope of keeping them in check, but

T'Lo Dê could not stand feeling their unhappiness and quickly set them free.

R'Ang, therefore, suffered everything, in his own way. They could not break him. But when a little emotion affected him, when a little worry over a dear one hit him, he suddenly took fever—he shivered and cried and his teeth chattered.

If Ta appeared a little too cold, too busy, for example, to have time for him, then it was like he was struck by lightning. Slow tears dripped silently down his cheeks. Dê-Ta'Am, who lacked this sensitivity, always just stood there gaping.

It did not take many disappointments like this to sink him into total despair. He stopped talking, stopped showing up. When they worried about his absence they found him curled up on his bed, deaf to their appeals. He looked like he had given up on life. At these moments Dê-Ta'Am wept, begging him to answer, completely mortified at the thought of losing him forever.

Despite R'Ang's sensitivity Ta never forgot that it was necessary to be firm with him. And when he became too obnoxious, she hit him so stoutly that he could never dodge this kind of punishment in time.

R'Ang, in such cases, tried to justify his actions with a flood of jabbering because he did not like the Queen to think he was wrong. But he always said, with great dignity, rubbing the still red cheek or hand, "You're the only one I'll take that from, Ooh'Rou of Kobor Tigan't, since you can never be wrong!"

With real affection he fell at her feet and begged her to explain why she was so naughty. He thought to himself that he rather liked being hit by her...

And Dê-Ta'Am, who caught these thoughts, reluctantly sat near Ta, but she tried to rub dirt on her clothes without being seen. R'Ang saw. And then there were no more tender words! He lunged at the terrorized guilty girl who usually managed to escape. And the two children disappeared, one chasing the other, cursing furiously all through the Palace.

Dê-Ta'Am only got safe with T'Lo Dê who knew how to assuage R'Ang's anger. He held the two children and cradled them together until they calmed down and felt like little babies again before falling to sleep.

Until they reached puberty, which unleashed different kinds of incidents for them, the two children had some notorious adventures. It was always Dê-Ta'Am who was the architect and advocate. R'Ang jumped right in to do it.

As for T'Lo Dê, he was a limitless, tireless collaborator. He knew all kinds of ways to get around the prohibitions. His hyper-sense served marvelously! He encouraged, therefore, the worst escapades and took part in them with obvious pleasure.

Less obedient than ever, he liked to do his own thing and so he joined in on all the childish pranks. He became arrogant and promised himself exclusively to Dê-Ta'Am and R'Ang.

Sometimes Ta scolded him severely. He did not argue with her. But it was worse since nothing lasted because he agreed, gave all the polite signs of being truly sorry, except that he forgot it all as soon as he left the room.

The Queen ended up ordering the Guards to follow the children at a distance, to watch them without being seen and only interfere in cases of real danger.

T'Lo Dê undoubtedly knew they were there but he never did any-thing about it. Their presence did not bother him. He figured there was no use telling R'Ang, who would definitely feel mortified by the protec-tion. As for Dê-Ta'Am, although she sometimes suspected something, she never discovered anything—the Guards were clever!

And so R'Ang set out on expeditions around the realm. With his companion and his T'Lo he went everywhere, hunted, climbed, ran and splashed around, too, because he loved the water—there was no river, waterfall or pond where he did not soak himself at least once.

Dê-Ta'Am fanned his fires and sought more. She liked danger and, as fearless as she was, she always figured out how to push the limits of their adventures. But beyond her rebellious spirit and her taste for anar-chic freedom, she liked these things because they opposed the legitimate authority of Ta over R'Ang.

With real ferociousness she envied their emotional bond and above all the respect for the Ooh'Rou shown by the boy. She had no fear of vy-ing with the Queen. In fact, she rose up as an adversary, determined to triumph one day!

It was surprising to see how cleverly this child, by pure instinct, could plan it so that her companion was always doing the opposite of what Ta asked. She managed to always keep him at odds.

She was madly hoping to make him despicable. Then, maybe, Ta would shut her door! And he would be all alone, cast off. He would live only with Dê-Ta'Am and T'Lo Dê. And when he grew up, he would go and kill the Ooh'Rou... Every time she went to this place in her reverie the girl paused. Wouldn't it be so much better to save the exhilarating act for her alone?

Dê-Ta'Am had refused once and for all to obey the Queen. The only family, the only parent, the only bond she recognized was T'Lo Dê. She knew that he could be everything for her. But in servitude. Whereas R'Ang always had to be vanquished. She wanted him on her side. She already had T'Lo Dê. She was striving to vanquish R'Ang. She had to do it. She loved him. She wanted him to be her future triumph.

Needless to say, during her whole childhood, these were only reactions reflecting the secrets of her subconscious. They rose up to her conscious mind by slow degrees, transforming gradually into coherent thoughts. In any case, she was soon able to evaluate the issue and order all her thoughts around this goal: to beat Ta and win R'Ang.

Therefore, she railed and rebelled against Ta or she cringed, pouted, brooded, but always aggressive, whatever the circumstances, however indulgent the Queen was.

At the time she was still almost a baby and R'Ang too. But his reaction caused the rebel in her to stop when he had pushed her off the terrace! She owed her life to the quick thinking of Hé-Nark who was able to save her in time.

The incident worried everyone. They saw bad omens in it.

For Ta it was a pall of gloom, she was devastated.

For Ata-Réè it confirmed her foreboding suspicions.

Hé-Nark, who shared her opinions and who, like her, was always anticipating trouble for the queen, told her that the direct enemy was living next to her, hiding under cover of that fragile, child's shell. Dê-Ta'Am was the danger, which would grow in proportion along with her...

Ata-Ré, Hé-Nark and Gan'd too discreetly tightened their vigilance around the Queen.

The chaotic state of R'Ang worried them as well. But they all felt that the day would come when the nobility and especially the predestination of the boy would triumph over all the upheavals of his personality and he would emerge like a sun from this molten paste that he was now.

Dê-Ta'Am never forgot her fall from the terrace. What struck her was less the fear than the grievous surprise at having been assaulted by her companion, thus revealing by this pure reflex where his real heart was heading.

Not against R'Ang but against Ta she held a grudge that clung on silently since she could never openly talk about it.

She also became jealous—burning with fever!—of the evening trysts that R'Ang had more and more often with Ta. Over the years he became so fond of them that the anticipation could interrupt their playing. It often happened that in the middle of wandering in nature he would run back, out of breath, in order not to miss a meeting, as if his life depended on it. Nothing could hold him back. Dê-Ta'Am would trot furiously alongside him, swearing to lead them farther away next time.

But this emotional submission to Ta did not go so far as to bridle the boy's mischief. It was not going to stop him gobbling up Dongdwo eggs, which he got away with stealing even though he almost got stuck in the swamp countless times. It was not going to stop him either from bringing back to the Palace, to everyone's fright, an armful of Aâz leaves, those dangerous, vegetal intelligences that no man risked challenging alone but that he picked as innocently as could be without the slightest harm while the Guards assigned to his safety hid nearby trying to muster enough courage to stop him!

This exploit was the talk of the town throughout the Cities. They started keeping a close eye on this extraordinary child because his adventures always seemed to conceal a secret meaning that they tried to decipher.

Ta did not complain, she just asked R'Ang how he managed to pick the leaves. He answered that he had seen a big crystal cloud above the Aâz and he went in to pick the leaves—a cloud like the ones in the House of Great Faces but a lot bigger.

Thus Ta learned that the child could naturally see what was reserved for an elite. She understood that the crystalline formations were protecting him.

After this she was a lot less scared for him. She knew she could have confidence. Nothing seriously bad would ever happen to him. This certainty would help her later because no matter how bad things got she kept this unbreakable faith in her heart. She also noticed, on careful questioning, that Dê-Ta'Am did not see the crystal formations.

Gan'd took great interest in examining the Aâz leaves. She discovered a corrosive sap of rare penetrating power and decided to find a useful application for it. Her inner voice soon told her how and at the same time Ata-Reé transmitted a message from the Angel Crystal saying, "It is the plant that sways the stone". She found out that stones soaked for a long time with these leaves became soft and pliable like clay but will harden again in time. They used this malleable stone afterward. It lightened the work of the sculptor while making it easier for him to work. This technique also allowed more precision in the art of building, making blocks fit perfectly together.

They only had to take precautions against corrosion in the preparation. Here, too, Gan'd found an ointment to protect the workers' hands.

They agreed that R'Ang's mischief often had a beneficial side.

One day he claimed he saw the foul birds up close, the ones called "Them" out of disgust (which was the same as giving them no name). To do this he went down at night into the carrion gulch where the birds slept. What he saw, what he did there nobody really knows but when he got back in the morning he requested, like an adult, a meeting with Ta.

Very seriously he told her that those birds had a name, that they had told him and it was only right that from now on they be called by it! It was passed through the Cities. They repeated the name. It worked. "Them" rose in rank by finally getting a name. They were the Krakoak.

But R'Ang had brought back from his expedition such a persistent stench that they literally had to bathe him in perfume. The whole thing went to his head.

He acted crazy. He was seized with uncontrollable mad laughter after a wild escapade when he started climbing on the golden sphere of Kob'Ooh'R where he used the votive banners like vines to swing down.

Ta was livid. Hé-Nark thundered. Ata-Réè looked stone cold.

The inhabitants of the Cities huddled together and looked up at the terraces. The Blacksmiths had stopped working. They all considered it a great scandal. R'Ang had really gone too far!

Dê-Ta'Am, who had obviously pushed him into this last stunt, slunk away to hide.

But T'Lo Dê jumped in and swept up R'Ang before he landed with such extraordinary dexterity and dignity that angry crowd just gaped in awe before doubling over with laughter.

There was a place, however, where R'Ang never allowed any nonsense at all. It was the House of Great Faces. From the time he could walk Ta took him there because he was generally believed that the transcendent presence of his Father was in the Crystal. They told him.

He attended the ceremonies. He loved them right away, his face turned solemn and sunny, almost transfigured, while Dê-Ta'Am cried in a corner.

Thereafter he himself asked to go there so that when he was bigger, educated by Hé-Nark and Ata-Réè who taught him as the Queen ordered, he was able to participate in the rite, not as a spectator but as celebrant, as the Sacred Son of the Crystal.

He played his part to perfection, in the middle and in front of everyone, with a majesty that enlightened all.

Ta often saw the crystal formation gather over him like a dome. She knew that he saw them too since he admitted it to her. But she was surprised to notice that he never spoke to Dê-Ta'Am about it even though she was forced against her will to go with him to the House of Great Faces where she suffered through the ceremony gloomily watching the door.

Ta realized that he had secret wisdom to call upon for things that were truly important. The crystal forms were one of those things.

Still, even though he had a privileged place in the ceremony they did not yet let R'Ang up on the platform of the Great Crystal, which was reserved for Ata-Réè. Respecting the sacred, he did not try to break this rule but took, for example, long meditation breaks in front of the different Faces.

He often stayed after the ceremony or when he was passing by the House he would enter as if answering a sudden call. Dê-Ta'Am got impatient and pulled his arm.

"Leave me alone!" he got impatient in turn. "Can't you see they're talking to me?"

She grumbled, shrugged her shoulders and pretended that he was lying to show off. "Bah," she huffed, "they're just rocks! They're all empty inside!"

"For you maybe," R'Ang shot back.

Feeling like an idiot, like a nobody, she ran off crying all the way into the ever-ready arms of T'Lo Dê who always found a way to reconcile the two children afterwards. For, it was unbearable for him to see them separated. He felt like he was the living "bond" of their union.

Finally, tired of being humiliated, the girl swore she would get R'Ang into real trouble. One day when they were alone in the House of Great Faces she lashed out at his pride.

"You think you're so important! Well, I don't believe it! If you were, the Ooh'Rou would already have said that the very noble R'ang should be on the platform like Ata-Réè since it's his father inside the Crystal!"

R'Ang stood there agape. He had not thought of this.

The blow was dealt.

He swallowed hard after glancing over at the Crystal, dimly luminous up in the darkness. Then he looked at the nearest Face as if to have a witness to his confusion.

"I don't have the right," he squeaked.

"Why not?" Dê-Ta'Am stuck out her tongue.

He was fidgeting, "I promised. I can't go up there. My Father is the greatest mystery of the realm."

"Stupid idiot!" she snapped back and then mocked, "You promised! You can't! The greatest mystery, ha!"

"It's the Queen who said I can't..."

"The Queen! What else? Admit that you're scared! You're scared that there's nothing there!"

He turned red and shook his head no, no. He was sweating, rattled, not wanting to look like a coward or to break his promise. And yet, if there was nothing?

Well played by his demon! After this good start she let loose with all her energy, teasing and nagging him with jeering darts. She danced around him like a little flame, her red hair ablaze and then extinguished as she passed through the light into shade and back again.

A few days before she had been reckless enough to climb up alone, secretly, onto the platform. She got scared and did not stay long as she felt herself enveloped in an eerily constricted atmosphere. She had seen nothing interesting in the Crystal except some thing clouded by a mysterious mist *inside*. For her there was nothing.

This phenomenon that hid Angel from view sometimes happened and for Ata-Réè it meant it was not a good time to communicate.

Dê-Ta'Am had touched nothing before scrambling back down pretty fast. She was annoyed but relieved (without admitting it) to get back on the ground. She still stuck to her opinion! She did not see the crystalline formations gathering around her. But the sudden panic that made her run away had no other cause...

For now she kept dancing around R'Ang, "Wimp, flunky, lower than a Krakoak, you're as dumb as a Mouh-Tou and as ugly as a Dongdwo when you do nothing! You disgust me. They're hiding something from you. Ata-Réè in league with the Queen is keeping it all for herself. And you don't have the right, ha! They won't let you go because they think you can't handle it! There's no Father of yours in the Crystal!"

She had hit the mark.

R'Ang turned pale. "Who says so?"

"The Queen of course. She said the baby R'Ang would die of disappointment. So, you see, you're just a baby. Without a Father!"

R'Ang jumped. "Shut up! Don't move. I'm going."

She was reveling. She knew that Ata-Réè would arrive soon. The boy would be caught red-handed!

R'Ang had run straight up the steps. He was alone with the Crystal. The oblong thing was glowing faintly. He felt good, reassured. His angry excitement faded away, leaving him relieved and relaxed. He took a deep breath. He had completely forgotten about everything that was not this Crystal and especially about the nasty remarks of Dê-Ta'Am.

A trembling vibration like a fog of words came to him. His heart swayed with tenderness. Unable to resist, he lost his balance but he rose up. He was astonished but not scared.

He did not know where he was anymore. An exquisitely sweet radiance permeated him. He heard incomparable sounds. Still not understanding he nevertheless identified them as a speech addressed to him. He felt gentle grazes. They were welcoming touches, caresses. He smelled perfumes. And the starving hollow of his soul was thus fed.

In this state, he kept seeing before him the royal center of this universe: the Crystal. He did not look away because the mist was parting, gradually, from one end to the other like a thin gauze being pulled off.

R'Ang's heart was racing. He saw the marvelous Being that endured in the heart of the Great Crystal. He saw it and *he recognized it!*

Then he shouted with joy—it was all true!

Ineffable, unchanged, long, pale and blond, huge, under the soft folds of the white garment, Angel, the Beautiful Being, *his Father*, was showing himself...

R'Ang saw himself in him. At this moment he knew what he would *really* be later when he will have cast off the last remnants of the rough shell that was still giving him so much trouble.

Down below, Dê-Ta'Am could not understand his joyful shout. Vaguely worried about her plan she was stepping forward when Ata-Réè came in.

One glance was enough for her to understand everything. "You again!" she sounded menacing as she pointed at the girl.

The crystalline formations immediately gathered around Dê-Ta'Am who apparently saw nothing but suddenly passed out, dropped to the ground, while the Priestess hurried over to the platform.

When she reached the top she saw that the Crystal was exposed, that R'Ang was unharmed but he was immersed in ecstasy. Slow tears flowed out of his wide-open eyes. He was babbling incoherently but sometimes uttering this refrain:

"The same hands! Hands like mine!"

To give him stronger contact Ata-Réè stood behind him, wrapped her arms around him and put his hands on the Crystal.

R'Ang emerged from the radiance and *he saw his Father standing in front of him.*

He knew that Ata-Réè was helping him. All three of them were inside an ovum whose crystallinity was like a diamond.

"Approach, my Son, my only son, my beautiful child, approach! Oh, I recognize you. You delight my sight. You are already beautiful even though you still have some heavy terrestrialities from the body that your mother gave you. But the marks of our celestial origin are on you. It's up to you to release them. So, nothing has been lost. I couldn't know because I was too obscured, but you will do it. And much more... You must grow up, of course! But from now on I will advise you."

R'Ang felt the hand of the Beautiful Being touch him, "Come, let me consecrate you, my Son!"

The boy felt faint but Ata-Réè helped him up.

Something opened up over their heads. A ray came and touched R'Ang in the heart while the voice of the Beautiful Being said, "Receive my Promise! Receive, ahead of time, the royal secret. It will sleep in you until you have fully developed as a man. Then *we will come closer*. And a predestination will come out of you that will be like a bridge between Kobor Tigan't and the distant future."

The silhouette of the Beautiful Being faded but his voice, though thinning, still reached R'Ang's hearing.

"Remember this well: Ata-Réè is the spouse of my soul, so through it I will talk to her often. On earth she is the double of the very excellent Ta who is the mother of your soul. Remember these things well, my Son! They will lead you to your lofty destiny. But don't forget that nothing is

194

gained without hardship and silence is like the lid of a vase that keeps perfume from evaporating."

Everything got blurry in R'Ang's vision. He felt like he was fainting and very quickly coming down while everything around him turned dark. But the final words of his Father kept whispering in him:

"Don't talk about our meeting. Except to the Queen, the Priestess and the Master Guard. They have been chosen to help you. Don't let them down. Go. Be happy. Fulfill yourself. I am close by in the luminous pathos that forms the direct lining of your material life…"

An awful shiver ran through R'Ang. He was wet, like after a birth, in the arms of Ata-Réè. The Great Crystal had turned milky again. Nothing of the Beautiful Being was visible any longer.

The boy staggered down from the platform like a drunk man. He was surprised to see Dê-Ta'Am apparently asleep. Ata-Réè picked her up and carried her to T'Lo Dê. The girl slept peacefully all night long and did not wake up until the next day.

She quickly realized that she had been robbed of the final phase of the adventure but she could not recall how. Her memory was a black hole. She remembered nothing after R'Ang running to the platform. Beyond that, nothing. What had happened?

She asked R'Ang but got nothing out of him except teasing about her talent for sleep. Happy to get a little vengeance for all her meanness, he only said that nothing had happened because he had run back to her when she dropped off to sleep and the Priestess arrived to help him with her.

Dê-Ta'Am guessed that he was hiding a mystery from her. She had been foiled! She did not calm down for a long time.

T'Lo Dê had an inkling of what happened. He had picked up some traces around R'Ang. But his faithful devotion to Angel kept him quiet. The contrary would have been bad. He did not want to upset the Beautiful Being. So, he shut off his brain to Dê-Ta'Am when she asked him as she usually did mind-to-mind.

"I don't know."

She wondered whether he, too, was lying. Why were they all betraying her? It was a hard time for her.

Giving up the questions, she managed more than once to sneak into the House of Great Faces alone. She never got far. As soon as she went through the door she felt nauseous, her guts revolted. Every time it was as if the inside of the place started wobbling and making her dizzy. She tried hard to fight it. She stepped in, rubbed her eyes to see clearly, but she would have to run outside to vomit. Every time it was the same, a failure, the longer she stayed the sicker she got. On her last attempt she thought she was going to die.

Defeated, she acquired an intense hatred of the place and never again went in. Nobody forced her. Therefore, she stopped attending the ceremonies. Instead she waited, sad, wandering around, until she could jump on R'Ang when he came out.

Baffled by his new seriousness she felt he was escaping her and she wanted to win him back every time.

She showed up pretty and graceful. At the end of every ceremony she started offering him little presents. She was in an enchanting mood. R'Ang, who felt it, was immediately happy and flattered. Life was making sense. He was finding importance in it. His companion's apparent tameness made him feel like he had power over her. He was touched by her attention and always gladly accepted her offerings.

Besides, because of his awakening sensuality he started to feel Dê-Ta'Am's carnal presence. Sooner than him, she realized the full extent of her hold over him in this matter. While R'Ang was still just smoldering embers she was already crackling and blazing, bright and bold.

Puberty opened up a new field of experiences for them.

Paradoxically, however, where Dê-Ta'Am kept seeing just games of power (her psyche remained childish even in the midst of the excess that later triggered irreparable actions) R'Ang, with his senses both excited and numbed, felt them more like a man and soon took things seriously, if not tragically. He became a fanatic for whom everything took on a sacred character. Everything, therefore, became fraught with consequences.

Dê-Ta'Am was a player. Everything for her was a game. She quickly learned to control a series of events in which she could blow hot and cold. The early and total awakening of her sexuality made her even more jealous of Ta. For, becoming aware of her own vast powers of seduction, she spotted Ta's, just as powerful but of a completely different quality.

She knew how beautiful the White Ooh'Rou was, strangely young, untouched by the years and utterly desirable. She caught men sneaking peeks at her. She saw through Hé-Nark's unspoken love for his sovereign and while dismissing the Master Guard she was afraid it was the same for R'Ang. But she knew that he was not yet there because he could not yet tell the difference and for the Queen he just had a strong, hazy feeling that habit made cozy.

For R'Ang, Ta was first and foremost the incomparable Ooh'Rou, then his true psychic mother, but also the sister of his mind since they fraternally united their thoughts.

He loved her clear physical beauty but he saw it as the manifestation of her royalty, her sacred veil. He did not yet feel anything sensual here but he was very interested in her apparel, telling her that he preferred her wearing this instead of that. Ta listened to him. He had good taste. He knew how to pick out the right clothes for the right occasion to make the right impression.

However, when he was next to her in their evening rendezvous he never let go of her hand, which he laid his cheek on while talking casually. Sometimes also when they were on the floor he hugged her legs and put his head on her knees. Ta looked at him. She caressed his head. A blurry image of To took the place of the boy's. She sighed, happy and unhappy.

When R'Ang left to go to sleep she looked at herself in a big, polished crystal plate fixed to a golden plate. In the solar ambiance of this mirror she saw that she was still young and whole. Had not many years gone by? She knew they had! All her royal projects and duties had crushed her on the inside, but it did not show on the outside.

And it would never show. She was sure of it. The balms of Gan'd gave her eternal youth. But was it only those balms?

In the eyes of all her Race a divine halo graced her now. They liked talking about it. It made them feel stable and proud. They forgot about the other plump and fleshy Ooh'Rous who ripened like fruit.

The reign of Ta was like an eternal spring.

This White Ooh'Rou lived a little outside of time. Thanks to her the Race of Giants at this mysterious juncture of two eras, leaving the first without really having entered the second, was living in a kind of untroubled, intermediate Age—the Crystal Era.

It was no longer the matriarchy but it was not a patriarchy. The women were no longer so heavily dominant. The men were gaining importance, discovering theirs every day, with restraint.

It was a harmonious balance, still waters, equal forces. Men and Women. Not really in couples—although there were examples that Ta held particularly dear and on whom she lavished honors—but in principle, there were already single men and single women discovering together what their mutual destiny might be.

So, beyond the first matriarchal source, the two parts of the Androgynous were waking up from a sleep of the unconscious and seeing each other, recognizing each other.

The White Ooh'Rou took it all upon herself, hovering over the Race, with her ambiguous youth in which her male will and female subtlety were united, the ideal government of the Androgynous.

But she knew that she was but an image and that this reign would not last...

CHAPTER XIV

The two children reached the threshold of adolescence and quickly blossomed into their adult stage.

Sexuality developed early in their life. With new appetites, other curiosities, different kinds of adventures and experiences began for them.

It caused a great deal of drama. Driven by their young loves they ignite all their latent passions and in the destiny of the Giant Race they played the role of triggers, the catalysts of events.

First we must speak of Dê-Ta'Am because it was at this time that the full significance of her presence really started to show.

She had become almost as big as R'Ang who, despite his tender age, was already as tall as Hé-Nark. She was beautiful, unquestionably, but a vicious beauty because it was all aggressive, violent and savage.

The first shock: her red hair, thick and messy, often tangled up, bespeaking an erotic but warped emanation.

The second shock: huge, piercing eyes, yellow like amber, sometimes waxy with wickedness, but then they would hide behind her almost black eyelids. Most of the time, however, they were shiny hard like metal—a kind of warrior gold—two shields that revealed, unmistakably, her exceptional pride.

And then there were all the other shocks: a moist, red mouth, venomous and voracious with its sharp teeth, much thinner than normal humans—a bold and brash mouth—full of curses and words of love, bitter and sweet, but also mercilessly ravenous for kisses. Whosoever got one was its victim!

Long legs allowed her to escape any prison and conversely to imprison all possible lovers. And who would not have submitted to those seductively long arms of an expert archer, which she was, by the way, having gained a diabolical proficiency with the bow that she owed to no teacher since, as everyone knows, she shirked all discipline.

Her hands were long, too. Her supple fingers could grab something but then never let go! Predatory hands. Loving hands, too, skilled at caressing, at loosening the bonds of reason to cast the prey into a frenzy of mad love.

She choose to be nude, with massive jewelry and gem-studded chains—which she did not hesitate to steal, from anywhere, to the great dismay of the Queen and her entourage who long ago had grown weary of punishing such a creature!—Dê-Ta'Am flaunted the inverted triangle of her power: at the top her two breasts with their two hard tips in glistening aureoles, and on the bottom the smooth vertical and double bulge of her sex, clearly visible, which the rare, thin fuzz never veiled in the least.

Made like this, vitalized like this, how could she not, at her young age, be the idol and hope of the Devotees who adored her so much that they never dared to stand in the way of her whims. They just implored her, with devoted patience, to consent to lead them in overthrowing the Queen and establishing the religion of the T'Lo. But she held off. She liked stirring things up but she did not really care about them. She took great pleasure in prolonging this game. Real obligations only half-smiled on her. She had plenty of time. It was so fun to taunt everyone!

What was the use of fully committing herself since she saw the Devotees whenever she wanted. They were always waiting for her. Through T'Lo Dê who had calmly kept his friendly relationship with T'Lo Gâ, Oda-Néè sent her messages, advice or invitations to participate in celebrations at their House of Great Ancestors.

She went or not, it depended... She especially liked to drag along R'Ang who, since childhood, was always reluctant to go. Torn between two desires, one of erotic curiosity and the other of obedience to the Queen, to whom he had never confessed these escapades (never found out thanks to the collaboration of T'Lo Dê's transcendent senses) he was tormented by remorse.

Dê-Ta'Am thoroughly enjoyed it. It added spice to her wicked joy. Outwitting the Queen—nothing was more flattering to her.

Oda-Néè knew this and kept trying to instill the desire for a more glaring triumph. But Dê-Ta'Am was still too young to fully understand. The game she was playing satisfied her vanity. Besides, despite the bad blood, the conflicts between her and the Ooh'Rou were still not serious enough to make her, for example, live permanently with the Devotees.

Ta was smart and self-controlled in her reactions. The young girl who had drawn away from her, willingly, had not spent much time with her, so she had few opportunities to provoke her. In a way, Dê-Ta'Am realized that she had been caught in her own trap by refusing to be intimate with this Ooh'Rou who was constantly hovering over her childhood and whose kindness had let her and T'Lo Dê not only survive but put them a privileged place.

Whether she liked it or not, she was subdued—for the time being—by Ta's finesse in giving her freedom, which prevented serious confrontations. She understood, of course, but since the idea of making a decision bothered her, she pretended not to think about it.

All the Devotees were informed by Oda-Néè and bemoaned the situation. They agreed that it could not last long because having gained strength and an organization in their confinement, they were aching, every day more and more, to destroy the limits imposed on them by Ta for too many Ooh'R cycles.

They were independent now. They had copied all of the Queen's achievements in derision. Not only did they have their "temple", the House of Great Ancestors, but also their artists and their B'Tah-Gous to glorify their religion and their Guards to defend them in case of attack.

The mystery surrounding them had attracted adepts from outside.

Some Giants had not got used to the new eroticism. Still intoxicated with the old "mana", infatuated with the nether regions of sexuality, they felt Ta's government was too stale to their liking. The kind of simplification by the light that she cast on them made them feel stripped bare. They got bored and believed the White Ooh'Rou was barren of love.

Well, the covert propaganda of the Devotees found fertile ground among them. Total love, outrageous love, perpetual ecstasy as well as the secrets of traditional power that they claimed to have inherited, the orgiastic rituals of the House of Great Ancestors, the beguiling lure of the T'Lo, all these attracted weak souls whose indecision had already pushed them into the wake of the evolutionary wave.

But this they did not know. Just like they did not know that a selection was being made, for a long time, throughout their Race and that only the strong would survive after bravely stepping off the beaten path. The old plants of the Race of Giants were depleted and their sap was slow. Before being withering completely, they had to gather up the best to make a healthier graft that would raise it to a higher level of the Great Life...

The White Ooh'Rou knew these things. Little by little her spirit grew stronger. From the crystal formation in her room she started receiving the framework of a transcendent concept. It was not yet a telemental dialogue, but it was contact with an Intelligence come from Elsewhere.

All this was far, very far from the preoccupations of Dê-Ta'Am! Surrendered to her appetites, utterly sensualist, determined to suffer no frustration, she was like rampage made woman... But was she really a woman? Did she even have a soul? Nothing was less sure! From her actions, the Queen doubted more than once about her humanity, as Ata-Réè agreed who, despite her gentleness, could not stand the girl, and also Hé-Nark who had already seen the counter-queen in her, which she would in fact become.

Dê-Ta'Am was a bad breed. In her, like at the time of her conception, the revolt of her parent, Amo, momentarily deceived by magic and trapped in T'Lo Dê, was battling the blood of the T'Lo. And it was this hyperactivity that made her so diabolical.

Basically, she knew no rest in her vital sources so she was unable to be at peace or even to tolerate it. Therefore, the special T'Lo gentleness, that quality that might have been passed on to her, she had not a drop of it!

No, she had no soul. In her the place for it was formed a vegetative hollow. This meant that she did not really understand the consequences of her actions and maybe, basically, she was not responsible.

R'Ang, therefore, served as a kind of borrowed soul for her. Because she loved him.

She desired with all her might to unite with him. Not to make a pact, not even to be a partner, but to take him, to have him. A ludicrous desire after all since she was not really capable of blending with him.

R'Ang loved her, too, with all his passion, with all his youthful blindness. He believed that she was a part of himself. They had grown up together, never separated. Hence, again and again, he let himself be devoured and perish like this, miserably, in the midst of being!

But ultimately nothing happened, he resisted. Every time the misdeed was so serious they thought he was lost, he managed to escape by some miraculous burst of energy, a kind of lightning-quick reaction that cast the frightened demon far from him. His angelic nature, inherited from his father, lit up in him like a lantern of salvation at the darkest moments in the wildest storms.

Frustrated and furious, still Dê-Ta'Am had to admire him: for her he was perpetually to be conquered. Her nature compelled her to hate almost immediately everything that had been conquered. This was a large part of the feeling, this having nothing left to conquer, that was holding her back from consenting to the supreme desire of the Devotees.

However, she did not hate T'Lo Dê even though he was entirely under her thumb. But this was something else! Their bonds were different from regular people. She was projected in him and he was projected in her. There was practically no distance between them. Neither conquered nor to be conquered, it was with her, made part of her. Like her shadow. Like her double. She cherished him like a territory of herself with whom she played a kind of masturbatory game, in a closed circle, giving or refusing herself to this personal transfer of herself but without suffering for it.

There was an absolute intimacy between them that only certain dreams, located beyond any idea of good and evil, of lawful or unlawful, could give us an inkling.

T'Lo Dê was her place of origin, her land, her fiefdom. Born of him, fed on his milk, raised and protected by him, she found completely natural the first thrills of the caring flesh, of waking up to more and more caresses he gave to her and of knowing, finally, at first through him, the peaks of erotic revelation. Was not their flesh identical?

Secondly, after mastering love, she naturally expanded to R'Ang whose senses were suddenly aflame. Thus they were joined in strange bonds that the young man often saw as torture. He quickly found that he could not do without her. His spirit suffered, being in perpetual conflict with Dê-Ta'Am with whom he shared none of his thoughts.

Most of his youth was spent trying to break free of this hold only to fall back into it once freed!

He hated to go with the girl to the Devotees. But to hold her back a little, he jumped on her, consumed by jealousy to find this sight that made him half-crazy: Dê-Ta'Am, radiant, teeming with love, responding to all the caresses that the T'Lo and the Devotees were bestowing on her like a ritual.

But the anger aroused his desire and soon, with a red veil over his eyes, he succumbed with her, he too aided by the diligent efforts of the erotic entourage.

He left exhausted and furious, sneaked back to the Palace thanks to the web of accomplices that the Devotees had woven around them and where the psychic powers of T'Lo Dê and T'Lo Gâ averted all unwanted encounters.

All along their covert return Dê-Ta'Am made fun of him. Insatiable, she shined like a flame. So, they fought and R'Ang ran away from her... for a few days...

This distinctive quality of never being tired out by eroticism earned Dê-Ta'Am a legendary reputation among the Devotees. In fact, she never showed the characteristic fatigue that everyone got from abusive use of the T'Lo who were growing more toxic every day, making their users look like drug addicts. Which they really were.

But Dê-Ta'Am had inherited from T'Lo Dê a veritable immunity. This made her formidable because under her influence the Devotees were soon going beyond excess. She loved it. Their "temple", the House of great Ancestors, became home to an orgiastic cult that turned immeasurably cruel.

All that was needed was a spark to trigger the chain of events.

Amidst all this T'Lo Dê, in the haze of his consciousness, suffered the tyranny of Dê-Ta'Am without even thinking of complaining. All her whims, all her demands, he suffered them and satisfied them. All her maliciousness he forgave without even knowing what there was to forgive because he never held a grudge no matter what she did.

He could accept what she gave. He could also accept her tormented passion for R'Ang. Loving him like his own child with devoted tenderness he always did all he could to get them back together.

T'Lo Dê was always ready for anything. To give love when they asked him for it and as much as they wanted, as well as putting up with the cold shoulder or callousness because Dê-Ta'Am did not spare him her sulking and her tantrums when she took sadistic pleasure in withholding all intimate contact.

T'Lo Dê put up with everything without batting an eyelid, with indestructible patience. Above all with unwavering kindness.

Maybe deep down inside he had the embryo of a soul that another kind of sharing, a higher kind, might have aroused?

No, it was not in him that the shadow was hiding, but it was Dê-Ta'Am in whom the hybridization of T'Lo and Human had resulted in psychic monstrosities. So, in this case, was she really responsible for her actions? Not completely, perhaps… And yet she was very aware of herself; she had a strong sense of her character; she knew the extent of her actions. Did she not plan things in advance with great relish?

Whereas T'Lo Dê felt barely any limits to his psychic boundaries. Everything, feelings, vibrations, lights, smells, thoughts from others came through him freely. He almost could not tell the difference from the atmosphere around him. It was a cloud made up of various mists. Therefore, he was not in control. He was always at the disposal of others.

But although the fatality of his state as a T'Lo had made him the same as his kind, harmful to the touch for human vitality, he had their other qualities as well. His intentions were always positive. He liked harmony and especially communion in ecstasy. To be happy he had to share his entire being. To cause suffering was impossible. Besides, he would not have known how.

It was totally the opposite with Dê-Ta'Am. She was selfish, loved fighting, could not be trusted, took pleasure in hurting others, liked seeing people cry because of her. Take everything and why give? That should have been her motto.

CHAPTER XV

R'Ang was heading for the royal rooms, aware of nothing around him, with only one thought in mind—to be with Ta.

He had just fought with Dê-Ta'Am worse than usual. The night before she had dragged him once again to the Devotees. After the pleasure plunge, which he himself shunned, his return to consciousness had been unbearable. He could not stand it! Far from suffocating in the orgiastic lassitude, as he was cowardly hoping for, his lucidity only increased so that the more important Dê-Ta'Am became for the Devotees as she arrogantly adapted to the role they were hoping to see her play, the more R'Ang revolted.

He realized that not only was he forcing himself to live in an environment that his deepest nature condemned, but also he was betraying the White Ooh'Rou!

He was naive enough to voice this thought to Dê-Ta'Am. She had a good laugh, open-mouthed, beautiful and wild. "O R'Ang, you're as stupid as a Mouh-Tou! Don't you see that I will be queen whenever I want? Don't you want to be the favorite in my Chamber of Men, to be at my side and share my glory always and forever? I just have to give the signal, see, and everything will happen!"

Things had gone this far! The young man was flooded with terror. But he teased her, "You, reign! Come on, you're just a filthy animal who thinks only of her own pleasure! To reign you have to be white and shine like Ta. Besides, she is impregnable!"

After that came the insults. Then Dê-Ta'Am pounced, baring her claws. R'Ang threw her to the ground. And there, under him, suddenly transformed, she turned all kind and gentle, assured him of her love, babbled sweet nothings so that the young man was subdued by the intensity of her erotic magnetism and believed their harmony was back, mingled his tears with hers, sought her kisses.

He was still breathless from having had her when she sat up and whispered, "See then? That's how I will reign! In comparison Ta will have been just colorless little fuzz!"

In a rage, he slapped her. T'Lo Dê came running to separate them while Dê-Ta'Am, in no way humbled, threatened to leave the Palace to go live with Oda-Néè and prepare everything.

R'Ang felt nauseous. So, they were falling back into the same rut!

It was the hundredth time that she pulled out this threat. Blasé, even though his heart sank, he just shrugged his shoulders before leaving. "Ha, you always say the same thing. And then you never do anything. You're too lazy."

He put an end to the discussion by walking away.

She yelled after him, "If you leave watch out!"

This, too, he had heard before! But, contrary to habit, Dê-Ta'Am kept quiet after that and just stood there, livid, her black eyelids masking the yellow oil of hatred permeating her gaze.

Of course, T'Lo Dê had sensed trouble and tried to stop R'Ang by grabbing his ankles and putting his head on his feet. But the young man raised him up gently, "No, my T'Lo Dê, no, believe me, this time it's better that I go. She'll do what she wants. But she can't do anything, don't worry."

Alas, he was mistaken!

T'Lo Dê stayed there, dangling his arms. His eyes moistened as he trudged back to Dê-Ta'Am who had not moved.

Hé-Nark had witnessed the scene from afar. He waited for R'Ang to come in reach so he could put a hand on his shoulder. The young man, who had not seen him, jumped.

"Listen," the Master Guard told him, "I never caught you, but I guess you've been going to the Devotees with Dê-Ta'Am. All your problems come from that."

R'Ang tried to excuse himself, but Hé-Nark waved off all his denials.

"I'm not asking you to justify yourself, but to open your eyes. For Dê-Ta'Am to do these things is not too dangerous. Using T'Lo will never weaken her. She's more than half T'Lo herself. And even if it were dangerous, it wouldn't be a very big loss."

This irony from such a level-headed man surprised R'Ang. He went on:

"But R'Ang, for you to mingle with the Devotees holds more than one danger. You weaken yourself for one. Another is that if people find out it'll be a huge scandal. Haven't you considered that you're putting our Ooh'Rou in danger too? Would you, unwittingly, become an ally of Dê-Ta'Am against the Queen?"

R'Ang gaped at him, feeling exposed by all this insight. Then he got upset, not yet recovered from his nocturnal excess and the subsequent quarrel, he reacted badly to Hé-Nark. He regretted it right away but it was done. Shaking off the friendly hand on his shoulder, he said:

"Yeah, all this because you're jealous of me! Everyone knows, right, you never got to have Dê-Ta'Am. She told me so."

Which was false. The opposite had happened when the demon was humiliated seeing the Master Guard remain unmoved by her advances. But she twisted it to her advantage.

Hé-Nark let go of R'Ang and sighed, "You're wrong. You'll find out one day. You have to grow up some more to understand. From now on you can rest assured that I'll be even more careful and any danger, no matter what it is or where it comes from, will be severely dealt with by me. Think of loving our Ooh'Rou better, O Royal Son, and go more often to seek counsel from the Great Crystal."

R'Ang had to admit that the Master Guard had really left nothing out.

So, it was in this sorry state that he showed up at the door to the royal rooms. Everything was mixed up in him. He had urgent need of purity and calm, of certainty. Ta represented all these for him.

He went in. Right away inhaling the light, fruity scent, so familiar to him, he felt the almost immediate beneficial effect of the exorcism he sought. Here he escaped everything and especially himself! Here was the sacred world of Ta where nothing ever grated, where everything always held together in peace and harmony. Like her.

After every visit he wondered what aberration of his senses kept him from living nearer the Queen instead of running off on shady adventures that he had to hide from her and that gave him no glory, but rather the opposite. The excess of sexual pleasures left him irritated and the image of Dê-Ta'Am was almost repulsive!

He walked in slowly, called by the Queen. She was waiting for him. It was the time for their daily meeting, a habit dating back to his childhood. A wonderful habit...

Ta was reclining on her bed. Tired from her day she smiled a little languidly. Around her were arranged the details of her refined universe: fluffy cushions; white furs on the ground among thick, vegetal, light-colored mats woven with down by skillful artists; long, spotless wall hangings inlaid with gold and silver filigree; delicate jewels embedded in mineral cups; flowers blooming in vases on tables next to baskets of rare fruits all cheerful pink and yellow.

The door at the back was cracked open onto the leafy garden where flowing water murmured in her favorite pool. On the ledge of the main window a carefree bird was singing a little medley of notes, then smoothing its wings, its neck, stretching a foot before starting another musical phrase, meandering peaceably.

"It's a M'Li," Ta pointed at it. "A charming friend. It's tame all by itself. Come and sit down where I can see you. You're sad."

R'Ang obeyed and in response lied so awkwardly that it made her smile.

"I missed you a lot today."

She patted his cheek, "That's not exactly true, my Son, but it's nice of you to say."

She often called him "my Son" and it was not remarkable but this time, hearing it, he felt a kind of inner shock. He suddenly realized that she was not his mother and she still looked like a young lady. How had he not recognized this before?

While talking to her about various things, he caught himself eyeing her. It was like a revelation to him and he became more astounded. Who would have believed, on seeing this very young, shapely woman, that she was a queen, governing for many long cycles of Ooh'R, often overwhelmed with troubles and who was alone to contemplate and alone to watch over the future of an entire Race at a critical turning point of the ages.

Of course, R'Ang had already thought of things like this but only superficially. He was also telling himself that he should help the Ooh'Rou. And yet, this never got out of the planning stage. He had plenty of time! She asked nothing of him.

Then he suddenly realized that time had passed. He thought that, judging by her famous paleness, she really needed help now. He saw that he himself had matured, but he hid it. He understood that he was already fully capable of assisting her. But, feeling intimidated, coming up against other truths that were more troubling for being so deeply buried, he lowered his eyes, wanting to stay a child, "the Son", for a little longer.

He had stopped being.

For her part, Ta always saw him as younger than he actually was. She did not fathom the reasons for his distress. She took his hand, put it to her cheek and said, "Well, what did she do this time?"

He sighed, "Nothing, nothing…"

Ta figured it best not to press him. She watched him sitting on the edge of her bed, sighing, playing with the gold chain that fastened the royal robe.

"Do you want me to tell you about my day?" she offered.

He nodded. While listening he remembered that she had, in a way, raised him since childhood. Year after year he had learned from her what it was to govern. He knew all about the realm, the Race, the Ancestors. She had patiently explained what the future had to be and how, when the time came, he, R'Ang, would have to take over the burdens that she was preparing him for.

Up to now he had listened to these things like a pretty, complicated story that hypnotized him a little, pleasantly, glamorously, full of images that he imagined living. He did not truly realize that it was about objective realities that were bound to happen.

This evening he understood that these things he had imagined living in a serene fog were still going to be lived but in a very near future!

He jumped because the Queen had just laughed loudly, "Oh, R'Ang, really, you're barely listening to me! You're as tired from your day as I am. But for different reason, I guess."

Still laughing, she got up. "Come and help me bathe. Then, you'll be free... to go and sleep."

He helped her undress. This, too, was a familiar habit for them. He had often seen her without clothes. The nudity of the Queen is a royal state. And was not he himself of royal blood? So, there had never been the slightest erotic insinuation between them.

She was everything for him! His mother by patience and tenderness. His sister by youth and vivacity. His everyday friend, his advisor but above all the miraculous, the white sovereign who never grew old, never changed. An image of stability that he, always changing, had clung onto since childhood.

Well, this evening, as usual, in the delightful, domestic tranquility, he helped her bathe in the pool in her private garden. They laughed, as usual, at the stubborn bejeweled fasteners and at the familiar bird that pretended to bathe in a puddle and at a scented vase, always the same, that was hidden, that they searched for, like a game, but could not find while it was there in plain sight the whole time.

Real joys! Ta splashed R'Ang. He ducked in time but he slipped on a towel and laughed like crazy, which spread to her too...

Ta got out of the bath completely relaxed. "You see, if I'm young it's thanks to you."

She had held his head in both hands. He felt himself trembling and wondered why while she went back to bed. He closed halfway the big window like she asked and let down the shade. When he went back to her bed he stood there speechless: Ta had just fallen asleep.

Lying there wet and refreshed, she had fallen into one of those typical poses of Dê-Ta'Am on the nights when, by chance, she played at being sweet and lovable. Her head thrown back languidly, the light casting a flowery reflection under her chin, she exposed her body beneath the open robe.

This sleep, this abandon, troubled R'Ang. The thoughts that he had been holding back came rushing in, uncontrollable...

All of a sudden, behind him, the oval body of the crystalline formation materializes, touches him without him knowing, lost in contemplation.

This is no longer the White Ooh'Rou! This is no longer the mythic female whom no male desire can touch. This is a young woman who is sleeping like in springtime with gentle sighs and vaguely sensual movements of her legs that stretch out and spread. Then R'Ang thinks about her loving, about her being with a man who was called To and in his arms she vibrated and screamed. Like Dê-Ta'Am when she gave in. Better than Dê-Ta'Am…

This is something tremendous! He does not dare move from his place. His heart is beating against his ribs so hard it hurts. And yes, a desire for her, mad and painful, strained, like he has never felt before, explodes in him.

His true feelings, so long sealed up in his soul, are breaking free.

R'Ang teeters. It's the Queen, he loves her! It's his mother, he loves her! It's his sister, he loves her! It's her, it's her—he loves Ta!

Devastated, he's crying, standing up. What's he going to do now? He still cannot see the sparkling crystalline presence behind him. All of a sudden it disappears.

Ata-Réè is coming in for her evening visit.

R'Ang pulls himself together in time. His reflex is to put his finger to his lips. She understands, sees Ta sleeping and curbs her enthusiasm. But the young man's distress does not escape her attention. Does she understand what is happening? R'Ang wonders anxiously. She is so mysterious! Her contacts of mystical union with the Great Crystal have made her move as if gliding. Her clothes float on her as if wafted by a breeze from another world. Sometimes she seems almost luminous and when people speak to her she listens not so much to their words as to their echoes refracted in the invisible.

But this time, on seeing R'Ang, she livens up and gives him an exquisite smile.

Her wise eyes, hard to stare into, dive deep into the young man's gaze. She murmurs, "Don't stay here."

She has put an arm around his shoulder. Maternally, calmly, and irresistibly she leads him out while he cannot stop crying again.

"Quiet!" she says. "The Ooh'Rou needs her rest no matter how you feel." Her eyes light up as she squeezes his shoulder. "The time has come. You've touched the substance and felt the secret of your role. The time has come. Should we welcome it? I don't know. We fear so many ordeals even if they are for our glory! Alas, before any glory, a night full of screams and horrors must be spent…"

She stops, overwhelmed, it seems, by the excess of the event she sees. But R'Ang urges her to continue. She pets his head, unwilling, already distant again and thus so majestic that he does not dare question her more. She is the Great B'Tah-Gou!

Now she seems to have decided to leave him alone. Before going away, however, she says, "No, Royal Son, truthfully, I don't really know what this terrible event is. But I can tell you that it will be yours alone to decide."

R'Ang is alone again. He feels dizzy. He shivers. Is it a fit of fever? His recent reactions, the thoughts they bred, and the other thoughts that are coming now, everything is amazing and upsetting him.

He feels guilty, regrets his surge of desire and yet, inexplicably, he is proud of having felt it. Of having dared to feel it.

The fit fades. He feels older and also more important. His true importance. That of R'Ang.

Even though he has not managed to gauge the full extent of what is happening because he gets dizzy just thinking about the start of it, he keeps it jealously to himself. He has no desire to share it. He does want to mention it again.

He also has no desire to go back to his rooms even though he catches a worried thought searching for him. It is T'Lo Dê trying to send a message and, as usual, to alert him.

Another trick of Dê-Ta'Am! R'Ang grumbles. The thought of seeing her sickens him. Let her wait! He is afraid she will discover his secret. She is dangerously intuitive. T'Lo Dê has given her some of his powers: telepathy, foresight, clairvoyance are natural to her. Except she uses them for bad, never to help, always to baffle, to surprise, to raid the private garden of the mind.

R'Ang remembers bitterly all the dreams she ruined forever, just for fun, by slipping in without his knowing. There is no one like her who breaks out laughing at the sweetest moments of a reverie and tears them apart with some ironic comment. Obviously he learned to close his mind. But he dreams less behind this closed door! As for Dê-Ta'Am, she became furious... once again.

To put all this out of his mind, R'Ang refuses to hear T'Lo Dê's call. He needs to gather his thoughts. Therefore, he heads for the House of Great Faces. It is never closed. Anybody can enter, day or night.

For a moment he is afraid of seeing other people. As soon as he pushes the door open, he is relieved. It is empty with its velvety shadows fluttering under the starry flowers of the yellow nightlights. Scented smoke drifts lazily in cloud-like veins at different levels. Like golden oil the streams of light soften the contours of the Faces—a jutting nose, the angle of a cheek, the curve of a mouth or an eyelid. The young man knows them all and loves them. What mute discussions have they had together!

But tonight the Faces do not call out to him. They know that R'Ang only wants to see the Great Crystal.

The young man runs up the steps to the pedestal on which the Great Crystal sits. The familiar crystalline formations go with him. He likes to feel surrounded by them. Sometimes when he meditates they form a dome over his head.

But tonight they just float a safe distance from him. Seeing this he suddenly feels unworthy. He collects himself and leans over the Great Crystal, pleading. But nothing comes except a dim glow that barely lets him see the hazy interior, masking the Presence.

He waits. In vain. The crystalline clouds have gone away, down below, into the nave behind the Great Faces that they halo now.

"Father, help me!"

No response to this prayer. Nothing but a severe peace.

Then R'Ang thought he heard, *"Help yourself!"*

That was all. Disappointed, crushed, he descends, goes back down the aisle without even glancing at the Great Faces, and leaves. He wanders off through the cities. Dawn finds him far away in the countryside, sleeping on a grassy mound protected by a rocky outcrop.

When he wakes up he sees a group of hunters passing by. He joins them and sends back one of them with a message to reassure the Queen.

He does not return for three days.

When he got back to Kob'Ooh'R he found Dê-Ta'Am's rooms empty. She, too, had not come back. T'Lo Dê was gone as well. But the residual of his thought was floating: "Come find us! We're waiting for you!"

So, they were with the Devotees! Dê-Ta'Am had made good her threat. In a fury, R'Ang wrecked the rooms and went back to the hunt.

Ta sent Hé-Nark looking for him to summon him back to her. He came running back, quivering, like for a lover's tryst, spent ecstatic days at her feet but he dared not say or do anything that might reveal his feelings. The Ooh'Rou is beautiful! The Ooh'Rou is beautiful!

CHAPTER XVI

The night R'Ang had left befuddled from the House of Great Faces, he had not seen that T'Lo Dê was lurking in the shadows. The T'Lo had come looking for him. He was supposed to take him to Oda-Néè's where Dê-Ta'Am was now. He wanted to succeed with all his heart, but when R'Ang came out he felt such inner chaos, such a great tension that any interference seemed to him not only inappropriate but dangerous.

In fact, he did not budge, just watched him from afar with a pity that wrung his heart and made him cry. For the T'Lo, R'Ang was not "his" child! But feeling him suffer so much was a horrible thing. It was then that T'Lo Dê had a strange feeling.

The door of the House of Great Faces was left open. He thought he heard a call coming out of it, saying clearly: "T'Lo *Dê!*"

It was so urgent and yet so gentle that he went in. He knew very well that he did not have the right. As always he was overwhelmed with shame. In other circumstances he would not have disobeyed the prohibition but the pull here was too strong. His heart was pounding as if an old friend, missed for so long, was coming back.

Moreover, there was this drifting voice that seemed like the voice of the air itself or of the light. And this voice was calling him. It had always been calling him. Every time he passed by this place or every night he came out of the maze of sleep he heard it in his mind but never answered or obeyed it.

Well, maybe fed up with him doing nothing it came searching for him. All he could hear was it. The wind, the light, the shadows, the walls themselves resonated it. This time it said his name so clearly that to refuse would have meant disobeying.

Now he was standing still inside the House of Great Faces. He was not far from the door, but the mysterious and reverential atmosphere kept him back. Gusts of wind ran over his sensitive skin. His fingertips felt the vague outlines of another world. His golden eyes with dilated pupils saw the formidable Faces impregnated with magic by Amo and gradually being animated by devotion. They affected him but less than the other presences that he felt surrounding him and that were hazy *like dimly lit clouds*.

Some of these presences lingered in front of him like a group of people astonished by an unexpected visitor.

T'Lo Dê knew he was being studied by these presences whose questions came to him like a cool breeze. He was relieved to understand that they were not hostile to him but they wanted to know why he had come like this in the night to this place.

So, he opened up his thought as best he could for them and mentally he told them the truth, "It's calling me. A voice is calling me. So I, the T'Lo, come in tonight. I should have come sooner."

His message was clearly received. The glowing clouds parted to either side with such exquisite kindness that it brought tears to his eyes. He felt their goodwill telling him, "Peace. Don't be afraid." And also, "Go in when you want. You are not unexpected. You do no harm. You are awaited, it's true."

T'Lo Dê was flooded with joy and without a sound he headed into the back of the sanctuary. He did not hesitate because the voice was calling again and it was coming from there.

"T'Lo Dê, T'Lo Dê!" it kept calling and calling.

It was talking as if from inside his own chest and yet T'Lo Dê knew that he was not talking to himself. Nor was it a normal train of thought. No, this sounded clear and independent. He had no power to change it or stop it. He had to listen and obey now. The voice was becoming more urgent.

"T'Lo Dê, T'Lo Dê!"

He reached the back of the nave. The shadows were dark. He felt completely isolated in the place. He bowed low to the ground, trembling.

Then he noticed that in the shadow on its pedestal that kept it away from him and that he dared not even look at, the Crystal was starting to emit a sparkling blue glow.

T'Lo Dê was irresistibly attracted. He stood up. Like in a dream he started climbing the steps reserved for the celebrants until he was level with the precious thing.

The glowed grew brighter. It completely surrounded him and it started pulsing though he dared not look inside the Crystal and to the rhythm in his consciousness he heard this order: "T'Lo Dê, come forward. Come closer. I want to talk to you, my friend…"

The T'Lo threw himself wildly against the Crystal, avidly scrutinizing what was inside—he had recognized the voice of the Beautiful

Stranger. *And indeed, inside the Crystal, Angel, his friend, was there, frozen in translucent immobility!*

His face had not changed. His pale hair shimmered. He was stretched out, stuck in his crystal sheath like in a cradle. He was not moving at all. T'Lo Dê started weeping, his fists in his mouth.

Silence came again. He heard nothing. The glow from the transcendent sarcophagus had dimmed. For a moment there was nothing but the uncontrollable grief of the T'Lo who was curled up at the foot of the Crystal. Then the light brightened again while he picked up a new order:

"Take off your jewelry, T'Lo Dê. All your jewelry."

He quietly stripped it all off and put it on the ground.

"Put your hands on the dark part of the Crystal in front of you."

He leaned forward. Indeed, within the Crystal's radiance there was a small, unlit area. He put his hands up to it.

Straightaway he felt pulled to it and infused with strength. He could not take his hands away. A little panicky, he felt nauseous briefly but was quickly over it. The voice came more clearly but he did not understand what it was saying. Everything was scrambled up with melodious sounds that were transposed around him into bright flashes. They dazed and distracted him, crisscrossing and blending together. Layers of efflorescence, phosphorescent waves, everything sprinkled with fireflies, speckled and shimmering streams that drove him out of his mind!

All of a sudden it was ripped open in the middle. He saw before him, between two blinding sheets opened like double doors, Angel smiling, gesturing to keep calm.

"Whatever you do, don't move from there, my dear T'Lo Dê. Just listen and, watch. Trust me in everything. I promise I'll take care of you no matter what happens. Above all, I want you to remember this promise that I'm making to you now. Let your heart tell me if it's understood."

T'Lo Dê's speechless heart must have told him because T'Lo Dê saw the happiness radiate from his friend's face before he started talking again.

"Good friend, listen to me. Pay attention. I'm very worried about your son R'Ang, about the White Ooh'Rou, about Kobor Tigan't. Terrible times are coming, which you're unaware of because you're good and simple. But I'm telling you, the danger will be great for Ta, for R'Ang, for all the Race. A wind of chaos and madness is going to rage. My friend, dear friend, promise me you'll be only love for the boy you fed with your milk, for the queen who always protected you and for Kobor Tigan't where your life was made easy."

T'Lo Dê nodded. He was shaking from the announcement of all the misfortune that Angel was saying was nigh. Nevertheless, he did not understand very well. He could not imagine the horror. Still, the speaker went on:

"Promise me to be only love and kindness! Promise me you'll do all you can to avoid ruinous actions. Warn the queen. Warn Hé-Nark. Warn R'Ang. And if the calamities still come and Ta is threatened, promise me you'll do your best to eliminate the danger!"

T'Lo Dê's heart spurted out a promise.

Then a cloud covered his eyes. He felt wobbly while Angel's voice pulled back, away, seemed to rise up into space.

"Remember!"

The T'Lo found himself standing stunned in front of the opaque Crystal. He went back down the stairs, stealthily, afraid of being caught. But nobody came. He left safely.

Outside, the night was black. An intense solitude washed over the forecourt of the House of Great Faces. T'Lo Dê was caught in it and stood still. Only then did he realize that his marvelous Friend had not once mentioned Dê-Ta'Am.

He could not admit that this meant any kind of condemnation, but the omission made him so sad that he ended up lying down for a long time not far from the temple where no more messages were coming to him.

Dawn's first darts pricked him. He jumped up and ran to meet Dê-Ta'Am whose telepathic calls were harassing him.

"Where are you?"

CHAPTER XVII

There followed for R'Ang an incoherent period due to himself as much as to Dê-Ta'Am. And because he was the key figure of the time, whatever he went through spawned a mimetic magic that cast a copy of his torments over all of Kobor Tigan't. The young man's chaos, by all appearances very personal and intimate, was embodied in the whole Race. To one degree or another, everyone was affected.

Without knowing why or how the people were confronted with the most glaring problems of the evolution, which seemed to be accelerating. The origin of this forward thrust was located among the Devotees who had turned fanatical by the presence of Dê-Ta'Am. After she moved in with Oda-Néè they proclaimed that the time for daring had come. Dê-Ta'Am played the role of catalyst.

They snapped out of their sluggishness. Neither the wishy-washy speeches of old nor sporadic actions were enough for them. Out of them sprang the flame of Dê-Ta'Am's nature, the huge fire that would soon ravage all of Kobor and whose suffering would produce profound changes. Nobody could survive by procrastinating! Nobody could refuse to take sides!

All the undecided who had smoldered under the ashes for a long time suddenly flared up, out in the open. Everyone had to make a final decision. There were violent tumults. Old problems reared up, clashing with the new ways of living that were not yet fully assimilated.

Emboldened by their passions, the Devotees came out of their seclusion. In short time, relying on the secret support that they had kept here and there, they spread all over in the name of tarnished Tradition and oppressed love. People listened. They rekindled old eroticisms. Then they started recruiting. But these recruits still hid. They were smart enough to guard their secret for the moment. Little by little it formed hubs of influence in the heart of the population.

Acting in the shadows fired up the imagination of these neophytes.

The Devotees did not openly attack the White Ooh'Rou, but they appealed to the past, to the carefree and voluptuous life, to the universal happiness due to the absence of efforts. They especially boasted of the merits of their traditional practices founded on the love for which their cherished T'Lo were the living instruments.

They explained what their religion was, saying that the mythic Very Huge, Abim herself, watched over them from the depths of their House of Great Ancestors and that in passionate rituals carried out by the T'Lo for them, they reached long, erotic ecstasies like nobody else. They spoke of revelations of transcendence, of infinite climaxes.

In groups, in Kob'Iâm where they made many adepts, in Kob'Râm and Kob Vâm where they made fewer, while swaying together with their B'Tah-Gous they came as lascivious women from the purple times, distorted priestesses who did not hesitate to mate with their T'Lo in public, something once considered holy.

Their brightly colored clothes, their heavy jewelry, the deluge of perfume they used, their excitement, all this amazed the crowds. Their demented eroticism was contagious due to the very fact of its excesses.

Everywhere they went they handed out concentrate of Dot'Ooh'R, the hallucinogenic, stimulant drug they used.

All of their events were interrupted by the Royal Guards. But since the people had denounced all violence long ago and the Devotees were not attacking the Queen, the Guards could only send them away or escort them back home. Interventions without any real consequences because they were bound to do again and again.

The first deterioration of Ta's authority was that a large part of the public rose up against the fact that the Devotees had been so long deprived of their freedom. What harm had they done after all? In Kob'Iâm they criticized the Guards.

A dark shadow was cast over Hé-Nark. He ordered his men to stay strong. They patrolled Kobor Tigan't from top to bottom, but they could not be everywhere at the same time. The Devotees played cat and mouse with them. And they enjoyed it. Because of this people went to see them a little more. They did not realize the seriousness of the game and of the danger they were playing with. Wasn't the White Ooh'Rou being a little too severe? The Devotees were looking more attractive to many.

However, the Low City, Kob'Lâm, which had given its whole heart since the start of Ta's reign, rejected these ploys. There were enough shameful encounters there that they quit risking it, saying that Kob'Lâm was of no interest, peopled by the dregs of society, just a roost for old fogies and a storehouse for food. There was nothing worth getting there. So let it rot!

In fact, the City was very aware of the situation. It sent delegations to the Ooh'Rou to guarantee its loyalty. This example was later followed by others, like Kob'Vâm and Kob'Râm. But these two were still very much undecided since the Devotees had adepts there.

The Royal Nursery did not escape the trouble. There were many and influential Devotees there because all of them, to some degree, were descended from the royal family. Higher than the others, they called on them for a return to the Traditions.

Gan'd, who lived there, isolated but not ignorant, provided the Master Guard with details. In Kob'Ooh'R the new court tightened around the Queen.

For R'Ang, torn between the seductive charms of Ta and Dê-Ta'Am, the crisis developed in a series of conflicting episodes that never got resolved, only worsened, one after another, with no sign of slackening. Paradoxically connected to the whole, all his actions and reactions, like stones thrown into a lake, caused endless repercussions in the very substance of the racial events.

On one side Dê-Ta'Am was trying to get to R'Ang. She was backed up by the Devotees who wanted to enlist the Royal Son whose total conversion would surely hurt the Queen badly.

On the other side, R'Ang steered clear of Dê-Ta'Am. He did not want to yield to the calls she sent through T'Lo Dê and T'Lo Gâ who could still sneak by the guards and pop up on his terrace begging him to follow them. As a token of sincerity they brought with them a piece of Dê-Ta'Am's perfumed clothes or some of her jewelry. R'Ang sent them away. Then he wept furiously, ripping the clothes that were intentionally left behind by the T'Lo.

Furthermore, on every visit, the visible grief of T'Lo Dê tore him up inside. Countless scenes from his childhood spun around in his memory. He had to run out of his room and could only find a little peace in Ta's garden. He spent the night there, lying by the pool, his face buried in the towels used by the Queen to dry herself.

Sometimes when she could not sleep she found him there and scolded him gently. But they ended up talking about all the problems of the moment. R'Ang was aware of the danger of the Devotees and he shared Ta's opinion that they would not attack directly. He thought it was better to wait things out and over time everything would slowly go back to normal. Both of them were sure that the power of the Royal Guards was enough to maintain order.

Talking like this, in this intimacy that she still believed was parental, though it was not for either of them, Ta felt a deep tenderness rise up inside her, which she could only compare to her memories of To. Caressing the young man's hands and shoulders she did not notice...

He trembled all over, captivated by the sound of her voice, the magnetism of her gaze, the smell of her skin, the nearness of her body! Happy and sad, he was both.

He bathed in his love for Ta, but when his feelings flared up, he divorced them from desire, which he reserved solely for the she-beast Dê-Ta'Am!

His resistance ended up breaking down.

One night he went to Dê-Ta'Am. But just when she thought she had triumphed, he escaped at dawn, sickened, with a horrible sensation of peril as if he were slipping out of a trap.

The girl's rage was indescribable.

Oda-Néè, who had aged a lot and was preening Dê-Ta'Am as her spiritual daughter, used this to fan the girl's hatred of the Queen.

Dê-Ta'Am listened. She started to get a glimpse of how to overthrow Ta, to take her place...

As a result, the Devotees' daring grew stronger.

R'Ang pulled himself together for a while. Before events reached their climax, he would break down again and pick himself up, many times.

In each of these crises and with every repercussion on the Race, the White Ooh'Rou stepped in, calm and controlled. The young man was enthralled and straightened himself out but could not admit the real reason for his torments. Ta guessed the truth, of course. But maybe she did not give it enough credit. With very royal disdain, she underestimated Dê-Ta'Am. It was a mistake.

Hé-Nark saw it, was distressed and tried the same old song to get her to recognize the danger of the situation. But Ta, whose recent speeches had been cheered and who did not stop seeing delegations at the Palace demonstrating their loyalty, thought she knew all about the Devotee problem, which she had been dealing with from the start of her reign. She was unconcerned. Besides, most of her thoughts gravitated toward R'Ang. She felt a little light-headed, all the time. Happiness was brushing its wing against her. The stress of being queen, which she had suffered for so long, was being relieved...

Furthermore, at every one of her interventions, all the turmoil simmered down. There was a general lull; the Devotees went back to being more discreet; the people focused their admiration on the Queen again.

They went back to living quietly, a little dumbfounded by what had happened. They really did not realize that they had gone down a notch, that the peace was delicate and what they took for a return to tranquility was, in fact, just a resting stage, a little lower than before.

Ta wanted to live. A passion was inspiring her. She yearned for happiness. Often her gestures, the tone of her voice, her dancing, graceful walk was strikingly similar to the girl she had been, that princess whom they used to call fickle.

More than before she sought out the company of the B'Tah-Gous, going with Ata-Réè to participate in their songs, in their simple ecstasies. She smiled, felt calm and relaxed. Much more often than usual she even laughed, cheerfully. The jokes of her Young Servants amused her—she was very forgiving.

She paid more attention to how she dressed. Her influence made the clothes and jewelry in the Palace even more refined. Now they were wearing finely woven fabrics because over the last few Ooh'R cycles repeated dreams had visited and inspired young people by revealing the secret of weaving whose likeness they immediately recognized in nature where insects wove the threads of their traps.

They delicately dyed these fabrics with soft hues of petal blue, dawn pink, water green. They wove in metallic threads. They embedded gems to look like flowery ornaments. Ta loved to gaze upon her young court decked out in delicate garb that contrasted prettily with their beautiful bodies, gold or bronze, the high-breasted women and the men with chests bulging like shields. The flowing tunics and light robes flattered their strength, their ripe flesh, their haughty stature.

More and more often the Queen organized hikes in nature. In educational games they looked for plants under the direction of Gan'd. They tried new fruits. They crowned themselves with flowers.

They participated diligently in the ceremonies of the House of Great Faces. Ta loved the crystalline formations that gathered around her there. Their contact made her feel good, almost voluptuous. But it was a voluptuousness of calm, harmony and peace, motionless, without activity, without climax. A permanence that might have helped to reassure her because she knew that nothing ever could truly cause her real harm.

"Do not fear. Ever."

That was what the intelligences were telling her.

The Crystalline formation that she had watching over her in her room said the same thing but it was more intimate. Ta perceived the meaning of its influx better. She got the messages. They were weird.

"I am devoted to you. We have chosen you. You are beautiful, strong and pure. I am receiving you. Reflect yourself without fear in me. I yearn, oh how I yearn to infuse in you the fire seed of my nature."

She listened to these things. She was troubled. And even more by this continually repeated promise:

"Patience! The time is coming when I will be near, when I will speak better, when I will truly unite with you in a way you could never imagine..."

Then Ta felt a kind of vast caress pass over her, blowing a kiss on her soul, awakening (but as if from very far away) her femininity, which was still numb and cold since the death of To.

But she was startled because the crystalline watcher always added, "With you but also with the Royal Son."

Ta smiled without really understanding and she caressed the hand and shoulder of R'Ang who, of course, was there beside her as usual and had not heard the message nor seen the fluidic presence even though he was aware of all the crystal formations in the House of Great Faces since he was a child!

"You were dreaming," he caught her looking off into the distance with that strange look she got when she was listening to the silence.

She did not correct him. She nodded, "I was dreaming. I became again like when I was your age and running all over Koh'B'La on wings of the wind, a young girl as carefree as ever."

R'Ang laughed, madly in love but hiding it in shame. She laughed too. Maybe already falling in love but unable to see the signs.

That night, on the terraces, the priestesses were singing, occasionally interrupted by conversations between the White Ooh'Rou and the couples of the new nobility that she had formed and was fond of.

To live, to live slowly, gently, to live again, to live at last!

In this climate of blindness Hé-Nark's bitter clarity seemed overblown because of his easily pessimistic personality.

He came to Queen with a smile. The Master Guard held nothing against her. He was careful to restrain his dark forebodings in her presence. His deep tenderness had shown him what she was going through. Touched, he respected her fragile blossoming. And he admired her all the more from the depths of his frantic patience, from his real martyrdom.

The love that he felt for faithful Gan'd helped him burn off the excess of this passion that otherwise would have been unbearable. He did not tell her that in her arms he imagined holding the Queen… He felt as guilty as a criminal. Nevertheless, his delightful affliction was a compensation he could not give up.

A passionate fire was kindled in Kobor Tigan't. It ran, crawled, spread out, pulled back, reacted in accord with the intrigues of the Devotees. Certainly, thanks to the Master Guard and his Men, they snuffed out local outbreaks that were too intense. But they were only superficial victories as the fire moved on, underneath, hotter than ever, to spurt out elsewhere.

Thus it went for R'Ang, struggling inside, afflicted by the ever-growing needs of his increasing awareness.

Thus for all the Race, forced to choose *for* a side and therefore *against* another. The egregore of the Giants, to pass the threshold of the New Age, was forced to maim the corrupted part of itself represented by the Devotees.

Only following the White Ooh'Rou was not going to be enough. They would have to stand by her side, maybe go into action for her… who for so long had acted in place of her lazy people!

Gan'd often told Ata-Réè and Hé-Nark that the Queen's inaction and her sudden desire for distractions was a symptom of great fatigue more than real contentment. The Master Guard thought that she would not last. He was yearning to help her.

The sorting out of Kobor Tigan't had begun at the start of her reign. It was now entering the active phase. Enduring for the Race was not enough. It was necessary to decide, to choose. A collective gesture in favor of the Queen was becoming indispensable. Events were soon going to come to a head.

Just like the Race, R'Ang faced gut-wrenching alternatives between the grip of Dê-Ta'Am and the lure of Ta because although he loved the latter with everything that was noble in his being and although he knew it, nevertheless he refused to accept the feeling and its consequences. He continued to be bound sensually to Dê-Ta'Am. She was his weakness. She was his drug. His remorse as well.

He rejected her only to make his desire for her that much more bitter! So, he ran back to her and right away hated her and missed the

Queen. Then he returned, was surprised he had ever left her and for a time believed he was truly exorcised.

He tried to distract himself with rough physical exercise. He went off on hunting trips, on Dongdwo egg hunts where he amazed the others with his endurance. Hé-Nark, on the Queen's command, vigilantly accompanied him everywhere and saw this waste of energy as a kind of desperation.

Ata-Réè tried to help the young man pull himself out of the rut. He listened to her and buried himself in all-night vigils in the House of Great Faces. But no messages came to him from his divine parent: the Great Crystal remained impenetrable. The mysterious inner mist did not dissipate and Angel stayed invisible.

R'Ang, therefore, found no answer anywhere. The cries of his soul made no echoes. His sentiments and sensuality would not reconcile.

Agitated by such momentous transformations, he felt like he was going crazy, especially faced with the abrupt maturing of his thoughts that his frivolous recklessness would not come to terms with.

He suffered because imperative orders—he must try—were harassing him but he knew not where they came from. A ruthless fist was pushing him forward. He wanted to run to the goal, to outdo himself in action and glory, but he kept holding himself back.

He was ashamed. He hated himself. And Dê-Ta'Am enjoyed pouring acid on his wounds!

On the other hand, Ta's tenderness was a balm. Unfortunately, the Ooh'Rou's domination paralyzed his passions. He did not want to know about it. The revelation of a new and different kind of femininity from what he had known so far disturbed him so much, body and soul, that he was scared.

He was stuck in a horrendous battle of thoughts and feelings. Chaos reigned in him! He could not control himself. His own violence, his rash reactions frightened him. In truth, everything was too much for him.

He found no peace or contentment anywhere. He was under siege with no escape. Wherever he turned he saw a mob besieging him. He went from the heights of excitement to the depths of depression. He endured the dark rage of loneliness facing the bed deserted by Dê-Ta'Am whose ironic victory he perceived from afar: "Go on, you'll come back to me!"

He suffered the oppressive weight of sleepless nights when everything was empty, when nothing responded.

He felt how impossible it was to express his torments, words could not translate his agitation and this despite the attentive concern of those around him trying to help but to whom he dared not reveal his depraved thoughts.

He suffered through the dire flames of his unsatisfied desires because the need to have Dê-Ta'Am left him no respite.

But when he was with Ta, he also heard the mysterious murmur that predestined souls shared with each other. He experienced the rapture of feeling with the Queen in a divine state of interpenetration where the movements, the voice and the smell of the body become invisible organs of love, coming together to merge as one.

And during this whole time the certainty flashed through him like a whiplash: "Conquer the Queen! Dare to do it! It is your destiny and hers! Reject Dê-Ta'Am! You do not love her!"

He could not reject her!

Meanwhile, Kobor Tigan't complacently tolerated the ever-growing waves of Devotees!

CHAPTER XVIII

Among the Devotees, Dê-Ta'Am has discovered what it means to be drunk on power. She is no longer the wind-borne demon doing nothing but frisk and frolic. She, too, has matured. Her ideas have clarified. She fully espouses the cause of the Devotees. They have always been her real family.

They shower her with honors. Nothing is done or planned without her. She is the living symbol! She is hope! She is righteous victory!

An erotic devotion follows her around. They anticipate her desires. Nothing is refused. They think that everything is finally possible with her. They are willing. They are dying to act, to triumph.

It is because they have been waiting for this moment since her childhood, since that exceptional night when the great T'Lo Dê had come to present her to Oda-Néè!

The strangeness of her birth made her superhuman in the eyes of the Devotees. She became a mythical creature come down from the paradise of the T'Lo!

So much adulation has given Dê-Ta'Am boundless pride. Was she stupid before? She wonders now why she had waited so long. Here she has already been queen!

So, she rises to cause, aggressive, ready for action. She shares her flame. They are seduced and aroused by her magnetism.

Deep in the House of the Great Ancestors, at the foot of the incredible statue of Abim whose head is lost in the dark heights of the vaulted ceiling, Dê-Ta'Am is reeling off her plan. It must be put in action. The White Ooh'Rou is a usurper. Free the Race! Bring back the traditional customs, the worship of the love T'Lo without which there is no happiness! Who better than Dê-Ta'Am could be a real Ooh'Rou!

In the shadows Oda-Néè is throbbing with joy. The long-awaited time has come!

She is on the way out. She feels it. She has seen her best years slip away without being able to get to the Queen even though she went after her with relentless disdain and, paradoxically, with unrelenting admiration. Oh, how she dreamed of being her equal! But it is too late for her now. She has passed on her flame to Dê-Ta'Am. She wants to see her win, to see her reign.

Therefore, she has insinuated all her own arguments to stand against Ta. R'Ang gave her the main reason. She knows how upset the girl was, usually so sure of herself, that her brother-lover will not stand at her side. She knows that a nagging concern is eating away at her. She knows that she suspects Ta of having a secret Chamber of Men which Hé-Nark is certainly part of. And what about R'Ang?

Worried, Dê-Ta'Am is going to ask T'Lo Dê about it mentally. He must know since he is often up there spying on the Palace in the shadows at night.

In fact, he does know. Candidly, naively, his thoughts come through. "Yes, R'Ang is always with Ta, on strolls, during meetings, in her room, not only the evenings as usual but at night now. He even sleeps in the royal garden near the pool and in his sleep he rolls around moaning on the towels that dried the Queen... Yes, T'Lo Dê believes that R'Ang loves Ta. But R'Ang still desires Dê-Ta'Am. And he misses T'Lo Dê. And T'Lo Dê's grief hurts him..."

With this last thought the mental message gets fuzzy. Dê-Ta'Am grows impatient because the T'Lo's eyes are clouding over. She hates seeing him suffer for anyone else but her! So, she hugs him in a friendly way, using her agile fingers to caress the T'Lo's female parts, which, for them, is a sign of tenderness and binds them on a purely feminine level. It is time for... the ploy.

"Take comfort," Dê-Ta'Am says, "I know how to deal with it. Soon he will be with us, at our side, like someone waking up, surprised that he had left us. And we can love him again. When I have freed him. When he sees that he is free and that the queen is just a lie... for the Power just like for love. When I am the new Ooh'Rou of Kobor Tigan't R'Ang will be free and awakened! Oh, I can tell you, that too white woman will melt in my fire!"

The T'Lo's eyes twitch. He draws away from her, unnoticeably. He dares not look at her. A new suffering is nagging at him. He knows her only too well! All these foolhardy projects he unravels in the young woman's feverish imagination are scaring him. He sees only hidden cruelty. Where does it come from? Has she really inherited none of his qualities? Love of peace, mercy, the will to please, patience, she knows none of these! Everything in her is swirling and burning: flames of pride, fumes of anger and pale flashes of irreversible actions.

She will not stop at bloodshed. T'Lo Dê knows now. And he thinks again of the promise he made in the House of Great Faces. Abruptly, he shuts down his mind to Dê-Ta'Am.

Alas, what can a T'Lo do when he is torn between everyone he loves? To save one he must, perhaps, betray the other and maybe even put them in danger!

After this meeting Dê-Ta'Am decides to go into action at once.

She talks with Eqin-Go and Oda-Néè. A plan is hatched. The Devotees' knowledge of certain drugs should do the trick. It will make it easier and keep things quiet. They agree to use the volatile juice, a powerful narcotic, from a kind of mandrake apple called Dod-Him. What could be easier than to snatch away a sleeping queen!

Within a few days Dê-Ta'Am and her cronies are ready. By chance the perfect opportunity presents itself: the Queen is going to leave Kobor Tigan't for a few days on a recreational outing to Kah'B'La and beyond. She will have a very small escort.

Dê-Ta'Am, Eqin-Go, Ka'Ok and a few others with some extra-sensitive T'Lo will follow them seretly at a distance. They will certainly find the right time to capture Ta.

To the great surprise of Dê-Ta'Am, at the last moment, T'Lo Dê insists on coming with them. The young woman accepts with a smile on her face.

It was decided that after the Queen left all the Devotees would spread into all the Cities to wreak havoc and convince as many people as possible of their imminent victory.

Everything goes according to plan.

The Queen leaves and Kobor Tigan't quickly turns into chaos.

CHAPTER XIX

Na-Nood was shining softly on Kah'B'La. The sky was clear, deep purple. It was a beautiful night, fit for dreaming.

The night unfurled everything, leaf by leaf, like a vast, sensitive plant, with the whistling of birds in muted flight through a symphony of rustic scents, bitter bark and fragrant flower all at once sublime. All the nocturnal animals were going about their business discreetly but in a flurry of activity. A constant rustling, the hum of stealthiness stirred up all of nature.

Halfway up the mountain, in a well-sheltered spot in front of the Ooh'Rou's camp, the white banners fluttered, signaling the presence of the Queen. Snatches of quiet conversation arose from the small group huddled around the fire over whose yellow screen crept the tired shadows of the Guards.

The day had been very busy, full of simple pleasures that they all had to experience at the rhythm of the Queen's new thirst for life. Lead by her whose infectious energy never relented, they had run, jumped and climbed, laughed and shouted, call out to one another to hear the echoes. Nature had countless resources for fun!

They had all worn themselves out to please the Queen. For, alert and alive and tireless, Ta seemed to be back in her youth. Maybe because of this place where she had come so often and that was once so dear to her.

Was she thinking of To, of her lost love? It did not look like it. Her cheerfulness made her even more inscrutable. Hé-Nark, who was keeping a close but secretive eye on her, could puzzle nothing out. But how can you even think about it when a wonderful woman, drunk on freedom, waves you over with her golden arm sticking out of the big, white sleeve:

"Come here, Hé-Nark and R'Ang, come quickly, everyone, I've found..."

What did she find? They ran over, rushed over, and always farther, like that, they went across the beautiful land of the Holy Mountain.

Ta wanted to see! Everything interested her, captivated her. To see, smell and touch. She picked handfuls of plants and flowers that were not easy to carry back to camp. She swam in a lake. She visited a mossy grotto that looked like a jewelry box.

It was as if she was trying to make up for her labor as queen, to recover from the psychic lethargy that had afflicted her over the long years devoted to the callousness of the reign. She hungered for life.

For her entourage, in this new light, she looked more surprising than ever, glowing with magical tenderness that made her hair lighter, her eyes more magnetic. Youth itself, indestructible, invincible!

R'Ang hung upon every gesture. Hé-Nark was smoldering, more patient than ever. Oh, he saw very well how much sadness all this good cheer was hiding...

But in the end, this first leg of the trip to Kah'B'La, decided and desired by the Queen, was a success and they all agreed in the evening that everything had gone well. They made plans for the next day because they had to hunt in the woods, farther up the mountain, which would take several days.

Ta, apparently, had been looking forward to this. But now, at night, she sat passively, silently, apart from the main group. She held R'Ang's hand as he spoke excitedly about the expedition. He did not notice that she hardly heard a word, sitting there gloomy and tense. She felt tired and disappointed. The day had offered her pleasures that she could not fully absorb. No, everything stayed outside of her. Her soul was not nourished, not satisfied. She did not want to start all over again the next day, the games and thrills that had once been so dear because To was there. This evening the darkness was clutching her. Too many memories were stuck here. Every rock, every bush, every path...

"I'm not going tomorrow," she blurted out, cutting off R'Ang in mid-sentence.

And so it was! It was useless to insist, to protest. The Queen had made up her mind. She would wait here for the hunters to come back. She would keep Hé-Nark and a few B'Tah-Gous with her. It should be enough to keep her safe. What was there to fear on the Holy Mountain, in this nature where wild beasts were unknown!

R'Ang obeyed against his will, as a lover who had just been sent away on a whim—and, in fact, for the Queen it was—she herself realized but could not resist the sudden desire for solitude.

However, she was sorry for causing the young man so much disappointment. Nevertheless, there was no way that she would rescind an order. She was riled up. The presence of R'Ang in this place was making her feverish... His initial, bitter reaction was to promise himself to stay away longer than planned. Thus, the Queen would have to wait for him, maybe to worry about him...

He shuddered at this thought right away! Besides, he had to admit to himself that he would not stand being away one day longer than necessary. Before leaving he was already eager to get back!

And still, after a short rest his bitterness made him leave with the rest of the escort well before sunrise pretending to get a headstart. Ta was barely asleep at the time. She woke up to fully understand the meaning of this hasty departure. She smiled with compassion, "He's still just a child."

She knew very well that this was no longer true. Her smile vanished. She pricked up her ears. The sounds faded away. Silence. She did not go back to sleep.

Why did she not go with him?

The blatant fact flashed through her mind: "With To, in bygone days, when I was with him, I would've done the same."

She sat up on her makeshift bed. The flurry of thoughts in her scattered like a flock of birds. From the midst of this bewilderment she saw fact that pure reflex drove her away. She was up and dressed in no time. She had to leave, get away alone. Absolutely alone!

In the milky mists of dawn she almost ran right into Hé-Nark. "No," she sputtered, "I don't want you to go with me. I won't go far. I'm very familiar with the area, you know that. I want to be alone. Leave me!"

He kissed her head, heavy-hearted.

She rushed off, feeling free, like she had just escaped some insoluble problem. Yes, an escape... But come now, the Master Guard upset her too, always dragging around the fear of a storm that never came!

"And that never will come," Ta mumbled furiously as she marched through the high grass. A surge of pride welled up to measure her power. "I hold them in my hand, everyone, have for a long time. It's not because I think a little about myself that everything is going to fall apart!"

She was trying to convince herself. Her inner voice was still as severe but Ta no longer listened. She revolted!

"Don't I have the right to breath, maybe even to be happy, to think of my life that is beating here in my chest?"

Alas, this right she was claiming aloud so as to convince herself, she knew she did not have it... not really.

It angered her to know it.

So, it was better not to think about it! She wandered farther and farther, took paths that she suddenly recognized from the past that had led her to a cave where she slept with To.

She was focused now on this one desire: to find the cave.

All of a sudden she saw T'Lo Dê in front of her. He had an unimaginable expression of distress on his face and was waving around his arms. He was panting.

In fact, he wanted her to turn back, to go back to camp as quickly as possible.

But Ta did not understand. On the contrary, to the T'Lo's horror, surprised by his weird behavior, she thought he was in trouble and she went to help him. She tried to calm him down, speaking softly, "T'Lo Dê, don't worry, I want to help you. What's wrong with you?"

The T'Lo's eyes got so big, staring at a point behind her, so that she tried to turn around, but it was too late. An arm wrapped around her, a hand covered her mouth. She struggled but could not break the hold. Rendered powerless, she saw T'Lo Dê crying on the ground and next to him stepped out Dê-Ta'Am, triumphant!

She felt bitterly humiliated for failing in her royal vigilance. "Hé-Nark was right all along!" She was prepared for the worst. But despite the situation she was surprised by her young enemy's attitude—she stood still after giving the T'Lo a kick and hissing, "That's for being so stupid!"

Ta figured Dê-Ta'Am must have been drugged because her eyes glistened strangely. Her face was stiff, frozen like a mask in an expression of such intense, such strangely satisfied cruelty that she looked almost demented. The heavy folds of her garment with its clashing colors only strengthened this impression of drugs and eroticism because her breasts and belly were left bare. Gold chains were tied around her waist and fell all the way to her ankles. She wore all kinds of gaudy jewelry.

For a moment, therefore, she stood perfectly still in front of her victim. Then the onset of a laugh creased her eyes and parted her lips.

Ta saw her raising her hand and guessed right away what she had in store for her. Dê-Ta'Am was holding something spongy, glistening a little, soaked with an oily liquid. When she saw that the Queen understood, her laughter broke out, merry and light-hearted, making a weird contrast with her former expression.

"The laughter of Play!" the Queen thought.

It was true. As always Dê-Ta'Am was playing. Other laughter echoed hers. The man holding Ta was laughing too.

In one graceful leap Dê-Ta'Am was next to her. Ta struggled. She had time to see her attacker's face up close, especially the parted lips that laughter was stretching to bare her teeth. "The Devourer!" But she was already shoving the sponge against Ta's nose. At the same time, the man clutching her squeezed her ribs, forcing her to breathe out and then, half-suffocated, she was released. Her relaxed lungs inhaled by reflex. The sweet, pungent odor of Dod-Him sap spread inside her... A sudden pressure in her head and a thousand crazy images came spilling in... She had passed out!

Ka'Ok, who had lifted her up, stared at the limp body gravely. The other Devotees formed a circle. Dê-Ta'Am tore off the white robe, revealing the secret nudity of the Queen, so incredibly young that all of them gasped at the sight.

"As young as me, really!" the irate Devotee lashed out. Her jealousy had just come rushing back and her savage plans suddenly stood out sharp and clear in her mind.

The women all gathered round. They were heavily perfumed. Their eyes glistened like their leader. They touched the Queen with lewd hands, testing the firmness of her breasts. Their nostrils flared and they giggled. Dê-Ta'Am and the men watched them doing it, obviously excited. The white flesh fascinated them. They followed the progress of one indecent hand, bolder than the others, slipping its fingers between the Queen's thighs.

Dê-Ta'Am barked out, "Later! You'll have her too. You'll all have her. I'll give her to you. We'll weaken her to nothing. In our temple. We'll weaken her with love. With our love!"

She laughed wildly but stopped abruptly to impose silence with a wave of her arm.

One of the men posted to watch the surroundings came running in. He had seen Hé-Nark, alone, obviously looking for Ta. Dê-Ta'Am's eyes flashed. She barked out orders. In short time the Master Guard was caught from behind. Bent double under the weight of his attackers, he was forced to surrender to the swift effects of the Dod-Him.

Rejecting the camp, the Devotees carried their prey back to Kobor Tigan't where they arrived at night and went back to their main fief in Kob'Lâm thanks to a network of conspirators and secret passages that they had had plenty of time to build over the years of semi-hiding.

The continuing troubles in the streets also helped. All the Cities were still in turmoil, invaded by parades of Devotees, out of their minds, singing and dancing and giving away drugs and perfumes. The contaminated crowds started mingling with them and clashing with the Royal Guards who tried to hold them back.

At daybreak, when the Guards were on the verge of violence from the rising excitement, losing hope of reestablishing order without causing more trouble, the Devotees scattered as if by magic and went back to their domains, mainly that of Oda-Néè where the House of Great Ancestors was lit up with countless fires. The doors here and on the other domains all slammed shut.

Then for the first time people noticed that the Devotees had tough-looking Guards posted behind all the points of access in all the domains, a clear message that no one but their own could enter.

With the Queen as their prisoner, they were preparing for a siege. Their domains were all connected by underground passages so they could visit one another.

The great sacrificial feast in which the despot was to be loved to death in the temple of the Ancestors had just begun. Dê-Ta'Am had seen to all the details. Dances, chants, orgies, already in preparation everywhere under the protection of the armed militia whose strength was boosted by stimulants.

Dê-Ta'Am figured that time was in her favor. Before Ta died, she would have to be used to strike a mighty blow: bring back R'Ang, demoralize him by showing him the nervous wreck fallen into disgrace and, better still, reveling in it!

Were not the drugs all-powerful? Anyway, an erotic dose of T'Lo, wisely employed, would be added to the mix. But she could not work too fast if she wanted the results to be deep and the pleasures to last longer.

Her whole body shuddered while she went to prepare the drugs. Plus, she had Hé-Nark!

So, she was decapitating both the Power—in the mythic person of this White Ooh'Rou whose image she had to blacken for good—and the Strength by taking the Master Guard whom she had wanted to win over to her cause for a long time. And here, too, the potent drugs and well-dosed eroticism would do the trick.

As for R'Ang—Dê-Ta'Am cooed sensually, which ended in laughter—that was her own affair!

She scolded T'Lo Dê who was shuffling around looking devastated, "As for you, don't even think of starting up again what you tried to do on Kah'B'La!" He bowed his head.

Nevertheless, the memory of the Great Crystal and the face of Angel would not fade away. Thinking of what lay in wait for the Queen he panicked. He also thought of Hé-Nark. He did not understand how the Master Guard could have been rendered so powerless. For him, too, his heart was already bleeding. He shivered smelling the luxurious perfumes and hearing the groans of pleasure everywhere. Everything around him sickened him now.

He also felt like he had to save Dê-Ta'Am from the dangerous slope she was so foolishly sliding down. But how to save her? She herself was the danger and he could not separate her from herself!

And R'Ang? What was going to become of R'Ang?

He abruptly shut off his mind from Dê-Ta'Am's mental probe. And he cried freely. He would have to be clever.

CHAPTER XX

That night, before dawn, the explosive situation was very troubling to Ata-Réè who, in the absence of the Queen, was temporarily in power as usual. The massive and unexpected but certainly planned outbreak of Devotees spreading through the Cities at the same time as soon as Ta had left had not particularly surprised the Grand B'Tah-Gou. It even corroborated some of her recent visions.

In fact, before these events were triggered when all was still calm, with no sign of foreboding, Ata-Réè was very reluctant to let the Queen leave. She even tried to hold her back, which was surprising to Ta who quickly got annoyed at the opposition to her will.

The Priestess, in fact, felt much more than reluctance—she felt disapproval, which she had trouble understanding. But the feeling was there, giving her the impression that the Queen should be more vigilant than ever and, unfortunately, deny herself the simple pleasures that she had been obviously craving for a while.

It was clear to everyone when saying goodbye that the Queen's faithful companion was hoping for the party to delay its expedition. Hé-Nark, always quick to pick up on all nuances, was on her side, inwardly. His eloquent eyes locked onto the anxious gaze of the B'Tah-Gou.

But Ta was in no mood to hear anything of the sort! Even though she was fully aware of what was happening, her impulsive state of mind prevailed. She had, therefore, deliberately suppressed the regret that was already starting to weigh on her conscience when she gave the signal to depart.

A mutual uneasiness sprang up between the Queen and Ata-Réè, almost like grief for the latter whose eyes suddenly misted over as she instinctively held out her trembling hand to grab the Queen's grim face. What, turn down every little pleasure! She turned and left, cutting short all the rituals.

Hé-Nark had time to shoot a sympathetic smile at the girl standing there helpless and confused...

Ata-Réè remembered these details as she wandered through the Audience Hall. She had got no sleep that night, either too nervous or too glum and also tormented by the fact that she could not bring herself to go the House of Great Faces where her premonitions would no doubt be explained by the voice of her oracle.

Her thoughts were constantly disrupted. She could not concentrate enough to see more clearly because messengers kept bringing news about the insurrection. No matter that they did to restore order, the fever kept rising, the chaos kept spreading, the people seemed fascinated by the demonstrations of "love" that the Devotees surrendered to.

The Royal Guards were more and more urgently begging the B'Tah-Gou to let them take more decisive action. Containment was not enough. They demanded precise orders from her because soon they would be able to do nothing about it.

Ata-Réè procrastinated so that she would not violate the tolerance that the Queen wanted to maintain. But she knew that this leniency had expired, that other, darker forces were at play, changing the game. The time had passed, which makes everything evolve!

She seriously doubted that the Devotees had remained inactive during those years of hiding. They had been planning in secret, concocting all kinds of treacheries. They had seen to everything for the day when they could come out in the open, drunk on power, with all their passions unleashed.

Don't they have now what they have always lacked: a flame to light fires everywhere? This flame was Dê-Ta'Am.

"It would've been better if she died at birth!" the distressed B'Tah-Gou mumbled gloomily. She had said this before on that bygone night she still remembered so well…

More Guards arrived, panting. They were outraged now. If they could not attack or even defend themselves, what did the B'Tah-Gou imagine would result from this madness that was raging through the five Cities? Did she think the Devotees would respect the Palace?

Their irony was harrowing. They hurriedly explained that the Devotees were giving drinks (obviously drugged) to the crowds and they were going into houses, showering boys and girls with caresses and then easily leading them out because they had brought their own children along who were practiced in lecherous ways since birth and could seduce the others as if it were a game.

Everyone thought they were just playing! The atmosphere was insane. Nobody seemed to be in a normal state of mind.

They did not know how or why but the Guards themselves felt their reason wavering. They figured that the drinks being handed out by the Devotees as well as the perfumes were deranging the senses.

They said everyone was laughing. But the laughter almost always degenerated into fits of anger, into aggression that they had a lot of trouble controlling. Every time they stepped in the crowd jeered and hooted.

The Devotees were capturing men by their strong, uncontrollable eroticism. The Devotees were offering themselves to the women. The many T'Lo were giving and taking. Licentiousness was everywhere.

Amidst these endless collective orgies the Devotees were proclaiming the future of the time of love, the end of frigid limits and the liberation of all for which this gala was just a prelude. They were urging people to join their ranks so they could freely enjoy the Long Ecstasy, to rediscover the ancestral practice of the T'Lo, the privilege of the Giants that the usurper Ooh'Rou lied about to enslave the people!

And the people followed them!

The Guards were racking their brains, feeling overwhelmed, powerless and furious too, convinced that Hé-Nark would not recoil from harsh reactions that were now necessary.

The B'Tah-Gou decided to order them to split up all the groups gathering together but without being aggressive, which could turn bloody. She also ordered them to close the Gates between the Cities. Like the Queen she did not know that this measure was rather useless because the Devotees' domains had been linked by underground passages for many cycles already.

The Guards left, shrugging their shoulders, unconvinced that these measures would do any good. Ata-Réè, now really scared, sent three messengers out to Hé-Nark on Kah'B'La to bring him back if there was still time.

Exhausted, haunted by dark forebodings, her anxiety now concerned for the safety of the Queen, she leaned out the window of the Audience Hall. She heard the loud, demented ruckus of singing and screaming. By the fires flickering in the night she saw the crowds milling about among the blue-tinted, aphrodisiac perfumes that the Devotees were billowing out.

Leaning out of all the palace windows, the royal court that did not go with the Queen were also looking on, scared. All the young B'Tah-Gou were huddled on a terrace in absolute silence, witnessing the spectacle that augured nothing good.

In the Cities, in the middle of the fracas at different levels, the Royal Guards were lined up, shield to shield, pushing back the crowd, breaking up groups that were getting too big. But the crowd was jeering at them, trying to grab their weapons. The Guards were all itching to surrender to the hysteria, to strike, to shed blood, which the Queen used to say only one drop of which would curse the entire Race.

Well, the Devotees were egging them on with their lunatic laughter and their lewd propositions. The crowd laughed with them, uncontrollably. And they forced them to drink the brews that *everyone* was passing on to one another. They exploded. Fistfights broke out.

Ata-Réè started trembling. Someone came slowly out of the shadow of the room. She was relieved to recognize Gan'd who had left the Nursery at the start of the uprising to come to the Palace with her daughter Do'A'Roo. They held hands and hugged each other tenderly.

"Oh," she sighed, "worse than this sudden madness of the Devotees, I'm scared to death for the Queen."

And it was true. All her forebodings were concentrated into one: the danger looming over Ta.

They stayed like that for a while, together, talking little. Do'A'Roo said nothing at all. Her worries were all about R'Ang. She loved him… Then, unnoticeably, day broke.

And all the Devotees suddenly retreated.

CHAPTER XXI

The three messengers from Ata-Réè reach Kah'B'La the day after they had left, at night, without taking a break. They find the royal camp in total chaos. No one is sleeping. They are yelling, running around, going off in different directions on a futile search since Ta and the Master Guard have apparently vanished without a trace.

In the light of their flames they scour every nook and cranny, again and again. At first they had thought it was a joke, a game maybe, but the longer the enigma and absence continue, the more worried and then terrified they have become.

When the messengers arrive, it turns to panic. At the sight of them, everyone stops, hoping they will understand now. They gather round to hear news from Kobor Tigan't but it only adds to their sense of doom. The three envoys, immediately informed of the double disappearance, are devastated. They look at each other without saying a word. Yes, the impossible has happened!

It is obvious to everyone that the uprising of the Devotees and the disappearance of Ta and Hé-Nark are related events.

What will they do? Who will make decisions? Without Hé-Nark who will able to lead the forces of repression? What authority, what brave savior can they call upon?

Everyone has the same thought and agrees; R'Ang alone can act!

Leaving half the guards at the camp the rest of the group goes to look for the Royal Son and his men. But they do not know exactly where the hunting party went. Nature is vast. The messengers and the others will not see R'Ang until he comes back to camp at the end of their three-day hunt.

What he learns changes him. In the eyes of everyone he suddenly looks older. His face hardens. He is pale and mute. But only for an instant. Then his reaction explodes. A flash of rage in his eyes and then cold determination. He shuts everyone up and hushes the lamentations of the Queen's Young Servants.

Action is all that counts!

He gathers everyone together and they return to Kobor Tigan't without stopping.

During the long march back he has plenty of time to think. What has the insurrection turned into during these past three days? He is sure now that his Queen is a prisoner!

The others around him are thinking the same dark thoughts: are they going to find ruins, corpses strewn in the streets, blood everywhere? Is the Palace holding out?

Nothing of the sort! Which is, perhaps, even more disturbing. There is not a sound in Kobor Tigan't when they get there. But the silence is not a good sign. The people are locked up in their homes. The forges of Kob'Râm have gone out. The streets are littered. Kobor Tigan't is waiting, traumatized, for what comes next…

In Kob'Lâm the people come out to meet them. They immediately notice the absence of the Queen and Hé-Nark. Anxious questions burst out.

"Did the White Ooh'Rou and the Master Guard stay behind on Kah'B'La?"

R'Ang does not answer. He passes by them, rushes up the stairs toward the High Cities. In Kob'Râm the Blacksmiths fall in behind him without saying a word. They will soon be needed. A male determination vibrates around R'Ang.

Crossing through Kob'Iâm he notices that all the Domains of the Devotees are closed up, that a newly formed militia guards them and that some strange activity is going on. Especially at Oda-Néè's where packed crowds are constantly going into the brightly lit House of Great Ancestors. The bitter scent of the toxic Dot'Ooh'R lingers over the whole City.

It wrenches their hearts. The tones of the incantations they hears sound fierce. And then they can hear laughter, which sends a shiver down their spines.

All the patrols of the Royal Guards they meet ask the same question, "Did you bring back the Master Guard?"

R'Ang remains stubbornly silent.

When he has gone by, the Guards realize that the Queen is not there and the whole party is dirty and haggard like they have not slept for days. The rumor spreads quickly: "Where's the Queen?"

So, it is a trail of dismay that R'Ang leaves behind him. But he does not care. Action, just action! Find the Queen! Words and speeches, even feelings do not matter! He must save the Queen! The rest will follow, people as well as events.

He knows that he will turn everything upside down. He does not realize at this moment that he has become the master of Kobor Tigan't. Decide! Act! Charge straight ahead...

Ata-Réè is there to greet him in the Palace. So pale she looks like a walking corpse. Some of her girls are at her side. Her tears are fresh. The girls are still crying. The Grand B'Tah-Gou is holding a Devotee's badge that R'Ang instantly recognizes as belonging to Dê-Ta'Am.

The newcomers gather round silently. All the doors open and other people, a whole crowd comes flowing in to slowly fill up the Audience Hall. Not a sound. No agitation. Nothing but a swelling assembly over which looms an almost funereal dread.

In the middle of the wide circle forming at a respectable distance R'Ang stands alone before Ata-Réè. She finally finds her voice but it is weak, faint. The Priestess sounds like she is talking to herself, barely aware of those around her, a broken, droning monologue. But her red eyes stare only at R'Ang. She is explaining things to him.

"Terrible things have happened. We have entered trying and grievous days..." She holds out the Devotee badge. Everyone sees it. "See, it's her! No one else could have hatched such a plan! She was just here. I was alone. She came in. With her usual insolence. Like a flame shooting up and flitting around, relentlessly, everywhere, all at once. Like that she takes over an entire space. And her cackling laughter! T'Lo Dê was guiding her not to bump into anything... She sat on the throne. Still laughing. But quieter, like someone really having fun. She stared at me calmly. I didn't cry out. I thought I was dreaming... She was swinging her leg. And she was playing with the streams of gold chains trickling between her legs. With her eyes stuck on me, with a kind of patience, a kind of condescending arrogance. Me, I waited, unable to move. I saw the abominable thoughts knitting her forehead. Everything she had already done. Everything she was going to do... And she knew I saw. Smugly, she let me discern all her plans... And..."

The B'Tah-Gou swallows hard. Her voice drops even lower. The gasping audience leans forward. Still not a sound. They keep coming in through all the doors. Strangely, Ata-Réè's whispering breath flutters over all their heads, a gray bird with muted wings.

R'Ang started to reach out to her for support but she went on, "And these plans were so monstrous, so unbelievable that I couldn't tolerate the images anymore! And she just sat there in the middle of the throne, back straight, legs together, arms on the rests. No more laughing... Her voice cracked... I can't repeat..."

The painful speech chokes and stops. But the storyteller seems to finally recognize R'Ang. A glimmer of hope flashes in her eyes. She talks to him directly in a different tone, more urgently, more frantically.

"Listen, oh Royal Son, listen! It's been three days since the White Ooh'Rou was taken by the Devotees, handed over to the men, women and T'Lo, addled with toxic drugs in the House of the Great Ancestors..."

She stops, her mouth is dry, but R'Ang grabs her arm and squeezes hard enough to break it. Her eyes look up, colorless, astonished.

"Go on!" R'Ang orders.

She obeys, manages to finish. Very quickly. Every word burning...

"Dê-Ta'Am said that... if you want to see the Queen again... before she dies, you have to hurry. She's already very weakened by the consumption of love... You can go in unobstructed by presenting this badge... They're waiting... If you try anything violent against the Devotees, she'll kill..."

An "AH!" booms out of the crowd. The Guards, the Blacksmiths, the Young Servants of the Queen, all the other men who are there rush over to R'Ang who is now holding the badge in his hand. But he holds up his other hand to stop them. He wants to know more.

"Hé-Nark?"

They can barely hear the B'Tah-Gou. "Prisoner too... Drugged... Half crazy... the aphrodisiacs..."

R'Ang has to lean over closer to hear the rest.

"Dê-Ta'Am has mated him with the Queen..."

The Blacksmiths get it. Their faces turn gray. They say nothing, just clutch their weapons. Their eyes turn to face the leader, the master who is there before them, already brimming over with the repressed force that wants, that has to save the Queen.

And R'Ang tells himself that action is not enough for this leader that is in him. Shrewd intelligence has to pave the way. He glimpses a plan, a possible way out.

The strength, the support, he knows they are there: all Kobor stands by him!

Briefly he questions Ata-Réè to corroborate his idea, "How was T'Lo Dê? What did he do?"

"Nothing. He kept his eyes down while she talked. He was shivering the whole time. I think he was even crying, but hiding it from Dê-Ta'Am. When they left he finally looked at me as if begging me to understand him. I got a strong sense of his thought… T'Lo Dê doesn't want these horrible things."

"That's good," R'Ang said. "Get some rest, Ata-Réè. I know what I'm going to do."

Then R'Ang gathered the men together, only the men.

The women went off on their own.

The men who were still coming in joined the others, spontaneously, like magnetic particles, around R'Ang, who was talking, while the women, in the same fateful manner, mingled among themselves. They were all quiet, watching the men, confused.

Something extraordinary was in the air. It was the passionate stirring of masculine thought, of masculine will, of masculine boldness. The first signs of masculine action turned independent because of the events.

The Devotees' aggression sparked this reaction.

An unknown and irresistible dynamism emanated from all these men, polarized by a Leader and joining with him the cunning and the power of a rescue mission.

The destiny of Kobor Tigan't were in the hands of these men…

Silently the women watched, hoped, started to believe…

Among them Do'A-Roo kept her head down. She was wondering whether she felt humiliated because during the previous scene, she was standing next to Ata-Réè and not once did R'Ang, as close as he was, even look at her! But she was not angry, just sad.

She raised her head. When she looked at R'Ang his patient and stubborn attitude gave her hope again.

Nearby Gan'd was standing stiffly, thinking of the Queen and feeling terrible about Hé-Nark. She wondered skeptically: are these men going to rush into something regrettable? Can they save the Queen in time? And Hé-Nark? No, she did not want the Master Guard to sacrifice himself!

This last thought made her blush. Oh if only she could do something!

Ata-Réè touched her hand. "No, Gan'd," she whispered, "it's time for men now. The time that the Queen wanted. They have to prove themselves alone. It no longer concerns us. Direct action is theirs."

Gan'd nodded, apprehensive, "Oh B'Tah-Gou, it's true, everything was said in advance, long ago, with the double birth as you know."

"Yes," Ata-Réè said, "the dark and the light were born together. The White Ooh'Rou was the mediator. What reign is being prepared? Of Dê-Ta'Am or R'Ang?"

But Gan'd was startled, even upset by the appearance of doubt that darkened the voice of the Priestess. Forgetting her own fears, she replied, "But who bears the sign of Ooh'R?"

Ata-Réè smiled, "The Great Child is R'Ang!"

Do'A-Roo had stepped closer. She heard.

CHAPTER XXII

Entering the House of Great Ancestors is to find yourself thrown into the very center of the mental universe of the Devotees. It is being suddenly privy to their thoughts, enclosed within their particular dream and being captured by this dream, unable to turn back. It is also forgetting, automatically and immediately, the rest of the world.

It is—in a massive shock—being confronted with the wildest manifestations of eroticism raised to the level of a holy office. It is being contaminated and sacrificing (like the others who are there) to all the phases of the most excessive lust.

It is no longer being able to refuse the lecherous invitations (yours as well as others)—here they are holy, a pious duty.

It is no longer holding back any of the endless, delusive fantasies and whims that are aroused in you (like in everyone) by the intoxicating scents saturating the place.

Last but not least, it is turning oneself into the delirious fantasies, competing in multitudes with all the other deliriums!

On the sides of the nave are built something like chapels, fabulously huge even for the Giants of Kobor. The Devotees call them Chambers of Holy Love. Dug out half-domes, they are vast and luxuriously comfortable, floor, walls and ceiling padded. They all connect to each other by passages that one can open or keep closed as one wants. Heavy curtains mask their main entrance. Depending on the ceremonies, these chapels keep the curtains closed or wide open.

At this moment, on the sides of the nave, through the blue haze of incense, all are open. All except for one with guards posted in front of it.

And all, except for this one, are deep pinkish amber like shells. Between the open curtains the golden-eyed T'Lo lounge on cushions contemplating the devout crowd filling up the temple.

Every higher-class Devotee has her own assigned chapel where she sits with all the males from her Chamber and all her T'Lo. In these chapels the private rituals complement the collective ceremonies, which always take place in the middle of the temple and in which the Devotees of lower rank participate.

The T'Lo, whose place of honor is in front of the chapels, sometimes choose from the crowd. They give in to their desires without hesitation because it is understood that a T'Lo has only blessed and beneficial impulses.

Thus, part of the crowd mixes with individuals during simple ceremonies. They mix a lot more in euphoric fusion during major ceremonies, votive festivals and the like.

Today is bigger than anything they have done so far. It is a huge festival of the future for the Devotees who have been outcast for so long! It is the celebration of their coming triumph because in the closed, glowing red universe of mortal delights, they are holding prisoner the one who has oppressed them for so long—the White Ooh'Rou, the usurper of Kobor Tigan't.

They will entirely consume her in the merciless fire of their love, her and her impious reign. Nothing will be left but ashes!

Then the great, the glorious Dê-Ta'Am will bring back the splendor of old to Kobor Tigan't, the days enjoyed by the Ancestors in uninhibited delights of the Long Ecstasy given to humans by the beloved T'Lo without which nobody can truly live!

All the people will wake up as if from a bad dream. Freed of the barren illusions and the unhealthy influence of the White Ooh'Rou, they will welcome with open arms the waves of love, the gifts of love, the drinks and food of love from the Devotees and their T'Lo, the sole keepers of the Unanimous Tradition of Kobor Tigan't!

Such had been the gist of the passionate speech of Dê-Ta'Am stirring up the faithful after placing Ta, unconscious and drugged, in the most magnificent chapel of the temple, to suffer the first erotic assaults of the T'Lo who were supposed to continue non-stop unto death.

Then the curtains had been closed and the Guards put on duty. And the sacred orgy slowly started up in the plush chapels. The rest of the faithful plunged into their embraces in the nave before the bed where Ta would be ritually delivered to all when her vital forces had been weakened enough so that she would be breathing her last in the very place grazed by the enormous shadow of Abim's statue whose head touched the ceiling.

This pyramidal monolith resembled Abim only in the defects and not as she really was. It was more of a condensation of all her shadows and only of her dark side, neglecting anything that might have been poignantly noble in her lofty conception of the royalty and the servants that she harbored about the Race, which she saw weakened because of the abuse of the T'Lo and that Ta, rightly, was forced to suppress.

But in their chronic frenzy, the Devotees valued only excess and reduced everything to their own principles and practices!

Abim in this temple naturally looked like some enormous T'Lo with woman's breasts full of milk, a pregnant belly, and with a male sex stiff as an archetypal weapon as well as a female orifice, dark and gaping...

Gems embedded all over the black surface, bulging like eyes watching everything in the Temple.

Around Abim was orchestrated the pantheon of Devotees. Other statues, other figures extracted from all their erotic fantasies. As well as the representations of pious characters who out of grief or old age had chosen death by love consumption.

This was the fate reserved for Ta. A noble and sacrificial and purifying death, in the sacred opinion of the Devotees.

Everyone thought so, very sincerely. But Oda-Néè and Dê-Ta'Am, in the twisted depths of their bitterness, were savoring all the fruit of a premeditated vengeance and the annihilation of a rival whose spiritualized femininity was distracting from theirs and, truth to tell, terrorizing it.

Inaccessible Ta! She had been Oda-Néè's jealous obsession, throughout her secretly ruined life, since early on, as a youth, seeing it was impossible to equal this woman and all the while feeling enraged by her charm and beauty and also, more than anybody, her erotic purity, that unfathomable mystery!

Incomparable Ta! Oda-Néè thought so too, deep down inside. For, she had never stopped admiring the White Ooh'Rou. She kept stubbornly silent on this point. Who could have suspected such a sentiment? Who could have said that for Oda-Néè Ta incarnated the radiant glory of the sublime woman to which her own imperfection will never measure up?

On certain nights when the abuse of drugs got her floating in a nameless space, utterly alone, Oda-Néè understood that she loved Ta... Without her knowing, the only one who perceived this, who discovered her secret was T'Lo Dê.

Incomparable Ta! This is what she told herself when, full of resentment, she had helped Dê-Ta'Am prepare the Queen for the temple. While Ta, despite her resistance, was gradually surrendering to the effects of the aphrodisiacs that would plunge her into lascivious madness and break down her nature and her strength, Oda-Néè wanted to desecrate her with caresses in order to exorcise herself and maybe also to touch her dream.

The dreadful fire of a wild desire was already burning in the Queen's sex. Her consciousness was clouded. Already her self-identity was fading. She complained of suffering a ceaseless desire, a bitter thirst, a gnawing hunger. And the shameless mouth and experienced hands of Oda-Néè carried her over the edge of an expansion where she was shattered to pieces, which relieved her for a moment.

This was the only respite from her hell. Afterward, the drugs would burn more fiercely and the T'Lo would keep her at the climax of mortal ecstasy as their toxic activities would quickly and completely break her down.

But here, in Oda-Néè's Chamber of Men, in her embrace, she herself was surprised by a strange spasm. Ta opened her eyes. And the two women looked at each other. The Queen's lips were parted. An ecstatic glow radiated from her face, haloed her forehead. She smiled at Oda-Néè with that gentle look sick people have to thank someone.

Dê-Ta'Am stood there speechless, unable to understand the hidden meaning of this scene. The infectious eroticism in the room was fogging her brain a little.

T'Lo Dê was there, in a corner, and he remembered what he had once perceived. In Oda-Néè's consciousness he felt the same sentiment again.

But Ta's eyes closed right away. Her cheeks turned red with fever while the Devotee started cackling, jumping up and away, and saying, "White Ooh'Rou, Oda-Néè the Devotee has just given you, just once, more pleasure than you ever got from the one and only beloved of your cold existence!"

Unconscious now, Ta tossed and turned on the cushions, holding her breasts, spreading her legs, groaning. Ka'Ok, who had desired her for a long time, slipped behind her and raised her up. T'Lo Gâ was already penetrating her femininity, he himself possessed in his own femininity by Eqin-Go.

Dê-Ta'Am saw everything through dilated eyes. Her lips were bared, revealing a canine. She was grinning, off and on, briefly, cruelly, at the scene of ordinary mating before her eyes, which she goaded on with whooping and hollering.

Oda-Néè was hugging her, gently pawing her breasts, but she was pale and did not take her eyes off Ta's body that, despite everything, still looked graceful and harmonious even in the worst convulsions.

All of a sudden Dê-Ta'Am turned quiet and kissed her on the mouth. The two women called for T'Lo Dê. He came, obediently, with the other males of the Chamber. However, he had tried to get away. The call had come just when he was about to slip outside to search for help...

The temple is saturated with a scented haze.

Between the chapels children are proudly playing their role, tossing resins and aromatic mixtures on the braziers they are in charge of. They, too, are drunk on the strong vapors of perfume.

From time to time a T'Lo comes out of the chapel, swooning, and letting some envious other take its place.

The haze hovers under the vaulted ceiling in sheets drifting in different directions, more or less dense, through which can be seen the russet-brown halos of the lamps. The gems embedded everywhere and the gold in the floor and the walls flash faintly while the outlines of things are softened, appearing to billow in dreamlike slow motion so that every recognizable shape is distorted by the others, unknown, bizarre, made real by the hallucinogenics.

Sometimes the eyes of the possessed are spotted. Huge, they glitter like precious stones, hard. They are empty of all feeling, impersonal. Despite the body's frenzy they stare only at the altered consciousness of the Long Ecstasy, to reach it by excess in order to prolong it more than ever before.

In fact, there is little noise in this universe of rutting. A muffled, relentless, panting celebration. A hushed litany of the Interminable Act. Persisting in the continuity...

The bodies glisten with sweat and also with intoxicating balms. Everyone is nude but covered with jewelry. Many are wearing erotic devices as supplements to their nature.

The drifting clouds of incense get thicker and thicker.

Lined up behind the empty bed reserved for Ta, the Devotee B'Tah-Gous start chanting. Their low, hoarse song gives rhythm to the growing pleasure, shouts incoherently at the peak, then warbles back down to a level where a shadow of the sensation persists, which they recite in gasps only to go off again, in climactic cries, on the next flight that ought to carry them even higher.

Outside, the weather changes, making it lighter or darker. Here in the temple there is only, always the muted light from the continual carnal passion.

Time will be told by the climax of the rite—the death of the White Ooh'Rou.

For now, in the chapel with curtains closed, they continue to arouse the sensory possibilities of the victim whom they revive (when she is weary and stops reacting) with intoxicating drinks so that they can assuredly wring out the last of her reserves.

Dê-Ta'Am went in several times. Sometimes to join in the mating to take control. But her victim did not satisfy her because she recognized nobody and could not even speak. She screams, groans or pants. She howls, struggles, refuses or suddenly gives in to everything. She faints, too, out of breath, more and more as her strength diminishes. But that is all, it is just a body they possess for gluttony.

Nothing said can pull her out of her daze. She does not even know her name. The drugs were obviously too strong. But if they stop now, she will stop reacting! And Dê-Ta'Am wants R'Ang to see her orgasm to death, completely surrendered and more than anything in carnal fury until she dies in howling ecstasy!

Dê-Ta'Am's look of triumph has started to fade. What is happening is not enough. She was expecting more. Little by little she feels let down. The more she watches this diaphanous body twist and turn unconsciously in all the debauchery, the more convinced she is of being foiled.

She feels her vengeance has been thwarted since the whole purpose of this is not affecting the queen whose psychic mystery stays out of reach. How can you destroy someone with moral humiliation if they don't know who they are!

Dê-Ta'Am broods. Certainly this body is totally surrendered to her. She can destroy it. But where is the pleasure, the long-awaited joy, in annihilating flesh that retains only animal reflexes?

She seethes. She has to admit that Ta's mind remains inaccessible to her, that she has no way to reach it. Ta, as a thinking entity, has escaped her!

Something, in fact, has happened that she could not have foreseen and moreover that she cannot explain, even though it causes in her a lurking fear of the possible failure of her power grab. From that moment on she is scared. She can only react with frantic and increasing violence. She cannot stop envisioning the queen's death, but she should not rush things too much.

Maybe the eyes of T'Lo Dê are the reason? Maybe also the momentary pity that Oda-Néè is hiding shamefully deep down inside causing her to cry tenderly when she is caught trying to protect Ta's body while pretending to ravage it...

What has really happened is that the excess of drugs used to subjugate Ta has caused a split in her consciousness. The noble parts have fled the body, in which there remains only a vague, psychic afterimage, and they have taken refuge in a sphere of their own. In fact, Ta has been "raised up", in the full sense of the term.

She is in A CRYSTAL HEAVEN.

And at first she did not remember. She experienced a state of being there and slowly situating herself within it...

CHAPTER XXIII

LIKE THIS? HERE? Nothing is situated. But it is certainly HERE. Because she is here and not surprised to be so. Why would she since it is, in a way, A PLACE. Very high, very far above.

The earth down below is tiny. And Kobor Tigan't is just a dot. And yet, she can see everything clearly, whether she wants to or not.

Evidently! It is far, it is down below and it is also elsewhere. Nevertheless, distance does not exist. She sees up close, recognizes, remembers and even compares.

But she is not involved in anything. No. She sees with apathy and with the lack of passion bestowed by plenitude, satisfaction, the certainty of being perfectly safe, HERE, LIKE THIS...

Yes, HERE is A PLACE... A CRYSTAL ROTUNDA... She is at the center... Its clarity surrounds her. It is part of her. She is the small, slightly shaded point. An eye. A consciousness. THE SEEDLING, who knows?

"WE WELCOME YOU," THEY say. "Ta, we welcome you."

It's true, she is called Ta! Since THEY say so... WHO ARE THEY?

Many and one, that is what THEY are. A unity of light reflecting itself, that is what THEY are. That is what IT is, THIS ROTUNDA, THIS CRYSTAL. That is what she, Ta, is.

No, there is nobody substantial around.

Otherwise, they would be separated but they are united, infused in one another... But what circulates here, this animating fluid, is full of presences... Oh, she, Ta, knows them all! She is delighted to find them again as if after an inexplicable absence...

... Inexplicable, truly! For, who could ever desire to leave this Place, THIS STATE OF BEING?

Like a ray projected from a lamp, she was just projected DOWN BELOW, ON EARTH... And she forgot—in Time, which is there down below—she forgot her source. She got distracted. To the point of no longer knowing that she still remained complete in her source.

Essentially, she has left nothing. SHE WAKES UP IN THE ROTUNDA EVERY MORNING IN HER MIND.

It is her consciousness that comes and goes, descends or rises along the thread of her own light, from her own source to her fall, an extraordinary spider, a shuttle in the hands of Kébélé who is always weaving…

Below her are the foggy fragments of her nocturnance…

So, she looks at them, the terrestrial grayish things.

And since she did not know what it was, someone said, "It's the interior of the House of Great Ancestors."

A dark place! Night kept at bay by fire. Torches, in bundles, in bushes, in unleashed furies… Fires, consuming themselves… Hurtful lights, cruel lights! They lurch and attack. And human shadows every which way, stretched out, crawling, gesturing, lustily or twitching absurdly, which are equivalent in movements to onomatopoeia in language.

She looks at all this.

A multitude of prismatic shining: gems. Mineral eyes, so hard, so deprived of feelings! They are everywhere, in the walls, embedded, in the floor, in the paving, in all the statues—a huge forest of monolithic shadows… But who are the people there?

"They are the Giants of the Race of Kobor Tigan't," the patient voice speaks again.

"Oh?"

"They don't belong to the future. These of the Devotees of the T'Lo."

Weird words that she takes the trouble to remember. A valuable lesson, no doubt, to better understand… She forces herself, though rather dreamily…

No, she does not get all this hustle and bustle, the moaning and groaning, the frantic jumbling of bodies. All this action is so strange! Nothing means anything to her. She does not know what is happening. Absurd! Meaningless! A persistent profusion of a multitude with a multitude!

Does it matter that she cannot understand?

Does it matter that she is not very surprised that *her body is down there too*?

"What are they doing? What are they doing to me?" she asks.

"Nothing. They're doing nothing. They're doing nothing to you. Even if they believe the opposite. You are not there. BUT HERE."

She knows it perfectly well.

"You are HERE, REALLY. Down there is an image. Lean over to get a better look. Like in a restless stream. See, the reflection is distorted."

She sees the stream, the frothing waves, the passions of those down below. She knows what it is. She remains at peace even though she knows…

The voice, which is the color of her peace, resumes, "Down below, life churns on like that. It flows furiously. Its fever keeps it from knowing its goal. See, what strives everywhere is the terrific profusion of life! Yes, down there, at this moment, what is rushing through your body is this: the profusion! Those who are bringing it to you don't know what it is. Don't be afraid for your body."

She is astonished. "My body? But I AM HERE! I EXIST HERE!"

"Yes, your body is HERE TOO. YOUR TRUE SPIRITUAL BODY WITHOUT WHICH NO BODY ENDURES. WITHOUT WHICH NO BODY GROWS AGAIN."

She must listen to the voice because it is important.

"Your body down below is undergoing a necessary acceleration. It is getting power. Fire and lightning are attacking you through those human assaults. Lunatics who believe they are making you fade away! They know not that they are illuminating you! They know not that from your ashes everything will be illumined and that you will be recreated as a higher woman, alive with a multitude of life! Far from wearing down your true strength, they are consuming theirs. Beyond the broken pieces, your mysterious core is fusing all their climaxes! Accept the terrific profusion of life so that from this overactivated body we can, down below, create the Body of OUR ALLIANCE!"

The curtain, momentarily opened onto the flickering redness of the nave, closed again.

"I'll be back," Dê-Ta'Am said.

She had Hé-Nark brought into the chapel among the men and T'Lo. He, too, is drugged. His consciousness emerges rarely, briefly, from the torrid tempest where his senses are raging. All ablaze, he rolls around with the others, squirming and gasping. He rolls from wave to wave, froth to froth, sometimes suffering flashes, and wheezing, then foundering in pleasure under the surge of his own storm but still coming back to the surface. Thanks to his mighty strength he overpowers and is not overpowered.

In the middle of this sensual storm, blindly he joins Ta like being washed ashore on an island they know nothing about except that it is land, a kind and grateful land.

… The tide tosses him against her. Far behind him the storm recedes… He is lying on this white beach. He stretches out, welcomes the peace and quiet. He has returned to his native land. He will never leave it…

All around him, the Men and T'Lo watch this strange reaction unfold. The tender gentleness surprises them, makes them pause and then stop moving. They do not dare move a finger! No one will act. What is happening there is too much for them and disturbs them. They look on. They feel like strangers, intruders. They want to be somewhere else. They do not understand why.

Oda-Néè is trembling, a hand covering her mouth.

Nearby, T'Lo Dê is in torment, searching with all his mental strength to find R'Ang who should be coming. He senses that he is preparing something. And he has to help him with it.

T'Lo Dê promised in the Temple of the Great Crystal…

She has turned away from the spectacle on land. A veil has covered the images. The Crystal Rotunda is delightful. HERE, love surrounds her. It is a love that expands with her. The divine waves flow through her consciousness. She knows it. Fully. And, knowing, she enjoys it, rejoices in it. But in calm, in peace, in omnipotence.

She blesses what blesses her. She is filled with a seed of light and with this light she fills up THE LIGHT!

Ta has become the movement of the Spirit that is: LIFE.

"I am living!" she affirms serenely.

An echo: "YOU ARE LIFE. THERE IS NO DEATH. ALL MOVEMENT, ALL TRANSFORMATION, ALL IMMOBILITY, WHAT RISES UP AND WHAT DISAPPEARS, THESE ARE ASPECTS OF LIFE. NOTHING BUT LIFE."

Oh, it is the voice of the Grand Old Man I met long ago!

But "long ago", when was that?

"It is HERE. It is NOW."

… They were still looking at Hé-Nark. But even though a little consciousness had returned to him, he was thinking only of loving Gan'd and, as usual, of being joined through her to this image of the Queen that always, in spite of himself, is one with his joys. SO, he contemplated this image. He was in it. As always. A long habit. All his existence shared like this, which gives it its rhythm.

And he knew all about it. He was going slowly, in peace, towards the calm triumph of perfect orgasms...

It seemed to Ta, however, that some minuscule point was missing. She was not attentive enough. In all these spherical radiances that were carrying her into a unified pulsation, she had to remember, to recognize, to name...

She heard: "To". But she no longer knew what this meant. Besides, To was not here, OBVIOUSLY!

She forgot.

Hé-Nark was going slowly. Why hurry when it was sure to be a perfect orgasm, shared by two, like a fruit of light?

And when the sensation came, preceded by its inspirational dawn, it was boundless, and slow too, and its peak was full of gravity. His whole being was set free in the depths of this beloved, solar flower... They were secretly so loyal to each other!

It was then that she murmured, "To", smiling before closing her eyes and letting herself go completely, unmoving.

Everything is torn apart! He heard, understood everything, situated everything. Awareness blazed forth in him like another kind of orgasm, but this one cruel.

He sees the Men and the T'Lo, Oda-Néè who is recoiling from his gaze, he sees the rumpled cushion and the body of this woman in his arms, naked and desecrated. But *by the others*, not by him! From him, he knows, nothing can defile her.

His Queen, his Queen! He cradles her. Against his chest no one will hurt her. He holds her, settles her, brings her back into his shelter, into his shadow, into the fortress of the Master Guard! Precious child. Suckling prey. Unjustly hunted. Unjustly wounded.

His Queen! What did they do? And what do they want with him? He cries. Out of anger. Out of love. Out of despair. But not out of shame. No. Nor for himself. Especially not for her. No, no. Between them this has been pure. Pure and mysterious. The union of the Queen and her most faithful, it happened only once. And it will last forever...

A cry of rage explodes above him!

From among the shadows and the shimmering lights that are still blurring his vision, he identifies Dê-Ta'Am, livid with fury because of the tenderness she observes. She has been thwarted in every way!

"Separate them!" she howls.

Unhypnotized, the men jump to it and obey. But Hé-Nark covers Ta's body to protect it. They cannot pull them apart. They cannot unknot their embrace. Moreover, they are clearly reluctant to do it.

Then Dê-Ta'Am moves swiftly. Her arm slashes through the air. The sword is buried in the back of the Master Guard. Hé-Nark grunts and rolls to the side. How fast the blood does flow!

Coldness has settled. The men recoil. Oda-Néè's frightful scream is still reverberating. A hesitation, condemnation. The T'Lo hide their eyes in their hands.

"Well, what," Dê-Ta'Am scoffs, "it's the blood of a man that made you scared? The blood of a man, the blood of a beast, what does it matter! Maybe you've never hunted before, you men of my Chamber of Love?"

She lightly kicks the body of the queen who is breathing feebly. "Come on, pick her up! It's time. Everything is ready in the Temple. Everyone is waiting."

Horrified hands have lifted Ta up. Now they are fearfully skirting around the pool of blood that is spreading.

"Come on, come on, faster, you oafs!"

She yanks apart the curtains to make way while a commotion arises to welcome them. The crowd presses in around them but they carve out a channel to approach the raised bed at the end of the nave.

The air in the temple, heated by the countless torches, blows like a furnace into the back of the chapel where Oda-Néè lies low with T'Lo Dê. They did not follow the others.

After a silence, yelling and screaming and the chanting of the B'Tah-Gous resumes louder than ever. The drunk Devotees spin in circles and hang garlands around the bodies that are once again intertwining in the nave. All the chapels have emptied into the crowd. Soon the T'Lo are gathered around the bed on which the queen lies motionless, a solitary victim besieged by the multitude.

Oda-Néè cowers. Her mouth is filled with a bitter taste. She is unable to move. And yet inside her head is hammering away, "Do something, do something!"

Her eyes meet those of T'Lo Dê who has stopped crying. She holds out a trembling hand pointing to all this disaster. He flinches, then resolutely slips out along the wall and disappears through an exit leading outside.

After a moment Oda-Néè crawls over to the Master Guard. She touches him, timidly. He is alive, he is still alive! She thinks that R'Ang must be close by now and that T'Lo Dê is going to meet him… Do something, do something!

She stares, dumbfounded, at the blood on the ground… the blood that is starting to flow over Kobor Tigan't.

She listens hard. Death is coming… Many, many deaths!

CHAPTER XXIV

Mercilessly opened, Ta was laid out on the main bed. They decorated her with flowers and jewelry. They put a Devotee badge on her arm. They anointed her body with balms and perfumes. In a half-circle behind the bed tall lamps were lined up into a hedge of fire. On both sides, from top to bottom, the braziers billowed out incense.

Now the White Ooh'Rou is one among the Devotees. Victim turned saint, she can be sped to her ecstatic death with everyone's help. Each of them wants to have her. Touching her is a blessing.

Servants, therefore, have been presented to her as an offering. They have posed her as demanded by the faithful. She is the object of communion. They must unite with her. The last traces of her life that they will pluck from her are a precious gift.

Dê-Ta'Am is leading, supervising, strictly controlling the progress of the ceremony. On her orders the servants lift up the victim so she will experience it standing up. They bend her over, open her more, spread her thighs. They support her on the cushions.

Countless hands pinch and squeeze her, tracing spiral caresses on her breasts, her belly, her buttocks. Innumerable mouths touch, suck, inhale, kiss passionately and share this kiss with other mouths.

Countless phalluses abuse her religiously. Mass insanity, the culminating point of all the excitement! Every lurch of the victim is revered, endeared, accompanied by identical lurches that spread throughout the crowd. Like her they scream, they groan, at the peak of a pleasure whose spasms will come faster and closer together.

And then this body in which the drugs have done their duty, stops shuddering, stops feeling, stops participating. It wheezes softly, that is all, its eyelids half-closed over dull eyes that are rolled up. A pearly sheen rings her mouth. Her toenails and hands are mauve. Purple hollows dimple her temples.

Then Dê-Ta'Am gives a sign. They move away for the final act.

The temple is buried in shadows. They have extinguished all the torches except those fanned out behind the sacrificial bed where all the T'Lo have gathered. The strongest of them, doing his duty, starts to finish off the victim by skillfully stimulating the final orgasm that will take her life.

With his stiff sex he burrows deeply into her searching for the last sparks. There is no emotion on his face. No feeling at all appears. His golden eyes are just vigilant. With apathetic mastery he performs the sacred work that they expect of him.

At first it is the only movement in the temple, which seems to grow bigger from the shadows surrounding the mute and motionless audience. Then, little by little, silent concentric circles all around the sacrificial stage, the front rows first, then the others, closer and closer, the Devotees are affected by the movements of the T'Lo and sway to their rhythm, deep waves that start from the center and roll out to the edges.

Then the T'Lo start jangling and clanging their bracelets.

Then the B'Tah-Gous strike up the funeral chant.

Then the audience hums along to the leitmotiv a moaning echo that reverberates under the vaulted ceiling.

New and stronger drugs burn in the braziers, which will unleash all the energy of the Devotees for the final jubilation that will soon crown the death of Ta and consequently the torrential future of the new Ooh'Rou—Dê-Ta'Am.

They are watching the latter as an idol standing on a high pedestal between the torches and the body of the queen whom she can look down upon. The passiveness of her face and attitude contrasts oddly with the obsessive rocking and rolling that spreads through the crowd. Her eyes stare straight ahead over the dark mass of heads, riveted on the door of the temple.

Oda-Néè, who had snuck into the crowd, suddenly pops up near her as if wanting to whisper something to her. But it is already too late. Dê-Ta'Am's eyes are sparkling—R'Ang has shown up!

He enters slowly. He has sworn to control himself because he wants to give T'Lo Dê time to open all the doors for the men of Kobor Tigan't who are surrounding Oda-Néè's domain. But he cannot resist. The heartrending white spot he sees over there before the arc of lights in the middle of which Dê-Ta'Am's demonic face is laughing breaks all his promises.

He has to get hold the trembling creature who is evaporating over there, if it is not too late!

R'Ang lunges so suddenly that nobody gets in his way. The B'Tah-Gous' chanting stops. The crowd parts. All the T'Lo recoil. The one holding the Queen scrambles off of her. But R'Ang is already there and throws him to the ground, kicks him and curses him.

Dê-Ta'Am has not moved. Her eyes are mere slits above a nervous grin. No one else dares utter a sound. Like her they watch R'Ang.

His frightful face with its masculine fire is so shocking to those around that it keeps them at bay. This is really a new man. They barely recognize him. Before even thinking of reacting they look at him first because his movements and his voice are no longer those of a man of Kobor!

He is something else, something they have never seen before or even suspected could exist.

He has the nerve, the ability, the will to do anything. An invisible force drives him. Everything in his way will be bowled over and destroyed!

A noisy commotion breaks out and the crowd thickens around him, but at a distance. The T'Lo run away, hunched over, into the shadows. The armed Guards are worried but advance slowly, waiting for a sign from Dê-Ta'Am.

"Wretch!" R'Ang spits out.

The grin on the face of the demon widens. She reacts unexpectedly, maybe because she sees that all is lost. She pulls out her sword to strike the Queen.

But R'Ang grabs her swinging wrist, twists it and throws her off balance. The crowd screams because the Royal Son is already on her, brandishing his own sword. The blade descends.

Oda-Néè jumps in to take the blow. "It's over, save yourself!" she whispers to Dê-Ta'Am whom she has fallen next to.

But instead she crawls, then runs, jumps on a statue and yells, "Grab him! And get the usurper!"

The Guards pounce. As R'Ang is picking up the Queen he turns to face them. And that is when all the doors pour forth the men of Kobor Tigan't. Royal Guards, Young Servants, Blacksmiths and others of every age and class, from every City. Almost all the people of Kob'Lâm have come to attack the domain of Oda-Néè. Battles are already raging outside, all over, spreading throughout Kob-Iâm with unbelievable speed.

Blood calls for blood and so it runs in rivers to answer for the Master Guard and the imponderable sacrilege committed against the White Ooh'Rou.

Everywhere, weapons for hunting turn into weapons for war. Everywhere, the enemy is prey for the other. Man for man, kill or be killed. They are no longer equals, one of them is a deviant. Deformed, he is a danger to the other who himself hates the one who is not a deviant. Their vision of each other enrages them. They attack each other in their fraternal home.

The healthy part of the Race of Giants fights to cut away the corrupt part that is putting it in danger.

No, there is no longer peace in the Realms of Mothers! Times have changed. The former days have turned into a bloody purge. Here comes the Action of Man. If he does not act now, the rest of the Race will crumble in the astral quagmire where the Devotees are perishing.

The White Ooh'Rou was not wrong: the matriarchy is finished.

The lazy sun of the ancestors has slept too long under the ashes of the old nest along with the Phoenix during its concealment.

In the end, the purple dawn of blood will precede the zenithal growth of the striking male light, the new Phoenix, the other sun cast out of the loins of the first, the Sun of Man over Kobor Tigan't!

It is the time of R'Ang, another avatar of the Sun Ooh'R, love in its armed purity!

From now on, the Mothers are less mothers and more Women since all of them gaze upon man revealed in his dynamism, all of them hope for salvation as a result and for the first time they are waiting for the return of these men, henceforth freed from their bosoms.

… In the Temple those who were trying to capture R'Ang turned away to face the invaders. Their numbers stunned them, like all the Devotees, as well as the fact of seeing them come in everywhere. But a worse shock was the forest of waving weapons, swords and spears!

R'Ang takes advantage of the surprise. Shouting loudly, raising his sword, he rallies his men, spurs them on and jumps through the row of torches that he knocks down on purpose to use the jumble of metal stalks and branches as a protecting wall of fire. He needs time to protect his Queen, whom he is still holding, until his men can reach him.

The Devotees are all howling in rage. Their Temple has been desecrated!

The excitement from the drugs turns into murderous madness. With all weapons wielded—and those who have none grab the heavy candlesticks or big metal objects—they attack the invaders who fight back, possessed by the desire to avenge the Queen.

Blades stab flesh. Skulls are broken by makeshift clubs.

The greater forces of Kobor Tigan't intensify their attack as the Devotees struggle to repel. In the middle of the action R'Ang's men are having difficulty fighting their way through to him.

And on the other side of the torches he is being attacked by the B'Tah-Gous who have gone mad and are trying to gash and gouge the body of Ta. Fearing for the cumbersome body he has to retreat. Backed against a statue he still manages to defend his precious package with his free hand swinging the sword, striking mercilessly at the spasmodic harpies who skewer themselves blindly on his weapon.

In the meantime, the men clash in total chaos. The thud of trampled bodies and the clatter of weapons. Shouts and commands. Curses and insults. Raucous howls too. With pent-up hatred the entire mass breaks down into roaring pandemonium. And a maelstrom of clashing bodies flood the sanctuary, rolling like dark waves from one end to the other.

The chapel curtains are torn down, trapping the fighters who slaughter each other blindly under the folds. The braziers are knocked over, scattering their burning embers to a chorus of painful shrieks. Heavy statues topple off their pedestals, crashing onto the floor, slicing through the knots of men. The reverberating ceiling magnifies and distorts everything, the bawling and the brawling, into an uproarious typhoon that both dulls and drives on the fighters.

Dê-Ta'Am is far away from R'Ang, crouched at the base of the statue of Abim. Her personal Guards are massed around her, defending her from the column of Kobor men, Blacksmiths and Royal Guards together, making every effort to reach her.

Now, faced with the magnitude of the enemy forces, she is gripped by fear. She is pale, realizing that her own troops are gradually falling into disarray under the unrelenting assault. However, she hopes that many of her men have escaped through the vast, serpentine network of secret passageways. She saw a lot of Devotees slip away and disappear in the confusion. The T'Lo seem to have vanished as if by magic. Few of their corpses lie on the ground. She turns to look horrified at Oda-Néè's body, crushed and burned under the torches.

Around her the fight to get to her is heating up. Breaches are made in her Guard. More than once she has to defend herself with a sword she picked up while her men regroup. She plasters herself against the monolith. Her fingers tremble along the groove that reveals a door in its back at the base of the statue. But this door only opens from the inside.

A thought flashes through her mind that she is amazed had not popped up before: "Where's T'Lo Dê?"

As an answer the door behind her opens. T'Lo Dê's hand sticks out and pulls her into the steep stairway. The door shuts again. All noise is cut off. She follows T'Lo Dê carrying a torch down the stairs. When they reach the bottom he clasps her hand hard and makes a mad dash. She goes along willingly. She understands that with all his paranormal senses on alert the T'Lo is searching for a way out. In the maze that smells of earth, he turns right and left without hesitating. But he suddenly freezes at an intersection. She sees him trembling. A faint sound in the distance.. They're coming!

T'Lo Dê stares hard at Dê-Ta'Am, handing her the torch and pointing down a passageway. His psychic message hits her like a hammer: "To Kob'Ooh'R! You'll find stairs that'll lead you there. I'll wait under the terrace of our old rooms. Meet me!"

She obeys knowing that there is a steep descent up ahead that leads under the Cities. They will save each other…

Alone in the dark T'Lo Dê lets the sounds come closer. At the end of a passageway men show up bearing torches. He was not wrong, they are enemies.

He takes off running; they chase him; he knows exactly how to lose them when the time comes!

Though they are still fighting with growing fury inside the Temple where small fires are breaking out and though the Royal Guards are possessed by homicidal rage when they find their Master Guard stabbed in a chapel, they are fighting just as ruthlessly outside where they have to trample corpses and in the immediate vicinity where groups face off or are sometimes surprised from behind, spewing out of some secret passage.

They are fighting in the area crowded with people. They are fighting all over the Domain that burst its seams and pours its war throughout Kob'Iâm.

The magnificent gardens of Oda-Néè are ransacked! Blood splatters the leaves under the slanting rays of the setting sun filtered by the trees.

They are fighting here, there, everywhere, in the flowering bushes where they crouch before pouncing while marred petals rain down on the wheeling weapons.

The gravel crunches under the wild pursuits through the winding paths where hordes chase unarmed fugitives already wounded whom they catch in dead-ends where they collapse or whom they toss off terraces or massacre in pools of water or skewer against trees with the blades of their swords.

The lavish home of Oda-Néè is devastated! They are fighting in every room. The cushions in the Chamber of Love are stained red. They are fighting on the roofs. They are fighting in the basements, pouring into the tunnels built by the Devotees who are ready to die (claws out) to protect the flight of their beloved T'Lo.

The people of Kob'Iâm track them down, thus satisfying an old hatred. No T'Lo knows how to defend himself. Panicking in the flurry of murder, they hide rather than save themselves and when they are found, if they do not throw themselves on the mercy of the enemy, they cower on the ground, huddled together, not even fending off the knife that takes their life!

In the Temple, R'Ang has been joined by his men. Their bodies make a wall to protect the Queen whom they must get to safety as soon as possible. It is hard going.

But the Devotees' inner defiance has weakened since the disappearance of Dê-Ta'Am. And the Kobor fighters are spurred on.

R'Ang finally reaches the chapel where the Master Guard's corpse is being protected by the Royal Guards. This enclave where no Devotee has managed to get into is the first safe place they can lay the Queen before the total defeat of the Devotees opens the way back to the Palace.

CHAPTER XXV

Dê-Ta'Am had problems getting to Kob'Ooh'R. Several times she had to change her underground route, barely escaping her pursuers who were fooled into thinking she had vanished in the dark. Now she was exhausted. Her nervous stamina had snapped.

Coming out too far from her meeting point, she wanted to take a short cut and boldly headed along the edge of a terrace. All of a sudden the Grand B'Tah-Gou was standing in front of her, blocking her way. Such powerful determination, such icy hostility emanated from her that Dê-Ta'Am believed she was face to face with death. She whimpered in surprise before pulling herself together.

She felt incapable of opposing this obstacle. Ata-Réè moved forward, looking stern, staring at her with metallic glints in her eyes. Dê-Ta'Am recoiled, in turn, imperceptibly.

The Priestess slowly raised her arm. The folds of her sleeve slipped back, uncovering a slender hand whose fingers were stretched out.

Dê-Ta'Am felt a ghastly horror. She tried to turn around, but something was already affecting her movements. She felt numb all over. Then, as she was trying to keep her balance, an agonizing pain shot through her heart. She wobbled, her sight grew dim, she tripped and unable to catch herself, with an horrific scream, she fell.

T'Lo Dê was underneath them where they were supposed to meet. She crashed to ground not far from him. He did not move. Just opened his mouth. He grunted when he felt a blow to his chest.

Up above, Ata-Réè had disappeared. The fighting went on, pretty much everywhere, in the distance, faintly.

A light rain started falling, which blurred things. Soon the body of Dê-Ta'Am glistened in the water. The few clothes remaining on her clung to her form. The ground under her was soaked in the hollow made by the impact of her fall. But T'Lo Dê was coming over, bent double. For the moment there was no expression on his face. Nothing but a kind of absence due, perhaps, to the pull that was bringing him closer to the strangely inert body on the ground. He paused and started trembling all over.

Very slowly, after the blackout, his consciousness was waking up. But too late. Because now he was really hearing the scream that Dê-

Ta'Am had let loose. He heard it! It would not stop! He covered his ears and closed his eyes. He was shivering.

The rain started pouring down, lashing and stinging. Everything around melted.

T'Lo Dê opened his eyes. After a weird leap he was kneeling next to the body. He reached out, touched the cheek, touched the breast...

Then he knew that she was dead.

He pulled back his hand. A whimper escaped his clenched teeth. He cried, slapped the ground with open palms, splashed the water, rocked back and forth, twitched and jerked, screamed and howled but with no other noise than his gasping breath made ludicrous by the excess of tears. He shook and bobbed his head like a lunatic. Suddenly he jumped up and started stomping the ground in mad rage, his face twisted out of shape. Then he collapsed. His body convulsed. He vomited, urinated. He held his belly with both hands. And he passed out.

When he came to and saw the mess he had created, the bodily fluids, the scratched and trampled ground, the thought occurred to him that he was just an animal. It finished him. It was over. What was the use! He had to die too, very quickly.

He calmed down then, went and leaned over the dead girl. He admired her. What a difference between the graceful pose of the young body being washed in the rain and all the lamentable wreckage left by his despair! He realized this. In a very bitter feeling of humiliation.

The fall had not mangled Dê-Ta'Am. She remained beautiful. Her eyes still glistened under the eyelashes, each still dangling a drop of water. Her head was tilted. A willful crease shadowed her forehead. "I'll start over again!" she seemed to be saying. Her legs were slightly parted. Part of her hip and buttocks was visible, nude because she had fallen on her side. T'Lo Dê remembered how she used to make love...

He kissed her, held her, then lifted her up. He started walking with purpose. He had to cross the Cities then leave Kob'Lâm... He feared nothing. No one would stop him. He was sure of it. And he was right.

At one point, even though he was instinctively taking side streets and avoiding crowds whenever he saw them, he ran into some. Royal Guards came storming out to catch a group of fleeing Devotees. At the sight of him they all stopped together.

T'Lo Dê emerged from the rainy fog like a ghost. Quickly he was on them, then past them without them doing anything in the confusion of seeing the corpse of Dê-Ta'Am in his arms.

One of them, however, did make a move but was held back by another who said, "Leave her to him. She belongs to him. The work's been done, the rest is his own business..."

By then T'Lo Dê was already lost in the maze of steep stairs, plunging into the dark heart of the rain.

But then the Guards reacted. After their amazement had died down, released from the shock of seeing the ghostly porter, they understood the full magnitude of the sight. The infamous Dê-Ta'Am was dead! They cried out in triumph. The Devotees had been decapitated!

With increased energy they ran off to spread the news everywhere: "The infamous Dê-Ta'Am was dead, dead, dead!"

... Yes, it was raining, vast, sluggish, relentless. A torrential cleansing in the heart of which T'Lo Dê was running, like swimming, completely lost.

Amphibians were coming out all over the place, secret and silent witnesses of his tragedy. Living slime, rippling ooze, green and yellow, they poked out their flat heads at his approach. Their soulless eyes watched him.

When he passed by, all of them, big and small, fell in behind him. Little by little they formed an endless swarm that other amphibians kept joining.

But T'Lo Dê was utterly unaware of this. His lips parted, swallowing mouthfuls of rain, he ran instinctively towards a halo of light he glimpsed at the end of his night, at the end of his sorrow. For, this halo, this hazy, round glimmer, calm and gloomy, was his goal, the end of his suffering, his peace. He knew that it was a way out. Over there he could leave and fade away, beyond, fast, in the weak shimmering that he alone, the unworthy, the T'Lo, could lay claim to.

Now he was not crying anymore, the rain was sobbing enough for everything. He was grateful, vaguely. It washed his wounds, cooled his fever. He was completely numb.

His agonizing grief was staying at its peak in him, but he did not really feel it—all feelings were suppressed. It only felt like an extremely thick, heavy weight at the bottom of his being. He ran.

Even though Na-Nood changed the rain into a kind of luminous sheet, he took no notice of anything around him. He thought only of the pale halo awaiting him.

271

He had to run, simply run, desperately, anxiously, run because it was the time for it, because the time had come and in the end, as his life collapsed, there was nothing else for him to do.

Dê-Ta'Am's head bobbed in his arms. Suddenly he noticed it and stopped as if shocked. He had forgotten!

He looked at her there, naked, limp, squeezed against him, all exposed, all revealed in the hazy glow of this liquid universe.

He panted: Dê-Ta'Am, his glory, his love, his amazing creation, all him! Strangely, in his stupor, he examined her with horrific sharpness that spared no detail. She still had that haughty, cruel frown. Dê-Ta'Am, water dribbling out of the corner of her mouth... She had not given up, even at the last moment when her life was over, splattered on the ground after the fall... No, he saw very well, Dê-Ta'Am had remained focused on herself. Intact finally. Not broken. Above all, not vanquished. Just frozen in a kind of suspended intensity that would be hers henceforth on the other side of things.

Her hair hung in ribbons, snakes of glistening fire, purple algae. A bloody star stamped on her shoulder: a fatal sign, the seal of death—the only one visible, which T'Lo Dê suddenly touched while gaping dismally...

With his mind wandering he confused everything now. All his memories were mixed up with this young corpse. Dê-Ta'Am? She was Amo through her aggressive redness; she was Opak with her snootiness and uncontrollable eroticism; she was the magical gem, the creation of the Chamber of Love; and she was also him, everything he had been, everything he had loved, she was his fruit, his child, his little girl whom he had fed with this femininity, and his big girl, the Woman, born of him but whom he had then penetrated with his male sex, joining them together in a terrible mystery. All this, she was all this, here in his arms among the obscurity of reflections, refracted in every direction... broken reflections...

He was screaming, with his mouth open, him the mute, him the T'Lo, he was screaming, without uttering a sound: Dê-Ta'Am! He tilted back his head in the rain, choked on the water that poured down his throat...

Then the inner scream quieted down. Only a shudder at the end whose slow waves saturated the T'Lo's brain. Dê-Ta'Am, the sole link, the failed attempt at joining the pariah race with human triumph... Dê-Ta'Am, dead!

He hugged her hysterically. She was growing cold. He had the dreadful realization that she was losing her human part, that warm blood that he adored.

He started off again. The energizing current, paused for a moment, had surged forth again without any transition.

He remembered only one thing: at the end of the night, of the rain, there was a halo in the middle of which he was going to enter.

The whipping winds were easing up. In its place, gradually, came a watery mist, a vast dampness that, more than the crazy downpour, turned the earth into liquid mud where the (ever-increasing) amphibians banded together. It looked like a gelatinous bridge flowing in bunches out of a huge, invisible frog that was blanketing all of nature with its spawn...

T'Lo Dê, then, went back to his primitive state. Finally and fully vanquished, he left the daylight land of the warm-blooded, the miracle of man whom he had only been able to live alongside.

Maybe the white halo is the door to his origins? He feels himself growing cold, his damp skin feels slimy. He will never again see the sun Ooh'R! What for? Na-Nood understands him, she who guides him... He is heading toward the original sludge, the blind, gentle, slime, the swamp.

T'Lo Dê comes to the edge of the cliff that overlooks the Dongdwo domain. He stops. He straightens up, his toes gripping the rocky vein above the chasm. Far below is the clammy, peaceful dark. Fog hovers above. The light of the moon reflects off it. Into this halo T'Lo Dê wants to go!

He glances down at the one he is carrying. With clumsy fingers he combs her long hair, brushes it from her face, which is now pale and hard with mauve lips. One last surge of memories floods him, chokes him, he moans. The images march by too fast, overlap, get mixed up, then they slow down. Ah, here's a happy one, timeless! He remembers how sweet it was! Yes, he was weaving flower crowns for the head of the Beautiful Stranger and he, T'Lo Dê, how proud, he had the idea of mixing in bird feathers. Oh, the smile of the Stranger! Marvelous human world!

T'Lo stiffens: now he is entering the world of outcast T'Lo.

Roughly, as if with a paw, he covers the face of Dê-Ta'Am with all her hair. And then, he jumps...

He did not hurt himself down below. He just sank, with his load, up to his shoulders. Dê-Ta'Am is already sunk.

He waits. He feels nothing, no fear, nothing. Everything is empty inside. He is in no hurry. He waits patiently. He who has nothing more to do, no more worries. The swamp is gently sucking him down. It is good. It is this. T'Lo Dê descends with confidence. The mud has reached his neck.

He waits. He is thinking of trivial things of no importance that he sees around him: the ridiculous remains of Opak's funeral that took place here not long ago… Some scattered ends of shiny fabric hanging onto the rare plants sticking out of the swamp, a scrap of a votive ribbon, a spear embedded with rubies planted weirdly at an angle.

T'Lo Dê does not know what any of this is.

… Dreary indifference. His gaze falls upon the pools of water around him. They are quivering in the dripping mist… Then, suddenly, their surface remains smooth. The thin layers of fog in the air are gone. All is blurry and quiet.

T'Lo Dê looks up. From where he jumped, on the sharp edge of the cliff, extraordinary—countless amphibians are lined up pointing in his direction. Their staring eyes are fixed on him. They are all perfectly still. His cold witnesses.

Wearied, T'Lo Dê lowers his head. It is too long. He waits nonetheless. And as time passes, without him being aware, masses of Dongdwo start to appear on the edge of their island.

More time passes. The Dongdwo are all there now, facing him.

Thus posed on the swamp, the head of T'Lo Dê looks like some aquatic plant, a pale, bulbous fruit. The mud covers his lips. He keeps his eyes closed. His sinking continues. He will not move when the mud reaches his nostrils. Maybe by some wild force he has already gone, dead before completely sinking?

Up above, the slimy amphibians all shudder for a moment, then suddenly withdraw and disappear.

The top of T'Lo Dê's head glistens like a piece of sunken moon. And is eclipsed… There remains only the gloomy swamp where the Dongdwo gather, slowly, to start their service.

Huge dark masses, decrepit, obsolete shapes, the Dongdwo lament as from the depths of time. What are they, really, these mourners? Out of the night in lumps, out of the black, frozen suffering, they bellow-fog, they bay-moon, they squeal, grunt and chew the vestiges of the past.

Their one-voiced lament started quietly. It was gentle and patient, lengthy, before rising up. It got gradually louder. Then it grew excessive until it threw into a panic all the awakened birds that flapped their wings and soared off in every direction, until it chased the reptiles into an exodus from the swamp. They alone, the Dongdwo, will stay there on this woeful night, they alone know how to weep!

All of nature hears them. No animal will sleep this night.

And the Dongdwo's lament, in the end, reaches Kobor Tigan't, carried on the wind that blows like a prophetic whisper through the final battles.

Yes, Dê-Ta'Am was dead and the Devotees vanquished!

But Kobor Tigan't will not savor the joy of victory over the Devotees. The White Ooh'Rou is dying, they say.

The flurry of the last battles was winding down on this gray morning under the vast swathes of dripping fog. Through the insomniac fatigue that gripped everyone, the grief-stricken convoy carrying Ta wound its way furtively back to the Palace, leaving a trail of woe behind it. A second group followed it, which was the Royal Guards bringing Hé-Nark back. It was a double lamentation that affected the onlookers. The crowd had become huge, pressed to see and understand. The people of the three lower Cities fill up Kob'Iâm, overflowing into Kob'Ooh'R. They are going to stand before the Palace waiting for news.

They are mostly women, children and the elderly from Kob'Lâm, all the men having joined the troops of R'Ang to comb through the territory in search of escaped enemies. The indignation against this coup attempted by the Devotees is immense. The tolerance they had shown for quite a while now is gone, replaced by vengeful anger. Likewise, the revelation of their dark nature was an unpleasant surprise. They realize, in hindsight, how dangerous they are.

"Didn't the White Ooh'Rou say so!"

They repeat this. They harp on it.

All attention is focused on R'Ang. Without fully realizing it, they are expecting everything from him. They know that he acted, fought, won. His radiant figure is deeply engraved on their psyches.

The waiting crowd is sure they will see him soon. Yes, who is he really, this Royal Son raised so carefully by the Queen? Who is he whom they have known since childhood but whom they do not really know, this R'Ang who suddenly over-leaped them all and whose glorious strength vitalized all the Men!

Following his orders, in Oda-Néè's domain where the isolated nests of resistance surrendered, one by one, the prisoners are already penned

275

up. They have stopped killing the T'Lo. With the passions of combat calmed down, that passiveness facing death ended up discouraging the fiercest fighters. Therefore, they picked them out from the surviving Devotees and set them apart. They will all be thrown into the Ananou Pit under the Palace.

With this news scenes of hysterical grief explode among the Devotees. The idea of being separated from the T'Lo is unbearable to them. They weep and wail loudly. The docile T'Lo do not react. They close their eyes and stop their ears. Certainly they are crying but silently.

The underground network of the Devotees is searched. Its extent, its numerous branches is no surprise. It fans out from top to bottom of Kobor Tigan't, ending in the many openings in the allied Domains. Crevices and caves were cleverly used for storage—stocks of weapons and provisions were found. It also leads all the way to the Royal Nursery where many influential devotee families lived.

The Royal Guards, the Blacksmiths, the Young Servants and all the men who swelled their ranks have soon emptied the big houses of their families who are brought with the youngest children to Kob'Iâm, the Domain of Oda-Néè where they will be held with the others.

Skirmishes break out, relatively brief, more or less fatal. They capture more T'Lo. They find others died of fright. Some Devotees whose favorites are snatched away choose to commit suicide rather than live without them. Others kill them with their own hands and must be captured in bloody battles.

But the coup is over. Everything calms down.

Devastated from carrying the Queen, the Royal Guards and Young Servants leave the royal rooms where Ata-Réè and Gan'd take charge of her as R'Ang looks on with forlorn eyes, disheveled and dirty and bleeding.

Gan'd sees those carrying Hé-Nark pass by. She sends Do'A-Roo to go with them because her first duty is to the Queen.

The two women gasp pitifully when they see all the bruises on Ta's body. R'Ang cannot stand being idle during this urgent care of their poor martyr, so he starts helping the two women who are both, unconsciously, moaning while washing the abandoned body, so easy to lift up.

Together they clean all the inflicted wounds. R'Ang applies perfume and soothing balms. Ata-Réè prepares the finest white tunic and puts it gently on the Queen. They smooth out the bed, lay her down, wedge cushions around her, cover her with light blankets and dim the lights. Gan'd trickles a restorative drink between her lips.

How calm everything is all of a sudden in this huge room where the walls are hung with the serene folds of beautiful fabrics woven with gold and silver!

R'Ang has plopped down, exhausted. Ata-Réè is kneeling against the bed, one hand on the Queen's forehead. Gan'd is coming and going, without a sound, diligently preparing her remedies, pouring them patiently into Ta's mouth. All three watch her intently, continually. She is breathing, quietly, in short breaths. They all fear lest it stop! Their own breath is strained. But it goes on, this shallow breathing…

Gan'd clenches her teeth for the first time. A passing thought flashes in her mind in response to an imploring glance from R'Ang. "She'll live… I think."

Ata-Réè cannot hold back any longer. She breaks down in tears and turns away.

Ta's face is strangely thinned down. It is the face of a very young girl, exuding a kind of childishness.

"Death is near!" thinks R'Ang despite what Gan'd just said. He watches passionately. Her mauve mouth, her pinched nose, her lowered eyelids that are like fragile bird's eggs with transparent shells. But all around them, the deep, dark circles, tragic…

Her breath quickens. A sudden flush in her face. Beads of sweat on her forehead.

Gan'd leans over, "Yes, she'll live," she states affirmatively. "My cures are working. She's going to burn, but it'll be the fire of life."

Ata-Réè looks up.

R'Ang stammers, "Are you sure?"

Gan'd nods, smiles bravely, piously, "Yes, she'll live. I'll save her. I swear to you, Royal Son!"

Outside, the people are clamoring for R'Ang.

Ata-Réè stands up, radiating authority, "Come, Royal Son, let's go together to tell them what they want to know and what you do not yet know yourself. Let's go tell them why our Queen has worked for this day to come, prepared by her for you since childhood. Let's go tell them that you are the Great Child of the Reign, the first male to bear the solar cross: the Mark of Ooh'R in the only shade the Sun tolerates when at zenith—under the feet of Man!"

R'Ang mutters, "The marks on the bottom of my foot is therefore the…"

"The Mark of Ooh'R!" the B'Tah-Gou finishes, proudly. "Come, Great Child, the Power belongs to you!"

The sun was reaching the summit of its course when Ata-Réè, escorted by R'Ang, stepped onto the main terrace of the Palace. With a firm voice, despite her emotion, she first announced to the people that the White Ooh'Rou was alive and that everything was being done to keep her so.

The crowd instantly burst out in cries of joy and hope.

Ata-Réè demanded silence. After a long wait, more emotional than before, she revealed the true identity of R'Ang, proclaimed him the Great Child of the Reign, the Chosen of Ooh'R and he himself, from now on, the Ooh'R of Kobor Tigan't.

"As the Queen wished, she who knew everything and who worked only for this future!" she emphasized with authority.

A stupefied silence fell over the crowd. Then, suddenly, like an explosion, the enthusiasm was unleashed, indescribable!

It was then that a remarkable celestial phenomenon occurred. A thick cloud that was blocking the sky right above Kobor Tigan't instantly dissipated. And they saw, in its place, very high up, *a huge crystal dome*, which reflected the rays of the sun majestically!

Was this not the miraculous sign of Ooh'R's favor approving his Son R'Ang and the victory over the Devotees?

The Giants were carried away and could not stop cheering this apparition.

R'Ang and Ata-Réè contemplated the thing solemnly. They likened it, reasonably, to the crystalline formations in the House of Great Faces and thought that mysterious beings, like the one who had been The Beautiful Stranger to them, were watching over their destinies.

Several days later the dome was still there. They marveled at it tirelessly.

Even though they were not aware of the crystalline presences of the House of Great Faces, which were seen only by the Queen, R'Ang and Ata-Réè, the people came in droves to the Temple.

As time passed, as the dome remained there, they got used to it, feeling proud of the solar privilege.

CHAPTER XXVI

Indeed, Ta survived.

But as Gan'd had foreseen, she burned for a long time (days and days) in the grip of an uncontrollable fever. Spasms and shivering shook her body constantly. Her muscles seized up. Her heart, often, seemed to stop from exhaustion. It started up again, however, beating against her ribs with irregular strength, sometimes racing, sometimes fading into weak, intermittent beats.

She grew thin, almost emaciated. R'Ang got scared. But Gan'd, trusting in the power of her plants, repeated that it was a good sign, a reaction that assured a happy ending, the progressive return to health. Still, she did not hide the fact that it would take a long time.

Unceasingly, with an extraordinary resistance to fatigue, with the support of her knowledge, she stayed by the Queen. She moistened the body several times a day with herbal preparations that cooled it down. The skin peeled off, revealing a new, pearly white epidermis.

Then the fever subsided, washed away by excessive sweating. The Queen's body relaxed, stopped shivering and, for the first time, they saw her move on her own, albeit unconsciously, to get more comfortable.

R'Ang, who was leaning over her, looking straight into her eyes when they finally opened. She was feeling for his hand, grabbed it and spoke clearly, as always when giving orders:

"Now it's your reign, isn't it? Hold the power and wield it! Don't be afraid to command! I worked only for you, R'Ang..."

Her eyes closed again. She seemed to be sleeping. R'Ang was beaming, buoyed by hope, imagining that when she next awoke she would regain consciousness. Gan'd frowned doubtfully. He did not believe her but waited patiently for her awakening, which promised so much happiness.

He was disappointed. Time passed. Ta's skinny body slowly repaired but she did not speak again. She opened her eyes only briefly and stared at nothing in particular.

Her convalescence dragged on. Ta acted like a Traveler who was far away from her homeland, who was coming back, of course, but in small stages, dawdling, wandering around wherever she was.

In fact, the link between the spirit and body was not really restored. Ta was floating between two worlds.

Her body was reviving with stunning beauty and grace, and in another mystery. So translucent, it seemed, day by day, being purified and rejuvenated. The luminous severity of the White Ooh'Rou was disappearing to give way to a simple sweetness that feminized her more.

R'Ang was dumbstruck seeing a young girl take shape. Was this, really, Princess Ta coming back? He liked to believe so as he was filled with tenderness for this fragility and ready to defend it, already feeling a kind of possessive pride.

His love for the Ooh'Rou had been strangled by respect. He would free himself of this and become the tender love of a strong man for the wounded girl... A brand-new feeling for a Kobor male but one that perfectly fit R'Ang's nature, which, by a surprising contrast to his rough features, showed an obvious maturity of body and mind. His authority, his decisions were not up for discussion. He was soft only in the presence of Ta.

This was spread all around him. The men were already copying his manners. New ways of being were quickly adopted. A whole reorganization of life was implemented after the Devotees' uprising. It persisted. Kobor Tigan't was thrilled with it... The elders from Kob'Lâm came to see him out of curiosity. The independent Blacksmiths of Kob'Râm swore by him alone. The Young Servants were truly fascinated.

Furthermore, the women of Kobor Tigna't saw in him a different being, a man with a new essence around whom they never would have dared to throw their belt if the Festival of the Choice of Men were still celebrated! One does not capture the Sun Ooh'R.

For everyone he was the Son. Maybe even the avatar...

The revelation of the Grand B'Tah-Gou calling him the Great Child on the morning of the victory over the Devotees had been received as a sign of the Times in a stupor that almost immediately replaced the vibrant energy of the general enthusiasm.

The people praised Ta's foresight, which they remembered had given them plenty of hints during her speeches. They thought a lot about the White Ooh'Rou. Gifts for her flooded the Palace. Materialized thoughts, wishes and goodwill that they really hoped would help her get healthy again. They knew it would be slow.

The one in the best place to know this was Gan'd. The slight improvement in the Queen's condition allowed her to go see Hé-Nark who was almost out of danger thanks to Do'A-Roo's care, instructed by her mother. When Gan'd paid a visit to the Master Guard, the young daughter took her place at the bedside of Ta. It was nice for the two to be alone for a little while.

The first thought of the wounded man was obviously for news of the Queen. Gan'd did not hold back the details, she was proud of her treatment and the progress of her dear patient who relied and was still relying on her skills. While talking she kept a close eye on Hé-Nark and was sad to see how weak he was, though she knew he would recover completely.

The massive, muscular body of the Master Guard was emaciated. When he stood up he looker taller, straighter and, in a way, more imposing. His hair had turned gray and there was a glint in his eyes that even more than before bespoke the weight of contemplating things and people. He was not cheerful. His thoughts were occupied by the White Ooh'Rou. He constantly wondered whether he had been negligent in his duties and the Devotees had taken advantage of it.

Gan'd, who easily guessed this, tried to appease him. No, his vigilance was not at fault! But maybe just wanting to leave the Queen alone had made him forget the growing danger and the perpetual need to watch over the Reign... He readily agreed. But plagued by remorse, to himself he said that he would have better served the Queen by loving her less and being just a Master Guard, brash and brutal who sounds the alarm without worrying whether the Queen needs peace and quiet! Oh, he too often remembered that Ta was always a woman, the most exquisite woman... At this point he always willingly stopped his train of thought because certain images surfaced too quickly and were too sweet—they were his mystical treasure. He knew they were part of him forever. He did not want to tarnish the flower by thinking too much about them.

After a while Gan'd left to go back to the Queen. She did not like staying away from her for too long. Hé-Nark agreed since he, too, was rarely alone with his loyal Men visiting him and with the constant care of a few Young Servants of the Queen who were strongly attached to him and truly revered him.

Then Do'A-Roo came back. He thought of her a little like his daughter and she, who had total trust in him, did not try to hide her sighs or the fire in her eyes when around R'Ang, who also came by frequently. The Master Guard had no trouble guessing her feelings. He knew but said nothing. He was worried, afraid of seeing her suffer a love like his for the Queen, an impossible love... For, he knew that R'Ang loved the Queen and could allow himself to do so!

For her part, Gan'd had developed a maternal love for Ta. Seeing her get better swelled her heart. She was happy to feed her, wash her, dress her. She combed her long, light hair delicately.

Ta's vegetative existence gradually revived in the hands of this healing magnetism. It was a docile recovery, without drama, almost unnervingly calm. She opened her eyes only rarely still. She mostly slept, with a smile on her lips.

Gan'd did not try to speed up the recovery with strong cures. She knew that a lot of rest healed not only the inflicted tortures but also—maybe especially—the great fatigue built up through her reign, secretly, by her spirit of sacrifice, which did damage to her own nature, her love of personal freedom, the boundless dreams she could not cherish and that she cruelly repressed.

But, in the end, every day brought progress in her recovery.

Ta opened her eyes for longer. She let her gaze wander around the room. She paid no more attention to the people than the objects. She watched them moving around like watching a sunbeam move across a wall. She lingered a little longer on her pet bird perched on the window sill or on the careful actions of Do'A-Roo when arranging flowers.

When they spoke to her she turned her head to the sound of the voice but did not seem to understand. Gan'd forbid anyone to tire her out by repeating anything too much.

Ta appeared to have no desire, no curiosity, no appetite for anything. Gan'd gave her everything to eat and drink.

Then one day she started talking, just saying simple things about the light, the bird in the window or the flowers in the vase. She correctly named all her friends when they came in. But she showed no particular reaction on seeing them. Calm contentment perhaps? In any case, no emotion, even when she saw the tears of joy rolling down their cheeks.

She did not ramble. Just sometimes she whispered as if to herself with her eyes half-closed. It was like a mysterious interview.

Do'A-Roo, who was very sensitive to ephemeral events, told her mother and Ata-Réè that the Ooh'Rou was most certainly being visited by invisible beings. The girl added that every time she had been alone with the Queen at one of these moments she felt a kind of nervousness, an emotion like when a great person walks into a room. In fact, for her, someone was really coming to Ta! That meant (she explained more clearly) someone suddenly just showed up! Then the atmosphere changed. She felt peacefully lethargic and thought she might fall asleep. All her limbs went numb, but she felt no fear. On the contrary, she started looking forward to these visitations.

Sometimes she glimpsed at the foot of the bed, most often at the head next to the Queen, a glossy shine, a kind of reflection, for example, that the position of the sun did not explain.

Gan'd narrowed her eyes. Ata-Réè nodded gravely—she was seeing nothing around Ta.

But Do'A-Roo was not wrong.

Ta was visiting with the Being of the Crystal almost all the time. It had become familiar and almost indispensable to her. She loved its caresses. Being enveloped by it made her quiver pleasantly. She needed this quiver, this vibration whereby all her senses were transcended and could savor the interpenetration of the Crystal. When this happened, she had access to a different existence than that of blood. She saw herself turning transparent. Her own being was expanded with light and the vital spirits of the Crystal circulated in her freely.

Consequently, she donned the Crystal like an extra part of her being, like something infinitely precious that she had been stripped of in an extremely dark past... And yet, even though it became an intimate part of her, the Crystal kept its independence, differed from her and talked to her...

It told her many a strange thing, this Being of the Crystal who swaddled her with its kindness. She listened passionately to everything it said because it was answering the old questions of her soul. She never tired of listening and she remembered everything.

"You see," it said, "we're not so much beings as living meeting points between your form of life and ours, between your evolution and ours. You need us and we also need you.

"We're free spirits who long to experience a personality by descending into the depths of your matter. You, creatures bound to the flesh, you long only to free yourselves of all the density in order to rise through the planes where you will expand, infinitely, in universality.

"We can give you our own experience of these planes and part of our free nature that is only clothed with light. In exchange, you can give us the incomparable experience of living on earth in the constricted clothing that demands of the spirit, to fulfill itself, more than anywhere else.

"As you know me in my crystalline form, I am a Mediator.

"To join you, as eager as is our desire for this alliance, we cannot become denser than this appearance that some, like you, might not truly see but can be aware of.

"We are called Evolutionary Powers. We search among you for those who will be the chosen ones. Through us certain humans on earth are granted the additional moderator they lack and who will activate them. Those we accept will be different than others. They will evolve, triumph over stagnation. They will dare. They will create. The mineralization of the antiquated races will not catch them in their snares of death.

"The chosen ones of our Alliance will cross the reefs of the engulfing age. The chosen ones will survive the obliterating times because by our endowment they will have been sublimated above all the others!

"Of course we should have waited for the possibility to clothe ourselves directly with a body of your flesh when it had been refined by your merits alone. The solar seed of Ooh'R, combined with the seed of deep earth, would have managed eventually since these two elements were received and develop by your fertile Ooh'Rous, true mediators, but you know what happened and how the Very Huge redirected the earth's fluid all for herself, ruined our plan and made a widower of the vital sun.

"Our compassion was concerned for you. We wanted to fix it, to extract from your fatally condemned racial masses the noblest elements so that they could survive elsewhere and otherwise. Thus my love chose you first, White Ooh'Rou!

"Someone different from us but who is close to us also desired to help you. He took a different path than ours to occupy an earthly body as soon as possible. It was a tragedy because your heavy shell destroyed his essential qualities or at least kept them from manifesting, the envelope being too coarse to answer to his subtle desires.

"This being you called Angel, the Beautiful Stranger. You found him again in the Crystal, the mineral him, like our Crystal of Light and he graces your Temple.

"This crystal is the symbol of his tragic failure. If we did the same thing, incarnating directly in a human link, we'd sleep and never wake up inside your crude shells.

"So listen, hear what is coming!

"We will linger on through your children. We will add a fertilization of light to your own fertile elements. These children who make up the New Chosen Race will be born of a Triple Union; Man with Woman by the Crystal.

"Understand this, you whom I love!

"I have chosen you, the first, and I have chosen R'Ang for you. I will ally myself to your union. And there will come from us a Renowned Son. He will reign over the new land. And all the Crystal Beings like me who will be allied to chosen couples will be born of famous children who will be the people of our son!

"I told you I love you, but don't get confused, o woman! I love raising your vibration to my level. I love bathing you in the living water of my light and blending you with it. But I don't love like a man does.

"We others have no feelings in the way you normally understand. Just like you have no personality—not yet—in the way we know.

"We are all alike. No Crystal is different from me. We are all like one. We all emanate from just one Crystal. It is our All and it governs us. Our rest is in It. It works through us. We are the parts of Its Body. But each of us is also It, fully.

"Can you understand a little, Ooh'Rou Ta, the effects of this universal harmony that is expressed in countless ways?

"We come to you because there is already a dormant trace of our nature in you. You bear our signature. It lies in you, sleeping. It is in our Alliance that by receiving us it will awaken and blaze up, finally active!

"Open your eyes so that I can unveil the mysteries you are entitled to!"

Ta obeyed. Her vision opened and the Crystal directed the insight on herself so that she would know herself better. It first showed her her own heart and the Flaming Spirit, golden red, that was the Directing Intelligence.

It showed her how this heart, alone in its work, pushed and pulled the flow of blood. It pointed out the luminous, living spheres that this blood transported. Then it suddenly showed Ooh'R at the summit of the clouds, like unto its heart, and it saw the same Flaming Spirit that validated the harmonic obedience to it. She saw Ooh'R, also alone in its work, pushing and pulling the torrents of luminous energy that sweep along, like a golden shimmer, the living, thinking spheres.

Ta understood the connections revealed to her.

Then the Crystal increased the rate of vibration unifying them. And at the limit of what was tolerable for an earthly creature, it showed her, at last, the Ineffable Center that neither words nor images can truly express but that, by grace, the creature can still receive and feel.

OMNIPRESENT. OMNISCIENT. OMNIPOTENT. TERRIFYING BEAUTY. TERRIFYING POWER. TERRIFYING LOVE. FROM WHERE COMES, INCESSANTLY, THE FLOW OF LIFE... AND THE FLAMING SPIRIT was there too!

The Crystal said, "Call it the Supreme Ooh'R! Everything comes from It. Everything goes back to It. LIFE-LOVE-SPIRIT, IT IS."

And Ta understood that It was in her too!

Several times a day, when he could escape the obligations of the reign, R'Ang went to see Ta.

The first time she came out of her fever, it was right there at her bedside. She stared at his face with clear, unblinking eyes. Her voice was the same Ooh'Rou, questioning to make sure her orders were carried out.

"Now, R'Ang, you are reigning, right? You hold the Power just like I've always wanted?"

As he nodded, touched and eager to please her, she sank back into her cushions and breathed a sigh of relief.

"Finally, finally, I haven't failed in everything. Man reigns!" A mischievous smile crossed her face. "Hold tight, Great Child, Son of Ooh'R, the reign is hard, it's tiring."

Her eyelids fluttered. She looked like she was getting numb again. She muttered, "Oh, the reign, the reign..." And she dozed off

But in the end she awoke from her semi-lethargy. R'Ang double his visits to be sure not to miss one of her moments of consciousness.

When he got there he would lean over and fondly brush his hand over her forehead. She would recognize him right away, show no surprise but smile with obvious pleasure. She would talk to him, but contrary to his expectations she never again broached the subject of the Reign or of government or anything specific about the Race or even Kobor Tigan't. She spoke in short, cheerful phrases, carefree and frivolous, talking about how a sunbeam was moving or the manner in which the bird in the window was sharpening its beak or the weird way the beautiful flowers were wilting so quickly this morning...

This childish talk delighted R'Ang, gave him pause from his daily activities, but they were not without cause for worry. Would Ta's mind ever come back from this long drifting where she seemed happy enough?

To his great relief R'Ang soon realized that he had been too pessimistic. Ta's mind was recovering. But it was gradual.

First of all she stayed awake for longer and longer periods. Then, instead of just talking inertly in her bed, her face started showing signs of her mood. She made gestures to punctuate her comments.

She started asking for certain flowers rather than others, picked out her favorite fruits, refused food she did not like, wanted to change the wall hangings, had certain cushions and carpets brought in, the ones she had known since childhood, she put on perfume and wondered where they had put the last jewelry she had ordered before becoming sick.

She questioned everyone about what had happened to the Devotees. She knew that R'Ang was now the ruler but wanted to know the details, a lot of details. They told her everything by degrees. They saw that she had no memory of the horrible abuse she had suffered. She suspected something and pushed her friends into a corner demanding answers to her queries.

During these sessions R'Ang was tortured. Hé-Nark, usually so bold and clever, used the excuse of a painful wound to get away as soon as possible. It was Ata-Réè, helped by Gan'd, who found the fitting responses to avoid traumatizing the Queen. She listened, intently, but without a trace of emotion. They even saw a smile flit across her lips, touched with a hint of compassion.

"Oh, really, the poor White Ooh'Rou," she proclaimed.

Her two companions could not believe their ears.

She noticed their reaction and said, "How solid the body is and you've taken great care of this body here, my faithful Gan'd."

Gan'd was a little upset and corrected her, "I took care of Ta!"

The Queen smiled, more mysteriously than before, "Ta is not in this body. What happened to this body does not bother me, quite the contrary. Nothing could have defiled me—I am not really in this body!"

She looked with gratitude at the Being of the Crystal nearby. She remembered everything. Never had her mind been clearer.

Ata-Réè and Gan'd were alarmed. They believed that the fever had come back!

That night, when R'Ang went into Ta's room he felt like something mysterious had taken place. A wave of irrational happiness washed over him and he wanted to blurt out, "You're healed!". But he could not do it, stunned as he was by the weird ambiance that surrounded the Queen.

She was sitting up in bed on her cushions, watching him come in and smiling at his emotional reaction. She was calm and beautiful, with a rested beauty beyond anything he could have imagined. A light haloed her as if radiating from her now translucent flesh. Her eyes sparkled with expectation and promise. The tassels of her thick hair snaked lazily along the curves of her breasts that were visible under the light robe that barely covered her.

R'Ang was both taken aback and carried away.

As soon as he got through the doorway all his daily cares vanished in the feeling of being welcomed into her world, this intimidating, other world on the borders of which he had been confined for a long time, waiting, never daring to believe that he might be allowed to enter one day.

And now it was done! The garden of the wonder was open. Ta, in the center, was holding out her arms. And not like a big sister, certainly not like a mother and even less like a queen seeing her favorite, but like a lover, with a simple passion that was beyond compare.

"I was waiting for you," she said, "it felt so long but now you're finally here."

The new tones of her voice deepened the meaning of this remark. And R'Ang understood that, in fact, Ta had been waiting since the day he was born.

Younger, fresher, lighter than ever, she had stood the test of time without being affected by it so that she would be worthy of him.

"Oh, my one and only," she exclaimed while hugging him, "you're younger than me."

He knelt next to her bed so that his dazzled eyes could gaze more closely upon this fragile wonder, a victor over time and suffering, this unbreakable woman whose face and body bore no traces of the abuse endured or the distress of power.

"How perfect and pure you are! In truth, I knew nothing could conquer you!"

She was still smiling, calm, happy, looking deeply into his eyes almost greedily. Then, like a curious girl, she ran a finger over his face, the shadows, the early wrinkles, all the signs of the sudden maturing etched into his features on the morning of the Devotees' uprising.

"You've become a rough man," she commented. "That's good. You'll need it, you know…"

She paused and lowered her voice.

"And you'll need even more."

"When?" he was startled, already worrying.

But she waved away this cloud and cooed, "Oh, later, much later." The fearlessness in her eyes aroused R'Ang's desire. She whispered softly, giving him shivers, "Come, come, my beloved, don't make me wait!"

She leaned back a little, pulled him closer, beseechingly.

Shaken up, he saw her cheeks turn the color of rose petals, a sight he never believed possible on the legendary skin of the White Ooh'Rou!

Ta moaned with desire. With roving hands she urged him to join her.

R'Ang felt dizzy. He saw the big bouquet of flowers on the table grow through the room, colored suns that were coming to him joyously. Their magnified fragrance flooded him, exciting his senses, intoxicating him like he had never known.

Quiet sounds beguiled his ears, mixed with the loving words of Ta that he did not understand, murmurs, tinkling, babbling.

The feast of color melted away into a pink mist that turned pale but started glimmering *before being reabsorbed in a single, crystal sphere, living and thinking,* in the center of which a shining woman was beckoning him, but whom he could not yet join even though she was naked in his arms, under him, and the kingship of desire illuminated them both! Then—and this was extraordinarily intense for him—Ta ran her fingers down R'Ang's neck, fluttered over his shoulder and laughed with joy when he shivered, causing a spasm that flung him onto her.

He sensed that the echo of this shiver and of the laugh were reverberating in the Crystalline Presence that was sheltering them.

He felt that his tense virility, on the cusp of the Queen's open femininity, was a transcendent bridge over which the light of the Life bequeathed to him by the Crystal was rushing. Unspeakable rapture filled him. The Power added to his power. *He was then truly made King* while a storm of ecstasy carried him away, fully lucid, astonishingly aware of acting according to divine law.

The crystal envelopment throbbed along with him, to the same rhythm of love, the rhythm of all creation.

The Barriers fell. The Worlds opened like fruits. There was no more distance or differentiation. The divine Universe was mirrored in him.

The King and the Queen were united by the Crystal in the womb of Life.

In the loins of the King where the cosmos swirled the fiery pulses of the light were activated, joyful, casting their galactic flow into the shining night of the royal belly.

"I love you, R'Ang!" Ta said.

"I love you, R'Ang!" the Crystal said. "I love you, Ta!"

Countless cosmic voices: theirs!

His own voice mixed with the others, an echo of echoes, "I love you, Ta! I love you, World!"

And then he knew that he had become the Crystal. Ta was also this same Crystal.

… That night, the ecstatic leap that energized this Triad in fusion carried them so high that they contemplated, face to face, the Vital Spirit of Worlds and Beings of which their personal Crystal was a pure representative. They saw how this Spirit of Creative Love constantly emanated representatives of itself and how these went below searching tenderly for human alliances.

The dawn in Kobor found Ta and R'Ang regenerated and transformed.

They were lying in each other's arms, not yet untangled, listening in gratitude to the fire of love, which had initiated them, growing in them.

That morning, when they entered the room still pulsing with light, Gan'd and Ata-Réè bowed very low at the sight of them because they were radiating joy and power.

"In truth," the B'Tah-Gou said, "you were both born a second time!"

This exceptional union remained hidden.

Only very close friends knew, such as Gan'd, Ata-Réè and Hé-Nark. They did not speak of it, obeying the Queen's wish since she had asked them for total discretion.

Nothing, therefore, happened. Kobor Tigan't learned of it, with great pleasure, only when the White Ooh'Rou was finally healed. She showed herself to everyone on the big terrace several times to make the people happy. But she did not show the slightest desire to take again an active role, even next to R'Ang who, as she clearly expressed, had to stay the only Ooh'R for the Race of Giants for the time being.

The people were very surprised, as well as saddened, by this announcement. But they knew that for a long time, once Ta had decreed something, she rarely went back on it. Besides, as she had hoped, they were already used to R'Ang. They felt and appreciated the beneficial effects of his vigor and determination. They even liked his severity. In short, they like fearing him.

The White Ooh'Rou became, more than ever, for everyone, the mysterious figure of legend who enlightened Kobor. The people were more devoted to her than before.

And seeing her less often in public they imagined her even better. They quickly thought that she was still governing through R'Ang, whom she had trained over the many years and whom she had obviously inspired.

But out of great tenderness to her he did not confide all his worries for the moment. Always eager to be with her, not wanting to bring her anything but pleasure and happiness, he went to her every night in her rooms where she usually kept herself not forlorn like when she was sick but dreaming and with her spirit withdrawn from the world.

It was this state that let him deal with the affairs of the realm, which she seemed not to think about at all in being more concerned with loving him, caressing him and reawakening every night with him in their communal infusion of the Crystal Being, the ethereal spheres where the Revelation was offered to their amazement.

R'Ang felt like he was living two lives because these sublime nights were a strange contrast to the daily difficulties of the reign. They had turned dramatic. In fact, since imprisoning the Devotees inside Oda-Néè's domain, a major problem cast its shadow over Kobor Tigan't.

R'Ang figured it was traumatizing for the Queen so he forbid everyone to whisper a word about it to her. It was a kind of epidemic, spawned among the Devotees. They could not stand being deprived of their T'Lo who had all been thrown into the Pit.

Corroded by the psychic drug whose continued use made them artificially hyperactive, the Devotees had been afflicted with very violent convulsions that from the start twisted their limbs and burned them with fever. They became delirious, quickly turned into a frenzied erotic madness that made them attack each other. Screaming, tearing their clothes, refusing to eat, they ran ragged in bloody sexual excitement until they died.

Some did not die right away. They had many fits with lulls when they would just sit around in a daze. They lost their minds for good. They had to take away their children. But they were horrified to see that even when taken away the children got the same symptoms as the adults.

The deaths multiplied.

Oda-Néè's domain became a camp of lunatics!

It did not stop there. Quickly, the sickness seemed to spread outside the Devotees. At first there were isolated cases among the Guards who were watching the camp. Then, within days, before they had time to realize the danger, like a sudden wildfire, cases broke out everywhere, at the same time, as if noxious air had contaminated Kobor Tigan't from top to bottom.

Faced with this new ordeal, a wave of panic swept in. R'Ang had a lot of trouble reassuring his people.

At one point they were hoping for an immanent halt to the sickness thanks to Gan'd's herbal remedies, but unfortunately they proved ineffective. The sickness prevailed, even got worse. It struck at random. Healthy one day, laid up the next.

Everybody affected became frenzied maniacs. They drooled like animals. A film covered their eyes. They stopped eating and, like the Devotees, they killed each other out of savage eroticism.

Was this, then the curse of the Devotees visited upon the whole Race?

They put chains on the madwomen to keep them from attacking their friends and family.

Only one of Gan'd's remedies had any small effect. It just limited the damage by putting the sick ones to sleep which they did not even come out of to die.

The desperate people rushed to the ceremonies of the House of Great Faces. One day, finally, R'Ang and Ata-Réè got a message from the Great Crystal. Angel, the Beautiful Stranger, appeared in the middle of the sparkling gem. He bid the Royal Son to ask Ta for the cure. She alone knew it. She alone had the power to apply it.

R'Ang decided to obey, considering it an emergency.

When he went to see Ta she was very calm. She welcomed him with her enchanting zeal and wanted to be the first to talk but he spit out his message. She listened to the whole thing with great interest. As he spoke she turned pale. At the end, when all was said and the room fell silent, heavy with sadness, she murmured:

"In truth, my Very Huge Mother didn't lie… The horrible thing she prophesied has come to pass!"

Ta suddenly straightened up. She had found and donned her Ooh'Rou mask. R'Ang saw that famous paleness come back.

"It's true," she said, "I know the cure. It is strange and terrifying. But there is no other. Waiting longer will endanger our whole Race. Therefore, I will do it. And right away!"

She ordered R'Ang to bring his best Royal Guards led by Hé-Nark and follow her.

"Out of respect for the Very Huge," she said, "we won't go into her rooms unescorted."

At the door, she held back R'Ang for a moment and hugged him. He felt suddenly calmed. She looked him in the eyes with an extraordinary radiance. What he read therein took his breath away. He could not believe it!

He was even more astonished when he saw the Crystal Being appear around them.

And Ta said, "O R'Ang, our love is fertile. Know this: I am with child."

CHAPTER XXVII

When the door to Abim's rooms closed—the Queen had entered.

It gave the Royal Guards a bad feeling huddled together in the hallway outside. They snorted, anxious and tense, then they started listening. They knew, however, that no sound would reach them. Their labored breathing betrayed their nervousness. Some of them, more attentive than others, stared at the flickering flames of the torches as if the movement might hold some oracular power.

The sound of the door closing had reverberated in the chest of R'Ang. Without saying anything he looked at Hé-Nark. The Master Guard seemed not to see him. He had a distant expression, dreaming of another time when in this same place the White Ooh'Rou was behind him as he opened one door after another until they reached this one, which had not been opened in so long. At the time the torches crackled in the same way. Oh, he remembered!

… When Ta entered she could not help feeling an almost physical horror. Her whole being revolted at the thought of performing this foul task.

Thoughts swirled around in her head. Still, she forced herself to stay calm, scrutinizing the mineral mass of the Very Huge sitting askance in the middle of the room. She had to admit that the angle had grown.

Abim was a wall of shadow on which the torch flame seemed to lose its ability to light as if the gray-black matter absorbed its rays.

Ta snapped out of the evil spell, the gnawing sadness, and to further break the hypnosis taking hold of her she spoke out loud.

"Greetings, Very Huge Mother! I come to tell you that you were right. I come to tell you that I'm going to use the Klimm to save the people like you predicted. May your spirit aid me in my task!"

She went into action, purposefully, around the room, lighting torches. When it was bright enough, in front of Abim whose shadow looked like a lake of black water, she lifted the slabs one by one to reveal the chests. She pulled them out of their hiding place and opened them to take out the various objects, which she lined up carefully and made an inventory in her head. She knew exactly which ones were needed for her work.

Here lay the royal finery of the Very Huge: weird jewelry, archaic ornaments, combs and pins made of a black, translucent metal that is found nowhere in all of Kobor, an extraordinary breastplate of the same metal with a design, attached by small chains, of a tree of rubies wrapped in the coils of a black snake.

There was also the unusual crown, like antlers, black and gold, whose multiple tips vibrated gingerly, emitting sounds, either a swishing together or separate notes.

Bracelets joined the rest of the ornaments.

From another chest Ta took out pots of the same unknown metal. They contained the perfumes of ceremonial magic. Powerful balms that intoxicated as soon as the covers were off.

From the third and final chest she removed The Dress: an entity! Heavy, commanding, a cone of red orange with a mantle of satiny black reptilian hide.

The Queen put on the clothes, feeling oppressed by their brutal splendor. The metallic fabric of the dress shimmered faintly with the hues of burning coals, blending with the ruby glints that edged the mantle with alternating gems of dull green and gold stripes.

Everything was ready. Ta paused a moment.

"You have to help me, Mother," she muttered, "otherwise I won't manage."

She sensed a murmur come towards her. The memory of Abim's words flooded her mind. Echoes surrounded her. The torch flames seemed to ring. Indistinct voices seeped out of the depths of the walls.

She believed she saw waves rolling over the floor—a silvery sheen like water.

Then she noticed that in the slit of Abim's eyelids a purple ray was forming.

"I'll help you. Begin!"

Did she really hear this? Without wasting any more time she obeyed. Strength was added to her strength, penetrating her with a strangely dense energy that gave her body an uncommon weight. She felt herself becoming other. She accepted it. She had to for the magic to work!

Fire was drawing on her veins. She saw through a purple fog.

She took off her clothes, then carefully started applying the required balms all over her body. As she did so, she lost awareness of her individual form. Her sense of touch was both numbed and intensified. She felt herself growing in volume, dilating to fill up the whole room... The room? It had no limits! A red fog replaced the walls. There was no ceiling above her but the immensity of a kind of sky, a total blackness—the sky of an abyss, the sky of the center of the earth!

"There will come a time when the force from below will be necessary to you... for the people... great danger and within Kobor, sickness..."

It really was Abim's voice, the one she had at the end, whiny and childish, when breathing was getting hard for her and paralysis was setting in on her mouth, when she was predicting the future in spite of everything and the Reign of her daughter and the ordeals she could have to face when she was harping on the details of the magical summoning of the Klimm.

Ta finished anointing her body. Her nausea was gone, dispelled by the pungent strength of the balm, so strong that her psychic power went wild and she felt herself regressing to the dark, seminal powers of the Race!

"So, you will put the breastplate on your chest."

She did so. The cold metal stuck to her skin. In the kind of cloud that she had become, it formed a fixed, firm point, a plexus. Right away she felt infused with vigor.

"You have to put on the bracelets... Without them you couldn't stand it... You're not as strong as Us, the Ancient Ooh'Rous."

Ta slipped on the bracelets one by one. They jangled. They were heavy. And they too, like the breastplate, embedded themselves in her, dense and present. And full of power. The ability to command by moving her arm was starting to possess her.

"The jewelry will protect you... The Force from below will recognize you... The diadem!"

The Queen put it on her head. Heavy, very cold, it whispered countless words mingled with those of Abim; *"The Force from below... You will bring it out, send it out, all around, as you want... You will bring it back once the work is done... Tell me you understand!"*

"Yes, yes, yes," the Queen repeated, perceiving her own voice now like some distant thing that did not belong to her.

Her voice now sounded like metal and every word created whirlwinds in the fog of flame where she was moving.

"You will light the bowls."

She had already done it! In the four corners the powdered scents thrown on the fires were spewing the smell of pepper, of bitterness, of musk.

The fluid flames rose higher. In the middle Abim was burning without being consumed. Snakelike apparitions started coiling and uncoiling. They came from all sides, slithering, available, submissive, ready for the next command...

The Queen had just wrapped the heavy, gold-red robe around her covered with the black mantle. She was standing right up against Abim and could no longer tell how she was different from her Mother. She no longer knew where she began and where she ended!

In fact, having become non-dimensional she was bathing in an ocean of tremendous forces whose elemental aggressiveness was waiting only for a sign of weakness on her part, an error in the ceremony to split her off as a foreign element and thus enemy to be devoured!

But Ta wore the Robe of Power like armor and the magical ornaments made her chest, arms and head instruments of her will before which the dark spirits, constantly rising from Below, flocked and bowed.

"Are you ready?"

She said, "I am ready."

But wasn't she talking to herself?

Then Abim—or Ta?—ordered the work that would cleanse Kobor Tigan't of all the miasma of corruption.

"Klimm."

The First Word!

The floor turned transparent like rubies.

"Klimm!"

The cloud of spirits started seething.

"Klimm!"

And spun out from the volcanic bowels of the earth, rose the Klimm, like a serpent-dragon, terrifying and glorious!

The storm raged. Space opened. Through the night the formidable crew unfurled its sails of fire, just like when the Very Huge went about her business of tearing down obstacles!

... Below the Palace in the Pit, the prisoner T'Lo who had become passive like the Ananou had fallen to the ground. They were writhing in place while their vital fluid left their bodies to join the force passing by.

Is the Klimm this scaly dragon covered in metallic ripples whose tail sweeps away the stars like mere embers?

Is the Klimm what Ta is riding, fiercely guiding its movements and direction?

Or is it not rather her Very Huge Mother who is lending her spine and submitting her legend to help her in her reign?

But what is the Klimm, what is Abim, what is Ta at this moment when nothing is different anymore in the heart of this Plutonian tempest that suddenly pours down a rain of purifying fire!

And then who could remember the particular details of a magical storm after it has been unleashed!

It seemed to the Queen that she had been whirling around in the chaotic twists and turns of an occult war… Still, the disassociating fire sought to consume the shadowy pockets, the pus-filled pouches that looked like rotten brains and on which two maniacal eyes sitting bizarrely on the ends of stalks glimmered before fading out.

Gradually, the dark battlefield was cleared off. On the terrain, as far as the eye could see, burning bushes were flourishing under the rain of fire, which was like zesty dew for them!

And then… And then it was over all of a sudden. And maybe had been for awhile.

Ta was standing next to her Mother. Most of the torches were extinguished, leaving the room in semi-darkness.

The perfumes had stopped rising from the ashes. The Robe was crushing, the jewels painful. Her head under the circle of crown felt wounded.

Teetering, dying of thirst, Ta managed to run back through the details of the ceremony as she took off the vestments in reverse order. She put them all back. The slabs were dropped over the chests. Before leaving, torch in hand, the Queen took one last look at the mineral mass of Abim.

"I know, my Mother," she muttered, "I have to come back one more time. It'll be the last…"

She opened the door and left.

When R'Ang took her in his arms he found her ice-cold.

The cure was merciless but effective. The next day not a single T'Lo was alive.

A few days later the last Devotees died along with all the effects of their sickness, which disappeared completely.

Kobor Tigan't was in a daze, shocked by the remedy, but it quickly got back to living. Its devotion zeroed in on Ta, but she deflected it onto R'Ang.

He appeared in her place. His speeches revived the Race. They considered him radiant and splendid. Men touched by his light surrounded him. He really was the Ooh'R of Kobor Tigan't!

The child in Ta's belly fidgeted.

She wanted rest, to be alone, to stop working directly on the realm. Without hesitating, with her customary frankness, she expressed her desire to R'Ang to leave him completely in charge of the government so she could go live in the Royal Nursery.

He bowed to her wishes, which did not split them up since he was free to join her every night in the Nursery.

Once the decision was made, Ta did not want to put off moving. She immediately set up in Gan'd's house while they finished the Palace they were building nearby. She led a simple life, tolerating few people around her.

At her request, Hé-Nark had come along with a small Guard and a few chosen Young Servants.

Gan'd was there with Do'A-Roo who, as she was following the teaching of the B'Tah-Gous given by Ata-Réè in the House of Great Faces, came and went between the Nursery and Kobor Tigan't.

There were also some court couples made up of only two, a man and a woman, the new habit formed in the Palace over the past few Ooh'R cycles that was quickly spreading now among the customs of the Fivefold City. Ta liked hearing about them, of how many there were. The B'Tah-Gous married to a single man (almost always a Royal Guard) took care of these couples and taught them. They were often invited to live in the Palace in Kob'Ooh'R. They fascinated the people. In droves now more and more young people accepted only this love between two.

The disappearance of the Devotees and their T'Lo was a blow to the tradition of the Chambers of Men, most of whom wanted to be free like R'Ang. The mistresses of the Chambers looked more and more like the keepers of an outdated tradition that the youth wanted no more of.

Ta saw how things were going. She had worked hard enough to set it in motion! But while keeping her informed, they had to be careful not to trouble her too much because she was quick to get annoyed.

She seemed to be going through a period of personality changes. She showed, almost flaunted, a brand-new apathy for the problems that had engrossed her life.

R'Ang understood her well enough that he avoided talking too much about the cares of the realm so she could enjoy the somewhat selfish peace of her maternity.

In fact, Ta had turned away from Kobor Tigan't. She was living her life with delightful serenity. It was another adventure, another kind of work to accomplish. She put all her attention to the task. She expected no frustrations at any stage. It all belonged to her completely. How possessive she was of it!

Her belly swelled. The baby's movements became more pronounced, sometimes brutal, like it was already making personal decisions. It had its rhythms, its habits. It jolted, like in protest, when she lay in certain positions it did not like. She enjoyed it.

Paradoxically, despite being pregnant, or maybe because of it and the life forces being activated, Ta was feeling her youth come back, independent and alive, almost savagely insatiable of freedom. She would sometimes rudely get rid of the ungracious person whose company she was in no mood for. Gan'd, from a distance, watched over her with sympathetic eyes and, without seeming to, minded her health.

There was only Hé-Nark who was always welcome. He was thoroughly practiced in the difficult art of always being nearby, ready to do anything, but still being so discreet that his secret thoughts never interfered with the dream the Queen wanted to live while napping in the garden or strolling under the trees.

Settled in like this, she enjoyed her blissful serenity without remorse.

She was aware, however, that it was only temporary, lasting only as long as it took for the final act in the cycle of the White Ooh'Rou. She knew that she would have to grapple alone with the events of this final act in order to finish it. But there was no point in dwelling on this matter...

She was happy to be in nature again. She got used to going on quiet hikes with Hé-Nark on her heels like a shadow—he was thinking of another time—or right next to her, a polite confident when she chanced to feel talkative or had simply picked too many flowers to carry on her own.

Moreover, she made careful study of the plants under Gan'd's guidance. She had remarkable intuition about it, which never failed to amaze her teacher.

She also got lost in thought a lot, losing consciousness of her surroundings. It lasted for hours. She was elsewhere and no one dared to disturb her. She loved this state, which had been revealed to her during her long sickness. She accessed it at will.

The Crystal Being practically never left her. She was used to it like the air she breathed, like light.

They had longer and longer conversations together. It felt like everything she was learning was soaking into her child. She told this to R'Ang one evening when he was panting faintly, gently, at the memory of the mystery of their love that had made her fertile. Seeing him, hearing him, she laughed merrily, so incredibly young that he was still flustered by it. He loved her passionately. He wondered whether he was really joining her in her strange essentialness…

That night, the Crystal Being covered them with its light and the extreme rapture of their Triple Union illuminated their soul.

… The child was born one day at the moment of Ooh'R's zenith. It was an abrupt decision, a decree with no warning signs. Ta was ravished with light while the Crystal Being spread its intense radiance over her. She did not cry out even once.

The infant came, then, so quickly and so smoothly that Gan'd, informed by Hé-Nark, hardly arrived in time. When R'Ang and then Ata-Réè came running in, out of breath, Ta was laughing out loud while holding up her son.

"He's called Ta'El!" she announced in her queen's voice. The Crystal Being had told her this.

Leaning against the door, the Master Guard was crying with joy.

R'Ang could not take his eyes off the infant's little fingers, like his own, longer than the others.

Ta'El also bore the solar discs on the soles of his feet.

Ta did not want Kobor Tigan't to talk too much about her son. In fact, the news spread more like some fantastic tale. The devotion they had for the White Ooh'Rou fit this unusual birth into the legend surrounding Ta and her distance from the royal scene only helped.

After the birth of Ta'El, the Queen changed nothing about her new way of life. She showed no desire to return to the Palace in Kob'Ooh'R. She had just moved into her new Palace in the Nursery and was very pleased with it. It was entirely white decorated with gold forged by the Blacksmiths and formed into birds and whimsically twined plants.

Many garden terraces hung at various heights. Birds were frequent and faithful visitors. Artificial streams flowed pretty much everywhere, from top to bottom, forming stairways of bounding water.

In this bright home Ta fed Ta'El, weaned him, taught him to talk, to walk. Soon he ran. Jumping into the arms of R'Ang was his mighty feat!

He grew up. He was a bright-faced child with an intense gaze. His gestures were precise, never brusque. He always made quick decisions and went straight to his goal. He knew how to say no as well as yes and to explain himself calmly.

To hesitate teetered on nausea, which he hardly ever did. His father admired him enormously, remembering his own youth so muddled with his vague desires.

Ta'El was cheerful, but in moderation, without exaggerated dazzle. In truth, it was less a cheerfulness flaunting its high spirits than a joy whose silent smile readily flourished. But his feeling of joy was very real, coming from deep and truly mysterious source within him.

In this sense, he got along well with Ata-Réè. Together, very soon, the two had long debates in which the child's transcendent knowledge stunned the B'Tah-Gou.

From the start Ta'El had a royal demeanor, without trying, not at all vain, which Ta would never tolerate but she had little to correct in him.

He intimidated the Young Servants even though he laughed gaily with them and played their games with a marked tendency to lead them!

But he was full of natural majesty that radiated around him unwittingly. Because of this he was always a surprise. More than one Royal Guard passed out on seeing him suddenly appear, so calm, with a kind of light springing out of his forehead.

Unlike R'Ang, who was only intermittently aware, Ta'El always perceived the Crystal and became familiar with it. It was a natural companion for him, a presence he could not do without. He was very attached to it, fervently bathing his young thought in its superhuman Thought.

Having always seen the Crystal he was very astonished that others could not. But he did not talk about it openly. His mother and the Crystal had ordered him to be silent on this matter.

Contrary to Ta, who was always quietly young and seemed destined to escape the ravages of time, Ata-Réè had aged so much that the two women now seemed generations apart. It had happened quickly after long years of holding out. For the Grand B'Tah-Gou, age—and more than age, the complete spiritualization of her whole being—had come all at once.

Everyone was a little shocked. They felt like they had left her still young one night and the next morning found her almost decrepit.

Overnight she had lost a lot of weight and never gained it back. One could forget that there was a body under her veils. She was just a floating, gliding apparition. The wind could carry her away!

Her face had thinned, thus intensifying her big, bright eyes, two huge pupils that did not blink and that did not reflect anything but the transcendence of the lights through which her mystical spouse had progressively carried her.

Her skin turned transparent. Her body exuded sweet scents. Lights and sounds accompanied her everywhere.

She ended up living in the temple almost all the time except for the short periods when, by order of the Great Crystal, she went to the Palace or to the Nursery to speak with R'Ang, Hé-Nark or Ta. During Ta'El's childhood it was most often to meditate by his crib. She watched over him in silence, looking radiant.

After this transformation, they respected the Priestess of the Crystal even more than before. They approached her with a religious awe and awaited revelations.

Her voice had changed into an oracle: a word pronounced clearly, resoundingly, that even when she was not singing sounded like music, not coming from her throat but ricocheting off crystal blades mysteriously hidden inside her. They loved the lilt of this voice. They sought counsel from it, dreaded its disapproval and heeded all its decrees.

Outside of this priestly duty, in everyday life, for herself and others, Ata-Réè kept silent now, breaking it only on rare occasions, almost always for Ta'El whose young intelligence fascinated her.

Ta, in her semi-retirement, continued to adore her with loving care that never wavered. She asked after her health every day and every evening, by private messenger, wished her a good night.

The Priestess, who was always waiting for the messengers, welcomed them with an infinitely sweet smile. Every night, the messenger thought that the simple phrase, almost never changing, must have contained much more than he could understand. He felt that through the words the Queen and the Priestess were communicating together in eternal harmony. And then he saw a fold in the robes move, revealing a slender hand: Ata-Réè was motioning with her fingers, unveiling a source of light that he touched fearfully in order to receive it so he could transmit it. The holy robe closed up. The light was reabsorbed.

Disturbed every time like on the first day, the messenger went back to the Nursery as bearer of the blessing for the royal family. When he got there the Glorious Child Ta'El was still awake. He only fell asleep after the messenger had watched in awe his hand transmit the daily miracle of light from the Grand B'Tah-Gou.

In her Nursery palace, Ta remained up-to-date on the life of the realm. R'Ang, who governed wisely, made no final decisions without discussing them with her.

Ta always saw what was most important. Her distance gave her the necessary perspective not to get bogged down in details. Besides, she was dispassionate, which made her more insightful than ever.

Nevertheless, she still enjoyed, like at first, the benefits of being away from the Power. Her semi-solitude in the Nursery, her rest and re-laxation were priceless treasures.

But despite everything she felt like she would never really get rid of all the weariness of the reign built up over so many long, hard years dur-ing which she had to truly sacrifice herself. Thinking so often of this problem paid off one day in a moment of deep, inner detachment, when she realized that she was simply yearning for death and that her life, for a very long time, was too much for her.

She loved her spouse R'Ang. She loved her son Ta'El. But no mat-ter what she did, the one and only To, her soulmate, kept calling to her from the other side of things. She was longing to join him at last, finally to have this right.

She noticed that over the years her memories of him became more precise than before. She relived them in detail, one after another. She never tired of it. They became stronger, more vibrant every day, to the point of sometimes masking reality. Their clarity eclipsed her present life, made it dull.

Ta did not try to suppress them. On the contrary, she connected their brightness to the hope promised by death, the open door to To, to the in-effable Reunion!

She figured that her exhilarating youth and her longed-for death were of the same essence.

Between these two poles she had secretly remained herself, un-changed, more real than the White Ooh'Rou, who had only been a mask behind which Princess Ta, the free and independent spirit, had survived, always and forever To's soulmate, apart from which she was incompre-hensible because incomplete.

Knowing this, she still did not lose her head. She remained reasonable, knew she had work to finish before being free forever. And she knew she was nearing the end. She mustered her strength with the final task in sight.

The seasons passed quietly over the Nursery, like over Kobor Tigan't, which still had the Crystal Dome overhead from the day of the Devotees' defeat. It had become the heavenly companion of the Five-fold City.

Sometimes this immutable Dome, way up high in the sky, would suddenly come alive. A quick flash was the signal, then a bright sheen rippled slowly all over it, shimmering with pink and lilac and pale jade mixed with gold, studded with diamonds. It was like a silent storm whose explosive spirit would have been equal to holy rejoicing.

Down below, the people stopped what they were doing to contemplate the phenomenon with passionate but peaceful and reverential curiosity. Experience had proved that nothing bad ever came from the Dome's activity, quite the contrary since everyone felt a resurgence of strength, more zest for life and a kind of expansion of their entire being.

For the initiated, for those who were directly concerned, *it was a warning signal that one or more of the young couples had received the gift of a Crystal Being.* It was the Magisterial Dome's way of rejoicing.

Long, transparent tendrils, of every color of the rainbow, stretched out from it down to Kobor and disappeared in bright explosions as silent as the whole manifestation. Every conception made by the Triple Union of the chosen couples produced these reverberations of light, but only concerned couples saw this.

The rest of the population was unaware.

Likewise for every birth come from such unions there were similar manifestations that were seen by all the Crystal Beings already made real among the Giants of the Kobor.

All of them rejoiced at these births and hurried to give the news to their own parent couple. As a result, all the chosen couples were naturally informed of what was happening with the others. They were, therefore, inclined to know each other, to search each other out and meet together.

Thus they lived, drawn together, in the Palace of Kob'Ooh'R or the Nursery.

Ta together with R'Ang meet with them regularly. Ata-Réè was almost always there as well.

From now on, following the new custom, every nubile B'Tah-Gou
chose a partner from among the Royal Guards, Blacksmiths or Servants
of the Queen. The number of these unions, all of them fertile, increased
so rapidly that Ta saw the time approaching rapidly…

CHAPTER XXVIII

Ta especially liked relaxing in her garden a little before the approach of twilight. She felt very present and receptive. She reflected on what she had done and enjoyed putting her thoughts in order.

One day, on impulse, she decided to take Do'A-Roo aside at a moment when she was least expecting it, determined to clear up the situation so that the young lady might partake of the Secret and perform the role that the divine will assigned her.

Everything was calm and conducive to such a conversation. Nobody was around to disturb them. Ta'El was out walking with Gan'd. R'Ang would not arrive until later. Hé-Nark, being perceptive, stepped away toward the gate. The light of the setting sun was lingering in the garden. The slanting rays rebounded like splashing golden water, striking the statues and the ornamental monoliths whose contours were sharper against the leafy background. The birds, already perched, were holding their final conference before the silence of sleep settled over their feathered assembly.

Yes, this was THE moment. And Ta knew it perhaps from having already felt it during one of her meditations.

When she called, the young lady came over with the perky enthusiasm she always showed to fulfill the Queen's desires. As usual, when she got there, she was smiling pleasantly at the idea of one of those short talks that she loved and, as usual, she brought a present—always a gift of nature: a blossoming flower chosen for its perfect moment of beauty, some newly discovered plant or gem found in a rock and not yet fully extracted.

Today it was a surprise that did not look like much. She laughed and offered a handful of gray, unappealing roots, which she hinted at mischievously. "But," she was quick to add, "these roots contain a very sweet sap that you can boil and makes a beauty cream so potent that it only needs to be used once, O Queen, even though you have no need at all."

Ta fell back on her reclining chair, smiling, and wiggled a scolding finger, "Oh, I'm not so unique, young flatterer! You can prepare it not just for me but for your young peers and of course for yourself... even though you have no need!"

They giggled together. Then Ta turned serious. She gazed a moment at Do'A-Roo's face, appreciated the sharp features, its oval shape framed by the thick, smooth hair that she had inherited from her mother. The girl, in turn, turned quiet, opened wide her honest eyes, full of questions, which were both asking and fearing to put an end to this awkward situation.

"Leave your roots," the Queen ordered softly, "and come sit next to me. It's been a long time since I've wanted to talk to you about something we both hold dear even though you've never said anything about it and I, too, have not mentioned it until now."

Do'A-Roo lowered her eyes and turned pale, guessing where this was going. Her unease was so obvious that Ta paused to squeeze her hand gently to dispel any fears about her intentions.

"Come, come, young lady, let's start this important conversation with courage! I have to ask you a question because I might be wrong. Can you tell me why you're taking so long to choose a man to form one of those couples that I love and that you, too, often told me you admire?"

Do'A-Roo said nothing, her breathe faltered. Her hand became wet in the Queen's. Ta sighed sympathetically.

"Do'A-Roo, tell me, you understand, don't you, how important such couples are and especially their children? You know about the future and its ordeals?"

The young lady bowed her head in affirmation.

"The future lies in these chosen couples, my child… Your behavior surprises me. I see you as someone like these couples in whom the heavens want to lodge. You are, potentially, for me, the best of them." She emphasized, "Yes, the best, Do'A-Roo!"

But she wanted to get the required vow from her. So, she harried her with questions that she already knew the answers to, or rather THE answer.

"Isn't there a man you like? There are plenty around you! Isn't there one of the Royal Guards who are always so eager to escort you? And the Young Servants who study plants not so much to be near them but to be around you, is there no one? What about that Blacksmith, smooth and noble like molten gold, whom I've seen get so flustered whenever you pass by, doesn't he do something for you?"

Do'A-Roo was on pins and needles. "Oh my Queen, don't torture me like this!" she begged, almost crying.

Ta pulled her close, pressing her face to her chest. She murmured, "That's it, don't look, it'll be easier..." There was a pause, then, "Do'A-Roo, I know you love R'Ang!"

The young lady jerked in the Queen's arms like a young animal caught in a net. But she got hold of herself right away and raised her head bravely, staring at Ta who was smiling kindly.

"Please excuse me, my Queen," she pleaded humbly without trying to deny it.

"But why? I didn't say it was bad. And I've known for awhile. I've had a lot of time to adjust. I might have known even before you... When you were just a child and stubbornly trying to play with R'Ang but Dê-Ta'Am always distracted him like everyone else later. You loved R'Ang and you still do. Plain and simple. It's nothing new. You came into the world with this prospect and as you became aware, it condensed in you to the point that you live only for this feeling to the exclusion of everything else. Look, when you took care of me in the Palace, long before the birth of Ta'El, despite me being weak and silent, I knew where you stood, I saw your confusion, happy and sad, when R'Ang was around..."

Do'A-Roo was stunned and almost frightened by this new example of the Queen's proverbial insight. But she did not interrupt.

"How discreet you were, child, and heroic, too, to seal up this feeling in your heart! I admire you and I thank you. But above all how you nevertheless managed to preserve and nurture the hope of its fulfillment!"

This time Do'A-Roo's terror reached a peak. "I'm sorry! I'm sorry!"

"Not at all," the Queen replied, "since I said you were right to keep hoping."

At this Do'A-Roo gaped. She no longer understood. But Ta was already explaining.

"Listen and pay attention. Everything has progressed following the will of the heavens. Ta'El had to be born as the first of the line, descended from me and R'Ang. Now that this is done, you've seen it—other couples formed in the image of ours, chosen couples who give birth to children like Ta'El. To these couples, to their descendants is promised another kind of life than we have known here. They will go elsewhere, spread far from Kobor Tigan't into new lands. The best of us will thus survive in them because, Do'A-Roo, remember this well, of our Race such as you know it, of our Five-fold City, nothing will remain!"

This rang out like a blow to their conscience. Silence settled over them, giving the setting sun time to withdraw its light. They looked at each other now as brave allies determined to protect the future, each in her rightful place.

Do'A-Roo spoke up first, fervently, "I understand, my Queen. Teach me. Give me orders. Tell me what you want. I will obey you to the letter."

"Well, that's good. I never doubted you or your courage. I want you first to let your love for R'Ang run free. Go to him more often and for longer. Talk to him. Be his friendly, helpful shadow. Get him used to you, then needing you by his side. Show him what you know. Express the inspiration you have about everything. And above all, enjoy the moment when, after a long, hot day perhaps, he will take a rest in the Palace. He might be happy or sad... If he's alone at the time, go in without fear wherever he is. If he's sleeping, sit next to him on the bed, wake him up gently... The opportunity might be much easier since the radiance of your young flesh will shine beneath your clothes and he will have a sudden desire for a woman... Make sure you're there! Open yourself to his desire! That's my order: love him in the Palace, on the hunt, on Kah'B'La! Bind again and again the bound of flesh with him. Just be discreet. But don't dawdle, girl! The time is dreadfully near when I will have to go and finish my work alone!"

Do'A-Roo promised to obey. She left the Queen with stronger admiration and affection than she had ever had before. Her mind was running in circles but her heart was overflowing with hope.

A little later Ta figured, through signs that were clear to her, that Do'A-Roo had given herself to R'Ang. She was careful to keep to herself what she knew. She played with him a little about it as she felt his perplexity over what happened. He tried to be more tender and attentive to her but she knew that he had got used to Do'A-Roo who had become indispensable.

Gan'd, Ata-Réè and Hé-Nark were informed by the Queen and bound together by an oath to nurture the blossoming of this love.

After this Ta let her thoughts focus on the end of Kobor Tigan't that was fast and inescapably approaching.

Taught by the Crystal Being she knew now that the best of her Race would be saved. She also knew how.

Furthermore, she knew that all the young Chosen Couples, now grown plentiful, had been told of the final ends just like her. *Each of them received from their own Crystal Being the required teaching to prepare them for the life-saving exodus.*

During their regular meetings called by Ta they talked together in detail about the important points of the plan that had been revealed to them so that they could all be ready when the time came.

These couples were already essentially different from the rest of the population. They were characterized by an intense vitality whose radiance shone through their eyes. A spirited blood ran through their veins, giving their skin a kind of shine. They were calm and serious people despite their youth. The Triple Union had opened the eyes of their soul. They possessed the best faith, that of knowledge.

They were already privileged with the foundations of the Revealed Religion by the contemplation of the cosmic laws. Certainty was their strength. They were proudly aware of being chosen among all others. They wanted to prove themselves worthy *in order to perpetuate, beyond the inevitable catastrophe, the glorified race of the Giants of Kobor Ti-gan't.*

And even though their heart wept already at the thought of being separated forever from Kobor and having to abandon to its fate the rest of the Race who had not been infused with the crystalline seed, they heroically kept silent and determined.

Ta loved them. They vowed absolute respect to her. Wasn't she the first chosen woman! They also recognized R'Ang as their sovereign master who was responsible for governing them not just here, by the play of racial destiny, but also in foreign lands by the decree of the heavens.

And they all reckoned that their own children would live under the reign of Ta'El.

However, outside these contacts that were never neglected, Ta pursued the mysterious course of her meditations. Of course she mustered all her psychic resources to play her role to the end, but she did not want to let her action spill over into a flood of events that she was too tired to want to know. The more she contemplated her personal truth, the less fear and remorse she imagined. On the contrary, a great calm settled on her. She was firmly resolved that her life would end with that of Kobor.

When thinking about her people, those who were not part of the chosen ones, who were already damned, she found the bond that connected her to them, the old root currently scorned and rejected. And Ta, this White Ooh'Rou who had been the unexpected, anachronistic model of a Race for the future, accepted the truth that this future held no attraction for her...

She asked her Crystal Being to understand and help her. The Crystalline Entity did not try to curb her will and promised her its help so that she would be reunited with To.

Henceforth, the Queen worked on preparing everything, without saying anything, so that neither R'Ang nor Ta'El nor anybody else could stop her at the last moment.

She told herself that for the first time in her life she would betray the trust of her loved ones.

CHAPTER XXIX

The warning signs of the catastrophe whose purpose had to remain known only by the Chosen, arrive in Kobor Tigan't.

At first vague, they consist of a weird daytime darkening while at night the fat Na-Nood filling the sky with here pale presence, casting a blood-red reflection as a horizontal crescent that they had never seen before, this was the very signature of the Apocalypse.

The signs are clear. The earth shakes. Noxious storms rage out of Grand Va-Hôh. It rains mud. The ground splits open. It emits loads of harmful gas. The clouds thicken and stop moving despite the gusts of wind. They are totally black. Sometimes, ashes fall from them. The Crystal Dome is no longer visible.

The people hole up in their homes obeying an old instinct that compels them to await the end of what they again believe to be anger from the cursed West.

It was better to lock oneself in because they saw very old animals appear in nature. They came out of the caves in herds, bellowing and bawling dismally. They are trying to migrate. But they die in single file on the plains. Their carcasses befoul the air, which is already stinking of sulfur and niter.

Huge clouds of birds go racing off. They try to get past the inaccessible mountains surrounding the site of Kobor. Some appear to succeed. Most fall straight down the sheer cliffs.

On several occasions the big waterfall that flows through the Five-fold City goes quiet. Then it starts up again but its flow, like the color of the water, constantly changes. It is no longer drinkable, stinks of rot and corruption.

New, scalding geysers break through the soil crust. The bowels of the earth are in upheaval. Silos and cellars collapse into the gaping maws that open in Kob'Lâm. Landslides transform the surrounding terrain. The underground rumblings never stop. The storm never leaves.

The people have lost all concept of time. It was pitch black and no one dared venture outside because the wind was so strong that it would blow down or sweep away anyone foolish enough to tempt it. The trees were uprooted but the massive homes of the City held fast.

In the Royal Nursery all the Chosen couples, following their instructions, stayed together to wait for the grand exodus. Nary a one was missing. The few who were caught in Kobor during the worsening turmoil had miraculously slipped through the unleashed elements. *Just in time, the Crystal Beings had densified around them and their children. They had walked under shelter without feeling the wind, without a rock touching them, in a bright aura that showed them the way.*

Now, still, all the Crystal Beings were clearly visible.

This strange gathering filled the biggest room in Ta's Palace, which an invisible barrier seemed to protect from the black storm that was raging all around it.

Ata-Réè had just arrived, enveloped by all the Crystal Formations from the House of Great Faces *that had brought the oblong gem still encasing the intact body of Angel*, the Beautiful Stranger, the mystical spouse of the Grand B'Tah-Gou. She, too, was supposed to leave along with some not yet nubile B'Tah-Gous and the same number of adolescents mostly from among the Servants of the Queen.

Hé-Nark and Gan'd had also received orders to join the Chosen with Do'A-Roo.

R'Ang, very serious, you might say solemn, organized the groups, like a father fussing to make sure all were present.

The dusky room, lit only by the dim lights of the Crystal Beings cocooning each family, suddenly lit up with a flash coming from outside as if a star were casting its rays right into the Palace.

The huge Crystal Dome, which had stood over Kobor Tigan't for years, was slowly coming down towards the top terrace of the Palace.

This was the signal. A shiver ran through the crowd of the Chosen.

In order, led by R'Ang, they started off by taking the staircase to reach the terrace. As planned, Do'A-Roo, who was holding the hand of Ta'El, went looking for the Queen in her rooms because the Crystal Beings had said the first Chosen Woman should be the last to enter the Dome.

Do'A-Roo knew this. But she also knew something else. Her heart ached, but she would carry out her mission as promised to the Queen. Hé-Nark did not fail to notice her worried look. On instinct he waded through the crowd to follow her.

In her room Ta was sitting alone. A single flame lit her faintly. She was dressed in a light, loose robe fitted with a hood. Her son ran to her and she hugged him while he played, as usual, with stray strands of her hair.

But she was looking at Do'A-Roo. "Are you ready?"

With a lump in her throat the young lady nodded. She wanted to say something but couldn't. *It was then that a very bright Crystal appeared over her.* The Queen was startled at the sight of it and as always with her swift insight she said, "You have conceived with R'Ang!"

And it was true.

"You see, I was right, Do'A-Roo. All's well. Everything is going as planned. Have no regret of what you are going to do since it is my will. Let's go!"

Ta hugged Ta'El long and tenderly and calmly so as not to alarm him. She fought hard to control herself. She wanted to squeeze him hard. A flood of sorrow wrung her guts. She knew it was the last time. She was about to lose him. She choked back tears. Her maternal love was in revolt and started howling deep down inside. And all the heat left her body.

Ta'El was worried and looked up at her. He spoke a word that he had not used since he was a baby. "Mamata, why are you so cold?"

She almost cried out. Do'A-Roo broke down in tears.

Ta-El was astonished, "Mamata, what's wrong? I don't understand!"

She had to answer! Above all, answer with calm words, everyday words. Ta managed the miraculous feat. She used the name that awoke in Ta'El the resonances of the additional part of his spirit.

"O Crystal Child, I'm cold because my clothes are too light." She made the sign to Do'A-Roo who approached while she went on, "Do'A-Roo has better ones which she's going to lend me until I catch up to you up where you'll go with her before me."

They exchanged clothes. Ta gave hers to the young lady and pulled back the hood from her face. She also, unbeknownst to the child, gave her bracelets to her. Then she sprayed her with the perfume of the White Ooh'Rou, which no one else in the realm used.

"Crystal Child, obey me and behave yourself until I get to you."

"Yes, Mamata," he said.

"Until I'm there, you won't talk about our switching clothes."

He promised.

"Go on, then!"

She pushed him toward the door. Do'A-Roo stumbled and shivered. Ta hugged her and spoke firmly, "Girl, may the fruit of your loins be blessed! Bring forth for Ta'El a dedicated, honorary brother!"

She looked at her again and smoothed the royal vestment. "Yes, dressed like this they'll think you're me for long enough... Afterward, *when the Dome lifts up to carry you away*, it won't matter anymore."

In the hallway behind the door Hé-Nark had heard everything. When Do'A-Roo came scurrying out with Ta'El, he jumped back into the shadows.

Ta was listening hard. The noises in the Palace faded. She suddenly felt a great big void and at that moment *the vague glow that came from the dome had disappeared as well as the protective barriers around the Palace*, which was suddenly open to the raging elements. It shook on its foundations.

Ta was sure, then, that they had left.

She felt a jolt that froze her body instantly and every detail was wiped out of her memory. She no longer knew what was happening or even who she was...

After a moment of being deprived of hers senses, as it were, standing up against a wall, not reacting to the objects falling all around her, just watching apathetically as if none of it mattered to her, she suddenly shivered violently. She shook from head to toe.

"The earth... the earth is trembling stronger. It's already started. I'm late!"

This cry from her conscience snapped her back to her senses. She had little time to finish her work. She had to go the Palace in Kob'Ooh'R at all costs.

She had one last rendezvous with her people to keep.

From this point on she thought only of this. As she dashed out after wrapping herself in a thick cloak, her mind was already organizing everything she had to do up to the end. And without any fear. At no moment did she feel the slightest trepidation.

When she reached the outside stairs, the whole front of the Palace collapsed behind her. She did not even turn around. Head down, she charged forth.

People were fleeing in a blur all around her without saying a word, without yelling, almost without panicking, it seemed, streaming towards

Kobor Tigan't as fast as they could. For an emotional rendezvous perhaps?

"Shadows!" Ta pondered. "Already nothing but shadows! And all of nature already mourning us!"

Indeed, it was night, in a way, very dismal. The darkness was hideous, the air noxious. The sky was buried under thick, leaden clouds, lit only by constant pale flashes that threw into striking relief the land in chaos.

Ta kept her eyes half-closed in order not to be completely blind.

Pretty much everywhere yellowish swellings with frayed edges reflected the glow of fires coming out of the ground. Huge red clouds, so thick they did not move, swirled slowly, swelling more and more.

All of a sudden, a veritable wall of yellow smoke rose up before the Queen while the bitter stench of sulfur choked her. She dashed on without faltering, by pure reflex, covering her mouth with the cloak. She passed through it with her eyes burning. On the other side she doubled over with a hacking cough, but stumbled on.

She ran into people at times. They did not complain, having lost all agression. Like her they were just running. And they did not look at each other. Some were holding hands. When one fell, the other pulled him or her up. Who, therefore, would recognize the Queen among this fleeing multitude?

The earth did not stop shaking. Collapsing, crumbling buildings battered it non-stop. The shaking was so strong and so constant sometimes that Ta felt like she was staggering over thick liquid reeled by waves.

On either side, as she ran, tripped, fell down many times but always getting back up, she saw rocks moving, trees toppling over in rows, their roots in the air, their broken branches exploding.

The wind stopped blowing. Ta dreaded its return, an omen, for her, of the imminent end of everything. Right now, however, she still had a little time left...

She heard swishing. Almost right away she found herself wading up to her thighs in a flooded road. The current was so strong that she thought she would be swept away. She was spun around several times by the turbulence. She was already choking. Gravelly mud was battering her. Her hand felt a root, pull! She got out. A flash allowed her to see where she was.

In front of her was the start of a muddy hill where a tree was still standing. She grabbed a branch that hung down, half-broken off, and managed to climb up. She was near the stairs leading to Kob'Ooh'R.

She ran forth. It was crowded with people scrambling up it feverishly, still in that extraordinary silence. Sometimes, of course, a groan or a grunt could be heard when someone was hit by a rock or buried under a sudden upheaval of the earth. But this was only a result of pain and stopped right away in the silent bustle of shadowy figures trying to help the victim. Nowhere was there any outbursts of anger or curses. Nobody tried to push away or knock over their neighbor to assure their escape.

"Ah," Ta told herself, "they know they're lost." She felt an inner desolation, a repressed lamentation. She almost wept. Her poor people! But she got hold of herself. She had to get up the stairs.

She struggled through the middle of the throng. People were helping each other. For her too, anonymous hands reached out and hauled her over the tricky parts where the steps were already fallen apart.

While forcing her way up by, in a kind of split reality, her mind was washed in a bright light presenting her with countless images. She conversed with herself... Her last duty of love: to join her people. To be here with them. To confront with them whatever was becoming more and more present, these final moments, still so painfully mysterious. Oh, who knows how to die well?

Now a joyful energy was pushing her on. She was brimming with gratitude for the hands of men and women who were grabbing her own hands, wrists and arms to help her. She in turn pulled or pushed as needed.

Oh, her people! Her Race! Yes, she the Ooh'Rou was going to give them a wonderful surprise by giving herself to them, by being here.

She had a clear vision of the unanimous death mingling her own with all the others of her Race.

She feared nothing. She would have done anything, accomplished anything for them. One last effort still to reach the end of her reign. After this, the great weariness of existence, which she had so carefully hidden since the death of To, could have her. She would melt away into the infinite, into cessation, finally, finally at peace!

The stairs were done. To her left she recognized the yawning mouth of a secret passage leading to other stairs that ended inside the Palace. She dove in. No one followed her.

She kept running. The hallways were long and she knew it.

This sudden solitude after so much human contact startled her. She started feeling the anguish of a nightmare in which nothing ever ended. Strange sounds, a kind of hooting, came through the walls where the shaking earth was mutating horribly, making things unreal, including her bruised body that had lost almost all feeling.

The sudden shifts in air pressure that accosted her eardrums made her deaf at times.

Then the endless tunnels she was dashing through suddenly came out on one of the familiar terraces near her rooms in the Palace.

For a moment, from there, she could see the whole five-fold City where all the lights were lit up, incredible, heroic, a myriad of wild lights in all the houses, on all the terraces, in all the gardens, alleyways, along the stairways, torches stuck in the ground or carried by thousands of hands.

Kobor Tigan't wanted to die seeing clearly!

Even though the earth was still shaking, there was little damage. Everything was almost intact.

There was no fussing among those who had reached the meeting places. The people stood around in groups, more or less dense, waiting.

Frozen there, Ta felt that this image was engraved forever on the unalterable fabric of her soul. She would carry it away soon, very soon…

All of a sudden a great gust of wind came out of nowhere and blew out all the flames before disappearing, leaving everything dead calm, in total shadow.

One single groan rose out of Kobor Tigan't. It, too, was very brief. Already, here and there, they were relighting the torches.

But Ta, this time, had no more time to wait. After this first gust, others, stronger, fatal, final ones were coming. She knew it.

Once again mustering all her force, she ran to Abim's rooms, down the hallways with closed doors that her nervous hand opened one by one. She held a sizzling torch that left a wake of smoke behind her. Her feet within these walls that had been uninhabited for so long kicked up heaps of dust.

The last door swung open. There was a heavy silence, a dense atmosphere, a step back in time.

Ta was in the Center. Here, still, whatever remained of Abim kept vigil—this stubborn, monstrous stone. It was still leaning, not falling…

"This can't last much longer now," the Queen muttered. Then, more loudly, "Good evening, Very Huge Mother, I'm paying you one final visit."

With specific movements, *after* planting her torch among the others she had lit there, she started taking off all her soiled clothes. She carefully wiped off all traces of mud.

When she took off her sandals (because she did not want to keep anything on her body) she noticed that the ground was burning under her feet.

"Already."

Everything was going to speed up. But she was ready. For the last time she put on the only crown that existed in Kobor Tigan't, which she had only deigned to wear that one time for the evocation of the Klimm— the crown of translucent black metal that had once been in Abim's possession.

The earth's rumbling was getting louder. Jets of steam were springing out of the cracks between the stone slabs that were almost pushed up. It was getting hotter. But Ta paid no attention to these details.

Nude, slender, her stomach flat, her breasts firm, her hair flowing freely under the tree-like crown whose thin branches were vibrating and casting shimmering reflections over the crypt, she walked to the window, opened wide the stone shutters and climbed calmly onto the ledge to face her Race.

A long cry of astonishment greeted her. She spread her arms. Yes, she, the White Ooh'Rou, she was nude like the first Ooh'Rous used to be all the time. But like this, more than ever she was the White One, the special one, by virtue of the total purity of this body untouched by time.

A loving coo arose from the crowd, "Ooh'Rou! Ooh'Rou!"

It went on and on. They were really accepting death now that she was here, she who had loved them more than anything!

They stopped looking to the west where their fate was crouching. They wanted to see nothing but this bright figure. They wanted to know nothing but this Queen, completely devoted to them, whose pale radiance they absorbed eagerly. Her peace, already detached from everything, was blessing them. She appeared to them surrounded by a white aura. They did not even think of her nudity. Or that her body had never before been unveiled. No. Nothing like this crossed their minds. They moved towards her, those in the front rows under her terrace and the others climbing up after them, desiring nothing more than to get closer to her.

All of Kobor together rose up like this. They had all seen, all understood. The White Ooh'Rou, the mythic, had not left!

"Ooh'Rou, Ooh'Rou!"

On and on, the cooing of the crowd, in ecstasy...

Ta felt an unbelievable surge of joy inside her. "Ah, they will feel nothing when it happens!"

She rejoiced. Yes, she was succeeding in keeping them from feeling the impending death!

She spread her arms wider, "My Race, my People!"

The earth's rumbling had prevented her voice from carrying. Nevertheless, the smiling crowd heard her shout and answered with a louder cooing, "Ooh'Rou, Ooh'Rou!"

Ta was breathing shakily. The air was getting thicker. An unrecognizable stench accosted her nose. Underneath her the earth seemed to be coughing. In the room behind her she heard the grating slabs coming apart. There was a loud, heavy puff, a great gust of heat—the larvae!

Turning around would serve no purpose...

Farther away, still in the distance, there were muffled explosions, one after another. Ashes fell from the sky, mixed with sparks. Sulfurous patches drifted around the whirling black smoke.

But the hypnotized crowd kept pushing forward. "Ooh'Rou, Ooh'Rou!" A forceful but gentle movement. The front rows were getting packed in.

Ta noticed then that there was a tight wall of men, torch-bearers, standing still and straight, whom nobody was trying to push over. They were the Royal Guards and the Blacksmiths with them who had their backs to the Queen, facing the crowd as they used to on festival days. Her heart skipped when the strip of light revealed, right in the middle of them, an unmistakable figure—the shoulders, neck and gray hair of Hé-Nark. The Master Guard had not left!

She choked back a sob.

The underground explosions dispersed among the rumbling were getting closer. In places around the outskirts of the Cities the ramparts were crumbling. The dust mixed with the ashes and smoke.

One of the gates of Kob'Ooh'R suddenly collapsed. Its golden disc glistened on the ground for a moment, then rocks bombarded it and buried it.

Cracks in the ground yawned open everywhere. Walls split.

A thunderous noise could be heard while purple lights glowed in the shadows all around.

Now shrieks and cries of pain rose up.

Ta saw the people falling on their knees, all together, hugging each other and staying still, waiting for the end. Hands were reaching up to her. All their eyes, still burning with vital intensity, all those eyes were staring at her!

"Ooh'Rou, Ooh'Rou!" She imagined more than she actually heard...

The air was stifling. The shaking earth was not letting up.

Then a huge explosion erupted beneath Kobor Tigan't and while a part of the crowd was swallowed in a chasm that gaped open in Kob'Râm, volcanic magma came vomiting out of fissures in Kob'Vâm and Kob'Lâm.

With shrill hissing, the grand waterfall was evaporating, vanishing in thick white clouds.

The House of Great Faces was split in two, a tragic fruit, full of melting pulp, reddish gold, in which human forms were rolling and swirling, being crushed by the votive masks.

The foundations of Kob'Ooh'R were still holding. The front rows of the crowd, almost all on their knees now, stayed in front of the line of Guards. Hé-Nark was still there, standing straight, keeping his balance over the shaking earth that made Ta hold on with all her strength to the window frame, which was swaying.

The boundless anguish of her sacrificed Race was unbearable. She was weeping out loud without even hearing her voice. Ah, this was lasting too long. The end was taking too long!

"Hurry up, Wretch! Free us!"

She had screamed angrily, stretching her arms out to the west. Then it was as if the Grand Va-Hôh had heard her. For, everything sped up.

A maniacal uproar was unleashed. All of space was shaking. The Palace cracked everywhere. Behind Ta, in a fiery blast, lava gushed into the room. In one fell swoop Abim was uprooted and fell, making an awful sound—a gooey crash that splashed burning liquid everywhere.

The White Ooh'Rou knew that the Standing Stones on the shore of the Grand Va-Hôh were no longer and their engulfment was rushing towards them now.

The shaking air was getting stronger. While the storm front was hurling its initial blows against Kobor, Ta was the first to see the monstrous crest of foaming water rise up to attack the sky in one single, whirling column!

Kobor Tigan't, the Five-fold, the incomparable City of Giants split in two. The Palace wobbled. Ta saw all the arms reaching out to her. Hé-Nark swung around. He was holding his torch up, miraculously still lit. The Queen had time to meet his eyes. He opened his mouth...

Did he yell, "I love you!"?

The fire, the stones, the mad darkness where the tornado was lifting people, blocks and trees all together! Everything was being annihilated!

Behind Ta the lava flowed in and veered towards her while the wave filling the sky struck her head-on at the same time. The body of the White Ooh'Rou vanished at the exact meeting point of fire and water, at the moment when the two elements touched each other.

... Ta knew that she was dying... The Crystal Being had kept its promise. It was in front of her, right before the end: "Come!"

She leaps. ONTO THAT OTHER PLANE. *Her vital bonds snap, break, right before the fire and water conjoin. So, she is freed, right before.*

IN THE CRYSTAL, ON THIS PLANE THAT IS ALSO A BEING AND THAT ALSO REPRESENTS ALL THE CRYSTAL BEINGS, To, her one and only, appears, there in the middle. To, ALIVE!

Ta, ALIVE, *runs to him, free to join him while he runs to her, from afar, also free to join her!*

And the state of spiritual unity joins them at last in the supreme charity of the CRYSTAL, REUNITES THEM AND PUTS THEM TO REST.

"And now that the flood is putting an end to this Time of Kobor Tigan't, there is nothing left by me, Kébélé, the timeless, to witness the rest. Under my gaze nothing remains of the Five-fold City of Giants. In its place, fire and water are warring. But up above, a sun is growing bigger until it fills all of space. A terrifying sky of gold before which all sentiment is abolished!

"And here in the center of this final splendor, this last vision, the perfectly round spaceship, rutile like another sun, *a ruby pellet, full of seeds to sow, for them to multiply, in Another Time, for Another World!*"

www.ingramcontent.com/pod-product-compliance
Lightning Source LLC
Chambersburg PA
CBHW060424030726
47495CB00003B/730